THE MARGO CHRONICLES TOO!

CJ MACKINNON

THE MARGO CHRONICLES TOO!

CJ MACKINNON

Dedication

To my neighbours and friends who have enjoyed a laugh on me. Don't worry, you're not in the book. But some of what I see in you might have inspired me. I am amused most by what I love the best in people.

Imitation is the sincerest form of flattery.
- Oscar Wilde

TABLE OF CONTENTS

CHAPTER ONE

The Town Drunk

"Chilly out today," Michael remarked as he opened the front door. A gust of wind blew a yellow leaf in with him, adding an exclamation point to his declaration. He had spent the last week working in the garden, harvesting the winter squash that was starting to turn orange, pulling up the spent summer vegetable vines and stems and piling them up to add to the compost.

In fall clean-up mode, he worked methodically around the house to prepare the gardens for the long sleep till spring. This morning, he started trimming back the rose bushes that blossomed in vibrant colours, from yellow to salmon to dark red and perfumed the front deck all summer with their delicate scents. Michael found gardening to be a satisfying and—if a factual, by-the-numbers man could admit it—even a spiritual experience. "Warm in here, though! And smells wonderful!" He shut the front door and sat on the bench in the foyer to take off his gardening shoes.

"That's the bread baking in the bread machine," Margo responded without looking up. She was on her phone scrolling through recipes that used fruit and techniques for preserving fruit. The fruit trees in their backyard of the house were prolific. She and Michael had already canned three dozen jars of plums and two dozen jars of pears and had harvested three boxes of apples, which they stored in the coldest room in the basement.

Margo mused about her choices aloud. "Canning. No. Done that. Fruit leather. Maybe. Freezing. OK. Fruit cake. Not. Haven't eaten the one we were given last Christmas."

"What are you doing?" Michael asked.

"I'm riding a bicycle," Margo responded in a deadpan voice. It was their private joke. Her pet peeve was Michael asking this question when it was apparent what she was doing. So, instead of explaining, she often said she was doing something else, something absurd. Michael took his wife's sarcasm in stride.

"Ah . . . careful. You don't want to be a distracted driver. Sounds like you are talking to someone about what to do with fruit."

"Yup," Margo affirmed and continued scrolling through her phone. "Freeze-drying. Nope. Don't have the equipment."

Michael walked over to the cupboard, fetched a glass and poured himself a glass of filtered water from the jug on the counter. "You talking to Tina?"

Margo sighed. Her other pet peeve was that her husband wouldn't let go of a conversation until his curiosity was satisfied. She paused and looked up at Michael.

"No. Myself. I'm investigating different ways to use all the fruit loading our trees and potentially rotting on the ground in our backyard. I've given the food security bank and neighbours as much as possible. I'm sick of canning and juicing. What do I do now? That's what I'm trying to figure out."

Michael shrugged his shoulders. "The answer seems obvious to me. Rake them up and deposit them in the forest, far away from human settlement where they won't be an attractant to bears and other wildlife." He took a big gulp of water. "I just read that in a post in the Wannatoka Times. The community is posting reminders on Facebook and tacking up posters everywhere reminding us to deal with our compost and garbage as part of the bear-smart program."

As a rule, bears are passive and can coexist quite well with humans. The exception was the garbage bear. Habituated to humans, it roamed without fear, feeding on garbage left outside or going after the farmers' and gardeners' stock or harvest. In cases like that, farmers had been known to take matters into their own hands. Most shots fired were warning shots. But if a bear became a nuisance, it wasn't uncommon for a property owner to take down a bear.

Margo recalled an earlier time that fall when a report from a shotgun interrupted her pleasant read on her porch swing. Margo shivered and Chance crawled under the deck when he heard it.

"I agree with you about picking up the fruit, Michael. But I can't entirely agree with hauling it into the woods somewhere and dumping it. That's such a waste! We have never had such bounty. Think about what we would pay for fruit in the grocery store. It just doesn't make sense to throw it away. I'll talk to Tina. See what she's doing about their fruit. Meanwhile, you may not dump any fruit until I have at least a chance to devise an alternate plan."

Michael held his hands up in surrender. "OK, chief cook and fruit preserver! I will wait for your instructions. Just one request. Please don't wait too long to take action."

Michael was used to Margo voicing her strong opinions; even her mandates didn't bother him much. He was mild-mannered, and, as long as her demands didn't interfere with what he held dear—his garden and his music collection. He had learned that the way to deal with his wife when she wanted something was to step out of her way and let her do it—unless she stepped into his territory.

Margo was not a gardener. She enjoyed planning and planting flowers in the spring. From then on, she was happy to leave the maintenance and watering to Michael. She appreciated the gardens they had planned together from the comfort of the porch swing on a warm summer day. The exception was preserving fruit that grew on trees with little effort except watering, which satisfied her newly awakened sense of maintaining food security, a concept she had been exposing herself to since she moved to the Kootenays.

Coming from the West Coast, where fruit and vegetables were in plentiful supply year-round, she had never considered times when food would not be accessible. But with harsher, longer winters, travel costs that ratcheted up the food prices, and sometimes impassible roads delaying deliveries, she could see why people in the hinterlands coveted self-reliance and engaged in growing their food and preserving it for the lean times when there might be scarcities or food became unaffordable.

When they first bought the property Wannatoka Springs, which included almost a third of an acre of land, Margo looked out from the oversized windows in the living room onto the backyard below; she saw a desert of scorched lawn and patches of dead grass, with an old, twisted pear tree in one corner, a stunted apple tree in another, both badly in need of pruning and a row of young plum trees that had self-propagated from two overgrown plum trees in the back corner, forming an unruly hedge along the back of the property. The hedge of plum trees butted up against an overgrown garden plot, outlined by a sagging wire fence attached to rusted metal posts that a thicket of raspberry bushes and tall weeds had taken over.

When Michael viewed the same scene, he felt his hands tingle with the anticipation of getting in there and subduing and shaping this plot of land he was now the master. In the early days, when they were both staring out at the backyard, and Margo was bemoaning the lack of landscape and privacy, Michael had put his arm around his wife and said with assurance, "It may look like it now, but I have a vision. I promise you won't remember this in two or three years. You'll see a beautiful garden with flowers, fruit, and vegetables. Your own gardener will bring you bouquets of aromatic flowers and fresh vegetables and fruit to make sumptuous meals with all summer long, garden to table." That promise buoyed Margo's spirits; she loved flowers and was a creative cook.

Turning the backyard into the garden Michael envisioned, had proven to be one of Michael's most significant challenges in the past year, and an ongoing challenge to manage. But the work also became his passion. Margo admired the gardens Michael carved out of the blank canvas as he saw it, but she didn't share his passion for working outdoors. She eschewed any activity that made her sweat. She would passively listen to Michael's litany of accomplishments in the garden and make sympathetic noises when he talked about problems he was trying to solve (like getting rid of slugs and snails) but she didn't contribute much as the topic held only nominal interest for her.

After a while, when Michael came in from the garden, he simply put his harvested carrots or cucumbers on the counter and beamed like a cat who brought a mouse as a prize. Margo would remark how impressed and delighted she was with the size, shape, and ripeness of the produce and then busy herself with finding a unique recipe to incorporate the fresh produce into.

This arrangement would have been a little lonely for Michael had he not found a fellow gardener with whom he could share his gardening successes and head-scratching failures in their neighbour.

A wire fence that ran along the property line at the back of the properties on Spruce Street, dividing them from the backyards of the properties on Maple Street, was the only separation between Michael and Margo's property and their neighbours Joel and Tina, a newly retired couple who had moved to Wannatoka Springs the same summer Margo and Michael had.

Joel loved to work out in his yard and could be seen and heard on almost any day of the week both summer and winter. He turned his garage into a tool and equipment shed when they first moved in. He had tooled up with the latest implements he thought he would need to tame his one-third of an acre: a riding lawnmower, a gas-powered weed-whacker, a battery-operated hedge trimmer, long and short-handled pruners, sprayers, clippers. You name it, Joel's tool shed had it. He even acquired a gas-powered log splitter for splitting logs to burn in his wood stove over the winter. Through several casual 'over the fence' conversations, the two men found a common thread that became a bond between them: tools and toys and growing and nurturing gardens.

In that first summer, Joel constructed a patch-work of square corrugated metal garden beds in the back of his hard that he layered with logs, branches, and other compostable materials to add bulk. The beds were then topped with soil and compost. The raised beds were arranged in a three-by-three grid with grass paths running between them, one lawnmower width apart, so he could keep the paths mowed.

He grew vining legumes on tripod stakes in the center of each square container. Joel explained that the peas and beans he grew would contribute to the summer vegetable harvest and replenish the nitrogen in the soil.

Around the tripod in each bed, he mass-planted a single vegetable crop. He said he had learned this technique in California, where access to land and productive soil was almost out of reach for the average homeowner, and the home gardener had to learn to maximize the potential of plants and the space where they grew them.

Michael was fascinated by Joel's technique. He was a conventional 'row' planter, and having cleared the weeds and rototilled his plot, working in compost and topsoil, he had planted neat rows of vegetable seeds with stakes at the ends on which he had scribed the name of the vegetable with a permanent marker. While they had very different styles, the two men bonded over their admiration for each other's work and passion for gardening.

While Margo set off on a mission to pick Tina's brain about what to do with the bounty of plums they had in their yards, Michael headed out into his sanctuary—his vegetable plot. Usually, he liked the systematic process of weeding or harvesting to allow problems he wanted to solve to percolate through his brain. But today, he hoped Joel was in his yard. He thought it might be beneficial to get another opinion. As Margo started her walk around the block to visit with Tina, Michael headed into his backyard garden, hoping to find Joel so they could discuss the best ways to deal with the excess fruit.

"C'mon in!" Tina chirped and opened the door to the kitchen. Margo propped one hand on the doorjamb and started to take her shoes off. "Don't worry about your shoes. The floor needs washing anyway. Come in and close the door! You're letting the cold air in!" Tina caught Margo's elbow and escorted her in with one hand while shutting the door firmly behind her with the other. Tina and Joel moved to Wannatoka Springs from California. When the temperature dipped below twenty-one degrees Celsius, she felt cold.

"Sorry, my fair-weather friend. We call this weather change the beginning of fall. It's one of the four seasons we enjoy in Canada." Margo liked to drive the point home to her neighbour, who had traded in the year-round sunny climes of California for the hinterland of British Columbia. Tina said they chose to retire in Canada to escape the escalating California wildfires that were encroaching more frequently on urban areas, and to escape the escalating political animosity in their country, which was nearing a flash-point. Either way, it was a fire escape they sought. Although she often complained about being cold, Tina never indicated that she regretted their choice. She said living in BC was much more affordable and peaceful. Tina always said they had made a beautiful escape.

"The weather is the only thing I wish I could have brought with me. I'm a California girl. Joel has a Canadian passport and upbringing in Ontario, not me. Anyway, a mug of coffee will take the chill off. Have a seat!"

Despite her comments about the cold, Tina greeted Margo with a warm smile. To Margo, Tina always seemed upbeat. Everything is 'terrific'! Tina would say if you asked, and she would flash an irresistible smile, revealing a set of perfect, white teeth. Margo admired Tina's naturally sunny disposition and adventuresome, spontaneous spirit. Their friendship worked because Tina's nature balanced out Margo's thoughtful skepticism. Margo was prone to ruminating on the pros and cons, as well as obstacles that might present themselves before committing. If left unchecked, her ruminations could often stall or stagnate an idea.

Tina benefitted from Margo's presentation of rational reasoning as it would frequently hone the concept into a much more workable plan. And Tina's enthusiasm pushed Margo to stop ruminating and hit 'send'!

"The usual?" Tina poised the coffee carafe above the cup. In anticipation of her friend's arrival, she had already prepared the cup with a heaping teaspoon of sugar and a generous dollop of cream. She knew how Margo liked her coffee but was always thoughtful enough to ask.

"Yes, please." Margo smiled and settled onto the stool at the island where she always sat when she visited her friend.

"Did you hear the latest?" Tina asked, setting a steaming mug of coffee in front of Margo.

Margo wrapped her hands around the warm mug. She shook her head. "No."

"There's a bear in the area," Tina said, scooting onto her stool beside Margo's.

"Seriously? This morning, Michael and I were discussing what to do with the plums littering the yard. He said he read a post about bear awareness in the Wannatoka Times. The suggestion was that we should all pick up and dispose of our fruit since it could be an attractant for bears and other wildlife. Michael thinks we should rake them up and dump them in the forest far from our village. I feel sad about doing that. It's such a waste. But honestly, I don't know what to do, so I came over to talk to you.

Tina took a sip of her coffee. "Hmmm . . . I thought you took care of all your fruit trees already. You've been canning for weeks now."

Margo sighed. "I have. But this year, the plums have just gotten away from us. Between the two old trees that Michael doesn't want to cut down and wanting to keep juvenile plum trees as a privacy barrier between us and our neighbours . . . " Margo stopped mid-sentence and winced. The neighbours Michael was trying to obscure behind the plum hedge he was training were Tina and Joel.

Tina caught on to Margo's unfinished thought. "It's fine, Margo. I want a little privacy, too! Don't want Michael catching me sunning in the nude." She giggled.

"Seriously? You suntan in the nude?"

Tina laughed. "No! Not now. But I used to when I was younger and stupider. We had a private backyard and a beach twenty-five minutes drive away in California. I didn't want tan lines when I strutted down the beach in my bikini. Sadly, fear of skin cancer has taken away the joy of that simple pleasure."

Margo concurred with Tina's wistfulness. But, while Tina described her sun-drenched youth in California, Margo conjured up a picture of herself sunning her body in the nude. She saw a Rubenesque woman with red hair turning an unbecoming shade of pink. She shut that picture down quickly and changed the subject.

"So, has this bear been spotted somewhere around here?" She asked.

"Up on the back road, I heard. Getting into someone's fruit trees up there. Breaking branches. Making a mess. Oh, and it broke into that abandoned house up on the hill and may be making a den in there. People are saying it's becoming a nuisance, bear." Tina said. "Going to get himself shot!"

Tina looked over her coffee cup dramatically.

Margo's eyebrows shot up. "What? Wow! Have people around here ever considered that *we* might be the problem, not the bear? It seems to me that our negligence creates a nuisance."

Margo and Tina sat silently for a moment, sipping their coffee. Margo was surprised at her passionate outburst. Tina pondered whether to change the subject since her friend seemed on edge.

"I'm sorry, I didn't mean . . ." Tina started.

At the same time, Margo asked, "So what are

you doing with your plums? That's what I came to you ask about."

Tina shrugged. " I've frozen some and made fruit leather for my grandkids. Not sure there is anything more I can do. I guess I'll let Joel clean them up and haul them away. What about you?"

Margo sighed and leaned on one elbow. "I am at an impasse. Part of me wants just to quit processing; it's becoming too much of a chore. Another part says, "You have been given a bounty. Do not waste it!"

Tina covered Margo's hand with her own. "It's OK. You can let go. You can only save so many plums in the world." The twinkle in Tina's eyes belied the seriousness in her tone.

Margo pulled her hand out from under and smacked Tina's lightly in reproach. "Stop it. I'm serious. I am out of ideas. I need help! I thought I would try making fruit leather next. I came over to ask you for your fruit leather recipe. You don't lace them with pot or anything, do you?" Margo grinned, remembering the pot cookies Tina made for her that Michael accidentally got too high on by eating too many. That was a trip of a lifetime!

Tina threw her head back and laughed a tinkly laugh that ended in an uncharacteristic snort. "No!" she said, collecting herself. "They're going to my grandchildren! But if you want some 'special' fruit leather," Tina said, inserting air quotes into the sentence with her fingers around the word special, "I'm sure that can be arranged." Tina ducked her head and tittered into her cup.

Margo held up one hand, "Thanks, but no thanks. The first (and last) trip we took down that road was enough of a memory. I thought of fruit leather because I've run out of canning jars and think I've juiced as many litres of plum juice as I care to drink. What else can you do with plums?"

"You juiced plums?" Tina sounded surprised. "I hadn't thought of that!"

"We've juiced apples, too. But I think Michael and I can drink only so much plum juice."

"So, you have a juicer?" Tina leaned toward Margo; her interest piqued.

"I have a steam extractor. It extracts the juice from the fruit, so you don't have to peel or pit them."

"Wow! That's perfect!" Tina slapped her hand on the table. "How much do you have already?"

"About 16 liters. I pour the juice into four-litre plastic milk jugs, which I freeze. But there is also a limit on how many you can store in a freezer."

"Ha!" Tina jumped up from her stool, nearly knocking off her coffee cup. "I know what we can do with our leftover plums!" she exclaimed, "We can make wine!"

Tina's sudden movement startled Margo. She reflexively pushed herself back into a resistant posture. "I know nothing about making wine," she said flatly. "Besides, Michael doesn't drink wine, and I don't drink enough wine to make brewing a whole batch worthwhile."

"Joel and I drink wine!" Tina countered. "And you and I drink wine on my deck sometimes. Picture us—you and me—sitting on the deck in our lounge chairs, gossiping over a nice glass or two of our homemade plum wine." Tina posed with an imaginary wine glass held up by the stem in one hand, a teasing smile on her face.

Margo looked away and frowned. She was already thinking of obstacles to Tina's crazy idea. "What if it became contaminated and made us sick? What if it killed us? We should probably leave wine-making to the experts."

"You're such a worry wort!" Tina dismissed Margo's objections with the flip of her hand. "I'm sure we could find plenty of wine-making 'experts' on YouTube." Tina made air quotes around the word experts when she said it. "Can't be that hard. Humankind has been making wine for thousands of years. Hey, even Jesus made wine! At a wedding! And no one was poisoned. Gospel truth!" Tina held her right hand up, set her left on the counter, and nodded.

Margo smiled despite her misgivings. Since she and Tina met, Tina had been prodding Margo to embrace retirement as a time to open up to possibilities. Admittedly, some of the things she had tried ended up in the 'Done that. Never do it again' column, but so far, Margo found herself saying 'yes' more often than 'no.'

"Why not!" Margo threw up her hands in surrender. "It can't be that dangerous if people have been doing it since time-immemorial. On the other hand, the dead can't talk."

Tina laughed and raised her mug in a toast. "To the new winemakers of Wannatoka Springs!"

Margo held her mug in the air, but before she clinked, she looked Tina in the eye and said solemnly, "But you, Tina, must agree to be the taste tester."

Tina smiled precociously and clinked her mug with Margo's. "Of course! I'm dying for a glass of home-brewed plum wine! Cheers!"

Both friends took a sip of coffee and sealed the deal. "Time to call up the expert!" Tina said enthusiastically while reaching for her cell phone. She tapped a few keys into the YouTube app search and then scrolled down the screen until she found a YouTube video that looked promising. Pressing play, Tina propped up the phone on the counter so both could watch it.

The video was descriptively titled "How to Make Practically Any Fruit into Wine," presented by a woman who called herself The Backyard Winemaker.

After the two watched the four-minute video several times, Tina clicked off her phone and slid off her stool. "That was awesome! Thank you, backyard winemaker! I think I'm ready! Let's go pick up some plums and get this ball rolling!"

Margo held her hand up. "Whoa! Just a minute, Tina. We don't have a plan! We don't even have the proper equipment!" Margo listed off the items she remembered the YouTuber mentioning. "Carboys, a syphon, a hydrometer–whatever that is–and a lot more I can't remember. We need to make a list." As a career teacher, Margo was a prepper and a list-maker.

"Right," Tina said, turning her phone back on and scrolling through The Backyard Winemaker's video channel. "Got it. Our new best friend, The Backyard Winemaker, has already made a list! I'll copy and paste it into my notes and text you a copy."

By the time Margo heard the ping of Tina's text landing and had opened the text to scrutinize the list, Tina was already shrugging on her fleece and heading toward the door.

"Let's go, Margo. I'm betting that we could buy a wine-making kit somewhere in Crystal Lake. With all the homesteaders around here, you'd think the hardware store would stock them.

Margo looked up from her list. "But I'm not ready. I can't go like this . . ." She looked down at the baggy grey sweatshirt and black leggings she had hastily pulled on to walk to Tina's house. I don't have my purse or wallet, and I need to change!"

Tina took her purse down from where it hung on the coat hook at her kitchen door. After a brief rummage through it, she pulled out her remote fob. Holding it up, she pronounced, "We can take my car. I'll drive around the corner to your house so you can grab your purse. Who cares what you're wearing? This is the Kootenays! People wear pyjamas to go shopping!"

Tina's enthusiasm was like a magnet; Margo had

never quite gotten used to Tina's spontaneity but was learning to lean into it. Margo stood up and smoothed the oversized sweatshirt over her thighs—vainly trying to disguise her size and shape. "OK. But I insist on changing my outfit."

Margo was self-conscious about the weight she had gained since retirement. If she happened to glance up when she dressed in front of her mirrored door closet, she would cringe. When she was younger and more svelte, she had disapproved of full-bodied women who wore leggings, saying to herself, *skinny jeans and leggings should be a privilege, not a right*. Now, she was on the other end of the spectrum. Like many women in her age group, Margo had hung on to leggings and stretchy jeans, choosing comfort over more flattering styles.

"Your chauffeur awaits, Madam Priss." Tina made a mock swish with one arm, leading the way through the open door. "I hope one day, you will accept the freedom retirement offers: a land where you don't have to care about what you wear or look like. But until then, I respect you as a woman bravely embracing the grand adventure! And I will happily drive you around to your place so you can change."

Margo and Tina set off in Tina's navy BMW SUV to shop for wine equipment at the only store they could think of that would carry it in Crystal Lake—the hardware store.

But the purple-haired clerk with a nose ring and a bright red polo shirt that bore the hardware store logo, disappointingly said they had no wine kits in stock. It was the wine-making season, and they were sold out. The youthful-looking clerk (whose appearance gave no hint as to a binary designation) squinted at the screen on their store computer and tugged absentmindedly at their nose ring. Unable to identify most of the apparatus that Tina read out from her phone, they shook their head slowly and said they were sorry but couldn't help.

Perhaps their colleague Deborah could, though. They called for 'Deborah' on the PA. In response to the announcement, a middle-aged woman with heavy thighs sausaged into black leggings and breasts that maximized the stretch of her red uniform polo shirt walked laboriously towards them down the aisle. She seemed annoyed at being interrupted in whatever task she was undertaking in one of the aisles.

When Tina explained their mission and showed her the list, Deborah sighed and sucked her teeth. Margo held her breath, but didn't hold out much hope. Deborah returned the phone to Tina and said, "Yer in luck. I don't know much. But I do know about wine-making. Me and my wife grow and harvest our grapes and all kinds of other fruit on our acreage. We usually bottle about 120 bottles of wine every year. Keeps us goin' through the long winters." Deborah paused. A brief smile sparked and then disappeared from Deborah's face. Tina and Margo smiled back and nodded in unison. "Now, I'd rather sell you a kit 'cause yer newbies. But we ain't got no more. And fruit won't wait for no wine." Another smile flashed and disappeared across Deborah's face leaving no sign that she thought she had just made a joke. "Let's see what we can do to improvise. Follow me. Oh—you'll need a cart." With that said, she turned and shuffled back down the center aisle, turning left into the fifth aisle that had a sign above it that read, 'paint supplies'.

Tina gestured to Margo to get the cart. Margo nodded in agreement. Margo returned to the store's front to fetch a cart and Tina followed closely behind Deborah, hanging on to her every word as she explained what to replace the listed equipment with and how to make it work. Margo brought up the rear, pushing the shopping cart, while Tina loaded whatever Deborah handed her.

Despite her first impression, Margo was surprised at how innovative and knowledgeable Deborah was. She suggested substitutions for some items and identified others as only available online. She instructed Tina on how to make an airlock with a plastic drinking straw and duct tape, sealing the hole of the carboy with duct tape around the straw so air could flow through. After the lesson on DIY innovation and lunch at a popular deli and coffee shop, Tina and Margo headed back home reviewing what they remembered about Deborah's improvisations and comparing their new list with the list Tina copied from The Backyard Winemaker's page. Margo was getting excited. This would be their first foray into wine-making.

This is the list Tin copied from The Backyard Winemaker.
2 Carboys
1 Hydrometer
1 Airlock
1 Siphon
1 fermentation receptacle
Brewer's yeast
1 Acidity tester
1 Bottle filler
Cleaners and sanitizers
2-dozen glass wine bottles

After consulting with Deborah, this is the list they came up with.
2 hard plastic water dispenser refills
1 Hydrometer (online order)
1 Airlock (plastic drinking straw with duct tape around it)
1 Siphon (a length of flexible plastic hose)
Brewer's yeast (online order)
1 fermentation receptacle (an empty paint bucket with a

lid and duck tape to seal it)
1 Acidity tester (Deborah suggested soil testing Ph strips
would work)
1 Bottle filler (kitchen funnel and a flexible plastic hose)
Cleaners and sanitizers (hydrogen peroxide + washing
soda, with instructions for oven sterilization of the glass
bottles)
Sulphates for wine-making (online order)
Two dozen wine bottles (From Tina's recycling bin)
Two dozen corks (Online order)
Corker (The hardware store had one left in stock).

***

"What are you going to do with all those plums?" Michael
asked. When he strolled around the corner from the front
yard where he was working on a flowerbed, Michael saw
Margo and Tina hauling plastic bins of plums they had picked
up to the patio, lining them up against the wall.

"Michael! You startled me!" Margo looked up,
wiping the sweat from her brow with the sleeve of
her sweatshirt. "Oh . . . ah . . ." She looked around
self-consciously. "Tina and I thought that we should
do our bit for the bear-smart effort, so we are picking up the plums so we don't attract bears. We're, uh,
doing it together." Margo smiled at Tina. "Both yards!"

Michael's spidey senses tingled. He couldn't recall
the last time Margo had volunteered to do anything in
the garden. Margo didn't garden.

"I was going to do that," Michael replied, walking
towards the women. "You just got ahead of me. What
are you going to do with them? Need me to drive out
to the forest to dump them?" Michael was always looking for an opportunity to take the ATV out. He didn't get
much practice, and he wanted to improve his proficiency at

handling it off-road in case one of the men in the neighbourhood asked him to come along on one of their forays up the
logging roads or along trails through the bush.

"Oh! No!" Tina replied too swiftly. She thought
of their hard work and dreams of wine-making being
hauled away. "Umm . . . we got this!"

"Well, you can't just leave it here," Michael
gestured around him. "It's pretty close to the house.
That's not smart. Is Joel going to help? We were talking
about taking a load of plums into the forest—maybe
tomorrow if the weather holds. Good excuse to fire
up the ATVs and have a boy's trek," Michael swelled
with pride.

Tina felt trapped. If she didn't come up with an
alternative, they were hooped. Her eyes cut to Margo.
Margo shook her head in warning. "Not necessary. We're
going to make wine!" She blurted out and directed her
most disarming smile towards Michael. "You know, waste
not want not!"

Margo glared at Tina. She was hoping to work
on Michael slowly. Get him warmed up to the idea.
The drip method, she called it. Michael would be
skeptical about wine-making. He would probably assume
that wine-making would lead to more wine-drinking. When
they lived in the city, they bought a bottle of wine
for special occasions and when they had guests over
for dinner. But it was never something they thought of
stocking in the house.

Now that Margo had met Tina, she drank wine
with Tina when Tina invited Margo to sit on the deck on
the long summer evenings. She had formed a new habit
of buying a couple of bottles of wine when they went
shopping at Crystal Lake and stocking them, so when
they invited Joel and Tina over to play cards or watch a
movie in the winter, they had wine to offer.

In many ways, Michael thought Tina was a good influence on his wife. Tina had become the friend who took Margo out of her comfort zone, not drastically, just enough to allow Margo to open the window to her new life a crack and breathe in the fresh air. Tina also saw the lighter side of things and had a relaxed disposition, contrasting Margo's seriousness and anxiety-filled anticipation of what could go wrong. But Michael was worried that, following Tina's example, Margo would normalize drinking wine to lighten her mood or relax. That was his only reservation about Tina's influence.

Michael crossed his arms. He was about to say what he thought but held back his remarks. Instead, he calculated the probability of their success—less than fifty-percent, since they knew nothing about wine making. He mentally weighed the consequences of either scenario. Success: cheap wine, happy wife. Failure: another experience for Margo, and another story for her next book. "So, you think you know what you're doing," Michael said instead.

"How hard can it be? Humans have been making wine since the beginning of time!" Tina repeated the argument she had used with Margo and flashed her infectious smile.

Margo jumped in with, "We found an expert home-vintage winemaker on YouTube who demonstrates the step-by-step process and lists all of the equipment you need to make wine."

"Besides, we are doing this as part of the bear-smart initiative in our community," Tina added. "Removing the attractants that might entice the bear I heard is foraging around some neighbours' properties."

Michael raised his eyebrows. "A bear?" He had heard that a bear was seen up the hill, along the back road. He hadn't seen a bear since he moved to Wannatoka Springs.

He hoped he would one day. But not in his backyard. "In that case, I'll leave you two bear-smart volunteers to clean up the fruit in our yard and make wine, for a good cause."

He saluted the two women with a grin and turned to go. Hesitating, he turned back toward them, "Just one word of caution. Please review the instructions carefully and follow them explicitly. Wine-making is a science. Also, after extracting the juice, please give me the pulp and fruit waste to dump far away from our community. We don't want to attract bears with compostables, either.

Margo and Tina nodded their agreement with sober faces. When Michael started walking away, they looked at each other and smiled, giving each other a silent thumbs-up. They felt like schoolgirls whose chemistry teacher told them to approach their experiment respectfully and to be cautious not to blow anything up.

Serious wine-making requires finesse and experience. Margo and Tina, having neither, carefully followed The Backyard Winemaker's directions and example on her YouTube channel.

When they processed the juice with the steamer that sat on a hotplate on a table set up on Margo's patio, they poured it into the fermentation receptacle—a twenty-litre plastic paint bucket with a lid. They then sprinkled the brewer's yeast over the top of the plum juice and sealed the lid with duct tape. Then they hauled the bucket in a wheelbarrow to the shed in Margo's backyard to let it sit for three weeks in a warm, stable environment to start the fermentation process, as instructed by The Backyard Winemaker. The shed, still full of junk left over from the previous owner, was largely disused and rarely visited. They thought it would be the perfect place for plum juice to sit undisturbed to ferment in the first stage of wine-making.

Margo checked on their brew every few days,

crossing off the days on the calendar one by one, anticipating the countdown to day twenty-one. Though the pail was sealed, Margo's nose picked up a whiff of a sweet-yeasty odour when she opened the door.

More than once, Margo had the urge to open it to see how the wine was fermenting but held her discipline. The tutorial had explicitly said not to open the fermenting receptacle lest the wine be exposed to bacteria or wild yeast that could contaminate it.

Whenever she went to Tina's for coffee or to sit on her deck with a glass of wine, Tina would ask, with a wink and a finger tapping the side of her nose, how their 'hooch' was brewing. Tina had become enchanted with the idea of being a homesteading Kootenay hillbilly with an illegal wine-making operation deep in the woods. Margo would roll her eyes and report to Tina that nature seemed to be taking its course.

Margo never worried that what they were doing was illegal. It wasn't. She googled it. But she did worry about the efficacy of their makeshift equipment. She lamented that they didn't live near a city with u-brew establishments where they could have used proper equipment, or big-box and specialty stores where they could have purchased a wine-making kit. Tina dismissed Margo's worries with a wave of her hand as if she were waving a magic wand that would make everything work out right.

"Just think," Tina said one evening when Margo was stewing about the outcome of the wine brewing in her shed. "We are making wine like our ancestors may have, like people here in the hinterland probably still do. We are so on trend!" They were sitting on Tina's deck, each with a glass of a British Columbia VQA wine bottled in a winery in Kelowna, BC. Tina had only bought wine from an Okanagan winery since they started making their own wine. She may have left most of her California airs in California, but Tina still liked to think she was 'on trend' even in Wannatoka Springs.

"Right," Margo retorted. "Just what I always imagined, being 'on trend' with the hinterland home-steaders, wearing long flowing dresses and Birken-stocks, living in the woods and having my own label of homegrown wine."

Tina laughed. "Have you had a look at yourself in the mirror lately? Isn't that a long flowing dress you are wearing? And Birkenstocks would be an upgrade!" Tina frowned at Margo's crocs in mock disapproval. Margo looked down at her dress and then up at Tina reproachfully.

"Embrace it!" Tina enthused, lifting her glass. "Think of it as a cultural shift. We are actively engaged in our community bear-smart program and in establishing food security and sustainability. If the world around us turned to chaos and political uprisings, we could unplug our phones and thrive in our little isolated community nestled between forested mountains at the edge of a lake, living off the land, hunting, fishing and growing our vegetable gardens, and cheering ourselves with a glass of our backyard wine, totally oblivious to what was going on out there!" Tina tilted her glass of wine towards Margo. Margo smiled despite herself and lifted her glass, clinking it with her friend's glass.

The thoughts Tina expressed resonated with Margo. She had moved to avoid bombardment from the media and the noise of construction, the ever-expanding building projects usurping arable land in the lower mainland, skyrocketing housing costs, an increasing number of home-less people calling for their right to squat on concrete and in parks. Gang violence and reports of crimes were an almost nightly news item. As were incursions and wars around the globe. Since they moved, Michael and Margo have sworn off listening to the nightly news, and Margo rarely opened her news app. Her spirit had shifted from a constant undercurrent of anxiety to a center of calm broken only by the occasional breaches of neighbourly respect that personally affected them.

On the twenty-first day of fermentation, Margo woke up early to a bright, crisp fall morning. Michael was still asleep, so she quietly stepped out of the bedroom and went downstairs. At the rear door, she pulled on Michael's garden boots to protect her feet from the cold ground. Chance, their dog, had followed her down the stairs. He whined when he got close to the door and started sniffing and scratching at it. "In a hurry, boy? Can't cross your legs anymore?" Margo opened the door, and Chance squeezed past her and bolted outside, barking in earnest. Startled, Margo stepped out quickly to see what had warranted his urgent attention. "Chance! Quiet! Stop barking! You'll wake the whole neighbourhood," she hissed, conscious of the level of her voice.

And then she caught a glimpse of what Chance had been so eager to confront. She stood stalk still. Heart pounding. At the other end of the yard, a massive black bear's huge hairy rear end was stuck in the tangled wire he had broken through on his way into the yard. The bear twisted and tugged his powerful body until he had finally freed himself of the wire that had trapped him and made his ungainly retreat through Tina and Joel's yard.

As the bear broke free from his entanglement, Chance exploded with a volley of barking at the bear, from a safe distance, as if to say, "And don't come back! Or else!"

"Chance!" Margo called out sharply. "Come!" She was afraid the bear might turn around and attack her dog. Or worse! She had been told that sometimes a dog would turn and return to their owner if the bear started chasing them, bringing the bear back with it. At her command, Chance obediently returned, still growling and whining in protest. Margo watched as the bear sauntered through Tina and Joel's yard, then onto the street, where he hesitated, swayed to the right, and disappeared from view.

Margo shivered and pulled her robe tighter. "Michael!" she shouted toward the bedroom window as she crossed back toward the house.

A tousled-haired Michael appeared at the window. "What's all this hullabaloo?" he yelled back.

"A bear!" Margo pointed at the fence. "It came through the fence. I saw it before Chance chased it away. Huge hind end." She stretched out her arms as she tried to estimate the size but couldn't stretch her arms out wide enough. "It broke through the fence between our yard and Tina and Joel's." Margo pointed at the gap in the fence and the tangled wire.

"Is it still here? In the yard?" Michael queried.

"No. It left the same way it came in. And then crossed Tina and Joel's yard and up the street. I can't see where it went."

"I'll be right down," Michael said, disappearing from the window.

He threw on a robe over his pyjamas. Not waiting to find his gardening boots, he trudged outside in his slippers. Michael was a meticulous man who had clothes and shoes for every occasion. He was already annoyed that he had been woken up with a cacophony of barking and yelling, so navigating the dewy lawn in his slippers only raised the level of his aggravation. "What's going on, Margo?" He stopped in his tracks. Margo was staring down at the pile of bear scat beside the metal compost box Michael had purchased. It was supposed to be a bear-proof. Michael made a quick assessment. It looked like the damage was limited to a series of scratches the bear had made down the side, and a dent in the top where the bear had climbed up to try to pry open the lid but couldn't figure out the lever system that locked him out.

"Looks like the bear might have smelled something in the compost bin and tried to get at it. There's no real damage."

While Michael examined the compost bin and the surrounding area, Chance moved on. Nose to the ground, he followed a trail that led him to the shed. He stopped to investigate at intervals, sniffed, peed on several grass patches, and then went around the corner of the shed.

Margo heard a sharp bark from Chance, who had disappeared around the shed. She huffed across the lawn to catch up with her dog. "What's up, boy? You find something?" She stopped just short of stepping into a pile of fresh bear scat near the entrance to the shed. "Think I found some more evidence here," she called back to Michael.

Michael caught up with Margo who tiptoeing carefully now, following Chance's sharp barks. When they rounded the corner of the shed, they both stopped. The shed's wooden door was ajar, swinging away from the opening on one hinge. The other had been torn off.

Margo looked at Michael, and Michael looked at Margo. At the same time, each said to the other, "The wine!"

"Did you forget to latch the door?" Michael demanded.

"No, Michael!" Margo protested. "Look! The door has been pried off its hinge, and the latch is broken off!"

An indescribable stench wafted from the shed. Margo took a tentative step forward and peered in. The bucket was tipped over, and the lid with the duct tape had been wrenched away and Chance was half-way inside, gingerly sniffing and licking something on the floor.

"Oh no! My wine!" she exclaimed. Then, "Chance! Stop that! Come out of there!" Chance looked up and swirled his tongue around his jaws. Reluctantly, he backed out of the shed, following Margo's order. Margo held the sleeve of her robe against her nose and backed away.

"My wine! The bear drank my wine!" She screamed when she backed up far enough to escape the stench.

Michael's arm encircled his wife's shoulder to calm her, while his eyes swept through the inside of the shed, calculating the damage. "And pretty much turned this shed into a brewery and outhouse doing it!' He said with distaste.

"I'm sorry, Margo. But there is nothing we can do now. Let's head back to the house and put some distance between us and this reeking mess. I'll put the coffee on." He steered them back towards the house.

Later that morning, the following posts appeared on the *Wannatoka Times* Face Book page.

Tina: A bear is sprawled out on our front lawn, belly up. He won't move. We tried scaring him off by shouting or banging pots, but he just rolled over onto his back and started snoring! What do we do?

Michael: This morning, a bear broke down our fence, entered our yard, forced open our shed door, and got into Margo's homemade wine. Our dog, Chance, chased him off the property. The bear was last seen making his way onto Maple St.

Tina—replying to Michael: What? The bear drank our wine??? So, what we have here is a drunk bear sleeping it off on our lawn?! Laugh/cry emoji

Spliff—replying to Tina: Don't do anything. He'll sleep it off and then go. Sorry about the wine. If you want to start over, we have plums! Smile emoji

CHAPTER TWO

Michael, Michael, How Does Your Garden Grow?

"They have been at it for months," Margo told Tina. The two women looked out Margo's living room windows at their adjacent backyards. Below, they could see their men toiling in their backyard gardens. A camaraderie based on the love of growing plants and a friendly competitiveness had developed between their husbands, Michael and Joel.

They were very different men and came from different backgrounds—Michael had been an insurance actuary. He had worn a suit most days and commuted to work on the sky train to his office in a high-rise in the city's business sector. He had never punched a clock and was expected to work overtime without overtime pay to meet a company deadline. He regularly won bonuses for high quotas and outstanding results. Michael liked the conformity and predictability of numbers. His steady progress forward and the confidence of his peers provided all the satisfaction he needed at work.

He was different when he loosened his tie, took off his suit, and hung it neatly in the closet. He enjoyed listening to rock music, of which he had an enviable collection of record albums. He played Scrabble with Margo some evenings. He also liked to stay active and enjoyed the camaraderie of sports. In the winter, he played hockey in a community league, and in the spring and summer months, he played golf on men's nights.

Michael was also a passionate gardener. During the long growing season on the coast, Michael would be in his garden after work, planting, nurturing and harvesting cucumbers, squash, and anything else he could persuade to come up in his postage-stamp garden plot. He proudly brought in the fruits—and vegetables—of his labour for Margo to prepare.

Joel was born in Canada but relocated to California to pursue his trade in high-voltage electrical engineering. He hung on to his Canadian citizenship; however, because he had enough of the big city and wanted to retire in British Columbia.

For Joel, off-work time was adventure time. He loved the outdoors. He loved hiking, mountain biking and camping with his wife, Tina, and when they lived in California, he loved to surf. Tina was as active as Joel was, so the two enjoyed an outdoor lifestyle that they thought would work well in their plans to retire in the hinterland of British Columbia.

When it came to gardening, Joel found container gardening and hot-house gardening on their small plot in the big city was the most efficient way to grow edibles. He found his niche was growing salsa ingredients—peppers, tomatoes, chives, onions and cilantro—plants that thrived in the hot climate of southern California. He bragged that he made the best salsa north of Mexico.

The climate in Wannatoka Springs was a challenge for Joel and Tina to get used to. It's similar to the west coast of Canada, with mild temperatures and heavy precipitation in the winter and spring. Unlike the coast, the winter precipitation usually comes in the form of snow. Summers are generally mild, with occasional rainy and cloudy days. However, in recent years, the weather seemed to be getting hotter and drier, leading to increased forest fires. Some attributed this to climate change.

Being adaptable and resourceful, Joel designed a garden of raised beds in their backyard in their first summer in their new home. He drew from his experience of growing in pots on a balcony to adapt to a larger scale. However, he faced challenges adapting to local weather conditions, such as dealing with cold snaps and fungus on his tomato plants, which he hadn't encountered before. Luckily, he found a valuable source of gardening advice and knowledge in his neighbour, Michael. In exchange, Michael often sought Joel's expertise for home projects. Joel was skilled with tools and had the right tools for the job.

The over-the-fence consultations led to a strong bond between the two men. As their gardens flourished, their produce became a source of friendly rivalry, competing to see whose tomatoes were tastiest or which squash would grow the biggest.

This summer, the two had taken on the challenge of growing the tallest sunflower. Michael had mentioned to Joel that he thought he would grow sunflowers this year and hoped to enter the competition for the tallest sunflower in the annual fall fair in the neighbouring town of Crestview. He had come across a post advertising a local fall fair the previous fall, but it was too late to enter the competitions. However, the idea piqued his interest, and he noted it for next year. When the two men were discussing what they were planning to grow that next spring, Michael mentioned that he had decided to grow sunflowers with the hope that he would be able to place an entry in the 'giant' category, which included, among other things, the heaviest pumpkin, the heaviest potato, the biggest zucchini, and the tallest sunflower. As it happened, Michael had some experience growing sunflowers when he was a boy. His parents enrolled him in a 4-H club to round out his education. He had grown a very tall sunflower that won a prize. His record-high sunflower was seventeen feet high, and the seedpod was fourteen inches in diameter. His picture with the sunflower was published in the local paper: twelve-year-old Michael standing stiffly beside a monster sunflower that towered over him, formally holding up a blue ribbon.

When Michael proposed that he would enter the tallest sunflower competition, Joel jumped at the idea. He knew nothing about growing sunflowers, but he was up for the challenge to produce anything—especially if the challenge was pitted against his new friend.

"It's dead easy, Michael said when the seeds arrived, and they had split them up. "All you have to do is plant them outside in a sunny spot with good soil—although they will grow in almost anything— and fertilize the heck out of them."

Joel's ears perked up at the mention of fertilizer. He had experimented with various fertilizers and had developed his own unique concoction over the years that produced the plumpest tomatoes and glossy peppers.

"What kind of fertilizer?" Michael shrugged and smiled at Joel, saying he wouldn't reveal his secret. He threw out the standard comment, "20-20-20 will do. It's an all-round fertilizer."

Joel nodded but knew Michael would add ingredients he wasn't telling him about. From experience drawn from his own experimentation, he was confident he could develop a sunflower-raising concoction.

The only other piece of advice Michael gave Joel was to plant them in a sheltered, south-facing spot—preferably against a structure so they could be protected from the wind and tied or staked when they grew tall and their seeds grew heavy.

In May, Michael and Joel made a shallow garden bed along one wall of their buildings. Michael chose his shed in the backyard because it got the most sun. Joel dug a trench along a south-facing wall of his house and filled it with topsoil and compost. They each planted the seeds from the same packet, which they divided between them—just to be fair. As the sunflower plants grew, the two gardeners nurtured them, watered them, and often compared them with the others. But, talk as they would, openly sharing gardening tips, failures and triumphs, they each guarded the secret concoction they used on their sunflowers. However, they attributed their sunflowers' success and growth rate to their personal fertilizer blend.

It was now August. The sunflowers in Michael's patch had reached the height of the shed and were still growing. Joel's line of sunflowers against his garage had grown above the roof line, dwarfing all the other land-scapes in the yard, their giant golden heads nodding in agreement that they were the giants.

Margo and Tina were looking through Margo's living room windows down at their husbands' sunflower stands. Margo had the binoculars focused on Michael's patch along the side of the shed. "I wonder if Michael has a winner there? Do you see that one on the left? It looks to be a head above the others." She handed the binoculars to Tina.

"That's one giant sunflower, all right!" Tina remarked, holding the binoculars to her eyes. "When did you say the fall fair was?"

"The weekend of September tenth."

Tina turned her binoculars to her husband Joel's sunflowers growing against the south side of their house. "Hmm . . . looks like Joel's Giants are doing pretty well too. I wouldn't be surprised if that one in the middle is as tall, if not taller than Michael's."

"Seriously? Let me see," Margo frowned. Tina passed the binoculars back to Margo. She focused the binoculars on Joel's sunflowers growing against their garage wall. The tallest one was already weighed down as it was with its large seed head. "Hard to compare. Especially from this distance." Margo kept her tone nonchalant, not wanting Tina to hear a twinge of concern that perhaps Joel's was higher than Michael's. Throughout her teaching, Margo emphasized to students that it's not winning that counts; participation and having fun are the most important things. And yet, when it was personal, she felt a competitive instinct tingling.

"They have both put so much effort into cultivating these flowers. I say good luck to both of them. May the best sunflower win." Tina replied. "Thanks for the coffee—and the gawk at what our husbands are up to. I'd better get going, though. I've got to get my gear ready for the women's day hiking trip. We are hiking the Huckleberry trail to the Cascade peak tomorrow. Sure, you don't want to change your mind and come along? Chance could go, too. Dogs are welcome."

Margo smiled and declined. "It would mean I'd have to break in my new hiking shoes, someone said were a must-have here in the Kootenays. So far, they are still in the box. I'm sure they'd give me blisters. Maybe next time."

Tina laughed. She was used to Margo's excuses for avoiding outdoor activities—even though when she had suggested one—like hiking together—Margo had initially embraced the idea and bought the shoes online and cargo pants and a backpack. But after outfitting herself, her enthusiasm was spent.

Michael came in the front door just as Tina was leaving.

"Hi, Tina! How's it going?" Michael greeted her. "Super Awesome! And you, Michael? How's your sunflower garden growing? Tina's eyes twinkled.

"Wonderfully! I couldn't be more pleased." Michael answered. "I'm confident in the probability, projecting their daily and weekly growth rate, collated with the number of days they have left in their cycle, that at least one will grow a head taller than Joel's tallest one. Only a probability, of course. We actuaries say we can't predict the future, but we hedge our bets." Michael couched the pun in a self-conscious cough.

"I'm impressed!" Tina said. "Awesome! As I've already said to Margo—may the best sunflower win!" Tina sat on the foyer bench to lace up her cross-trainers.

Michael then turned his attention to Margo but spoke theatrically, intending to let them both in on the news. "Just got back from the garage. I was right. When you step on the brake, the tires' squealing sound indicates worn-out brake pads. I'll book a time to take it in next week for the garage to replace them. I'm glad I was tuned in. It would be a disaster waiting to happen if I hadn't had the foresight to have them checked out. Can you imagine brakes going out from under you just as a deer crossed the highway?" Michael was buoyed by his diagnosis being corroborated by the mechanic and having the foresight to have them checked out. Michael knew nothing about cars but had always taken on vehicle maintenance as his duty, even if he could only defer to a mechanic with more knowledge than himself.

"Oh, my goodness!" Tina's voice was tinged with alarm. "I'm glad nothing happened!"

Michael's chest swelled slightly. He appreciated

Tina's responsiveness to his indication that he had faced potential danger and faced it down.

Knowing Michael tended to exaggerate slightly when playing the hero's role, Margo responded coolly. "That's good. I'm sure they will take care of it. Oh, Tina, there was something I meant to ask. Does Joel have any habanero peppers growing? I want to make a Jerk Chicken recipe tonight. I thought I had some . . . just a second, let me check.

I'm pretty sure Joel does," Tina offered, waiting for Margo to check her inventory. Both women had lost the thread of Michael's story.

Undeterred, Michael went on. "That was quite an ordeal, you know. Driving nearly forty kilometres to the nearest garage, not knowing if the car would stay on track, worked up an appetite."

"Mmmmmmmm," Margo muttered in response to Michael, her head still in the fridge. She shuffled a couple of bags of greens and threw out her response to Tina, "I guess I'm out."

"We have tons!" Tina threw back.

Feeling ignored, Michael amped up his act. "A man could use fortification for his labour. What's for lunch, good-looking'?" With that, he patted Margo gently on her rear. Startled, she jerked up, and her head bumped into the top of the fridge compartment. Margo turned and grinned at her husband, gingerly rubbing a spot on her head that came in contact with the fridge.

Tina yelped and then stifled a giggle.

"Then a man can go forth and forage!" Margo commanded as she swung the fridge door open and stepped aside so Michael could see for himself what was there if he cared to make his own lunch. "C'mon Tina. I'll walk you back to your house and pick up a couple of peppers. Let's get out of here before I turn into Samantha in

Bewitched and twinkle my nose to put a sandwich in Darren's hand."

Michael played his final hero's death scene—staggering, he pulled out the imaginary knife from his heart and then poked his head into the fridge.

Tina stopped when they got to the corner and turned to Margo. Putting her hand on her friend's arm, she said. "Margo, what do you say to a friendly wager on whose husband grows the tallest sunflower?"

"I don't know. . ." Margo hesitated. She didn't like committing to a wager unless she was confident of the outcome. She hated losing.

"It shouldn't be money." Tina went on, thinking Margo's objection was money. "Not between friends. How about something like a dare-bet?"

Margo's eyebrows rose. "Aren't we a bit old to dare each other to do something ridiculous?"

"No, we're not too old! Think of retirement as circling back to your childhood. You are free to do anything you want—within legal limits, of course," Tina winked. "You get to play! Nobody's supervising you. Nobody cares!"

Margo didn't respond right away, so Tina explained her proposed dare-bet. "I propose that if Michael's sunflower is higher than Joel's when measured at the fair, you get to dare me to do something. It could even be something I would never do or hate doing. And if Michael's sunflower wins, I get to dare you to do something you would never do or even hate thinking about doing."

"I can think of a hundred things that would be," Margo said dryly.

"Oh, I can think of one you might hate." Tina smiled mischievously. "You told me once that you hated camping. Even the thought of it made you queasy. You said you couldn't imagine why people would pay money to sleep in unsanitary conditions on the ground under the flimsy fabric that hardly protected you from rain, let alone wildlife. You said a lodge or cabin was as close as you wanted to get to camping."

"Oh no . . . no! Absolutely not!" A shiver went up Margo's spine as she thought of the idea.

"It would just be a dare. If Michael wins, you won't actually have to go through with it."

"He's pretty confident he will," Margo answered. "But if he does, I would have to think up a perfect one for you." Margo wondered what she could dare Tina to do if Michael won the competition. "Got it!" She snapped her fingers and announced her dare. "You said you hated golf. A game of golf was a great way to spoil a good walk, you said. If Michael wins, you must spend the weekend golfing with us. You and Joel and Michael and I. And you can't moan about the game being a good way to spoil a great walk."

Tina grimaced. "All right. Deal. But I don't plan on playing golf." She sang out cheerfully. "Joel and I love to camp, so get your gear ready!" Tina linked arms with Margo as they walked. "You and Michael will be our guests when we go camping in September. You'll love it! Joel knows some beautiful places right on the lake." Then she stopped, turned for dramatic effect, and said with a serious face, "But you have to watch out for bears. They're hungry that time of year." Margo drew her arm out of Tina's and pulled both around her chest. She shivered at the thought. Tina laughed and stuck out her hand to shake Margo's. Margo gave her hand to Tina and shook on the deal. Looking Tina in the eye, Margo said, "I hope you have an extra set of clubs. If not, I'll let you borrow mine," and smiled.

Margo and Tina decided not to tell their husbands. Whoever lost would be a good sport and would do what the other one dared them to do as couples, so the men would not need to know about their side bet. However, they were both certain their husbands would wonder what got into them when they suggested doing something they had always said they'd never do.

Later that evening, after a satisfying dinner of jerk chicken legs and callaloo, prepared with Michael's freshly harvested swiss chard, Margo and Michael sat in their matching recliner chairs, watching the orange and pink of the setting sun streak across the blue sky and the sunflowers at the side of the shed nodding their shaggy yellow and brown heads in the soft breeze as if being lulled to sleep.

"Your sunflowers have taken off!" Margo remarked. "The one on the left especially. I bet it will beat Joel's tallest one, hands down."

"Or by a head," Michael responded. "Right now, by my calculations, it's half a head shorter than Joel's, but it's not the end of the contest. We have another two weeks of growing yet. And sunflowers can grow four to six inches a day."

So, what do you feed your sunflowers, Michael?"

Michael scratched his chin. He had grown a stubbly beard in the last month. Now that he had retired, he felt he could experiment with a more casual look. Margo admired Michael's experimentation but didn't know if she loved the result. But she couldn't argue with it since she had traded her 'teacher' clothes for more generous garments that moved freely around her figure.

"Sunflowers like to drink what we drink: water, coffee and whiskey." Michael winked, got out of his recliner, walked to where Margo was still sitting in hers, and kissed her on the top of her head. "Nature is full of wonders and miracles, Margo. I am constantly amazed." With that, he went out to the backyard for his nightly ritual of saying good night to his plants, tying some up, watering others, and inspecting them all.

Margo was left alone in the living room to ponder Michael's fertilizer cocktail. Water, yes, that's a given. But coffee? And whiskey? What would the proportions be?

Margo watched Michael exit the shed with a plastic milk jug half filled with a murky brown liquid. She saw him carefully pour it around the roots of each of his sunflowers. As she watched him, she mused, "What if their daily intake was doubled? We grow fatter when we eat twice as much, so it would make sense that the sunflowers would grow taller faster with twice the nutrients!"

Her motives were split between wanting Michael to succeed so he could show dominance over his more athletic friend and not wanting to lose to Tina and have to face her fear of camping. For either or both reasons, Margo resolved to support her man. To accomplish this, she first tried to find evidence of what Michael mixed up in a plastic milk jug before he poured it on the sunflowers, but all she could find in the tool shed were bottles of 20-20-20 fertilizer and a couple of canisters of old, dried-out coffee grounds Michael had collected, evidently to add to his fertilizer recipe. When she stuck her nose into the empty milk jugs she found in the shed and sniffed, she was assaulted by the acrid smell. But she did think she got a whiff of coffee. "Coffee, maybe liquefied compost," she whispered to herself. "But what is that acidic smell . . . could that be whiskey?" She couldn't keep her nose focused long enough to determine the origin of the objectionable odour. Whatever it was, she recognized the jugs he used to feed his sunflowers every other day. The formula must be here somewhere, she thought. But after an hour of looking through jars full of receipts, drawers crammed with odds and ends and notes pinned on the cork-board where Michael kept gardening ideas and lists of things he needed to buy, she found no recipe for his special plant fertilizer. "Damn! It must be in Michael's head," she surmised. "And unless I can get him to talk in his sleep, I know he won't divulge it to anyone, not even his wife."

With the competition only two weeks away, there would be no time to research another fertilizer concoction on google. She would have to go with what Michael told her were the three key ingredients Michael said plants like to drink—water, coffee and whiskey.

For the next twelve days, Margo's routine was to express a shot of espresso in the morning, and, instead of drinking it, add a to-go cup then fill the cup with water, leaving a 'two-finger' measure at the top to accommodate the last ingredient: Michael's scotch. She set the to-go cup on the windowsill in the kitchen. At some point in the day when she knew he was out of range, Margo would sneak out from the buffet, Michael's single malt scotch.

Michael was not a regular drinker, but he kept a bottle of scotch for special occasions like impressing male friends when they came over. Margo didn't like to drink scotch, but she thought it was sexist of Michael to only assume men did. However, she had no desire to join him when he only asked Joel if he wanted a nightcap— just to make that point.

After Michael had settled down with a book as he did every evening, Margo would grab the to-go cup and make an excuse that she wanted to take advantage of the long evenings (after the wasps had gone back to their hives) to take their dog, Chance, for a walk—which she did. But she also snuck around to Michael's sunflower patch and surreptitiously poured her libation over the roots of the sunflowers and cheer them on, humming the song 'You are my sunshine'. She had read somewhere that plants liked it when you sang to them.

Every morning, Michael would focus his binoculars

on Joel's sunflower patch and then try to compare them with his. Given that Joel's were farther away, they looked smaller than Michael's, but when he factored in the height of Joel's south-facing garage wall that they were planted against, and the roof, which was twelve feet high at its peak, he estimated how high the sunflowers were relative to the height of the building. He did the same for his sunflowers growing along the shed wall. The top of the shed was ten feet high.

Every day, after he estimated their daily growth, Michael marked the increments of growth for his sunflowers and the growth of Joel's sunflowers in a notebook he kept beside his chair. It was an imperfect calculation, but so far, their growth seemed to be parallel. Some days, Joel's would be higher, and then his would have a growth spurt. And then Joel's shot up another couple of inches. It was amazing how fast a sunflower grew to reach its astronomical height in a few summer months. Michael's sunflowers were thriving. And so were Joel's. He didn't know what Joel was feeding his plants, but Michael was satisfied with his own formula's performance, so he had no intention of altering it.

It was the last week before the fall fair. Michael noticed that his sunflowers were not gaining any more height. Worried he was going to lose and decided to make one last effort to saturate them with his secret concoction. Not only did the sunflowers not respond with another growth spurt, they seemed to be bending toward the ground as if they were weary of growing. A droop of the head is to be expected as the weight of the seed bends the flower downward, but Michael's sunflowers were actually curling down from the stem as if they had no will to support themselves anymore. He felt desperate. He applied his secret formula twice a day. He tied the stalks up to screws he fastened to the wall of the shed right to the head of the flower, but nothing seemed to stimulate them to grow any higher. In fact, they looked like a row of stooped old men sitting on a park bench.

The day before the Crestview Fall Fair, Joel strolled into Michael's backyard, hands in his pockets, whistling a tune Michael recognized as *We are the Champions* by Queen.

"Michael, Michael, how does your garden grow?" He hailed cheerfully. Michael was untying his tallest sunflower from the stake. As he untied each section, the stalk drooped limply over his shoulder. The head bobbed up and down in a lackluster nod in Joel's direction.

"Um, not as good as I had hoped. If I didn't know better, I'd say this one has a hangover!"

Joel barked a short laugh and then quickly regained his composure. "Can I help?"

"Sure. Can you hold on to the head while I untie the rest of the stalk?" Michael asked, struggling to keep the drooping stem on his shoulder with one hand and release the tie with the other.

Joel carefully held the head of the flower to support it while Michael untied all the strings that held it upright. When he was finished, he cut the stalk down at the base, making sure he could account for every inch above ground. Then the two men stretched it out on the ground, full length.

"I see what you mean," Joel said. Is it supposed to be that bendy like that? The stalk on mine is stiff. Had to be careful not to break it while I was taking it down. But then, what do I know about sunflowers, coming from California." Joel said with a shrug.

Michael looked at the sunflower forlornly. "Lying down, it might be longer than yours even if it is a wet noodle." Joel barked out another short laughed. Then stood back and eyed it up.

"You might be right! Not over 'till it over!" Joel slapped Michael's back heartily, almost toppling Michael over his sad looking sunflower.

Michael recovered himself and straightened up. He stuck out his hand for Joel to shake. "May the best man win"!

"Come on . . . we're both good men, Michael. So, here's to the best sunflower winning! And you're right. It will all be measured while lying down on a table, so it will be an even playing field. Got to love retirement when the biggest competition is over a sunflower, not a job!"

Michael smiled and shrugged, trying not to let his disappointment show. "It's just a friendly competition," he reminded himself. "Whatever the results from tomorrow's competition, it'll be another story and another chapter in our retirement to reminisce over." To punctuate his camaraderie and sportsmanship he slapped Joel on his back.

Joel didn't budge. He just grinned back at his friend and nodded in agreement. "Why don't we get these girls in the back of my pick-up. I'll drive around." Joel had purchased the half-ton truck when he moved to the Kootenays. He envisioned using it to haul firewood, tree trimmings, and booting around on adventures in the woods. He wanted to be prepared for the adventure!

The Crestview Fall Fair was a highly anticipated event for the retirees, newly transplanted from the city to life in the hinterland. The highlight for Margo was seeing the farm animal competition that the youth under eighteen entered. She loved how knowledgeable the kids were about the animal they raised. The farm animals—calves, pigs, sheep, goats and even an emu were all well groomed and looked healthy and well fed. She didn't know how the judges would choose which one was the best, but it delighted her to see young people taking responsibility for their animal and making a connection with them.

Tina's favourite event was the rodeo. She couldn't decide if she liked the bucking bronco or calf-roping event the best. But she sure liked the cowboy attire! She couldn't stop talking about how the cowboy hats, the plaid shirts with snap buttons and embroidery over the pockets with engraved silver belt buckles holding up their jeans were so handsomely worn on these fit men. She especially liked to see the cowboys in their leather chaps worn over jeans when they were riding the bull or chasing their calf in the ring. "Man, those cowboys sure know how to show off their assets to their best advantage!" she exclaimed as she watched the competitors through binoculars from her seat in the wooden plank stands.

Michael spent much of his time at the produce displays—eyeing up the largest pumpkins and zucchinis. He enjoyed chatting with the exhibitors sitting behind the tables of ripe, healthy-looking produce, gleaning tips on how to grow vegetables in this area.

For Joel, the highlight was the spectacle. Wherever he walked with his wife—along aisles of the tables set up to display such a diversity of hand-made items from cakes, knitwear, quilts, and flower arrangements to photography, artwork and wine-making, or through the barn where the prize animals were penned, or sitting in the stands watching the rodeo contests – he kept making remarks like, "Is this for real? Where are the cameras? Pinch me and tell me I'm only dreaming I'm in an old western movie!" He could be forgiven because he came from California, where he only saw setups like this in movies made on sets in Burbank and Hollywood.

When the sunflower judging was announced on the PA., Joel and Michael went to their table (which was in the giant class of the vegetable division) and stood by their sunflowers. Michael thought it perhaps wasn't the most popular of competitions. Theirs were two out of six entries. The three judges carefully measured each plant, made a note, and then moved to the next. After taking their measurements, they went to a table at the back to discuss each other's calculations. After their conference, all three stood up with clipboards in hand. The head judge announced to the contestants, "Before we can make our final decision, we must measure two sunflowers together, as there is a discrepancy between our measurements," All three walked over to Michael's sunflower and measured his specimen. They huddled briefly, talking in whispers to each other. Then they moved to Joel's and repeated their measurement. Back at the table, the head judge quietly conferred with her colleagues, who nodded in agreement. When they reached a consensus, the head judge cleared her voice and said, "Attention contestants. We have measured the flowers and, after deliberation, have reached our judgement." Michael and Joel beamed at each other. They could see that their sunflowers far outgrew the others in the competition.

"First of all, we would like to thank the contestants for your enthusiasm and good-natured competitive spirit. You have produced fine specimens. I hope you have all enjoyed seeing your sunflowers come to fruition." She droned on for a few more minutes, complementing each one and recounting the competition's history. Michael was sweating and Joel was scuffing the cement floor with his right foot. Both men were wishing she would get to the point.

"At this time, we will declare the prize placement." She cleared her throat for dramatic effect. "In third place, and at fourteen feet, two inches, is Slade Dillon's sunflower. The contestants and onlookers clapped as she walked toward a chubby twelve-year-old boy with red hair and freckles. His mother, who he resembled, was beside him. She hugged him and said something in his ear. He scowled and accepted the prize with a sour face, ungraciously dangling the ribbon upside down as he made his way back to his mother.

"Probably told him she was proud that he participated," Margo said in Michael's ear. Michael smiled. She and Tina had come in late. They were each standing beside their husbands.

"Second prize goes to Poppy Enns," the judge announced as she walked toward a young teen. The girl squealed with delight when she accepted the prize, exposing her full set of braces. Her girlfriend, who was standing next to her, squealed, too, and the two of them went into a spontaneous dance, holding hands and twirling. The judge beamed when she gave her the second prize ribbon. "Congratulations, Poppy! I knew you could do it!"

"Must be her teacher or a neighbour," Margo whispered to Michael. She squeezed Michael's. "Here it comes . . ."

The judge paused after she congratulated Poppy and referred to her notes. Michael and Joel waited expectantly. Since they were both still in the running and their sunflowers were taller than the second and third place, Michael was certain that they would tie.

"We had to decide between two sunflowers for the first prize. Initially, we considered a tie, but upon closer inspection, we found that one of the specimens didn't meet the competition standards. The stalk was porous and seemed to be weeping, indicating it couldn't support its seed head. We made the unanimous decision to disqualify the sunflower entered by "Michael—uh— Gaetor." She looked down at her notes and stumbled over his last name. "I'm sorry about this, Mr. uh . . . Gaetor (she tried again to pronounce it correctly). This must come as quite a blow since you have obviously invested a lot to achieve such a height. We ruled it out because it does not look healthy. Our advice to you is to reconsider your growing techniques including the fertilizer you use. She looked at Michael, whose face had taken on a questioning look, and lowered her shoulders in disappointment. "We thank you for entering the competition and most heartily encourage you to enter the competition next year."

Michael's face fell. He, too, had been concerned about the lack of fibrous structure of his sunflower but thought it would be disguised if they were all lying down, but it may have been that the giant head, which extended beyond the length of the table, was drooping as if falling asleep in class. At any rate, it was apparent that nothing escaped the experienced sunflower judges' notice.

The judge turned her attention towards Joel and smiled. "It is our pleasure to announce this year's winner of the tallest sunflower in Crestview fair, Joel Fender"!

Everyone clapped and Joel's smile grew wide. He gave Michael a look that read 'Sorry buddy' and then walked forward and proudly received the blue ribbon.

Margo winced when she heard the judge's pronouncement of disqualification over the specimen's ill health and withdrew her hand from Michael's. She immediately regretted her effort to help it grow by giving Michael's tallest sunflower a nightcap of coffee and scotch. That might have pushed it over the top or, as it was apparent to everyone, pulled it down to the ground. Margo felt so bad for Michael. She had only done what she did because she didn't want him to lose. And the competition was so close! She debated about telling Michael about her fertilizer concoction. She didn't know which would make him feel worse, thinking he had misjudged his fertilizer brew or knowing Margo had sabotaged his project. Margo decided she would fess up later, when the whole thing blew over. Maybe sometime in the winter when they were sitting in their chairs reminiscing about what a novel experience the fall fair was. Perhaps Michael, himself, would bring up the subject when he thought about what he would plant next year, and Margo could casually preface her confession with 'a funny thing happened last fall . . . "

Joel stood beside his sunflower, posing for pictures with his winning specimen with the blue ribbon pinned to his chest. Tina stood apart from Joel so she didn't get into the picture. This was his time to shine. She waved and made a sad face, indicating her sympathy. In return, Margo sent Tina a bleak smile and continued her task. Stooping over Michael's sunflower, she bent the noodling stem into a garbage bag while Michael was stuffed it in.

Michael was still dumb-founded about his loss, and particularly about the spineless sunflower he had grown. He kicked his shoes off at the door and hung up his jacket. "I think I'll have a scotch and unwind," he said, walking towards the buffet.

That alarmed Margo. "Oh! Sweetie. Are you sure you should? I mean, you don't want to go down that road, do you?"

"What road?" Michael stared at her.

"The road where you drink your sorrows away. You know, the road you have cautioned me about when drinking wine with Tina."

"I don't intend to go down THAT road or any other, Margo. I want a single scotch, not a bottle to drown my sorrows in. Besides, as disappointing as the contest's outcome was, I actually enjoyed the experience. So, get yourself a glass of wine, Margo, and toast our new adventure: Retirement. May it always be full of surprises."

Before Margo could think of something to stall him, Michael opened the buffet and pulled out his bottle of scotch. Margo held her breath. Maybe he wouldn't notice?

Michel noticed immediately. He turned to Margo, gripping the bottle. This scotch bottle is half-empty. I know I haven't been drinking it." He raised his eyebrows. "Margo? Don't tell me YOU are going down that road!"

"No! I mean, yes, but it's not what you think. It was another road. Oh dear, I can explain." Margo blustered. "But first, why don't we go ahead and do what you suggested? You pour yourself a scotch, and I'll grab a glass of wine. Then we can sit down, and I'll tell you the story of the scotch."

While she said that, Margo moved to the kitchen and opened the cabinet door to reach for a wine glass. Michael grunted in response and poured himself a fairly stiff three-finger scotch. Drinks in hand, the couple each sat down in their lounge chairs in the living room. After taking a sip or two in silence, Margo launched into her story, starting with Michael's response to her question about what he fed his plants, that they liked to drink what people like, "water, coffee and whiskey".

The next weekend, Margo and Michael camped for the first time at a provincial campsite, with Tina and Joel. Margo couldn't fault the campground. Located in the woods, a short walk to the lake, the grounds were kept was clean and tidy. Being fall, the campground was not at its maximum capacity and the campers were mostly adults. The summer had passed, and the kids were back in school, bringing family holidays to an end. Their site was shaded by tall trees and large enough for two tents with a picnic table off to one side under a canopy of trees and an outdoor grill between them. Tina and Joel had already set up their tent and announced that they were off to the beach for a while, inviting Michael and Margo to join them when they were set up. The neophyte campers had some difficulty setting up the tent they bought on an end-of-season sale at the hardware store, even though it said on the label: easy, three-step pop-up. When the tent was erected and pegged firmly into the ground, they had to take turns pumping up the air mattress with a foot pedal pump. The ordeal left Margo exhausted. So, she was happy to sit at the picnic table in and read while Michael wandered down to the beach to find Tina and Joel.

When the three came back, Margo was still reading at the table. Michael hailed her. "You look comfortable! No wildlife interrupting your serenity?"

Margo smiled sarcastically, "Not unless you count that squirrel who keeps chattering at me from the tree above. Apparently, I interrupted his sanctuary." In truth, Margo felt surprisingly comfortable in this cool sanctuary among trees, sunlight filtering through the trees, making patterns on the table when the breeze moved them, carrying the scent of pine. Even the squirrel, chatty as it was, became a source of comfort to Margo. As long as it was chattering away, she felt confident that there were no predators lurking.

Tina reached the cooler and rattled around through the ice, producing a bottle of white wine. "Wine, Margo?" Tina asked, lithely stepping over the bench seat with two glasses.

"Please! Love a glass," she responded, not looking at Michael, who she knew would be trying to catch her eye to warn her not to drink too much.

While the women chatted at the table, the men moved toward the grill. Joel rustled through the cooler on the way. "Here you go, Michael, catch!" He tossed a beer can Michael's way. Michael caught it in the cradle of his arms. Joel popped his can open, took a long drink, and wiped his mouth, "Ahhh . . . nothing like it. Don't you think? Communing with Mother Nature!" Joel raised his beer to the treetops.

Michael opened his beer, too, and took a sip. "Yup." The two men walked over to the grill to discuss dinner. Since this was an inauguration dinner, Tina suggested they pack steaks to grill and throw seasoned vegetables and potato wedges wrapped in foil into the fire to bake.

"Competition is still on, I see," said Tina, observing the two men stand over their steaks and discuss how to tell when they were cooked to the desired doneness.

"Indeed, it is," Margo agreed, taking a sip of her wine. "But I have come to believe a little competition is good."

"As long as someone doesn't try to tip the scale." She bumped Margo's shoulder gently and giggled.

Margo turned to Tina, "You know?"

"Michael came over and told Joel the next day that his wife soused his sunflower with booze. He said that Margo's interference should make the competition between them null and void."

Margo made a face and swallowed down the rest of her glass in one glass. "Another please, if you're pouring," Tina tipped the wine bottle into Margo's glass and turned it upside down to drain the last drop. Feeling a bit tipsy, Margo leaned forward and confided in her friend what she did. She ended the tale with, "Michael was so mad at me! But after a couple of days, we laughed about it. He admitted that he was leading me down the garden path with that flip remark about plants liking to drink what we drink—water, coffee and booze. How was I to know that booze kills plants?"

Tina stifled a laugh and looked over at the men. Engrossed in BBQ banter, they were sipping beer and ignoring the women. "He then told me what his real fertilizer formula was—coffee, and urine." Margo hissed.

Tina nearly spurted out her wine.

"What? He peed on them?" She said, wiping her mouth.

"Not directly. He peed into a milk jug and mixed it with coffee grounds and 20-20-20. That was his secret formula!"

"Ewww!" Tina made a face. "So, no booze in his secret formula?"

"No. That was just a joke, he said. Alcohol will kill your plants, he said. Just like daily drinking will for humans." Margo took another sip of wine and gave Tina a conspiratorial smile.

Tina laughed a twinkly, infectious laugh. The men looked up from their BBQ. "It's nothing," Tina called out, "Just girl talk. Go back to minding the steaks. And remember, Joel, I like mine medium-rare."

"That's so funny," Tina said, turning back to Margo, "He told me that when he was helping Michael get his sunflower into the truck, he thought the sunflower looked drunk!"

Margo covered her giggle with her mouth while Tina stifled a giggle to not break into the men's concentration.

Tina fished out another bottle of wine from the cooler, opened it. Pour herself a glass and then topped up Margo's glass. "A toast," she proposed and lifted her glass. "Here's to silver linings. If you hadn't made Michael lose, you wouldn't be here enjoying the beautiful outdoors. And we wouldn't be spending this time together."

Margo lifted her glass too but before she touched Tina's glass she said, Here's to the four of us. Maybe next weekend we can all go golfing since Michael's sunflower would have been the winner if it hadn't been so pissed!"

Tina guffawed. The two glasses tinkled. And the men came back to the picnic table with their prize steaks to show off to their wives.

Later that night in Margo and Michael's tent, the glow of a phone could be seen through the walls. Margo was texting.

Margo: Tina. You awake?

Margo could hear the ping of Tina's phone in the tent next to them and made out the phone's glow through the fabric wall.

Tina: Am now. Yawn emoji

Margo: Did you hear that?

Tina: What?

Margo: That sound. Outside. Listen. I think it's an animal.

Tina: Can't hear anything. ZZZ sleep emoji

Margo: You can't hear that? What if its a bear!!!! Scream emoji

Just then, a crashing noise caught their attention. A male voice, was shouting.

Margo: Do you hear it now?

Tina: Shhhh emoji

Margo: Panic emoji

Tina: Praying hands emoji

Margo sat up and listened for the sound again. She strained to hear what was out there. She barely made out the strains of country music coming from a few sites down. Then, another crash close to their site, as if a large animal was stumbling through the woods. And a woman's scream.

Margo pulled the sleeping bag around her neck. She was shivering despite the warmth of the bag.

"You hear that???"

"Oh Damn! Sorry ma'am! Didn't mean to scare you. I'll be goin' now. Truly sorry. I thought this was my tent. Sorry!" The man hiccupped. The next sound was a beer can crunching under a boot, then retreating footsteps crashing through the stand of trees between the campsite next to them and the one beyond that.

Tina: That's a beer, not a bear. Go back to sleep. Laugh/cry emoji

Margo: So, this is camping? Watch out for wild drunks. Eye-roll emoji

Tina: Night John-Boy. Laugh/cry emoji, heart emoji

Margo: Night Mary-Ellen—LOL! Heart emoji

Michael stirred as Margo clicked off her phone. He had slept through the whole drama. "OK, Hon?"

"Fine. I'm fine. Just thought I heard something. Nothing to worry about. It wasn't a bear, just a beer.

"Uh, OK. Go back to sleep then," Michael rolled over onto his other side. "I'm going to have a helluva backache tomorrow. This air mattress is losing air by the minute."

"Isn't camping fun?" Margo rubbed Michael's back until she heard him breathe deeply and knew he was asleep. What had she been so afraid of all these years, she asked herself? Then she put her arms under her head and breathed in the fresh, scented air and listened to the night sounds, frogs croaking, and coming from somewhere down the trail, the muted strains of a familiar country song playing, "I got friends in low places where the whiskey drowns, and the beer chaser . . ." Then she rolled over to find a more comfortable position. As she did, a hiss of air exhaled from the mattress. Before drifting off to sleep, her last thought was about the pancake breakfast she anticipated making with Tina in the morning and sharing around the picnic table with their new friends.

CHAPTER THREE

The Winter Escape

February in Wannatoka Springs was a quiet month. A blanket of snow covered the open fields piled up in the yards, and berms narrowed the roads as the snow was pushed to each side by snowplows. The ATVs were stored for the winter and replaced with snowmobiles loaded onto trailers, sitting in driveways waiting for the weekend, where they would be hitched to a four-by-four truck and hauled to various spots up the mountainside where the owners could chase each other as recklessly as they dared.

The traffic that passed by Margo and Michael's house consisted of a few habitual dog walkers following their usual route, walkers who were persistent enough to come out no matter what the weather, like the three elderly women clutching walking sticks and each other as they negotiated icy streets. But most folks preferred to drive wherever they had to go or, better still, not go anywhere.

During the doldrums of winter, Margo spent most of her time indoors, reading, baking, and, in the mornings, perusing the Facebook community page to see what her neighbours were up to or looking for activities and groups she could join. However, it seemed to be that the social calendar for Wannatoka Springs was as empty of signs of community life as the streets. Most of the notices were posted by individuals looking for a ride to Crystal Lake, asking if anyone had seen their cat, or advertising eggs or homemade baking they were selling. On one such February morning, however, Margo spotted a post in The Wannatoka Times that would spur her on to take social action.

URGENT! My parrot, Precious, escaped from my garage this morning. She was last seen around the motel. If you see her, please call or pm me immediately! SHE WON'T LAST THE NIGHT!!!"

Margo had met Birdie on one of her first walks around the community the summer they arrived. She had been walking their dog, Chance, around the neighbourhood and Birdie's house was on the corner of Willow and Maple. She was such a chatty, cheerful person and always stopped what she was doing in the yard for a friendly chat.

Margo learned a lot about the neighbourhood from Birdie. When Birdie learned that Margo loved flower gardens, she insisted that Margo come over and take cuttings and divisions of perennials from her garden. Birdie was almost always outdoors, rooting around in her gardens during the summer, and Margo immensely enjoyed her routine of stopping to chat with her whenever Birdie was outside puttering. But since the snow piled up in earnest, she didn't see or hear much from Birdie.

When Margo read the message about the lost parrot in the Wannatoka Times, she put down her phone and picked up the binoculars on the window ledge that were always at the ready.

Looking through the sites, Margo scanned the tops of the trees in her view. Margo and Michael's house stood on a higher bank than the houses on Maple Street; they could see down to Maple Street and beyond to the lake and the mountains. Having spent many mornings drink- ing coffee and looking through those windows at the trees below, Margo could identify the common birds in her and her neighbours' backyards.

She watched the Stellar Jays picking at the mountain ash berries, squawking and complaining, competing for the food they found. She noted the migration of summer birds and the return of the chickadees in the fall.

In winter, she was entertained by the antics of the crows that were attracted to Birdie's back door. The crows would gather in the branches of spruce trees, spying on the house below, waiting for Birdie to emerge. Every morning, she appeared in her house coat with a pail; she would reach in, pull out a fistful of bread cubes and litter the snow with them. As Birdie ducked back inside and shut the door, the crows swooped down and lined up, single-file, waiting their turn to claim their prize before flying off to the nearest tree to eat in peace. Then they returned for more. Occasionally, one or two would try to budge ahead in line. The birds ahead would scold and peck at the naughty bird who had attempted to hop ahead in the lineup, until it retreated, protesting indignantly, while it waited its turn at the back of the line.

That February morning, when Margo scanned the treetops below her, the only birds she could make out were crows and stellar jays. She put down the binoculars and picked up her phone again to see if there had been any new developments in the missing parrot post. A number of the neighbours had already replied to Birdie with sympathy and advice.

> Becky: Will look out for Precious. Praying hands emoji
>
> Sam: Think I seen it out my window. In the Collins's tree. An hour ago, maybe?
>
> Bev: So sorry. Heart emoji
>
> Tina: On the lookout for your Precious. Care emoji
>
> Howard: Have you tried birdseed to attract it?
>
> Sam: Responding to Howard—Birdie's got bird

food all around her place.

Glenda: Oh dear, Birdie. Hoping Precious flies home. Heart emoji

Jim: Sorry to hear. Hope you find her. Prayer emoji

The comments kept coming in. *The whole neighbourhood seemed to be on The Wannatoka Times Facebook page this morning*, thought Margo. She wasn't the only one with nothing better to do.

Margo checked back around mid-afternoon to see if there were any updates. Birdie had not posted since the morning, so Margo sent her a message.

Margo: Found your Precious yet?

Birdie: No. Sad face emoji

Margo: Someone should take action!

Birdie: IDK emoji—Thanks. Hope someone spots her. Fingers crossed emoji

Margo: Fingers crossed emoji, heart emoji

Margo closed that disheartening conversation and opened her Google app. When she didn't know how to do something or if she wanted to find out if something someone said was accurate, she would Google it. She typed, "How to find and capture a pet parrot."

Although she learned that parrots were social birds and developed a strong bond with their caregivers, and would return to them if they strayed, Google didn't offer specific help. She hoped the bond between Birdie and Precious was strong enough that they would find each other soon.

The temperature was dropping quickly as the day wore on. Margo didn't know how much she could do to help by herself, but in a neighbourhood like this, people looked after each other. Maybe they could find the stray parrot together if she could find a way to rally the neighbours together to look for it. Facebook, she thought, was too slow. Too much time is spent between posting a message and waiting for responses. It would have to be a neighbourhood APB. Margo's brain clamped on to an idea that might bring the whole neighbourhood out in a hurry.

***

Michael was napping in his recliner, head back and feet up on the footrest, when his phone's ringtone—a train whistle—hooted. Startled, he swivelled his chair around without pushing the footrest back into place, and collided with the coffee table. He swore when he stubbed his toe. Then he lowered his footrest and bent forward to reach for his phone, which was tooting and vibrating around the coffee table. Fumbling, he picked it up and swiped up to open it.

"Michael here." He said and cleared his throat. "Yes. Yes. Oh? Right. Of course. I can be there in two minutes!" He ended the call.

"Margo!" he called out. No answer. "Margo?" he called again, listening for a response while he walked to the closet to find his coat and boots. Chance was on Michael's heels. He had been napping, too, on his bed. When Michael slammed the footrest into place and rose from the chair he was reclining in, Chance woke up with a start. He knew by Michael's energy that something big was going down. And Chance didn't want to miss it. Michael scratched Chance's ear. "I guess she's not here," he said, "I think you have to stay here, boy. Got an emergency fire call-out to attend."

Michael opened the front door, trying to block Chance's way. But Chance went through his legs and bounded out on the front lawn, frolicking in excitement. After a fruitless minute or two of attempting to capture the dog, Michael threw up his hands in surrender. "OK, boy, you can come. But behave yourself!"

Michael and Chance walked briskly down the street to the fire-hall, Chance running slightly ahead and looking back to Michael for assurance that he was going the right way. Twice, Michael lost his footing on the slippery road, but stopped himself from falling. He wished Chance was a search and rescue dog. Or at least sympathetic when his owner slipped and fell. But Chance would stop and look at Michael until he regained his pace. After that, he turned and walked forward, sniffing the side of the road for signs only significant to and decipherable by a dog, then occasionally peeing on a spot where he wanted to leave a message.

When they arrived at the fire-hall, Michael saw the volunteer fire chief and his deputy checking that the equipment in the red fire truck was secure and operable. The antique red truck had been backed out of the garage and sat on the street, parallel to the curb, engine idling.

The other volunteers were in various stages of suiting up in their turnout gear, pulling on overalls, stepping into fireproof boots and adjusting their hard hats. Michael went to his locker beside Joel's to climb into his gear. Joel was stepping into his boots. Michael hurriedly took his gear down. In his panic at being late and in fear that this might be real, he forgot his training about how to get into his gear quickly and efficiently.

The fire chief shouted orders to the team. Joel and the other volunteers responded by running to the truck. Then, he slapped Michael on the back, "Duty calls! I hope you make it, buddy!"

Michael nodded. "I'll see you there." He stripped down to his sweats, socks, and t-shirt then tried to sort out where the top of his overalls were, since he had just pulled them off the hook without thinking.

The fire bell sounded.

Bewildered by the barrage of sounds and sights, Chance ducked under the bench to find a hiding place to wait out the commotion. Michael had pulled on one of his boots, but Chance had pushed the other in front of him as he scrabbled under the bench to find safety.

Hopping on one foot, Michael twirled around to locate the other boot. Not seeing it, he sat backwards on the bench behind him, and heard Chance whine underneath him. Bending down and looking between his legs, he came eye to bulging eye with his dog, who was panting, whining, and cradling his other boot. "Come out here, Chance! And bring my boot back!" Chance stayed where he was.

Michael muttered a curse on his dog and knelt to grab his boot from Chance's clutch. Chance hung onto it with his teeth, tugging back. "This is not a game, Chance! Drop it! Out!" If he understood either of those commands, Chance was ignoring them. Michael tugged harder, pulling the boot and the dog out from under the bench.

Without warning, Chance let go, sending Michael flopping onto his back, boot in hand. Chance looked around at the retreating volunteers who were listening to orders and scrambling to take their places on the truck. Chance barked once—as if to tell Michael to get going or he would miss the show!

"It was a big mistake taking you, Chance, you mutt! Now look what you got me into!" Michael said through gritted teeth as he pulled on his winter boots and shrugged on his coat. "I should've left you at home!"

Chance sat calmly looking at Michael, cocking his ears as if trying to make out what Michael was say-ing, but all he heard was "Blah, Blah, Blah. Chance! Blah, Blah, Blah, Home!" On the word "home," Chance pranced to the open garage door and waited for Michael.

As Michael fidgeted with the buckles on his coat and returned to the bench to retrieve his helmet, the red lights atop the truck started rotating and the siren cranked up. At a snail's pace, the red fire truck followed the Chief in the bright yellow-green first responder vehicle in a slow procession down Tamarac Street.

Michael stumbled out of the hall, weighed down and burdened by his turnout gear, which was meant to save the occupant from burning and was not designed for chasing after a fire truck. He stopped in the street, hands on knees, breathing heavily and sweating inside the heavy, fire-retardant suit. Looking ahead, he could see the back of the red truck make a wide berth and turn left onto Maple. He waved and tried to shout above the noise, but intent on their mission, all eyes were facing front. Michael stood for a minute in the middle of the street, to catch his breath, and then began to lumber down the street. "Chance! Follow that truck!" He called out to his dog. Michael needn't have said anything. Chance was already ahead of Michael. He was barking down the street in full chase of the trucks.

Michael followed Chance clumsily, his firefighter's boots and gear feeling heavier and more encumbering with every step. The conflagration of sirens and lights, a yellow lab running down the street barking, followed by a firefighter in turnout gear shouting for the truck and the dog to wait up, stimulated a chorus of barks from dogs tied up or in their backyards and propelled homeowners outdoors to see what was going on.

Later, a Maple Street resident, whom a reporter from the Kootenay Voice interviewed, described the event this way: "It was like watching a circus parade pass by my window and down the street. First came the fire chief in his high viz yellow rapid responder vehicle, flashing lights on the cab's roof and through the grill. Right behind, came the old red fire truck that should have been in a museum, siren wailing and lights flashing. And if that wasn't enough of a parade, after that came a yellow lab, ears flapping, tongue hanging out, and barking his fool head off. Bringing up the rear, maybe 200 meters or so behind, was a single firefighter in his fire suit chuffing down the middle of the street, yelling, 'Stop!' I don't know if he meant the dog or the fire truck or what. But no one stopped until they reached the end of the street, where, supposedly, the emergency was."

When a parade comes down the street, some people inevitably want to join it. Some who followed the procession were dressed only in indoor clothes, with a blanket or jacket thrown over their shoulders as a last-minute nod to the cold weather. Some had taken the time to don winter coats and had stuffed sweats or pyjamas into boots. Some even jumped into their vehicles and circled the block in the opposite direction, hoping to beat the fire truck to the scene.

The chief's vehicle, and the fire truck behind it, stopped slowly in front of Birdie's garage on Willow. By the time Michael caught up to them, heaving for breath, the crew had already disembarked and the fire chief was barking orders for the volunteers to fan out and search the area. Chance found Joel first. He sniffed around him, wagging his tail.

Recognizing Chance, Joel looked around for Michael. When he spotted him, he waved him over. As Michael passed them, the other volunteers cheered and clapped him on the back, congratulating him for making it and apologizing for not seeing him behind them. Red-faced, Michael limped over to stand by his buddy, Joel.

"Michael! What the hell happened? I thought you were right behind me in the hall." Joel said, concerned.

Michael sucked in a breath, his hands on his knees. "Just missed it. I thought they would stop." He sucked in a breath. "When they saw me running behind them . . ." Michael heaved another breath in, wiping the sweat from his mouth, ". . .it was all I could do to catch up." He hung his head and panted.

"Sorry, man," Joel commiserated. "We were supposed to take roll call, but everyone was so con-fused and excited about our first real call-out that we let that ball drop."

"We'll have to let the chief know . . . " Michael breathed in and out hard as he talked. "Not protocol."

"Yeah, well. Save it for the debrief. This whole thing is not protocol."

"What's going on?" Michael looked up at the crowd that had gathered around the trucks while the chief was attempting to call the disparate group to order.

"Dunno. I just got a call. Emergency at Willow and Maple. Not a fire. Medical maybe. Hope old Pete didn't collapse. He's a heart attack waiting to happen."

Joel was referring to Birdie's husband. Everyone called him Old Pete to differentiate him from his son, Young Pete. Young Pete was in his fifties, but he still answered to Young Pete. Old Pete was in his mid-seventies. Some people joked that Old Pete carried a beer barrel in front of him and would soon need a wheelbarrow for his beer barrel. He'd had a bad heart for years.

Four years before, he suffered a major heart attack. So Birdie was always watching out for signs of another one. The fire department responded to fires and attended medical emergencies and accidents as an auxiliary service if someone reported it to 911. So, if this wasn't a fire, a medical emergency was the following logical reason for the call-out.

Michael and Joel could see the chief talking to Birdie up ahead. They went to where Birdie and the chief were talking and the group of volunteer firefighters and other neighbours formed a circle around them.

Birdie, a small, spare, woman in her late sixties, no more than five feet tall, was standing toe to toe with the fire chief, a burly young man with a bushy beard and piercing blue eyes. Birdie was flailing her hands around and talking in a shrill voice fuelled by panic.

In contrast, the fire chief stood, feet planted shoulder width apart, arms crossed in front of him, firm, calm and resolute.

Standing beside Birdie was a woman in a red parka, the hood which was trimmed in faux-fur, over her head, covering half her face. Her black leggings were tucked into black winter boots. One gloved hand held Birdie's, while the other arm was wrapped around Birdie's shoulder to comfort her and keep her warm.

Michael squinted at the figure in the red parka. "Margo? Is that you?" he asked, pushing closer to the inner circle.

"It IS an emergency!" Birdie was saying, "It's a matter of life and DEATH!" To drive her point home, she stood on her tip-toes and poked her forefinger into his chest when she landed on the word death.

The chief took a step back and held up his hands. "Calm down, Birdie. I didn't say it wasn't serious. I said it might not have been serious enough of an event to warrant a call out to the fire department. But we're here now. When did you last see him?"

"Precious is a she." Birdie corrected and stepped back onto her heels. Making a gesture towards the open garage door, she said, "Precious flew out of here 'bout three hours ago. You gotta help find her. She'll be freezing by now! She won't last the night!"

"Where did you last see your parrot?" The Chief was looking around and scanning the skies above the heads of the small crowd that gathered.

Birdie pointed upward. "Up there!" She was pointing to a tall spruce tree that towered above her house. "But someone said they saw her at the motel earlier." Birdie gasped for air. Margo stroked her back. "I just stepped out of the house to get somethin' from the freezer in the garage. She was sittin' right here. On my shoulder." Birdie tapped her opposite shoulder with her left hand. "I don't know what scared her. Maybe a cat. She squawked and swore like only Precious could do—learned that language

70

from Old Pete. Then she flew out of the garage. I been callin' and callin' 'till I damn near lost my voice!" Birdie started to sob and Margo hugged Birdie while turning her attention to the Fire Chief.

"I was the one who called the fire department," Margo admitted. "I saw Birdie's post in the Wannatoka Times this morning. When no one had found her by the afternoon, I couldn't just stand by and do nothing. So, I called the fire department. I didn't think you would come out to rescue a parrot, so I reported an emergency on the corner of Maple and Willow. So now that I got you and half the village out, let's stop wasting time arguing about whether it was important enough to rate as an emergency—and start looking for the damn bird before we all freeze to death!" Margo stared defiantly at the Fire Chief while holding onto Birdie, who was sobbing into her shoulder.

Not wanting to lose face, the chief chose decisive action. He turned to the people listening to the conversation and turned up the volume on his voice, "Listen up, folks, we're looking for an escaped parrot. The bird is bright green with some red on it," he announced. "Last sighted near the motel at the end of Willow. Likely, it's in a tree somewhere higher up. The bird answers to "Precious". You might see and hear it before you see it. Birdie says she can mimic voices and sounds, so listen and look up. If you see the bird, don't try to capture it. I repeat. Do not try to capture it. Do not try to talk it down. You may spook it and cause it to fly away. Stay still. Hold your position and whistle, or call this number on your cell if you can. Keep watch. If it flies away, be prepared to inform us of its direction.

In a booming voice, the chief relayed his cell phone number to the crowd gathered. "I repeat. Do not try to capture it. You will likely scare it away. Just stay where you are and keep still. I'll escort Birdie to the location. Birdie's most likely the person Precious will come to."

With that, he sent his volunteers in three directions—up and down Willow Street and Maple Street, where they came from. The curious group of neighbours, who had gathered around, also joined in the search. Calls of, "Precious!" and "Here Birdie's bird!" and "Precious want a cracker?" could be heard through the neighbourhood, despite the chief's order.

The chief walked Birdie down Willow towards the motel, the last place someone said they had seen the bird. He was hoping she would attract her parrot's attention. "Precious. Mommy's here. Come to Mommy, Precious. Precious." Birdie cooed as she walked.

Michael stood with Margo, watching the volunteers spread out through the neighbourhood. With his hands on his hips, he confronted his wife. "What the hell, Margo?" You called in an emergency for the fire department to attend to a lost parrot?"

Margo stood her ground. "Birdie was trying to do this all alone. I did go over to look with her, but there's only so much ground two people can cover. I thought if more of the neighbours got out and started scouting, we could be of more help than just one or two of us. And what better way to get people together than to call in an emergency? When you see it through Birdie's eyes, it *is* an emergency. Precious is part of her family. Just like Chance is part of ours."

Michael allowed himself to decompress and then gave Margo a side hug. "OK, good neighbour. Let's walk this way and see if we can locate Birdie's precious parrot."

Margo smiled ruefully and looked around for their dog. "C'mon, Chance," she called to him, patting her side. "Let's go find a lost parrot," Taking his physical cue, Chance walked sedately beside Margo. And the three strolled down the street, Margo linking her arm through Michael's, expecting Michael to support her if she should slip, Michael shuffling along in his already too-heavy gear, scanning the mature Maple and Fir trees that lined Maple Street. And Chance, at Margo's side, playing the part of a faithful companion. As they walked, Margo shared what she had learned online about parrots. "Did you know that parrots bond with their person for life? And some of them can live to be 100 years old. And get this: when people get a parrot for a pet, they are instructed to leave the parrot in their will! Hopefully, to someone the parrot knows and likes because it will need to feel like it has a substitute for their person. Parrots mate for life in the wild. And they stay with their flock for life, too."

Michael listened to Margo with one ear. With the other, he tuned in to the world around him, alert for unusual bird sounds. Despite his annoyance that his wife had called in what would likely be deemed a non-priority nuisance call-out, he was secretly proud of Margo for caring enough about her neighbour's predicament to rally the neighbourhood together.

Michael's phone pinged. It was the chief. "Parrot Sighting. Willow St @ service rd."

The chief posted another message immediately after the first: "Volunteers, do not approach. Hold everyone back from the location. Birdie and I are on our way."

Michael and Margo slowed down. They didn't want to disobey the order, but like everyone else, they were curious and moved slowly but deliberately toward the location. Chance, who had, up till then, been keeping pace with Margo, sensed the tension in her gait and pranced ahead of them. "Whoa!" Michael growled. "Come back boy. Now! Or you'll be grounded. For a month!" Chance looked at Michael as if he was speaking another language or to someone else, not him. Addressing Margo, he said, "That's all Birdie needs: an excited dog chasing her bird."

"Chance! Come!" Margo called out, tapping her thigh with the palm of her hand. Chance heard his name, looked her way and recognized the command. Obediently, he resumed his place alongside Margo.

Margo patted his head in approval while Michael seethed. "Oh, Sure. Doesn't do that for me."

"Maybe he doesn't understand your language," Margo responded. "They say dogs learn sign or physical language first. You have to get their attention by calling out their name before telling them what you want them to do. Just like husbands." Margo looked up into the trees to hide her smirk.

When they got close to the corner, Michael stopped. Turning to Margo, he said, "I'll wait on the corner with Chance. You go ahead and see if you can do anything for Birdie." With that, he took Chance by the collar. "Sit, boy. We're going to wait this one out." Chance heard, 'sit,' and complied.

Margo walked faster towards the motel. She saw Birdie ahead, looking up at a maple tree's bare branches. In one of the branches sat a bright green bird with red streaks. Next to her, and in the branches above and below it was a sheltering ring of black crows. The crows were eyeing the people below suspiciously, screeching out their warnings. One of them dive-bombed the chief.

As he ducked, a blotch of white spattered on his helmet. "Shit!" The chief looked up as the bird flapped past him and resumed its perch on a branch above him, crowing all the way. "Looks like the crows think they're guarding the parrot!"

Birdie kept her eyes on the parrot, pleading with her bird. "Precious! Come to mommy, Precious. Mommy's here."

The parrot cocked her head, eyeing the human gathering below and then screeched. The sound she made mimicked a crow's scolding caw.

"Please, Precious," Birdie continued, "you're

not safe! You're not a crow! You'll die if you stay out all night!" Precious responded this time by imitating a siren wailing. Margo looked around. She thought the fire truck was driving their way with its siren on.

"It's just Precious," Birdie said, patting Margo's arm. "She imitates everything she hears. She must have heard the fire truck coming down the street." The siren sound stopped abruptly.

Birdie approached the tree base and raised her hand, signalling the parrot to alight on it. "Come to mommy, Precious!" She said in a singsong voice.

Seeing the signal and recognizing the familiar voice, the parrot swooped down and landed on Birdie's outstretched hand. Then, she jumped up, wings fluttering, to Birdie's shoulder. There, Precious settled and preened herself as if nothing was out of place except her feathers.

The crows flew, in formation, above the parrot on Birdie's shoulder and then flapped up to perch single-file on the wire strung between street lights, cawing as if they were taking credit for the rescue.

Turning to Birdie, the chief asked, "Is it OK?" The parrot was perched calmly on Birdie's shoulder, blinking at the chief.

"SHE," Birdie said, "is fine." She turned her head sideways and stroked Precious on the beak. Birdie talked to her parrot like a mother scolding a naughty child who had run away, scaring her mother half to death. Then she looked at the Chief and smiled, "Thank you for coming to her rescue—and mine, Chief Kyle. You're my hero!" Birdie beamed a toothy smile.

Embarrassed, Kyle touched the brim of his helmet with two fingers, nodded, and then turned back to guide his crew and the trucks back to the hall to disassemble and debrief.

Birdie walked toward Margo with Precious bobbing up and down with her gait, keeping herself balanced.

Thank you, Margo," Birdie said, taking both of Margo's hands in hers and giving them a warm squeeze. "Thank you for caring about my Precious. Would you like to come back to my place for tea? Warm up a bit?"

"I'd love to, Birdie. It's freezing out here! But I'm so glad I could help. Did you notice all your neighbours coming out? Practically everyone who lives on Maple!"

Margo and Birdie, with Precious on her shoulder, walked down Willow with Birdie clucking away to her Precious and the parrot answering her in subdued coos, in a language only those two shared.

"He's a good man, that young fire chief," Birdie declared to Margo. And a good neighbour. Community is one of the reasons I feel proud to be a Wannatoka Springs resident." Margo smiled. She was beginning to feel that way about this tiny community they had moved to, too.

When they had all returned to the hall, disembarked, and changed out of their firefighting gear, the chief called the volunteers together. He stroked his beard, taking a minute to collect his thoughts and then addressed them. "This event may not have fit the criteria for a call-out, but it did turn out to be a good test of our emergency fitness. We worked as a team. And I'm proud of that. But we still have work to do—like ensuring everyone who shows up is accounted for."

Michael smiled. "Right! No man left behind! Now I know why we don't bring untrained dogs to an emergency!" The others laughed.

The chief nodded. "Like I said, this call-out didn't warrant an emergency response. That said . . ." he looked meaningfully at Michael, "when you talk about this to any-one, please emphasize that we are here for the community, but only in the event of a real emergency, endangerment of human life and limb, fire, or what have you. That does not include someone calling in 'cause their cat is stuck in a tree. That's what yer ladder's for. Or call a neighbour if you don't have one. Or wait it out. Cats know how to go up. Cats know how to come down."

A few of the volunteers tittered, stifling their laughter while Michael looked down at his shoes. The chief went on in a severe tone, "I'll clarify our position in the Wannatoka Times along with sending our thanks to everyone who came out to search for Birdie's parrot."

His colleagues would tease Michael for some time about the dog and pony show, as they called his and Chance's antics. But teasing and joking reinforced the bond Michael began to feel among his neighbours in his new community. Dusk was gathering, and the snow started falling as Michael walked home on the snowy street, shaking his head and laughing. *It must have been quite a sight,* he thought, *a volunteer firefighter in turnout gear chasing a dog who was chasing the fire truck. Not in bad shape for a retired insurance actuary,* he thought, congratulating himself.

A week later, on another cold February morning, Margo sat in her recliner looking through the binoculars at the scene before her. Birdie was on her porch scattering bread cubes on the snow for the crows. Having worn a path through the snow from the nearest apple tree to Birdie's deck, they were lining up single file, hopping and jockeying for positions until they got to the head of the line, where they greedily picked up their handout and then swooped up to the nearest tree to perch to eat it. After consuming one piece, they would flutter down again and join the line.

Beyond the roofs of the houses on Maple Street, on the far side of the lake, the snow-capped mountains rose to meet the sultry clouds that were beginning to crack and let in the morning sunlight. Margo watched Birdie's ritual feeding of the crows, sighed contentedly, and sat back in her recliner. She took a sip of coffee and turned to her crossword puzzle.

Suddenly, the peace was broken by the piercing wail of a siren!

Margo leaned forward in her recliner and scanned the horizon. "What's going on?" she asked Michael, who was leaning forward in his recliner beside her. He glanced at his phone. As if he conjured up a response, it pinged. The message was from the fire chief.

Chief: false alarm. The siren sound is coming from Birdie's garage. She called me. She let the parrot into the garage to fly around for exercise and forgot it for a couple of hours. Precious has learned to imitate a fire siren to call out an emergency. Eye roll emoji

CHAPTER FOUR

When Old Man Keppler's Beer Can Sees Its Shadow

It was mid-March. A grey lid had slid over the sky, shrouding the evergreens, the lake and the mountains. Due to the still-low temperatures at night, a constant drizzle filmed car windshields and turned the streets into skating rinks in the early mornings. The snow that covered the fields in soft white drifts shrunk in the early days of February whenever a glimmer of sunshine melted it.

The warm front coming in from the west, accompanied by the trickling sound under the ice in the ditches, filled the hearts of the residents of Wannatoka Springs with false hope of an early spring.

The remaining snow was stacked in hardened lumps of dirty white along the streets and walkways where it had been shovelled in the giddy first days of winter when kids built forts, and the community came out to skate on the newly cleared and flooded tennis court. Winter's welcome had worn thin even by the hardiest winter lovers' standards.

Impatient with winter's slow retreat, Margo and Michael turned their attention to making gardening plans. Margo, a lover of flowers and books, was looking through a book called *Award Winning English Gardens*.

What attracted her were the bright, glossy pictures of flowers planted in colourful arrangements along borders and in verdant beds. More than wanting to plan a garden, she yearned to look through her living room window and see the garden she imagined.

Margo remarked to Michael that she had enough of this monochrome landscape. She missed the advent of spring on the coast this time of year, when the ornamental cherry trees lining the streets blossomed, softening the grey skies with their gentle pastel hues and littering the sidewalks with pink petals. She even went as far as to threaten to cut out the pictures of flowers and paste them onto her window. But she drew the line at defacing a book. That was her family creed: no books shall be destroyed in the name of projects—not for school, pleasure, or any reason.

Her father had impressed upon her that pictures are meant to reference the words they illustrate and are arranged by the author or editor as their contribution to general knowledge. And so, a whole set of National Geographic magazines dating back to the 1950s were displayed on the library wall in Margo's family home. She had dared not request to cut out pictures of animals to decorate her room with a jungle theme or to use photos of people clothed in traditional garb or geographical features for social studies projects. Books and National Geographic were sacrosanct.

On one of an endless march of dreary days, Michael turned towards Margo and read her a post he had just read in the Wannatoka Springs Times.

HAIL ALL GARDENERS! It may be bleak outside, but spring is just around the corner! It's that time   to plan our gardens. The Wannatoka Springs Garden Club is hosting our tenth annual 'Seed exchange and Garden Planning Day' on Saturday, March twenty, at the community hall from ten am to two pm. Bring a bag lunch and come to share your seeds and garden tips, plans, and expertise. If you are new to our community or haven't yet established a garden, you are welcome to come and learn from experienced gardeners. We expect it to be a beehive of activity! Bee emoji, flower emoji, sun emoji

Michael looked at Margo when he had finished. "What do you think? Want to go?"

Margo's eyes did not stray from her book of flowers. It was open to an infusion of pink, yellow and white flowers popping out of green leaves that framed them. She didn't want to look at Michael because her eyes were filled with tears. She had been musing about spring on the coast. The cherry blossoms would have already fallen, replaced by an intense profusion of red, yellow and purple tulips, daffodils and hyacinths. While in Wannatoka Springs, only the earliest of spring flowers, the crocuses, and snowdrops were opening their faces to the dreary sky while the hyacinths and daffodils were up but shivering in the cold, begging for sunshine to warm their still tightly coiled flower buds.

"I don't know," Margo sniffed and blinked back her tears. "It doesn't feel like spring here. I miss the cherry blossoms and spring bulbs in bloom on the coast at this time of year." With her thumb, she whisked away a tear that threatened to fall.

"Maybe this is just the tonic you need," Michael said cheerfully, trying to entice his wife out of her doldrums. "We haven't seen our neighbours in months. And we can certainly benefit from the advice and ideas from seasoned gardeners about what thrives here." Margo reached for her cup of coffee on the table next to her recliner and took a sip, silently contemplating the barren backyard, noting that the plum trees and the apple trees had only just started to push out buds that would turn into leaves.

"C'mon! It'll be something to do. It might even be fun!" Michael cajoled.

Michael's optimism irked Margo. He always

seemed to find the upside of things that got her down. Today—and for the rest of March or however long it took, she just wanted to curl up in bed and read a book until spring arrived. But she knew that was just the winter blues talking.

She had also experienced that same nagging sadness on the coast during the winters of endless grey skies that leaked a steady stream of moisture, not quite snow and not quite rain. She had been looking forward to spending a winter in the hinterland with honest snowy days and more sunny skies than the dull. The sun did shine on more days here than where they used to live on the coast, but the winter was at least a month longer. She didn't know when she moved to Wannatoka Springs from the coast that bare trees and landscapes denuded of colour, save the dull green of the coniferous forests, would make her feel like she was frozen in time and space.

Struggling to contain her emotions and knowing that going back to bed would be a mistake, Margo nodded and said, weak in conviction, "OK, I'll go."

"That's great. It'll be like a breath of fresh air!" Michael's voice countered with booming enthusiasm, and he snapped back the footrest of his recliner to punctuate his endorsement. Springing from his chair, Michael rubbed his hands together. "Still a bit chilly in the house. How about I get you another cup of coffee and see about stoking the wood-stove downstairs. Nothing like the warm heat of the wood-stove to take the chill off."

"Good idea," Margo said in a monotone voice, holding her cup up for Michael to grab. She turned the page of the book on her lap to another chromatic layout of flower gardens.

Michael approached Margo, took the cup out of her hand, kissed the top of her head and then went to the kitchen to fill her coffee without saying another cheerful word. He had learned that trying to cheer up his wife when she was wrapped in the winter blues often boomeranged. The best he felt he could do at times like this, was to infuse their home with warmth.

***

On the morning of the seed exchange and garden planning event at the community hall, the sun shone warmly in a wide-open blue sky. Margo made egg salad sandwiches for the two of them and included an orange and an individual serving of yogurt in their bag lunches. Making bag lunches reminded her of her teaching days when she made herself one every school day. She smiled at how quickly the time had gone by and how many new adventures she and Michael had since they had retired and moved to Wannatoka Springs. She hummed a little tune as she wrapped the sandwiches and placed them in the mini-cooler.

Through the winter-clad days of February, Margo and Michael had kept their spirits up by pouring over books on gardening they had collected over the years. They discussed how they wanted to add to the landscaping this year and mapped out garden areas on graph paper. Michael's suggestion of using this community garden-planning day to consult with local gardeners seemed like a good idea to Margo once she had broken free of the hold the winter blues had on her. Hand in hand, Michael and Margo walked to the community hall. Upon arrival, they were surprised to see many vehicles parked outside.

"Old people." Michael glanced at Margo and winked, "Not like us spring chickens who can still walk around the block."

"Just remember, what they lack in mobility, they make up for in experience!" Margo smiled back and squeezed Michael's hand. She felt the joy of anticipation return.

They opened the door to see a room full of people, young and old, standing in groups around tables sprinkled with pictures, templates, gardening supplies, and even iPads. Margo recognized some residents who had set up displays, but others were unfamiliar.

"Where shall we start?" Michael asked but took Margo by the elbow before she could answer and steered her toward the table where their friends Tina and Joel were standing, talking to an older woman whose collection of seeds in marked envelopes was spread in front of her.

"Look who's here?" Michael said as they came up behind Tina and Joel. They turned around in unison.

"Well, look what the draft swept in! I trust your commute was safe?" Joel said, clapping Michael on his back. Michael stumbled forward a little and righted himself. Tina beamed and reached out to hug Margo in an enthusiastic embrace. It was a typical greeting from Tina that had initially put Margo off, but she was warming up to it. Tina's smile and hug took the chill off Margo's mood today.

"I'm so glad to see you!" Tina looked from Margo to Michael and then back to Joel. "Should we grab a table, do you think?"

"Sure, hon. You go ahead. I'll catch up with you. I'm wrangling Elsie's white fly organic pest control recipe out of her. It's been in the family for years." Joel winked. Have you met Elsie?" He turned to introduce Michael and Margo to the woman he was talking with. A woman of about eighty years old, with a close-cropped curly white cap of hair and clear blue eyes looked sharply at Michael as her face crinkled into a smile. She wore a purple floral fleece over loose-fitting black polyester pants and sky blue and orange hand-crocheted slippers she had replaced her boots with at the door. Elsie held her small frame erect, exuding the confidence of a life well-worth living. "Elsie here is a long-time resident. What, going back fifty years was it?" He looked at Elsie for confirmation. Elsie nodded and smiled.

"That's right," Elsie affirmed, "Came over here as a bride. Had my children here, buried my husband here, and I'm still here." She nodded emphatically with the last statement, and her eyes twinkled in merriment as if the secret to a long life was a sense of humour about it.

"Elsie, meet Margo and Michael. They moved here last summer about the time we did. Bought Leonard's old place. Elsie lives three houses down from us on Maple. And has two—no—three cats. Ritzy, Bitzy and Ditzy."

Elsie nodded again and crossed her arms in agreement with Joel's introduction. "Good to meet you. How are you adjusting to our little community life?" Elsie inquired. "Must not have all the bells and whistles you folks coming from the city must be used to. But we tend to improvise here."

Michael fielded that question right away, not sure how Margo would answer in the state she was in. "Great! We love it. Couldn't ask for a nicer place to retire! And we are learning so much! Especially, as you say, ways to improvise."

"Glad to hear it. I, for one, think its good for this sleepy community to fill up with young vigour!" She looked around, "Used to be thriving family community, don't ya know. When we were raising our children, and to go to school here. Lots of do's and going's on. The young'uns mostly flew the coop, looking for work and settling in cities that have more to offer their children. Some come back to visit, their kids in tow for the summer, but most of us still here from those times are a bunch of old geezers, still hanging on to our ways. Got some old coots 'round here that can be stuck in their ways and as sour as pie cherries on a Sunday picnic. But don't mind them. They'll warm to you newbies when they see the life come back into this place."

Margo had no idea what Elsie meant by that remark. She wondered what an 'old coot' was according to Elsie's standards. Certainly not the tidy little lady that stood in front of them.

"Well, it's a pleasure to meet you Elsie," Margo said, not knowing how else to respond.

"You'll have to come over for tea sometime," Elsie offered, patting Margo on the arm.

"Oh, I'd love to!" Margo replied and glanced at Tina. Any kind of touching made Margo feel awkward. She hoped her friend would intervene in the conversation.

"Nice to meet you, Elsie," Tina leaned forward towards Elsie when she said that, assuming that most octogenarians were slightly deaf. "But I must whisk Margo away. This gardening event is such a great community get-together, isn't it? I'm so fascinated by all the ideas for gardens! I don't know how we'll fit in time to go through them all!" And in her buoyant manner, Tina managed to elicit Elsie's permission to detach herself from Margo and steer Margo in the direction of the places at table she and Joel had saved.

Tina led them to a long table with four empty chairs—two across. The rest of the chairs were reserved. The claims had been staked with coats or scarves draped over the backs of the chairs and lunch containers set on the table in front of them. "Looks like the whole of Wannatoka Springs turned out for this!" Margo said, looking around. She saw people of all ages mingling together to discuss the one thing they had in common— their love of gardening. "I feel like such an amateur!" she said as she perused the displays she passed.

"Ah! The teacher becomes the student!" Michael released the cooler from Margo's shoulder and set it on the table. He helped her remove her coat and hang it on the back of the chair.

Margo busied herself by setting out the books and plans she had brought. "Oh, I'm all for that! You go ahead, Michael. Tina and I will follow you after I have laid out our plans. Unless you want to stay here to explain them."

"No, let them be for now. I know where they are if I want advice," said Michael, eyeing the tables he had perused and making his way to the one they had claimed as their own. "I think I'll catch up with Joel. See what he's up to." He excused himself and meandered over to where Joel stood, scanning envelopes of seeds, chatting with the people who were passing them on, and occasionally picking up an envelope of seeds he was interested in trying to grow. Tina and Margo followed his path.

"You know they will try to one-up each other in their gardens this summer again, don't you?" Tina looked at Margo and sent her a conspiratorial wink. "Michael is probably looking for an advantage—an heirloom tomato or pumpkin seed that promises to produce giant pumpkins right now."

"I'm sure they will try," Margo agreed. "I say, let them go for it. This time, I will not interfere. Scout's honour! Oh help me, camping gods!" Both women laughed at the memory of Margo's interference with Michael's sunflower competition last summer, which resulted in Michael's sunflower getting soaked in whiskey and Margo having to accept the consequences of losing her dare-bet to Tina to go camping with them. Margo swore it would be her first and last foray into sleeping among the wild animals—and drunks in the woods.

"I'm sure you will mind your own beeswax this time around. What say we head towards the coffee bar? There seems to be a small gathering around a little old man there. I'd like to hear what he's saying that's so interesting."

Tina was much more social than Margo, but that was one thing Margo admired about her, and she had begun to rely on Tina to introduce her to people in the neighbourhood and tell her where and when the next big thing was happening. Margo gave Tina the anchor she needed to avoid getting too carried away. For instance, Margo stopped Tina from impulsively buying toboggans she saw on display at the hardware store earlier that winter so they could go tobogganing down the hills at the golf course. She joked that they might end up taking a polar bear bath in the lake if they went too fast. Married to a golfer, she knew the golf greens were sacred grounds. Nothing aggravated a golfer more than coming to the golf course in the spring, only to see divots and ruts made by snow machines and other winter sports equipment. A sure way to make yourself unpopular was to tear up the golf course in winter. Even if it was a couple of retirees sliding down the greens on toboggans reliving childhood memories.

They made a good pair. Tina was full of ideas. Margo was the voice of reason. Though Tina listened to Margo's cautionary advice, she didn't allow Margo's conservative nature to douse her enthusiasm. Sometimes, Margo steered Tina away from acting on ideas that may not be as welcomed as Tina imagined, and sometimes Tina's playful nature galvanized Margo's resolve to take part in something she has never dreamed of doing.

As the two women approached the group huddled around the old man, they could hear people asking questions about gardening but could barely make out his quiet responses. Margo and Tina came closer to listen to what was being said. They could see that the old man in the center had almost no hair, just a white fringe around his liver-spotted scull. He was making feeble gestures using one gnarled hand with blue veins. His other hand grasped a diamond willow cane.

In a voice that was barely a hoarse whisper, he was saying, "Soil's got to be warm when ya plant, or yer seeds don't come up. They'll freeze just like you would

if yer goin' outside without a winter coat on. And the
sun has to be yay high." He pointed east with his cane at
about a sixty degree angle. Everyone in the circle moved
their eyes upward toward the ceiling of the community
hall in the direction he was pointing.

"When do you start to plant your garden?"
Someone asked.

"First cycle of the spring moon. As she waxes full,
start with yer annuals and yer crops that grow above the
ground—tomatoes, corn, beans and zucchini and such.
Then, when she starts her journey on the wane, ya plant
yer root vegetables—beets, carrots, potatoes, onions and
the like."

When he finished answering one question,
another person piped up. "What's the best method
to plant potatoes?" There would be a pause. The old
man looked down to the floor in thought, and the
group collectively held their breath, straining to hear
the answer when it came.

"Best to dig yerself a trench 'bout a hand's span,"
He stretched his fingers out till the thumb and baby
finger were parallel opposites, "And ya cut the eyes out
that are already sproutin', and face them toward the sky
so they can see the sun. Then you bury 'em till they cain't
see the sun no more."

The questions from the group tumbled one
over another, coming from gardeners eager to gain
the knowledge the old man held from years of experience on the land.

"What's your secret formula for organic fertilizer?"

"Don't have a secret formula. Didn't used to call
it that. Used to call it, using what nature provided. In one
end—out the other, recycle and repeat." He smiled a toothless smile at his small joke. Some of the people tittered in
acknowledgement. "Seriously though, aged manure is the
best for growing good vegetables. Sheep or chicken is best,

but I've used cow and horse. Whatever I can salvage from the farm. Oh, and I piss in a bucket and swill that around in the compost. I believe a man's piss is the best—'scuse me, ladies. Don't mean to offend. Mebbe yours is too sweet for them plants." The man nodded and tipped an invisible hat. A titter ran through the small crowd.

Margo and Tina looked at each other, and help their hands up in front of their mouths to stifle the giggles they felt coming on. The old man's reference to pissing in a bucket reminded them of Michael's secret formula for the sunflower contest. Tina nudged Margo and hissed, "Looks like Michael was on to something!"

Tina was fascinated with the old man's country wisdom. She told Margo she wished she had recorded the tips he was explaining while she was listening. But since she hadn't, she would find out where he lived so she could ask him if she could come over to talk about gardening. Margo was skeptical. She made a mental note to Google the moon phase planting system he seemed to believe in to see if it had any scientific merit or was just folklore. She was sure it was the latter but would keep an open mind.

Old Man Keppler, or 'Mr. Keppler' to his face, was revered as someone akin to an oracle in Wannatoka Springs. His reputation expanded, in fact, throughout the valley, as a garden and farming guru. He had lived in the community all his life. The Keppler farmhouse was moved onto its current property when BC Hydro appropriated the valley to damn up the river that ran through it to expand its electric service. Fertile land was flooded to create a lake that fed into the hydroelectric dam. The farmers who owned the land forfeited their rich farmland and were relocated to land above the water line of the man-made lake. They had to start over again and, in some cases, diversify their farming because the soil was far less fertile. When his parents passed, Old Man Keppler took over the family farm—growing vegetables and harvesting plums, apples and pears from an orchard his father had planted. He had also raised sheep for a time, grazing them on his acreage. He cut hay fields in the summer, seeded alfalfa for his horses to eat, and enriched his soil for next year's crop.

In that way, adhering to the ways his father and his grandfather farmed, he became an organic farmer years before it became trendy. At age ninety-four, he lived alone in the family farmhouse. His wife had passed away ten years previously, and his four kids had their own families that were scattered all over Canada, pursuing their careers.

It was said that Old Man Keppler could predict the advent of spring in this valley with certainty, and was the authority on exactly when to plant what. He was the unofficial draw to Wannatoka Springs' annual garden-planning event. Even though he never advertised his presence or intention to attend, he hadn't missed one in years.

***

Sitting in Tina's warm kitchen, hands wrapped around a steaming cup of coffee, Margo and Tina reflected on their experience of the seed-sharing and garden-planning event they attended the week before. Margo had taken some perennial flower seeds offered, hoping to expand the garden she and Michael had started the summer before. She had circled back to Elsie, even, and when she got past Elsie's tactile approach to communication, she found a rich source of information and advice about what kinds of perennials grew in this area. She left with several packets of seeds and promised to come by her house in the summer to look at Elsie's garden. Tina had flitted from table to table, chatting and gossiping mostly. She was not an ardent flower gardener, but she avidly gleaned what she could in local stories.

"Remember the old man who was talking about gardening? Old Man Keppler, they called him." Margo nodded, "Well, here's the most fascinating intel I got from talking to people there." Tina leaned forward to lend weight to what she was about to divulge. "He's the man to watch when it comes to planting gardens. Folks around here swear by his timing, like he's some water witch or garden diviner—maybe a garden gnome . . ." She snorted a laugh at her small joke. "Anyway, he never advertises when he is going to plant. But . . . maybe a couple of weeks or even a month before he does, he sets up a little round plastic table and one chair on his porch. And once a day—in the morning—he brings out a beer, sits on the porch, drinks it and then goes inside."

"He drinks a beer? That's supposed to be a sign or something?" Margo scoffed. "Next you'll be telling me people come to him to divine when to plant their gardens by what he sees in the bottom of his beer can."

Tina dismissed Margo's comments with a wave and a smile. "Close . . ."

Margo crossed her arms and sat back in her seat.

Tina went on in a confidential tone. "According to the folks I talked to, it has to do with Old Man Keppler's beer seeing its shadow."

Margo burst out laughing. "Are you high?"

Tina looked offended. "No! Dead serious!" People watch him closely when he brings out his long-handled spade and leans the tool against the wall with his gardening ball cap hanging on the handle. He's out there with a can of beer every morning at about ten o'clock, sits there for about an hour, drinks his beer and then goes inside. But! And here's the tell. Folks say that the day he sees the beer can's shadow point in a certain direction on the table, he picks up his spade and switches out his toque for his ball cap. You can see him out there after that, turning over his soil. They say that once he has seen his beer can's shadow, you can count on spring—and the start of planting season will be a couple of weeks away."

"Well, if Old Man Keppler can do that, why don't we try to put our beer can out?" Margo asked.

"Actually!" Tina tapped the table for emphasis, "I talked to Birdie about that. She says she's tried—even put a beer can out on her front porch. It faces the same direction as Old Man Keppler's, so she thought she would catch the same shadow. She said her beer can doesn't tell her anything except that it's empty and she needs another one. She said she has to go inside because it's too damn cold to drink outside!" Tina let out a giggle and a snort. Margo laughed along with her. They could see Birdie on her porch feeding her crows and drinking beer.

Tina leaned in again. "I hear the neighbours have been coming around his place for about two weeks already. Nothing. We may be in for a long wait for spring."

"I'm so tired of the cold and grey and dirty snow. All I can think of is hoping against hope that spring finally comes around here!" Margo propped her chin on her hands. "So, what do we do? Walk past Old Man Keppler's place every morning to see if he sees his beer's shadow?"

"Why not! What else do us retirees have on our agendas? Besides, it will make us feel more like part of the community. Some folks around here mark their calendars by Old Man Keppler's beer's shadow. 'Sides," Tina shrugged, "it will get you out walking. The air will do you good, as will the first signs of spring, like listening to the water gurgle in the ditches. C'mon. Put your student hat on, Margo. Let's call it a sociological study."

"Ha!" Tina seemed to know how to goad Margo into doing something she was skeptical about. All she had to do was appeal to the teacher and lifelong learner in her. "Okay. I'll go along with you. But don't expect me to convert to local superstition and malarkey for predicting spring. I'm just agreeing to walk past his place with you to observe, as an excuse to get out and walk. Chance is always up for a walk and it'll do me good to get out. But please, please, do not embarrass me—or interfere with Mr. Keppler's solitude—by inviting yourself onto his porch to ply him with questions about his beer can! Promise me!"

"I promise!" Tina smiled and held up her right hand, then picked up her coffee cup and took it to the sink to rinse. "I'll pick you up tomorrow morning just before ten. We will walk up Willow, around the loop, and casually peek at his porch when we pass his house. We won't disturb him, I promise, unless he invites us to have a conversation. I swear." Margo knew that Tina would use her wiles to charm the stoic recluse into engaging in a conversation with her sooner or later. That was just the way Tina was, and Margo was secretly looking forward to Tina drawing her in.

Margo decided to share Tina's theory with Michael, though. He would think the notion was absolute hillbilly bunk. He had a factual mind and had always based his predictions on facts, figures and probable outcomes.

Old Man Keppler lived at the top of the loop that Willow Street made as it arched up the hill that overlooked the two parallel streets of Spruce and Maple street. The homesteads accessed by Willow Street were acreages, some still working farms and some still occupied by the original families who were moved there in the fifties. The Keppler homestead showed signs of a previous life as a farm, with weathered wooden outbuildings and the battered frame of an old barn leaning to one side, a sagging roof showing its age and disrepair.

A dirt and gravel driveway led to the family home, a hip-roof farmhouse that dated back to the turn of the last century. The paint was peeling in places, and the green trim was faded, but that was part of its charm. The original four long rectangular windows across the front had etched glass borders, and the wooden door was scarred and scuffed from many years of comings and goings. The porch roof was sagging. The white posts and spindles of the railing were peeling, showing years of weather. Margo had passed the place on her walks with Chance the previous summer. She thought it looked like a comfortable old shoe. She imagined the rooms with windows on the second floor being occupied by the family's growing children. She could imagine the children screaming and laughing, spilling out of the house, slamming the front door and running down the worn set of stairs into the yard where they played.

The next day, Tina showed up at Margo's door to start their walk, carrying two coffees. "On my way here, I saw Birdie. She said she was going up to see Old Man Keppler. Asked if we were going there too. Nosy neighbour!" Tina was gesturing animatedly with the to-go cup in her left hand. It wasn't locked down and drops of coffee dribbled out.

"Steady, Tina." Margo was watching the cup in Tina's hand. Taking it from her, she said, "I guess that makes us nosy neighbours, too, then! C'mon. Don't want to miss anything!"

Margo and Tina walked past Old Man Keppler's porch every day for a week, observing him sitting at the white plastic table with his beer. They would say good morning to him as they passed. He would hike up his beer in exchange. With every passing day, more and more people walked past the house casually or stood at the foot of the raised porch, engaging the old man in predictions about the weather. He was always polite, but he didn't like to spend much time talking, so he would say a couple of sentences, stare off into the distance, and take a sip of his beer, contemplatively indicating the end of the conversation, and they moved on. After draining one beer, he would walk back into the house again.

Margo was getting impatient. "I don't care

anymore," she told Tina one morning. "It's April already. The weather is still below zero at night, and the ice has not broken up in the ditches. All this anticipation for signs of spring makes my anxiety even worse. I want to take a break from our route tomorrow. Let's walk down by the lake instead."

"Sure," Tina replied, reading the anguish on her friend's face. "Who cares about Old Man Keppler anyway? I'm sure spring doesn't. We can walk on the trails or along the lake-shore for a change and talk about something else."

"I'd like that," Margo said. "Poor old guy. Do you think he wants to be bothered with all those people? He seems like a recluse."

The next day, Tina showed up at Margo's door, two warm to-go cups of coffee in her hands. They walked together, this time going in the opposite direction on Willow, taking a route that took them through a wooded path and down to the lake. The sun was shining, warming their faces. Chance was in his element. He loved romping in the woods and enjoyed the freedom to roam and smell every bush and twig, leaving his 'I was here' sign at every spot where his keen nose read another animal's message.

"As they hiked back up Willow towards Margo's street, Tina said, "Why don't we walk past the park. I want to check out the tennis court to see if it is clear yet. Maybe we can play tennis soon."

Tina was being optimistic. Margo knew that the tennis course was still standing in a puddle of melted ice that was still freezing at night and thawing during the day. It had been flooded in January and February to make a skating rink, but for the last couple of months, the wet weather made the outdoor court unusable either as a skating rink or to play tennis on. She didn't want to spike the balloon of Tina's optimism, though, so she agreed to walk up that way.

Once there, Tina looked through the wire fence at the court with puddles pooling in the low spots, and saw what Margo already knew. "Nope. Too wet for tennis and not cold enough for it to freeze. Oh well. At least we got a few skates in this winter." She shaded her eyes and looked up the gentle upward slope of Willow. "Isn't that Birdie up ahead?" She queried. "Hmm . . . I've never see her walking. Wonder what she's up to." And before Margo could protest, Tina called out, "Birdie! Hey! Birdie! Wait up!"

Chance felt, more than heard, the anticipation of an adventure, and he strained at his leash to keep up with Tina, who was waving and walking towards Birdie, who had stopped when she heard her name and was waiting for Tina. At the other end of the leash, Margo felt herself literally being pulled into another one of Tina's schemes. Birdie called out something the women couldn't quite catch, gestured towards Old Man Keppler's house, and then went ahead.

Huffing and puffing with the climb, Margo followed Chance, who was doing his best to keep up with Tina, who was race-walking to catch up with Birdie. When they got to the top of the rise and around the bend, they caught sight of Birdie elbowing her way into front of a cluster of curious neighbours blocking her view of the porch.

"That's curious!" Tina said, shading her eyes. "I don't see the old guy. But there does seem to be some activity there! Birdie certainly seems excited about something. Want to go see what's going on?"

Margo didn't want to interfere in her neighbour's business, but she had come this far, and Tina and Chance were excited to go on. "Maybe he ran out of beer," Margo said wryly as they made their way down the driveway and stood at the back of the small crowd who were discussing the cause of the empty chair. The beer can was still there, but the man who sat there with it every morning was conspicuously absent.

Tina sidled up to Birdie and her husband. Old Pete stood with them, staring at the tableau. "What's going on?" she asked.

"Dunno. The old man didn't come out this morning." Birdie was stomping her feet one and then the other to keep her feet from freezing in her boots, and her hands were shoved in the pockets of her parka. "Damned cold today!"

Margo checked her watch. "Ten-thirty. So does that mean he's a no-show today?" Birdie looked around at Margo. The expression on her face was serious.

"He is never a no-show. Hasn't been since I've been here. And he hasn't picked up his ball cap and spade, so he's not in his garden either."

"Maybe he's sick," someone in the crowd said.

"Or dead."

Tina turned around and faced the onlookers behind her. "Has anyone checked on him? Knocked on his door to see if he's okay?" There was a murmur as the gathered neighbours looked at each other and shook their heads.

"This is silly just standing here. I'll go and check on him. Won't we, Margo!" Tina advanced towards the porch and climbed the creaky wooden stairs one at a time, listening for any sounds from within the house. Margo, pulled along by her dog, stumbled up the steps after Tina. In his keen anticipation, Chance nearly pulled Margo off her feet. She let go of her grip on his leash and reached for the railing to steady herself. Chance jumped up onto the porch and sniffed his way to the door. When he got to it, he started whining and scratched the door with one paw as if he wanted to be let inside.

Tina looked down at Chance and gave him a pet on the head. "Are you on to something, boy? Want to find out what's on the other side of the door?" Tina knocked. The onlookers became silent, waiting for an answer. None came. Tina knocked again with more force this time. Chance whined and barked once. Still no answer.

"He don't like visitors. He might not answer the door even if he hears it." a woman called out from below.

"Maybe give a call inside," someone else said. "He's quite deaf, you know."

"Open the door. He's an old man. Someone ought to check on 'im. He could be lying on the floor, injured —or worse—dead, and no one would know it." Birdie encouraged Tina from her vantage point at the base of the stairs. Margo shivered. That'd be all she needed to be famous for, the one to find the dead oracle. Tina tried the doorknob. It turned and was unlatched.

Margo put a hand on Tina's elbow, gently re-straining her. "I'm not sure we should go any further. Maybe we should call the authorities . . ." She was not one to invade someone else's privacy or trespass on someone's home, but Chance's behaviour was unusual.

"I'll just open the door and call," Tina reassured Margo.

Chance was standing beside Tina, near the crack in the door, sniffing. Tina opened the door just wide enough to stick her head inside and called, "Anyone home? Hello? Mr. Keppler? It's your neighbour from Maple Street. Tina. Just wanting to make sure. . . "

That was as far as she got when Chance squeezed in through the door. Margo inhaled sharply, "Damn it, Chance! Come back here!"

Tina looked at Margo and shrugged. "Well, I guess there's only one thing to do. After you, Margo. He's your dog . . ." She smiled and opened the door wider to allow Margo to step inside first.

The room was dark. Margo noticed that heavy curtains were draped over the windows at the front of the house. "Chance! Where are you, boy?" she called out in a hoarse whisper, hoping not to disturb anyone inside. She heard Chance respond with a "woof!" from inside the house but could not see him. She stepped into the room, letting her eyes adjust to the dark. "Chance?

Come!" she called. Tina called, too. They both listened and ran their eyes around the room, distinguishing large furniture pieces around it. It must have been used as a sitting room at one time, but by the musty smell, it didn't appear to be actively used anymore.

A figure materialized in the dark, gathering solidity as it came further into the room. Margo put her hand over her mouth to stifle a scream. She felt Tina's hand grip her forearm.

"Margo? Is that you?" Margo heard the familiar voice, but her ears were not communicating with her brain then, so she couldn't place it. "Tina?" the voice continued. "What are you two doing here? And why is Chance running loose?"

Margo stiffened when she recognized her husband's voice. "Michael?"

Michael walked over to the heavy drapes and parted them. Grainy light filtered in through the dust motes that had been disturbed when he had pushed them apart.

"Who did you think it was?" Michael asked as he stepped forward. She could see him now clearly. "What are you doing here, Michael?"

"I was just about to ask you the same question." Michael looked from Margo to Tina.

"We were just being good neighbours," Tina answered. "We were walking past and noticed the crowd gathered around the porch but didn't see the old man. They said his beer was there as usual, as was his spade, but the old man was nowhere to be seen, so we thought . . ."

"So, you thought what?" Michael queried. "That he might have had an accident?"

"Something like that, yes," Margo responded. "Tina decided we should come in and check on him. Like she said, it was the neighbourly thing to do."

"Let me guess. You were told that Old Man Keppler came out here every morning to drink a beer, and when his beer saw its shadow, spring was just two weeks away. Is that right?" Michael crossed his arms in front of himself, an amused look on his face.

"Well, that's what Birdie told Tina." Margo blurted out, looking at Tina. "I wasn't taken in by that kind of folklore nonsense, of course!" She scoffed, "But I thought I would just go along with it. To humour my friend." Margo gave Tina a pleading smile, hoping Tina would help her save face.

Instead, Tina shot back. "Thanks, friend. Next time I tell you I'm throwing myself under the bus, don't just go along with it, just push me!"

Margo looked at Tina, worried that she had offended her. Tina laughed and shot her imaginary pistol at Margo.

"Don't take it all so seriously, Margo. Your friend is just a nosy neighbour, that's all! Nothing else happening in Wannatoka Springs this time of year, so why not amuse ourselves with stories about an old man who drinks a beer on his porch every morning—until his beer tells him it's time to get up and start planting something besides his butt in that chair!" Tina flashed one of her mischievous grins.

Michael cleared his throat. "Now, ladies, whatever motivation brought you here, please allow me to interject with some facts. You may be interested to know that I brought Larry some beer this morning. That's his first name. Larry. I brought him the beer ans we're sitting inside comfortably, to discuss gardening. I have no love of sitting this butt on a cold chair. Besides, there's only one on the porch, so I invited Larry to join me and have a beer or two on me – inside." Michael held up the can of beer he had been holding. Margo and Tina looked at each other, and then Tina started to laugh.

Margo just stared. She wasn't sure what she was more surprised about, that Michael was inside talking with Old Man Keppler or that he was drinking beer at ten in the morning.

"YOU are why the old man didn't come out to drink his beer this morning? He was inside drinking yours? That is too funny!" Tina barked a laugh, then snorted. When she composed herself, Tina narrowed her eyes and crossed her hands over her chest, "So? Give! What's the scoop on Old Man Keppler seeing his beer's shadow?" She leaned in for the answer.

"Larry," Michael said emphatically, "has been updating me on the weather patterns in Wannatoka Springs. He says spring will likely be late this year based on the information he read up on in the Farmer's Almanac. I came over to ask when to plant because I started too early last year. At the garden planning event, he talked about planting during the phases of the spring moon.

His advice about planting around the moon's lunar cycle has scientific merit. I looked it up. See, the moon's gravitational pull, which affects the tides, also affects water in the ground." Michael used his beer can as the moon and circled his other hand around it, pulling it towards the beer as he explained the gravitational pull.

"Seeds will absorb more water during the full moon and the new-moon when more moisture is pulled to the soil surface. This causes seeds to swell, resulting in greater germination and better-established plants. It's a practice that goes back through the ages, even before people knew its scientific reasons. Larry's a pretty wise farmer."

While he was talking, the old man came out to stand beside Michael. He had Chance in tow. Chance sat beside Michael and smiled proudly as Michael delivered his lecture. Both women stood quietly, listening to him. Margo was try-ing to visualize the gravity pull of the moon on groundwater. Tina's eyes followed the beer can in Michael's hand, wonder-ing how you could tell when you saw its shadow and knew spring was coming.

When Michael finished his explanation, he looked at the old man. "Isn't that right, Larry?" he asked, clapping the old man lightly on the back.

"Can't say for certain," the old man responded, "First off, I didn't catch half of what you were goin' on about 'cause yer standin' on my left. That's my deaf ear. 'Sides I don't know science from the bottom of my boot. Got to grade seven, and my father figured I was ready to work on the farm with him. But my old man's methods haven't failed me yet. You seed yer aboveground vegetables as the moon gets fuller, and yer root vegetables durin' the time it starts to cut away. That's what my dad passed on to me and his dad before him." He stopped and shrugged. "I figure if ain't broke, don't try to fix it with any new-fangled ideas."

"What about the folks around here saying you see your beer's shadow and know that spring was about to arrive?" Tina asked, still curious.

The old man stared at Tina and cupped his left. "Sorry, dearie. Did you say you wanted a beer? Got lots back there." He pointed with his thumb towards the back room. "My friend Michael, here, brought some with him."

Michael leaned towards his new friend and enunciated loudly and slowly, "They want to know why you sit on the porch with a beer on the cold days of March and sometimes April with your spade and garden cap leaning up against the wall."

The old man's face was lit up with a wry smile. He raised his brows, revealing watery grey eyes and a nearly toothless grin. "It is my habit to go out on the porch every morning in March, to drink one beer, to take in the change in the air and listen for the signs of spring. The creek running again. The buds on the trees. That kind of thing. After that, I come back in. It's too cold to drink more than one. I get my spade out and set my gardening hat on it, waitin' for the day when I can get out to my garden. Always seems like a long wait. But everything has its time. Come spring, I don't have time to be sittin' around drinkin' beer!"

"But do you see your beer's shadow and predict when spring will arrive?" Tina fairly shouted at the old man. She was nothing if not persistent in her quest.

Larry Keppler began to laugh. His laughter turned into a coughing fit. Margo stepped forward, hoping to support him if he started to choke. He held up one trembling hand to his mouth and waved her off with the other. When he cleared his throat, he drew himself up, looked Tina in the eye and said, "Now, that's a mystery I cannot divulge. A man who has lived as long as I have and seen what I've seen around here is practically a ghost. So, let's just say I'm just keepin' up appearances. Gives folks something to talk about." He smiled and shrugged his shoulders. "Would you like to join Michael and me for a beer, ladies?"

"Oh, no, thank you. I try not to drink until the sun goes over my porch roof," Tina said.

'Not for me, either, thanks. Beer is not my cup of tea," Margo said.

"What's that? Would you like a cup of tea? I can do that, too. Come on back to the kitchen, ladies. I'll put the kettle on."

"Thanks," said Margo, "But I think we have overstayed our welcome as it is. I'm sure you don't need Chance bothering you."

"Eh? No bother. And don't you worry, ma'am? You won't be takin' much of a chance on my tea. Ever since my dear wife passed, I've been makin' my own tea. Never as good as she made, but I can guarantee it won't kill ya." The old man turned and shuffled back to the kitchen. Margo shrugged and followed him in. Chance followed her.

Tina looked at Michael. "I guess one of us should

go out and let the neighbours know that Larry is fine and having tea with us inside. And since I got us into this . . ." Tina went outside to tell the folks that Larry Keppler was fine. He was having his beer inside today with his neighbour Michael. With that, Tina popped back inside and closed the door before she was peppered with questions she could not answer.

After an hour of listening to the old man tell stories about how things used to look when he was growing up in Wannatoka Springs and how they had changed over the years, the three new neighbours left Larry's company, saying they would love to come back sometime, to hear more stories.

Margo and Michael parted ways with Tina when they came to Spruce Street. They turned onto Spruce, and Tina walked to the next street, Maple, where she and Joel lived.

"Spring's going to be late this year, isn't it," Margo said wistfully as she walked side by side with Michael to their house at the other end of the street.

"According to the Farmer's Almanac, it is." Michael countered, "Although spring comes later in the Kootenays than we were used to when living on the coast. Larry says that you'll know it's here for sure when you see the daffodils bloom, and they are already pushing up through the ground in your garden, Margo. Have you not seen them?"

"So, you are saying I won't see flowers and green grass for another month."

"Maybe not. But who knows?" Michael said cryptically.

Margo walked in through the front door first. Michael came behind her, stepping out of his wet boots and slinging his coat over the railing. Slipping into his soft fabric indoor shoes, he walked past Margo and into the kitchen. Early that morning, Michael had built a fire in the wood stove. The warmth enveloped Margo like a cozy blanket. By the time she had removed her boots, pulled on her cozy slipper socks and hung up her coat, Michael was turning on the power to the espresso machine and setting the dials. He looked up at Margo and asked, "Want a mocha?"

"Love one," she said.

"Go and sit in your recliner, then, and I'll bring you one."

"You are such a thoughtful man." Margo smiled affectionately as she watched him pulse the coffee beans, spoon the coffee into the basket, and press it down. He reasoned that investing in an espresso machine would pay for itself since they wouldn't be grabbing one from one of the drive-through coffee shops they had available in the city. Michael had made himself into a barista since they had established themselves in their new home and worked out their new routine as retirees. He enjoyed perfecting every step he had learned from tutorials on YouTube to make his wife the perfect cup of cappuccino, mocha and espresso coffee.

As she walked towards her recliner and the window to the backyard it faced, Margo stopped and blinked a couple of times, thinking her eyes were deceiving her. The large square pane of glass she had looked through this morning, lamenting the view of the drab grey scene before her, was covered with a collage of pictures of flowers and gardens. Flowers in cultivated borders outlining green lawns, soft drifts of monochromatic schemes, flowers and vines flowing from flowerpots on a stone patio, roses winding recklessly around trellises, and hedges blossoming in tidy rows.

"This is amazing!" Margo gasped. Michael came up behind her, her mocha in his hand. His grin stretched as wide as it could across his face.

"I thought you needed something to brighten your spirits," he said. "Now sit down. I'll hand you your cup when you're settled." Margo sat down as instructed, but her eyes still perused the riot of colours and shapes. "Until we can work on our garden this spring and continue to make our backyard the oasis of our dreams, this will have to do as a substitute."

"When did you do this? And where did you . . ." Margo leaned forward, recognizing some of the pictures. "Huh!" She caught her breath, "You cut these out of my book of English Gardens!"

"I did," Michael replied matter-of-factly. "I cut them up this morning long before you got out of bed, then taped them to the window while you and Tina went out for a walk this morning. I thought I timed it rather well, but when you took longer than usual to walk today, I decided to go over to chat with Larry Keppler. I know the rumour about his beer seeing its shadow as the first sign of spring, but I heard him talk about the phases of the moon influencing gardening, so I determined to lure him inside for a chat about gardening over a beer since that's what he seems to like.

That's where you found me. I expected you to come home to this by yourself, but I'm so glad I was here with you, if only to catch the expression on your face." And with a flourish, Michael handed Margo a steaming mocha, tilting his head towards his handiwork in the window. "I bring you Spring! For your viewing pleasure, my love. I sacrificed a book of flowers for this view, but don't fret I've already ordered you the latest edition to replace it with. You are worth every dollar!" Michael kissed the top of Margo's head affectionately.

Margo took a sip of her mocha, contemplating the collage. She was of two minds. She loved the colourful floral display that covered the drab view beyond her window and loved Michael even more for thoughtfully making the display just for her, but she also heard her father's voice lecturing about the sanctity of books and the sin of stripping pictures from their context. "You shouldn't have, Michael. I mean, you really shouldn't have."

CHAPTER FIVE

The Bear Came Back

It was that in between stage when winter had not quite let go and spring had not yet warmed its way into the trees setting off a trigger for them to loosen the sap that would push out buds and then leaves. Margo found this to be the hardest time of the year. Grey skies and grey landscape did nothing to improve her mood. She felt like there was no relief from the blues. Even her twice-daily routine of walking Chance, which often enlivened her spirits, became dull and routine. Michael felt the doldrums too, but had turned to looking a catalogues of vegetable seeds and had already started seeds in his makeshift greenhouse, a wood framed lean-to on the south wall of the house. He found the company of plants and ideas about what to plant kept his hopes up about spring being just around the corner.

Michael sat now in his favourite spot on the side of the couch he preferred, perusing seed catalogues. Roscoe, the cat Margo brought from the farmer's market one day, occupied the tight space between Michael and the arm of the sofa. They had established their territories almost as soon as they met. Michael mistook Roscoe for a throw cushion and all but sat on him. Roscoe's reaction was to scuttle out from under him and stare down Michael from the floor until Michael moved over and made room for him in the corner of the couch. Theirs was an uncomfortable but routine companionship. Michael never admitted it, but he felt like something was missing when Roscoe wasn't there. Not because he had grown to love the cat, but because he expected him to be there. It was the routine they had established. Michael was not a fan of disruption to routine.

On this afternoon, though, Michael's routine was about to be disrupted. It started with his phone tooting like a train engine, cutting off what he was watching and announcing an incoming call. Margo's name appeared on his phone.

"Margo?" Michael inquired, not because he didn't know the caller, but he wasn't used to Margo calling him.

"Yes, it's me." Margo's voice came through as a hoarse whisper. "Listen . . ."

Michael didn't wait to listen. He barged right in. "I can hardly hear you. Bad reception. Are you far away?"

"I'm on the street around the bend from our house. Just listen for a sec." Margo spoke in a harsh whisper.

"What? Why are you standing outside calling me? What did you do Margo? Are you bringing some stray home again? If you are calling to get my consent, my answer is no. You can take it back to where you found it. You're not coming in with another surprise pet you just picked up. Now, don't be ridiculous. Come inside if you want to talk to me." Michael pressed the home button on his phone and ended the call with an annoyed sigh.

He reached over Roscoe to put his phone down on the end table and to picked up his book. It was something he did on purpose, crowding Roscoe just to annoy him. His phone hooted five seconds later. Margo's name appeared back on the screen. He picked up the phone, and this time Roscoe pressed all four feet, claws extended, against Michael's side. That was his way of reminding

Michael that he only had dominance over the space because Roscoe allowed it. Michael winced and withdrew the claws from the fabric of his pants with one hand while pressing the home button on with the other.

On the other end, Margo was whispering again. "Listen Michael. Don't hang up. I can't talk to you inside. And I can't raise my voice. I'm afraid I will wake him up."

"What? Wake who up? What ARE you going on about Margo?"

His voice rose with every question. He strode over to the door while he was talking and was just about to depress the handle to open it when he saw through the clear diamonds in the window of the front door, a huge brown shape, butted up against the door.

Margo could see his shadow through the frosted glass and whispered as loudly as she could into her phone. "DO NOT OPEN THE DOOR!"

Michael took his hand off the door handle and put it up to his brow to cover the overhead light so he could better see through one of the clear glass diamonds that ran down the middle of the frosted glass window. When his eyes adjusted to the form, what he made out was a huge dark brown furry rump of a bear. Michael backed away, his heart pounding. "Margo! You still there? There's a bear sleeping on our deck!"

"I know!" Margo said emphatically. "That's what I was trying to tell you but you wouldn't listen!"

"Where are you now?"

"Chance and I are walking down the street back the way we came. I think we'll walk to Tina and Joel's house. Can you believe it? I think this is the same bear that visited last fall and got into our plum wine!"

"How did Chance react?" Michael didn't think he heard him and wondered why.

"He smelled the bear way before I could see it. A block away he started whining and straining on his leash.

When we got close enough so I could see the bear, I stopped and shushed Chance. I told him in no uncertain terms was he to bark at the bear! Or to disturb in any way. And then I led Chance away from the house and called you."

"Where are you now?" Michael walked towards their oversized windows on the opposite end of their front door where they usually sat looking out from their recliners in the mornings, looking down at the activity of the neighbours in their backyards and on Maple Street.

"Almost at Tina and Joel's."

Michael saw Margo and Chance then, rounding the corner of Maple St. and coming up to Tina and Joel's house. Their backyards backed on to the other's property, the lots separated only by a common wire fence that ran the length of the properties along Spruce and Maple.

Margo stopped at Tina and Joel's house. When no one answered the door, she went around to the back to see if they were on their back deck. Finding Joel there, setting out some pots, she told him about the encounter, and the bear still sleeping on their deck.

From his vantage point, Michael could see Margo pointing and gesturing excitedly while Chance ran around her in circles demonstrating the energy she was exuding. Joel looked their way, and then called to Tina inside. Tina came out and Margo's gesturing and pointing started again. He didn't need to hear what she was saying to know that Margo was in a panic.

Tina covered her mouth and stared at their house. She thought she could maybe see right through it if she had x-ray vision. Instead, she saw Michael standing at the window, looking down on them. She waved. Michael waved back, tentatively. He had always suspected, but didn't know for sure, that Tina and Joel could also see them. Now he knew. And knowing that would cause him to make a change in his routine later on, but right now, all he wanted was for Margo to come back home. But the bear was still outside on the deck.

The windows didn't open so he pressed her number on the screen of his phone and held it to his ear. He could see her there, fumbling in her pocket for her phone. When she answered, he said, "I see you from the living room window. Just stay there. I'll come and join you. We can talk about what steps to take when we all calm down (by we, he meant Margo) and talk about this rationally." Michael didn't want to admit that he, too, was nervous about the fact that a three hundred pound bear was sleeping on the other side of the front door. He needed to stay calm and in charge for Margo's sake.

"Over beer, maybe?" Tina leaned in towards Margo's phone. It was on speaker. "C'mon down Michael! No bears here!" She waved at Michael who was staring at the three of them from his window.

Michael signed off. He was about to go to the closet at the front door to get his shoes, but had second thoughts as he approached the front of the house. *What would the probability be of a bear breaking into your house?* He wondered. He shoved that thought to the back of his mind and quietly took the stairs down to the lower floor and, at the back door that led straight out to the backyard (as the house was built on a slope) and pulled on his rubber boots he kept there for gardening. Softly closing the door behind him, he moved purposefully through the backyard. When he reached the fence, he straddled it at the point where a bear had bent it down when he came through in the fall and drank Margo and Tina's fermenting plum wine. He wondered if this was the same bear coming back for a swig or two. Tina and Margo had learned their lesson about storing wine in the shed outside their house, when they found the door ripped almost off its hinges and what was left of the wine they left to ferment there, spilled on the floor. The plastic bucket had been abandoned a couple yards away next to the hedge. Retracing the bear's steps, Michael figured he had smelled the fermenting plum juice in the shed, clawed the door open, pierced the plastic pail and then dragged it out to the side of the hedge where he had drunk his fill.

Margo and Tina had learned their lesson, and started a second batch, gathering plums from the neighbours' yards. That fall, the plum harvest had been prolific. People were happy to give them away, especially as many of them fell onto the ground and became bear attractants. Their next batch was stored in Tina's basement bathroom, instead of the shed, where the temperature could be controlled and there would be no outside access for the bear to break and enter.

Michael did a mental check to remember if there were any full bottles or anything else left in the shed. His sharp memory, reminded him that the wine had been stored at Tina and Joel's house in the basement. So, it couldn't be the wine the bear was after. Perhaps it wasn't the same bear. Or it was, and had returned after a winter hibernation, to the last place he remembered getting a good snoutful of fermented plum juice.

The other three leaned on the railing of the deck following Michael's progress. When he got to them, he was puffing with exertion and adrenalin. He squinted up at them on the deck. "You are looking out of breath, Michael" Tina sang out from the deck. "Like you're running away from a little 'ole bear asleep on your deck!" Tina giggled.

Joel raised his beer bottle to Michael. "C'mon up Michael. Join me for a cold one." Michael climbed the stairs to the deck on the upper floor of Tina and Joel's house while Joel slid the door open and walked into the kitchen of their split-level home, to get Michael a beer.

Michael climbed the stairs to the deck on the upper floor of Tina and Joel's house while Joel slid the glass door open and walked into the kitchen of their split-level home, to get Michael a beer.

"Did you see it? What did it look like?" Tina asked.

Michael cut his eyes towards Tina. "What do you think? I was going to open the door to take his picture? Saw a huge hind end pressed up against the glass. That was enough of a view for me."

"Really?" Tina stared wide-eyed, "You were that close?"

"Well, there was a door between us. But yeah . . . saw him up close and personal and then I locked the door."

"What did he do then?" Tina asked quizzically.

Michael shrugged. "Nothing much. Snorted and rolled over to his other side."

Tina started to laugh, but Margo caught her eye. She was not amused that a bear had taken up lodging at their front door.

"What do we do now, Michael? Is there someone we can call? A game warden? A pest exterminator?"

Joel was taking a sip of his beer. When he heard, 'pest exterminator', he snorted. A picture of a pest exterminator in full HAZMAT with a pesticide canister, spraying the bear away leapt to his imagination. Beer foamed out of his mouth. He covered his mouth to wipe it away along with the smirk on his face.

Michael caught the look on Joel's face. He turned to Margo and said, "Pest exterminator? What you think they're going to do. Spray insecticide all over the bear so he'll crawl away coughing and eventually die of cancer?" Michael grinned and tilted up his beer to take another swig. Tina suppressed a giggled. Joel just stared out into the backyard, already warned that Margo was not impressed with their making fun of the situation.

Margo faced Michael, hands on hips. "Do you have a better idea, Michael?" Michael lowered the bottle and changed his expression to one of concern. "Sorry

Margo. I don't mean to make fun of your ideas, but we have to relieve the stress somehow, don't you think?"

Margo looked away, tears welling up in her eyes. Tina caught her by the elbow and said while steering her towards the sliding glass doors, "I think I have a stress reliever for you Margo. I still have some of that plum wine we made after Otis got tanked on our first batch. Remember?" Tina's sparkly laugh was contagious. Margo cracked a smile and began to relax. "Let's go in and pour ourselves a glass and let the boys talk about how they're going to defend their 'women folk'!" That got a laugh from Margo and she wiped her eyes.

Joel and Michael leaned on the railing of the deck and peered out at Michael and Margo's house, silently for a moment, simultaneously taking a sip of beer.

"He'll likely move on before too long." Joel offered. A bear's gotta eat. And to eat, he's gotta forage. Nothin' to forage yet in our gardens this year and the women got the wine making under control."

Michael took another sip of his beer while he contemplated that. "You're probably right. Probably just found a comfortable place to sleep in the warm sunshine."

As the two men stared out into the backyard in congenial silence, a conversation was going on in the kitchen, they weren't privy to.

"Remember last fall?" Tina poured Margo a glass of the plum wine they bottled last fall. "How he slept off the wine he drank from our stash, in full view of God and everybody?" She laughed. "Sure, was a funny sight to see. A bear drunk, sprawled out, belly up, on our lawn. At first, I thought he was dead! Then I heard him snore." Margo grinned at the memory. That's when they started calling the bear, Otis, after the town drunk in Mayberry on the Andy Griffiths TV show? Haven't seen that since I was a kid. Don't know why I thought of it!"

Tina continued, "Ha! I remember that show! Just

tells us how old we are! Too bad our Otis didn't just lock himself up in the town jail to sleep it off for the night. Haha! If there was one in Wannatoka Springs, since he can't bust anyone anymore for smoking pot in public anymore, Major Tom would have filled it up by now with illegal ATVers riding without permits." Margo grinned to herself at the memory of her and Michael's encounter with the RCMP officer. That thought triggered an idea.

"What about calling Major Tom?" Margo said out loud. "He's so keen on serving and protecting this community, why not call in an emergency and report that there's a drunk wandering around town, breaking into garden sheds and stealing stuff. And now he's been making a habit o sleeping on my deck!"

Tina slapped the table with her palm and laughed. "That would be a hoot! Yeah! We should do that! And if he asks for a description we can tell him, 'Officer, this, Otis, as we have heard he's called, is a big brown guy (no racial intention, just a description) about six foot, five inches tall with a menacing look in his eye. The women in town are scared of him and the men don't dare approach him. He looks like he's spoiling for a fight. Could be armed and dangerous!'"

Margo grinned wider. She was already forgetting that there was a real bear huddled on her deck. Tina continued her feigned helplessness "Honest to God, officer. He's massive! And mean looking . . ." Tina furrowed her eyes. "Massive!" She stretched out her arms wide and curled her hands. "Folks here have spotted him swaggering down the middle of the road at night, ignoring traffic. He poses a road hazard at the very least. Haven't seen him all winter, but he seems to be back skulking around the neighbourhood, peering into windows, prowling around the backyards, probably casing the joint to see what he can steal. Please officer, can you come and save us damsels in distress?" Tina put on a fake flirty eyelash flutter.

This sent Margo and Tina into peels of laughter. The two men were discussing the regular hockey season, which was winding down, and making predictions about who might win the Stanley Cup. Michael, having been an actuary all his life, was expounding on the odds of the top teams winning the cup. Joel listened attentively and nodded in agreement.

When laughter exploded from the kitchen, both men turned in that direction. "Another beer, bro?" Joel asked and took Michael's empty beer bottle out of his hand. Michael nodded. "Sure. I'll follow you in. Check on what the women are up to."

"Good idea. Their laughter is making me suspicious."

When they walked into the kitchen Margo and Tina were wiping tears from their eyes and repeating the fawning gestures Margo made playing the role of the helpless female tied to the tracks while the villain stood over her threateningly.

"Having fun, I see" Joel said. " You must be feeling better Margo."

" I am. Thanks." Margo sniffed and took a breath to regain her composure. Tina giggled and took a sip of wine to help regain hers.

"You should taste this wine Margo and I made last fall. It's wonderful!"

"So?" Joel asked, not willing to be sidetracked, "What's going on? You two are up to something. I can smell it."

"Who? Us?" Tina put one hand to her breast and fluttered her eyelashes at Joel innocently. Margo sipped her wine and looked down at the table so she wouldn't laugh.

"Margo?" Michael raised his eyebrows. "A little too much to drink?"

That straightened Margo up. "I'm fine, Michael." Maybe you've had too much to drink. Is that your third beer?"

Michael stiffened at the innuendo that he

couldn't hold his beer. "Second. And I'll be walking home," he retorted and took a deep swallow.

"So let us in on the secret, ladies," Joel prompted while fishing in the fridge for another couple of beers. "What were you talking about that made you laugh so hard just then?"

Tina put one finger to her mouth and said, "Top secret. On a need to know basis."

Margo swatted her hand away dismissively. "You guys wouldn't be interested. So, Michael, have you hatched a plan yet on how to get rid of the bear?"

"I don't think we'll have to worry about that, Margo. The bear will probably move on as soon as the sun goes off the deck. He'll have to forage for food. Nothing here for him this time round, so he'll probably move on pretty quickly." He looked at the sky. The sky was turning shades of orange and pink off to the side of the deck.

"I hope so," Margo responded doubtfully. "But I'd like to be certain. Why don't you go home first and text me when you check the front door? I'm fine here sitting with Tina, drinking wine."

Michael put his beer down and said. "OK. I'll be the man and secure the castle." With that, he turned and walked out onto the deck through the sliding glass door and down the street. The three were left in the kitchen watching Michael retreat across one lawn, then the other, and disappear into his house through the back door. It was like seeing the movie again but in reverse.

Soon after Michael disappeared into the house, Margo's phone buzzed. It was Michael texting.

Michael: Otis has left the building.

Margo: All clear?

Michael: Roger that. Over.

Michael thought of cell phone texting as communicating on a CB radio and used what he picked up of trucker-cowboy lingo from watching 'seventies classics like Convoy and Smokey and the Bandit.

Margo: TTYL, wine glass emoji, Leftover lasagna
in the fridge if you're hungry before I get home.
Kisses and hearts emoji
Michael: 10-4 over and out.

Margo turned phone upside down on the table, and turned her attention back to her conversation with Tina. Tina poured them both another glass. Joel had retreated to his 'man cave' making the excuse that he wanted to catch up on hockey news.

While Margo and Tina drank their wine, the scheme Tina had thought up with Major Tom saving the day, became more and more outlandish. And the more outlandish it became the funnier it seemed. When Margo left Tina's kitchen, she felt a lot more at ease. It may have been the laughter or it may have been the wine. Margo turned to give Tina a wave goodbye and stumbled on the track of the sliding door. She knew she was tipsy.

"You going to be alright, Margo? Need me to call you a cab?" Tina tittered.

"I'm fine," Margo pulled herself upright. "It's just a short hop, skip and a jump. Well, maybe a deliberate and careful walk." As she was descending the deck stairs, watching her feet and holding carefully onto the handrail, Tina called after her, " Sleep tight! Don't let the bear bite!"

***

A few days later, Margo called Tina again. The situation was getting desperate.

"Is Otis camping out on your deck again?" Tina asked. "Can you check?"

"What? What if he's there again?" Margo felt the panic rise in her throat and swallowed hard.

Tina sighed. "Margo. Just put on your big girl panties and go and have a peek to see if he's there.

119

Margo tiptoed to the front door hoping not to make a sound and stubbed her toe on the bench leg in the foyer. "Owww!" She whispered and hopped on one foot the rest of the way to the door.

"What's going on? You alright?" Tina inquired into the phone that Margo held to her ear. "Do you see the bear? Is Otis back?"

Margo peered through one of the clear glass diamonds that made a pattern down the window. As before, the bear's butt was pressed against the door. She could hear the bear snoring. Seeing the bear startled her and she stepped back. "He's here." She hissed into the phone. "What do I do?"

"Call the conservation officer. I'll text you the number. Happened to look it up just in case. And stay calm! Let me know what happens." Tina clicked off.

Margo paced back and forth, from the front to the back of the house, hesitating to make the call. She had heard that when a bear is reported in a community, the first thing they did was shoot it. She didn't want Otis camping on her front deck. But she didn't think he deserved the death penalty. She hesitated, and then thought she had to go through with it. Despite the consequences. She couldn't live with a bear sleeping on her deck.

Margo made the call and, at first started babbling incoherently about a bear on her porch.

"You just have to stay calm, ma'am," said the voice on the phone.

"I'm not sure I can do that. And please don't call me ma'am. It's Margo. Margo Gaetor. There's a 300 pound bear sleeping on my deck. What if he wakes up? Am I supposed to hit him over the head with a frying pan so he goes back to sleep?"

Margo could hear the officer clearing his throat. "Mrs. Gaetor," he began again (heavily emphasizing 'Missus'), "how often does the bear come around?"

"He's been here off and on for a week! We can't seem to get him to go somewhere else!"

"Is your husband home, ma' . . . Mrs. Gaetor?"

"You are assuming I have a husband, Officer. I do in fact have a husband. But, no he is not home." Why did male officers always assume she needed a man to protect her? So archaic. Margo was disappointed that in all the years women had been fighting for their rights to be equal, men still grew up assuming they were the half of the humans whose role was to protect the other half. Where were their mothers when they were growing up? Oh. Right. Protecting them. And doing a great job of it.

"I see. Are you alone in the house then?"

"No, not really. I have a cat and a dog. However, neither one seems to be too reliable as far as alerting me to strangers."

"I see. Do you mind if ask you a few questions about this bear?"

"What do you want to know?"

"A description would help." he said curtly, "Large, small, colour of the coat, any distinguishing marks., Any details that would help identify this bear would help."

" Let me think. He's a bear. So, he's big. I have no experience with bears, so I can't really compare him with other bear sizes. I didn't know they came in sizes, in fact. As far as I can tell, from looking at him through the glass, he is brown. Other than seeing no distinguishing marks on his backside (which is all I have seen of him) I couldn't tell you about his individual markings."

"OK. That's a start." Margo could hear the pencil scratching across the pad again.

"Oh, and he stinks."

"Stinks." The officer repeated. Margo could hear the pencil he was using to write with stop.

"Yes. You can smell him a mile away. Well maybe

not a mile away, but, when he lays next to the front door, a pungent odour wafts through and the house. Its revolting."

"Yes, bears do have a strong odour," the conservation officer agreed. "And where is he now?"

"In front of my front door! Passed out! I just told you that. Officer! I really need help here! I'm afraid to go out!" Margo hoped her voice reached that strangled timbre it did when she was panicked.

The officer plodded on with his questions. "You say he's been wandering around the neighbourhood for the past week? Probably coming out of hibernation, looking for food. You had best be very careful. Bears at this time of year are aggressive when it comes to hunting for and finding food. Very territorial. Give him a wide berth."

Margo was becoming impatient. "Of course, I'm giving him a wide berth! I can't even leave my house! What are you going to do about it?"

"Once we establish a location and the habits of the bear, we can make a plan. Can you tell me if he has damaged property in an attempt to get at food or garbage? Have you or your neighbours found empty garbage bags strewn around, or anything broken into? Chicken coops perhaps?"

"Yes!" Margo got excited. "He broke into our shed in the back yard. And made off with our store of wine!" Never mind that it was last year, the bear visited the shed. It was the truth. The timing was off. "And he damaged the shed. That should be good for break and enter and theft, right? So, are you coming out to take care of him?" Margo held her breath.

"Well. . . it looks like you have cause for an intervention. Can you ascertain that the bear still there on your deck?"

"Oh. . . I don't want to go anywhere near the front door. I'm in the basement. With the lights off." Margo bit her lip.

"I see. Mrs. Gaetor. Stay calm. Is your front door locked?"

"Yessss . . ." Margo hissed.

"Then please try to go to the front door and take a look. If he is passed out or sleeping, he likely can do you no harm."

"I will try, officer." Margo quietly climbed the stairs and tiptoed towards the front door. From four feet away, she could smell Otis. The bear moved and snorted. Margo screamed into her hand. The bear slumped down again, apparently needing to change positions in his slumber.

"Mrs. Gaetor? Are you alright? What's happening?" The officer's voice sounded sharp and alert.

"He's still here!" Margo whispered into the phone.

"Where? Exactly where is he and what is he doing?" The officer sounded urgent.

"He's on my deck! Passed out! Snoring! I think I woke him up! What else do you need to know?" Margo could hear her voice rise with anxiety.

"Calm down, Mrs. Gaetor. And tell me the address."

"304 Spruce St. Wannatoka Springs. It's easy to find, you just take the first exit . . ."

Margo's explanation was cut off. "I know exactly where that is Mrs. Gaetor. We've had other calls from that area reporting a bear prowling around their properties. We will dispatch a team to get rid of him, as he has become a nuisance to the neighbourhood."

Margo froze. "You-u aren't going to shoot Otis, are you? I mean he's sort of become part of the neighbourhood. I just don't want him hanging around on my deck!"

The officer coughed. "No. We don't shoot bears unless we have to. We will come with a live trap. When he enters the trap, we will relocate him. Somewhere far away from humans, in his natural habitat."

Margo let out a breath she didn't realize she was holding in. "Oh. Thank you, officer."

"Thank you, ma'am for your report. We will dispatch our team as soon as we are able. Is there anything else?"

Margo stiffened when she heard the officer address her as 'ma'am' again.

"Yes. Please stop calling me ma'am. In fact, stop calling all women ma'am. It's the twenty-first century. We aren't mistresses, or madams for that matter. That kind of address is demeaning, and patronizing and ageist and . . . archaic!" Margo pressed the home button to cut off the call before she could hear the apology she knew was coming. Saying that out loud, to a man, made her feel giddy. She was finally saying what she had wanted to say for years, but didn't because she felt some decorum was expected. Retirement meant there was no one to impress or expect anything from you. The thought made Margo feel empowered.

The conservation officer was good for his word. The live trap arrived a few days later on the back of a forestry truck. It was set up in a field not far from Margo and Michael's house, but far enough away from people that a bear might walk into it without endangering the folks whose homes and farms lined the road on the other side of the field.

Margo's bear story became the talk of the town, as was the mystery of why the bear chose their deck to sleep on. A number of folks drove slowly past their house, hoping for a glimpse of the sleeping bear and snapping a picture of it if they saw it there. The story even made the Kootenay News with the caption, "Otis the bear takes up residence in Wannatoka Springs. Someone had sent in a photo of a huge brown bear fast asleep in front of the door.

Letters about the situation were written to the editor, everything from advising that the only kind of good bear was a dead bear, to letters pleading not to destroy it, and indignant words defending bears. After all it was their territory first, before humans made themselves at home in the forest and cleared their habitat.

The trap sat gaping open. It had evidence of a visitor and had been on site for week. After a while, whatever the officer had baited the trap with started to stink. Fish, the village folks surmised. Or food garbage some speculated. Margo figured that if the smell of the bait was even ranker than the bear, it was time to call the officer to tell him to come get his trap back. The plan wasn't working.

It wasn't working, at least the way the officer had intended it to work. Otis was a seasoned bear and had been educated in the ways of humans over the years he had managed to survive among them. He had seen bears trapped in those contraptions. And he wasn't a stupid bear. He could smell the plot and knew how it ended. So, one night, after sniffing the air, and walking around the cage, he walked away and disappeared into the woods in search of food that smelled better than that. His favourite wallow deep in the woods was safe from human hysteria and looki-loos disturbing his daily nap.

One bright morning in August, after spending a carefree summer without a bear on deck, Margo had almost forgotten about the spring the bear who had camped out in front of her front door. She was getting ready to go to Tina's for coffee when her phone chirped indicating a message. She had set that particular sound to indicate a message from Tina. Margo picked up her phone.

Tina: The bear came back!!!!

Margo: What? Haven't seen him in months! Where?

Tina: On my deck! Snore—zzzz emoji

CHAPTER SIX

The Wedding Caterers

It was a dark and stormy night. Rain ran down the window. A branch was tapping at the window pain. The crack of lightening shot through the air. Startled, Jessica looked up from the book she was reading. A shiver went through her as she crossed the floor of the Bed and Breakfast room she had rented for the week, to close the drapes. She peered through the curtains to see what, if anything except nature playing havoc in the peaceful New England village by the sea. Jessica had come here to retreat from her broken marriage. The last thing she needed was . . .

What was the last thing she needed? Margo wondered. An intruder? Her lover standing in the rain asking her to come back? The ghost of her dead mother coming back to haunt her? Margo sat at her computer and stared at the blinking cursor, waiting for her to type the next word.   Margo had always wanted to write a novel. In fact, that is probably every English teacher's dream.

When she and Michael retired to the tiny village of Wannatoka Springs the year before, she told herself she would start on her fiction writing adventure. She had established a cozy room downstairs with table facing the window that overlooked the back garden. Pulled up to it was the ergonomic office chair she had spent many hours in, marking student work when she was a teacher. Photos and mementos of her school career, including a collection of mugs she was given as Christmas gifts over the years lined the windowsill where she could be reminded of their sentiments.

Margo printed off the first paragraph she had written and went out into the backyard to find Michael. She saw him bending over a patch of strawberry plants. Boots sunk into the mud; he was clearing the ground around them. A half bale of straw was stacked behind him, ready to be strewn around and under the strawberry plants as a weed deterrent. Michael had found his happy place in the garden. He had spent all winter watching gardening gurus on YouTube, and planning what he would do in the spring.

"Michael!" Margo called out. "Michael! I've finally made a start on my novel!" To reach him in the garden, Margo slogged through the rain soaked grass in her canvas shoes between the house and the garden. In her excitement, she forgot to change into her waterproof outdoor boots. She instantly regretted it. But even as the mud and water seeped into her shoes, she plodded on.

"What's that?" Michael curled his back upright and stretched it backward. Bending was not as easy as it used to be, he found. When he focused in the direction of her voice, he caught sight of his wife, green reading glasses pushing untamed curly red hair back from her forehead, and a single piece of paper flapping in her hand. Her favourite—too worn to give away to the thrift store but not worn enough to rip up for rags—faded flowered house coat was flapping around her knees as she strode across the lawn, exposing a pair of his cast-off plaid summer pyjamas, the bottoms of which were now wicking muddy water up to the ankles. The sight of his wife of thirty-six years in an uncharacteristically dishevelled appearance endeared her to him all the more.

Margo approached him, puffing from the effort, her face animated. She put one hand on a fence post to steady herself. "Michael. I've started writing! I actually sat down for an hour and started my novel!"

Michael smiled broadly. "That's wonderful, my dear. I am looking forward to reading the next bestseller!"

"Thanks," Margo struggled to regain her breath. "That's all fine and good. But the thing is, I have got the story to a crucial point in the introduction. Whatever my heroine needs, or in this case, doesn't need right now, is pivotal to the whole story. And . . ." she took a breath then released it slowly, breathing through her mouth to calmed herself. . . "I can't imagine what that is!" Margo paused, searching Michael's face for the answer. Michael maintained a sober, poker face, waiting for Margo to go on. He had learned years ago that the way to deal with Margo's dilemmas was to make as few suggestions as possible and keep any sign of emotion or preference that could be read as encouragement or disapproval out of his expression, while still looking engaged. Usually, she came up with the solution that suited her just by talking it through. Then she would thank him for lending an ear. "I think I am experiencing my first writer's block. Can I read it to you? Maybe you can see something I don't."

Michael kept his expression neutral, although his thoughts were jumping from one extreme and the probable outcome to the other at the speed of cell phone signals pinging from one cell tower to another.

"OK. Let's hear it. But keep in mind, I'm not your audience. I don't read fiction, so I may not know how to comment," Michael cautioned.

"It doesn't matter. You are a human. On some level we can all relate the needs and desires of others."

Michael cleared his throat and nodded. Clearing his throat was a nervous habit. He cleared his throat just before giving a presentation to a client. He cleared his throat when asked a question requiring a spontaneous answer. And he cleared his throat when Margo asked for affirmation about something he felt he could not answer without offending her in some way—like asking him if the dress she was wearing made her look heavy.

"Can't argue with that. Go ahead. You have this human's ear," he said, leaning slightly forward on his garden hoe and drawing his mouth into a tight smile.

Margo read the words she wrote with dramatic emphasis. The single paragraph took under thirty seconds to read. When she read the last unfinished sentence, "The last thing she needed was . . ." Margo looked up and searched Michael's face for some response. Michael's eyes shifted away from her gaze and then back again when he realized the sentence would not be completed. "Is that it?"

Margo's eyes narrowed. "What do you mean—is that *it*?" She emphasized the word 'IT'. "That is the pivotal to the start of a story. It is the make or break introduction— the point at which the reader will continue reading or put the book back on the shelf."

Michael cleared his throat again and wiped the perspiration off his forehead. His clothes were damp with humidity and sweat. He needed a glass of water. "I see. Well, as I said, I'm no writer—or fiction reader, but I think it sounds like a strong introduction. What comes next?"

"That's what I can't figure out, Michael! Jessica has escaped one world and is seeking to rebuild her life in another. What is the last thing she needs to happen?" Margo searched Michael's eyes as if they held the answer.

Michael shifted his eyes downward, and stared down at his muddy shoes hoping the answer would come to him. He was a literal thinker, and although he dealt in mathematical probabilities for all of his career as an actuary, the way his brain worked, he needed at least one or two facts upon which to base the probability of the 'X' factor.

"I'm sorry, but you are asking a man who deals in facts and probable outcomes based on those facts. I have no idea what a hypothetical woman who hypothetically left someone to start a hypothetically new life would hypothetically not want to happen. I have a hard enough time trying to figure out what the last thing you want would be. Unless it's me giving you advice." Michael grinned.

"Not helpful, Michael!" Margo bit her lip and turned to leave.

"Margo wait," Michael entreated, and reached out to grasp her shoulder. Margo stopped and turned. "You're a wonderful writer. Your description is engaging. I can picture the scene. I'm sure you'll be able to figure something out. Remember what you used to say? 'Authenticity comes through when you write about something you know.' You have a whole lifetime of experience!"

Margo felt hurt by Michael's words, even though she knew he was only telling her what she had taught. "But my life experience is so boring. No one would write about it, let alone read it.

"You may think that, Margo, but I don't. Just keep an open mind about who you are and where you are, and review the experiences you have lived to get your inspiration. That's all I'm saying." Michael could see Margo's lower lip tremor, so he wrapped his arms around her.

"Writer's block is not the end of the world. Look, why don't you focus on something else while you are waiting for inspiration?"

Margo's head was buried in Michael's shoulder, her voice muffled. "I always said that when I retired, I wanted to write. I don't play golf. I don't garden. What else is there to do here?"

Michael lifted Margo's head up. "C'mon. Let's go inside and out of the damp. I'd love one of your specialty coffees to warm me up. It's cold out here. And you're shivering." Michael rubbed Margo's shoulders, "We can talk about the last thing Jessica needs inside."

Margo straightened up and cleared her eyes with the sleeve of her robe. She sniffed and pushed her hair back off her face. "I'm sure the last thing Jessica needs is to be standing in wet feet in the garden in the rain sobbing into her husband's shoulder about how boring her life is."

Later, when they had settled into their matching lounge chairs, hands wrapped around steaming lattes, Michael broached the subject of Margo finding something to get involved in locally that might take her mind off her writing. He found the announcement he had read earlier on The Wannatoka Times Facebook page.

"I just read an announcement of an upcoming wedding. The Vanhouten girl, Brittany, is getting married. You know, the Vanhoutens? One of the old families of Wannatoka Springs? The announcement says they want to make this wedding a community event. They are asking for help with food and decorations and preparing hall. Maybe you could see if there is something you could contribute. You know, like you used to do for the high school grad. Making decorations or maybe bake something for the reception.

Margo stiffened at the suggestion. "I am a writer, not a decorator. So, unless the Vanhouten want me to write the wedding nuptials, I will be contributing to my own writing. Thank you for your suggestion."

Three days later, the cursor blinked impassively waiting for Margo's command to strike the keys, and complete the sentence, revealing what the last thing Jessica needed was. 'The last thing she needed was pie.' Margo typed in the word 'pie' to complete the sentence. 'Pie! A woman at a B&B resort, in the middle of the night when a storm was raging, thinks that the last thing she needs is pie? Why? Because her waistline is already expanding?' Margo laughed at her own suggestion. "No. Not Jessica. That's more like my problem! All I can think of is food!" The only one in room who heard her rant was Rosco, their obese rescue cat. Rosco stared at Margo from the nest he had made in a stack of fabrics on a shelf beside Margo's writing table, a stack representing a quilt project she was going to get to one day. He blinked once and then licked one paw carefully before putting it behind his ear and pulling it forward over his ear to groom his face. 'No comment' he seemed to say.

"Oh, what do you know!" Margo shot Roscoe a dark look. "You're a cat. Food is all you think about. You could care less about nurturing your creative side."

In response, Roscoe stood up, stretched backward and leapt down from the shelf. With a swish of his tail, he sauntered out of the room and made his way to his bowl of kibble. Margo could hear him crunching his food. "That's it! I'm done with you Susan! I have no idea what you want. But I know what I want! Pie!" With that said, Margo folded her laptop screen down, pushed herself away from her desk, got out of her chair and pushed it back in neatly, then and snapped off the light and shut the door. The end. At least for now. Writer's block would have to thaw before she came back to her writing. *And I think I've worn off enough calories just sweating out this writer's block to deserve that piece of pie!* Margo mused as she walked upstairs to the kitchen. *Perfect with afternoon coffee!*

***

Junuary. That's what the locals called this month's mercurial weather patterns. The last week had been cloudy and unseasonably cool. Intermittent breaks of sunshine teased out of the clouds, kissed the earth an infectious warmth. Then the watery grey curtains would abruptly close the gap, ending the precocious performance. It had been days since Margo had walked down to writing room. She felt a little guilty but held to her promise to herself that she wouldn't go back there until she knew what she wanted to write. This morning she leashed their golden lab, Chance and headed down Spruce Street, making a right turn onto Elm and then another right onto the service road where the only two businesses in Wannatoka Springs, motel and convenience store, were located.

Locals who had been living in Wannatoka Springs called this section "downtown". Margo thought that was charming. She started using the term herself. So, before she left the house, she called to Michael, "Michael! I'm going for a walk with Chance. We're headed downtown to see if there is any mail." Uptown Wannatoka Springs was the loop that circled a cluster of farms and home-steads above the two parallel streets, Spruce and Maple, which, by default must be mid-town—although no one called it that.

Chance, as always, was keenly aware of his surroundings, interrupting the pace of their walk to stop and sniff out some invisible sign. If he felt his comment was warranted, he squirted it out in the grass. Margo figured it must spell out something like 'Chance was here' to the other dogs that read it.

Rounding the corner of the service road was always a pleasant experience for Margo. She admired the line of mature oak trees planted fifty or sixty years ago. In summer they shaded the boulevard. In fall their splash of yellow and red leaves contrasted with the deep green forested mountain behind them and across the lake. In spring, Margo marked the advancement of the season to come by the new buds, then bright green leaves that formed on old, scraggly wood that had stood up to another winter. On this day the drizzle from above spotted the green leaves of the trees and darkened the grey asphalt to charcoal.

By the time they reached the post boxes—a grid of keyed metal boxes four high and twenty-five wide that stood independently at the side of the road, Margo's damp ringlets were beaded with water, while underneath her bright orange waterproof rain jacket she felt rivulets of sweat making their way down from her head to her neck and then down her back or migrating to the cleavage of her breasts underneath the loose cotton dress she wore.

When she recognized the woman stepping out of an SUV wearing a fawn coloured GOR-TEX anorak and lithely skirting her vehicle to get to the mail boxes she had deftly pulled her vehicle beside, Margo wanted to shrink away. She debated turning back and making a hasty retreat. Ronnie Vanhouten was the wife of a contractor, and mother of three, now adult, children. Ronnie was the sort of woman who always looked perfectly turned out for whatever occasion she was gracing her presence with. Her shoulder-length hair was pulled back into a casual pony tail at the nape of her neck; a sheen of peach lip gloss and a swish of mascara was that was required to compliment her unlined forty-something face.

Ronnie's unique, understated style, fit in effortlessly with both the wealthy landowner family she had married into, and the other locals without looking ostentatious. Ronnie was no snob. Quite the opposite, she established herself as the hub of the community with a welcoming, supportive enthusiasm for making Wannatoka Springs a community that worked together and played together.

"Hello Margo! Ronnie waved when she recognized Margo coming towards her. Margo waved back, but unconsciously she steeled herself for the encounter as she walked closer. She didn't know why she did that.

"Isn't this a dreary Junuary morning. But it may

surprise us yet!" She smiled widely, showing a row of even pearl-white teeth.

"Hah! Junuary. Good one!" Margo glanced at the sky as she said that. The grim façade overhead was not inclined to reveal its cards. Chance moved towards Ronnie and sniffed around her curiously.

"Chance!" Margo felt the tug of his leash and tugged to hold him back. "Mind your manners!"

"Oh, it's fine," Ronnie scratched Chance behind the ear. "I was just out riding, so it might be the horses he was catching a whiff of. Or the dogs. We have two border collies. Wonderful, intelligent dogs, but you can never quite get all their hair out of your clothes." Ronnie surreptitiously glanced down at her black leggings, which were tucked into chestnut brown leather riding boots, and picked off an invisible hair.

Margo couldn't see a hair out of place, not even a dog's stray hair. She didn't know why, but she wanted to find some flaw with Ronnie Vanhouten even though she was a perfectly congenial woman. Maybe that was why Ronnie made her nervous. Everyone should come with a little spot of something on their clothes or mussed hair, thought Margo, if only to demonstrate camaraderie with other humans.

"How are you doing? How are the wedding plans going? Is there anything we can do to help?" Margo offered what she hoped would be considered a neighbourly gesture. She expected a congenial decline and an exchange of pleasantries, not what she was asked next.

Ronnie touched Margo's forearm gently and looked straight into her eyes." Oh, Margo! Thank you for asking. There is something. My uncle Richard died on Wednesday. Heart attack. Very sudden. Very unexpected." Ronnie tightened her grip on her bag. Her eyebrows turned upward and furrows mounded in the middle of her smooth forehead.

"Oh, I'm so sorry to hear that, Ronnie," Margo's tone turned compassionate.

"Very sad. A loss for our whole family, especially for his wife and their two children. Unfortunately, his passing leaves me in a dilemma. Uncle Richard presided over the roasting of the meat for every Vanhouten special occasion. On Christmas, he was in charge of roasting and carving the turkey. Easter, it was ham. And when we got together at Thanksgiving—well that was always a special event. The Vanhouten men hunted every fall, and Uncle Richard butchered a steer he raised on his ranch. Oh, my goodness, what a feast! We had roasted venison and beef! And he always roasted the meat on the barbecues.

"Oh!" Margo broke in, "Uncle Richard's death must be a terrible loss. All those family dinners. He must have meant so much to the family. But at least you have the consolation of having those wonderful memories of those family gatherings. I have always been one to say that our best family memories are often shared around food."

Ronnie nodded. Tears formed in her eyes. "Yes, it is a loss and, you are right we will always have those cherished memories. But my immediate dilemma is that Uncle Richard was supposed to preside over barbecuing and carving the steer roasts he gifted us to serve at our daughter's wedding reception. And now I am at a loss to know who to fill that role." Ronnie paused and looked directly at Margo. "I've heard that Michael has done a fine job of handling the barbecue for the volunteer firefighters fundraisers this past year. So, we, my husband Brad and I, thought we would ask Michael if he would barbecue the beef roasts and serve them at the wedding reception.

I know this is a big ask. And you don't know us very well. That's my fault. I always meant to ask you over to dinner, but we have been so busy with wedding plans. My goodness! You have no idea how much planning it takes!" Ronnie flapped her hands. "First and only daughter and all. Do you have children, Margo?"

That last question took Margo by surprised. She was thinking about Michael turning over premade beef patties and inserting them into buns at the fundraisers. "No. We don't have children." Margo replied then pivoted off the uncomfortable subject. "Did your Uncle Richard actually barbecue roasts?"

"Yes, he did! Beef roasts wonderfully well on a barbecue. Even better than in an oven. I didn't pay too much attention to his technique but it looked fairly straightforward. I remember him, just slapping the meat on the grill and turning it every so often." Ronnie waved her right hand in the air. "I'm sure anyone could do it."

If anyone could do it, why ask Michael? Margo thought. Ronnie answered her unasked question in the next sentence.

"My dilemma is, my family and, of course, friends and families we grew up with here have already been invited to dine at the reception, and of course, we wouldn't think to impose on Aunt Beth—that's Uncle Richard's widow, at a time like this." Ronnie paused, perhaps to let Margo jump in and offer.

Margo made agreeable noises but held back her comments. She let Ronnie continue her explanation.

"So, since you are new to Wannatoka Springs" it could be a nice way to introduce yourselves to people here, and of course, we really want this wedding to be a community event."

"Of course," Margo smiled a half-convincing smile. "It would be an honour, for sure. It's just that . . . well, I don't think Michael has ever barbecued anything that complicated before. I don't know if you would trust an amateur to take the place of your Uncle Richard." Margo hoped casting a seed of doubt might be enough to get Michael off the hook.

"I'm sure you aren't giving Michael enough credit. He has already made a name for himself for his hamburgers! And beef is beef!" Ronnie shrugged her shoulders and tipped her open hands up. "I'll leave it with you to make a case with Michael. But please don't wait too long to decide."

"Of course. I'll run it by him when I get back home," Margo assured her.

Ronnie laid her hand on Margo's arm. She pleaded with her eyes when she said, "I honestly don't have any other prospects, but somehow, something will come through!" She raised her hand from Margo's arm and gave it a firm pat for emphasis when she said, "You know what they say–the show must go on!"

Margo smiled back at Ronnie and unconsciously drew her arm closer to her body. "I assure you we will get back to you as soon as possible—probably today. Thank you for including us, Ronnie." Margo didn't know why she said that last part. It felt like pandering. She wasn't one to pander over anyone—not even the wealthiest and most influential family in community.

"I appreciate that. Well, I must go. I just came to check the mail. Replies to invitations are coming in every day. So much to do!" Ronnie turned towards the mailboxes and opened her mailbox, which was indeed stuffed with mail.

Margo, still gripping Chance's lead tightly, even though he had sat and waited patiently throughout the conversation. Ronnie closed her box and pulled out the key. "All yours!" She said brightly. "Oh, and there is a $200 honorarium for Michael, if he chooses to do the barbecuing." She flashed her perfect-teeth smile and twirled away towards her SUV. Waving with the back of her hand like the queen as she walked to the other side of the road, she called out cheerily. "Hope to hear from Michael soon!"

Her mind reeling, Margo walked Chance back the

way they came. Usually, she would take the long way
around to their house for the exercise, but today, she
could hardly wait to tell Michael what they were asked to
do and by whom. She was both astonished and amused
by the proposition. Astonished that Ronnie Vanhouten
would ask Michael, an unknown, to handle the barbecuing
of her prime-rib. And amused at the image of Michael
labouring over huge slaps of beef on the barbecue.
Michael had never barbecued anything more complicated than frozen supermarket burger patties. Margo
was the cook, not Michael.

Margo opened and closed the front door in such
a hurry to tell Michael her news that she closed it on
Chance's leash. Chance was left outside on the deck,
his leash stuck in the door. She spilled the story of her
meeting with Ronnie Vanhouten and her request without
taking a breath. "Can you believe it? She wants you to
barbecue the roasts!"

"Barbecue roasts?" Michael echoed Margo's
last words without looking up. Michael was sitting in his
lounge chair studying his history of golf scores, averaging
the number of strokes it took for each hole and which
club he played in order to create a probability formula
for improving his overall score. Once an actuary, always
an actuary. Only now that he had retired, he could apply
future probabilities of outcomes just for fun.

"Michael?" Margo stood in front of him, hands on
hips. "Did you hear what I said?" Michael looked up.

"You said Ronnie wants me to barbecue beef
roasts at her daughter's wedding." Michael snorted a
laugh, then turned back to his numbers. "Clearly, out of
the question."

"Michael. Please. Can we at least talk about this?"
Margo was about to take a seat in her lounge chair beside
Michael's when she heard the soft whining coming from
outside the front door. "Oh, good grief! Chance. He's

still outside." She went back to the door and opened it. Chance sauntered in, waited for Margo to unhook the leash. "I'm so sorry, Chance. You've been such a well-behaved dog, too! Let me get you a treat." Margo went to Chance's treat cupboard and pulled out a denture stick. Chance, who had walked up behind her expectantly when he saw where she was going, grabbed it quickly from her hand and took it to his dog bed. He did not understand human behaviour or most of the words, but he recognized the word 'treat.' The rest didn't matter.

"Michael," Margo sat down. "Can we at least talk about this?"

Michael put down his phone. "I hope you told her that I didn't know anything about barbecuing roasts and that entrusting that job with me would be a mistake. You're the cook, not me."

"I did suggest that you were not experienced at barbecuing roasts and perhaps you might not be the right choice, but she raved about your reputation as the Burger Master for the fire hall fundraisers. The clincher was when she told me about her poor Uncle Richard, who died suddenly, leaving her in the lurch for the wedding catering since he was supposed to do it and there really wasn't anyone else who could fill in at this late date." Margo took a breath, "I couldn't bring myself to turn her down."

Michael sighed. He could feel himself being roped into one of Margo's schemes, but he was helpless to resist.

"You said I should involve myself in the community more, and, as Ronnie said, it would be a good introduction for us to be part of this community."

"Us? I didn't hear 'us' in the request. However, if you want to do it, I will support you. Barbecued beef roasts! Who ever heard of such a thing?" Michael shook his head and looked back at his phone, signalling that that was all he had to say about the subject.

Margo sat in silence for a minute or two, and then picked up her phone and found Ronnie's number in her contacts.

Margo, "Hi Ronnie . . . it's Margo . . . Fine thanks. How are you? Oh . . . I see. Well, in response to your request about Michael barbecuing the roasts for the wedding, how would it be if I took charge of the roasting. I'm actually a very good cook and have experience with roasts." Margo listened and nodded to Ronnie's comments. Michael squirmed in his seat. "Yes, well, Michael said he would support me if I did the prep so he would be on hand to handle the barbecue. With my experience cooking and Michael knowing his way around a barbecue, I'm sure we will make a great team." When she hung up, Michael huffed and rolled his eyes. Chance snored. And Margo stared out the window, thinking, 'I'll bet there's a YouTube on how to barbecue roasts.'

***

"I don't know how you got me into this, Margo," Michael stood facing a row of barbecues. He shook his head, looped his apron around his head and tied it at the back. Margo was beside him, her apron already stained with meat juice from her preparation earlier in the afternoon. She thought she have remembered to change into a clean one, something more presentable, if she was going to be in the public eye. But she had hurried out into the parking lot the community hall where the barbecues were set up, to watch over Michael and see how the roasts were coming along. Guests were already arriving. It was Ronnie's husband's idea to set the barbecues up in the parking lot, for safety reasons. In case sparks flew as the meat was roasting, the concrete was the safest place for them to land. The lineup of five barbecues was cordoned off with strips of crepe streamers in the bride's colours, sky-blue and lilac, wound around orange cones borrowed from the Vanhouten construction company. A row of orange cones also outlined where the guests could park at a safe distance away.

The guests at the reception would be seated in the Community Hall at long tables covered with white paper and trimmed with the same sky-blue and lilac paper streamers. Still, they would have to come out of the hall to the parking lot to fill their plates at the buffet table under a rented white canopy. It was a community affair, with an array of side dishes and desserts organized by the community club and brought into the hall before the guests went off to the church to attend the wedding. It was left to Margo to arrange the platters brought in, and fill the large stainless steel bowls with the bulk green salad, coleslaw, and macaroni salad prepared ahead and stored in the fridge. When they had gotten together to discuss the plans for the catering, Ronnie gushed over Margo's offer to work as a team, telling her how grateful she was for her help, as her aunt Beth usually took charge of the kitchen. In her urgency to fill Uncle Richard's role as the barbecue master, she had not thought of how his wife supported him by taking care that everything else was on the table, Aunt Beth would have done so if she was in attendance.

With a clean, bleached white apron on, Michael stood at the head of the serving table. Before him, a large oval silver platter sat empty, waiting to receive the first roast. Above it, the carving knife Michael would use to carve the roast for the guests. Ronnie had presented Michael with the knife the day before, telling him that it belonged to Uncle Richard, who had it custom-made for himself. He had used it not only to carve roasts at family dinners but to butcher and carve up deer and other game he hunted. His wife had mailed it express. She instructed Ronnie that it be used in her newly deceased husband's honour to carve the roast at her daughter's wedding, as he would have had he still been with us.

Michael picked up the knife by the handle and gingerly rotated the blade, feeling the knife's heft in his grip. It felt surprisingly light and balanced. The handle was made from a smoothly polished deer antler that curved ergonomically in Michael's hand. The slim, long blade was sharpened steel and ended in a fine point. Michael could well imagine what would happen if he miscalculated while slicing the roast with it, and nicked himself. He made a mental note to ensure a first aid kit was on hand with a supply of plasters and ointment in case of burns.

The morning of the wedding started out as a clear sunny day full of promise for a beautiful outdoor reception. By mid-morning, Margo was hard at work in the community hall kitchen, lining up slabs of raw beef roasts ranging from ten - twenty lbs each. She dug them out of the coolers they were delivered in, surrounded by ice, and slapped them on the butcher block to cut up the larger pieces into two so they would be more manageable and more evenly distributed among the five barbecues. She found that the hunting knife that was lent to Michael was the best tool for the job. The blade slipped through the sinewy shanks as if they were made of butter. After she finished, Margo stood back to examine her work.

Some roasts were smaller than others, so she would have to calculate the time they would take and stagger the start time so they would all be done at the same time. The kitchen was not equipped with a scale, and her kitchen scale at home was too small. It didn't even go up to twenty pounds. To solve the problem, she had sent Michael back to the house to fetch her bathroom scale to estimate each roast's weight. To be hygienic, she covered the scale with two layers of paper towel and then placed the first one on the scale. The digital scale kept blinking a scat of numbers, unable to decide where to stop. Unlike the human body, a roast didn't carry its weight evenly across.

Margo decided the most accurate way to get the weight would be to stand on the scale herself, read her weight and then step back on the scale with the roast and subtract her original weight from the weight recorded with the roast. She felt a twinge of self-consciousness doing this, but Michael had left immediately after dropping of the scale, so she had no one else to use to record the weights.

Taking a breath in, Margo stepped on the scale, and then let it out. She looked down to see where the digits settled. "What? Can't be!' She exclaimed out loud when she read the number. "I haven't gained that much weight, have I?" She hadn't weighed herself for a whole year since she retired. She told herself that she would let go of all the expectations and restrictions of her life before retirement—including self-judgment of her weight.

That first September after she retired, when school started without her and she was certain she would not step into a classroom she bagged up most of her restrictive, tailored teacher wardrobe and gave it to a thrift store, hoping that they would be picked up by women who still needed to make a good impression in the work place. After that purge, she went on a shopping binge, choosing roomy dresses and loose pants that flowed from gathered elastic waists. Permitting herself to let go of self-made restrictions, she relegated her bathroom scale to the back of a cupboard. This was the first time she had pulled it out. And now she stood on it in disbelief of the weight it registered.

Must be water gain. Or maybe its my clothes and shoes. I've never weighed myself with clothes on before. They must account for at least five pounds—maybe more! she thought. Stepping off the scale, Margo listened for any noise that might indicate someone else was in the building. Hearing nothing but the creak of the wind outside, she started divesting herself of her clothes. First, she kicked off her sandals, then undid the tie at the elastic waist of the long, swishy Indian cotton skirt and shimmied it down her thighs until it dropped at her feet and she could step out of it. She pulled the short-sleeved, loose-fitting cotton top over her head and stood barefoot in her bra and panties beside the scale. "Oh," she said aloud, "I forgot! My jewellery." After removing the swinging silver earrings, she bought at the Saturday market and the beaded necklace she found at the thrift store, Margo took a breath and stepped on the scale again and let it out. She was concentrating on the numbers that vacillated a decimal point up and down before it flashed and settled, so she didn't hear the door to the kitchen open behind her.

"Margo? Is that you?" Margo didn't need to turn around to recognize who was standing behind her. She blushed from head to toe and hopped off the scale, instantly grabbing at her clothes as she whirled around.

"Ronnie!" Margo emitted a half-laugh. "Uh—I must look ridiculous." She said, hopping into the puddle of her skirt on the floor to pull it up over her exposed thighs with one hand while clutching her top to her breasts. "This must look so weird. I can explain. I want-ed to weigh the roasts so I could time how long they had to be cooked. They wouldn't lay evenly on my scale so I thought I could get a more accurate read if I stood on the scale holding them, but then I had to read my own weight first . . ." Margo paused to push her arms through the armholes of the blouse and then pull it over her head. When she emerged, she pushed back the strag-gly red curls that had come free from the pins she had used to secure her hair so it wouldn't get into the food. "And when I weighed myself—I haven't weighed myself for

145

a year now—I was surprised that I have gained—uh—a little weight, so I thought, maybe it was my clothes. And thinking there was no one else here at all, I thought I'd like to see if taking them off would make a difference," she said while sliding into her sandals and straightening out her skirt. She held up her hands. "Honestly, I didn't touch the roasts with my bare body. And I'm not a naked chef." She didn't know why she said that. And she winced at how it must have sounded.

Ronnie stood silently arms crossed. A small smile played on her lips, and the corners of her eyes creased a little, which were the only signs that she was holding herself back from laughing. When Margo straightened up, Ronnie said, "No, no. I apologize for interrupting you. I had no idea that roasts had to be weighed to time them. Shows you what I know!" She giggled and flipped her hand and smiled as if dismissing the scene with a wave.

Margo giggled nervously. "I'm so embarrassed . . ."

Ronnie smiled wider, took Margo's wrists in her hands, and pressed lightly. "Not to worry. I'm no gossip, so your unique way of weighing roasts will stay between us." That broke the ice. Both women giggled.

Ronnie looked around the room, hands on hips. "Now, let's see. If I remember this kitchen right, I think there is a large scale here somewhere. I know they used it once for a pig roast the community club sponsored, but that was years ago. Ronnie snapped her fingers. "Ah! I remember now where it is. She walked over to a bank of lower shelves along the back of the spacious kitchen and crouched at the last one. Reaching into it, she pulled out a steel weigh scale, the style you would expect to find at the butcher's shop for weighing slices of sandwich meat. "Here it is!" It was heavy, so Ronnie grunted when she brought it out and set it on the counter. Margo went over to help.

"Wow! This is exactly what I need!" She exclaimed

when the two women had pushed it into place on the counter. Margo watched the red dial rotate around the round face when she pushed her hand down on the plate "I wish I had known before I stepped on my own bathroom scale. I wouldn't have had to face the shock of how much I weighed!"

"And I wish I had been around earlier to save you that fate! You know, I weigh myself once a week, early in the morning before I drink coffee. And always in the nude. Can't be too fastidious! Not when a pound or two sends us women into a tailspin!" Margo blushed as the chill of this perfectly turned-out woman defrosted.

"Anyway, the reason I came in was to tell you that the wind is gusting outside, and it looks like there might be a storm brewing." She looked out the tiny window over the parking lot. "I'm hoping it won't interfere with our arrangements."

Margo studied the weather through the window. Dark clouds were rising over the mountain tops and pulling a dark shadow over what started out to be a bright sunny day, perfect for a June wedding.

"The clouds coming from the west look a little ominous. But these summer storms usually blow themselves out before they cross the lake." Margo said, hoping she sounded more confident than she felt.

"Fingers crossed." Ronnie replied. "But just to be on the safe side, I thought we would move the barbecues under the canopy. They don't have to be close to the buffet table. I think the canopy is wide enough to accommodate a wide corridor between the barbecues and the serving table. That way, the whole business will be covered in case we have a smattering of rain. Although, hopefully, it won't amount to that."

"I think that can be done. Although, they will have to be situated right at the edge of the canopy so it won't block the smoke from above. That could be a fire hazard. But I'm sure Michael can handle it. They are ready to go, and moving them will be easy if we do it before we put the roasts in."

Ronnie nodded and smiled. "I trust you will both do what's best. I'm sorry I can't stay to help, but it looks like you have everything in hand."

"Don't you worry about a thing!" Margo said confidently, "You are the mother of the bride! You should be enjoying your day with your daughter. You just make sure your daughter and her groom make it down the aisle and say their vows! We'll take care of the rest. You can count on us, come hell or high water!

Margo thought she saw a shadow cross Ronnie's face, but in a flash, it was gone. "Of course, you will!" Ronnie beamed. "I know everything is in good hands." Margo later thought it was foreshadowing of what was to come. But at that moment, she felt buoyant with pride that this prominent family in the community was putting their trust in her and Michael, virtual newcomers.

The wind did not abate as Ronnie had predicted. By mid-afternoon, dark clouds moving across the lake towards the village indicated that a storm, a pretty big one, was heading towards the village.

When Michael joined Margo around noon, the time she had asked him to come, Margo handed him a bib apron like the one she was wearing and told him the rule of working together during this catering event. "There is only one rule," Margo pronounced in her authoritative teacher voice, waving the spatula in her hand as if it was a ruler, "You do exactly what I tell you to do exactly when I tell you to do it. You don't ask why and you don't try to work out the probabilities of success—at least not out loud. Got it?"

Michael could see that Margo was serious. There was not a flicker of a smile on her face. He nodded and lifted his right hand, palm up and solemnly said, "I do."

That broke Margo up. She threw Michael a towel and said with a grin, "Now, first I want you to dry those trays I rinsed and set them on the counter. We are going to make trays of crudités for the buffet.

Michael's primary job was to rotisserate the roasts. Since the meat was too large to spike onto an electric rotisserie, and that only two barbecues had the tools anyway, Margo instructed Michael to brown them on all sides with the flames turned up high and then turn the flame down to medium and close the lid. He was tasked with watching that the temperature on each barbecue did not deviate much and that, every half hour, he rolled each roast a quarter turn. Between rotating the roasts, Michael spent his time with Margo in the kitchen preparing the serving dishes and plating the rest of the buffet offerings.

As Michael was cutting up the raw vegetables that he was arranging on a platter, the alarm on his phone went off, interrupting his meditation. Michael wiped his hands on his apron and pulled his phone out of the pocket. "Time to rotisserate!" he announced. He exited the kitchen and went through the front door to the parking lot. Four of the five s showed active signs of roasting—meat sizzling, fat sputtering, and smoke emanating from the vents.

One did not. Michael went to that one first. The flame was out. When he turned the dial, he recognized the hollow hiss of an empty propane tank. "Damn! I wonder how long that's been off." He looked down at the roast. It couldn't have been more than half an hour. Or did he just not notice it during his last round when he turned them all over? The roast bled when he stuck his fork into it. "Damn and double damn!" he cursed out loud and then went on to check the others. All of the others seemed to be cooking as expected he thought—although his experience of what a roast could be expected to look like while going through the stages of cooking was limited. Michael looked at his watch. "Damnit!" Four pm. It was too late to find another propane tank. Margo heard Michael's ex- clamations through the window. She didn't like the sounds of his outbursts. One could have been a burn from touching the hot surface—but three meant something was seriously wrong. She rushed out to see what was the matter. As she did, a gust of wind hit her in the face, with a fist full of water. She wiped the rain off her face off and squinted up at the sky. It was iron grey, and the rain was starting to be sprayed across the parking lot by the wind. "What's the matter, Michael?" She forged on until she was standing beside her husband at the last grill.

"This little piggy will get none." He was staring down at a roast on a grill with no flame.

"What? What on earth. . .?" Margo looked into the grill. The flames were out and the roast looked quite underdone. "What happened?"

"The propane was used up. I can't say when. But there's no getting around it. It's not going to get done on a cold grill."

"Have you looked at the others?" she asked, walk- ing towards the next one and lifting the lid.

"I was just going to look." Michael said just as Margo shrieked, "Dammit! This one's gone too!" She flicked the starter a couple of times just to be sure.

"Hmm . . ." Michael said deep in his own thoughts. "I wonder what the probability of a canister of propane lasting four to five hours at a set temperature of 350 after being turned up to 400."

"No!" Margo said fiercely. "This is not the time or the place for figuring out what could happen. It's already happened. And now we have to fix it!"

Margo's idea was to rotate the five roasts be- tween the three still-lit barbecues, giving each time to roast and rest–as she called it. For the next hour, she and Michael rotated roasts from one barbecue to the next, with the last two sitting undercover on a wheeled cart while the others roasted for their allotted five minutes.

It was five o'clock. The guests were starting to drift in. The tables were set up in the hall; the sides and salads were artfully displayed on the buffet with a cutting board at the end set with a meat fork and the hunting knife. Michael took his place at the end of the table, ready to carve.

Ronnie appeared in an immaculate pearl grey chiffon dress that grazed her knees and four-inch heels that showed off her well-turned calves. Her professionally highlighted hair blended the grey with the blond. Her face was made up in understated blush tones that made her skin look youthful and bright.

Margo tried to visualize her own image through Ronnie's eyes–wisps of fuzzy, fading red curls sneaking out from the top knot she had fashioned her hair into with an elastic and clips. A worn but clean bleached cotton apron she had found in one of the drawers of the hall's kitchen over a roomy sleeveless cotton dress printed with huge yellow sunflowers against a navy back-ground. The dress grazed her ankles and exposed her neon green gym shoes. She chose comfort over style for the occasion.

"Hello you two!" Ronnie beamed. "It looks like you have it all in hand. What an artistic arrangement of crudités!" She exclaimed.

"Thank you," Michael and Margo said in unison. Margo looked at Michael, who was smiling ear to ear.

"So, we are ready?" Ronnie inquired, looking over the array of carefully positioned platters and then at the end of the table where the empty platter was set with the knife above it.

"I believe we are," Margo said, taking in the scene

to ensure everything was in its place. A low gust of wind flapped through the canopy, ruffling the fringe and rifling Ronnie's perfectly coiffed hair.

"Oh!" Ronnie exclaimed and patted it back into place. "I'd better get back in and let the master of ceremonies know to start. The head table will be first, and then he will announce each table, one at a time, so it won't overwhelm you, Michael." Michael nodded and smiled. Standing at his station wearing his bleached white apron over his crisp oxford-blue shirt with rolled-up sleeves and dark dress pants, he looked eminently competent.

Thunder rolled above and Ronnie's face showed signs of worry but she didn't allow it to tinge her voice. "Thank you both! I'd better get back inside." She walked briskly down the aisle between the buffet and the barbeques. Just before she reached the end of the canopy, she turned as if having forgotten to say something. "If you are not too tired, afterwards, please do join us for the dance." Ronnie rushed up the steps with amazing agility, Margo thought, considering she was manoeuvring in four-inch heels. Another gust of wind slammed the door shut behind her.

Margo transferred the first roast to the cutting board. Michael looked down at it's charred exterior and was about to say something when Margo held up her hand. . ."Stop! No comments or questions." Michael shut his mouth and nodded. "It just looks that way on the outside because it's barbecued. Now remember. Outside cuts are well done. Inside cuts are medium-rare. Ask them what they prefer. And always cut with the grain. Got it?"

"Got it!" Michael nodded. Margo had said no questions, but Michael still wondered how he would get inside without cutting it open. She didn't say he shouldn't, so he finally made his own decision. He would cut off the ends—which looked like charcoal—and then carve up the meat until he reached halfway. That way, the guests could just point to the cut that pleased them.

The hall door flung open with a bang against the wall. The bridesmaids who emerged, screamed at the startling noise, then shrieked in laughter at their response to the surprise. Then, fluttering down the stairs in their chiffon dresses like a puff of lilac and sky-blue birds, they twittered together as they made the short dash for cover under the canopy.

Behind them, the young men who had stood up for the groom, jacket-less with ties already askew, boisterously jockeyed for position, pushing each other playfully as they surveyed the spread on the table.

Their progress was impeded by the girls who were gathered around the buffet table, plates in hand, picking up a carrot stick or two or a piece of lettuce and centered it on their sparsely filled plates—all the while extolling the bride's amazing dress, her amazing mani-pedi, and her amazing do.

Margo wondered if there was anything left in the world that was truly amazing—or could the pyramids of Giza be as amazing as the latest mani-pedi.

"Follow me, boys", said the one who seemed to be the leader, "I'm skipping the rabbit food. Going straight for the meat!" That said, he skirted around the girls, who giggled as he passed. Looking a little sheepish, and with polite gestures and an 'excuse us," the other young men followed their leader. The boys surrounded Michael like a pack of hungry dogs, eyeing the meat platter he was filling as he was carving.

Margo's thought about how these rosy-cheeked girls with loosely curled hair that hung down past their shoulders, with floor-length, strapless lilac dresses clinging to their slender figures and accentuated budding breasts, were perhaps the prettiest they would ever be and didn't have a clue.

One voice cut through her reverie. The leader of the male attendants, a tall, skinny young man with thick black hair that fell into his eyes but otherwise was cropped short, complain loudly about the cut of the meat he was served. "I said rare! That's not near enough bloody! I meant bloody rare. Fresh kill, rare. Like where the blood drools down the side of yer mouth when ya take a bite!"

Michael scowled in concern. "Uh . . . maybe the center will be rare. Let me see what I can do." He stabbed the roast with the meat fork and slid the hunting knife down the center of the roast. The blade cut through the meat as if it were butter. Blood oozed out as he sliced down to the cutting board. Just as he thought. It was undercooked inside and charred on the outside. Michael hope this wasn't the last request for rare.

"Moo!" the young man bellowed. "Perfect! Slap it there!" Michael sliced off a thick slice and forked it onto the outstretched plate. He expected the young man to withdraw his plate and move to the back of the line. But when he didn't budge, Michael took his cue and began slicing another thick piece off, "Would you like another piece?"

"Yes, please! Load 'er up!" he said, turning to the other guys lined up behind him. "Look at that! Now that's what I call rare!"

"Moo.....ve over," one of the other guys bellowed. "We're hangry!"

One of the girls behind them looked like she was going to turn green. But the rest of the boys wanted to just like their leader. The girls were a bit squeamish when they saw the blood oozing out so they asked for well done. But as Michael sliced further into the roast it became clear that this was the one that didn't get enough time on the barbecue to cook through. The girls were making gagging noises and turning away from the bleeding roast.

"Can you bring me another roast, please, Margo?" Michael called without looking up from his cutting board. To the girls, he said, "I'll get another one. I'm sure it will be much more well done. Sorry about that, ladies. We had a little trouble regulating some of the roasts. But don't worry; we'll fix you up in no time." The bridesmaids giggled and turned away from the bloody sight.

"So gross!" said one.

"Right? I nearly hurled!"

"The sight of blood put me off. I'm becoming vegetarian. Starting now!" Another one chirped and stepped out of the line and walked back to the hall, a plate of sides and crudities delicately balanced in one hand while she held the side of her dress up, so it wouldn't get wet in the now sodden ground.

The rain was coming down in earnest now. Lightening bolts slivered through the sky, but the delayed thunder clap suggested to Margo that the storm was not close. At least not yet. Still, this whole operation seemed dicey and Margo was on edge. Not just because of the threatening storm, but because she had no idea if any of the roasts were cooked through. Having never had experience with barbecue temperature regulation and also the propane, she was doubtful of success. All she could hope for, at this point was that more of the guests liked their meat rare.

Margo chose the roast on the barbecue nearest the door. It was too heavy, she figured, to airlift it to Michael's station suspended by tongs. She would have to find a tray, slide it onto it, and walk it over to him. Margo found what she was looking for—a metal tray that was almost empty of crudités. She pushed the remaining vegetables onto the plate next to it with her fork and brought the tray back to the barbecue. As she worked with the roast, lifting it onto the tray with two forks she called behind her, "I'm coming, Michael! Make room. This one's really rare."

She didn't hear his reply. For at that moment the doors to the hall swung open, flinging forcefully against the walls where they banged almost as loudly as the clap of thunder overhead. In the doorway, holding onto her headpiece and veil with one hand and her train with the other was the petite blonde bride wearing a fitted strapless satin dress, and straining to hold up a ten-foot train by a fabric loop around her tiny wrist. She screamed and ducked back towards her groom when she heard the thunderclap and the doors slam.

Her groom, a fresh-faced young man of barely twenty, wearing a light grey cowboy cut suit, white shirt, black tie, and cowboy boots, rocked back on his heels when he caught her. Both were almost blown off the steps with the gust of wind that had just come up. He steadied them both and steered them down the steps to the cover of the canopy, the bride squealing that something was caught and her make-up was running.

So chaotically and simultaneously did the sequence that happened next play out, that it's probably best to describe each action and reaction in a slow-motion play-by-play like they do in a hockey play that's over before the crowd can follow the movements.

Pan to top of the stairs to the doors through which the bride and groom have just emerged to collect their plates of food: the thunder booms, a wind gust blows the door of the hall against the wall. The bride lets out a shriek and holds onto her headpiece for dear life. The groom takes her elbow and they descend the stairs as quickly as possible—in formal dress and heels.

Pan to Michael's station at the other end of serving table under the canopy; a gust of wind yanks one corner of the canopy up with a force that pulls the stake the guy rope is anchored with—right out of the ground. Now unsecured, the tent pole sways and then dangles uselessly from the pocket of the corner of the canopy and then comes free and clatters to the ground. The lightweight canopy fabric snaps and twists in the wind like a bird in a trap, furiously flapping its wings to free itself. Michael notices this and abandons his station. He heroically jumps up to catch the flapping corner and capture the flailing rope and the metal stake that swings dangerously close to his head. Fighting against the gusts of wind that threaten to yank the fabric and rope out of his hand before he can secure it, he grasps the pole on the ground with one hand while holding onto the corner of the canopy with the other. In a sequence of deft movements, Michael manages to stand the pole upright, secure the rope, and stomp the stake back into its place in the ground with his shoe. He tests the rope and deems it stable. Then looks up. What he sees alarms him . . .

Pan to Margo with the roast on the pan crossing the aisle towards the serving table, her back to the door. She sees Michael struggling to catch the flyaway canopy corner and the bridesmaids clucking over cuts of meat, then freezes when, in a lilac gaggle they scream and point to something they see behind her.

"Brittany! You're on fire!"

"Blade! Do something! Brittany's on fire!"

The peel of screams is echoed by the bride who was standing behind Margo, close to the barbecues. Too close. Hysteria broke loose!

Instinctively responding to the howling bride as the signal of an emergency, Margo pirouettes with the pan in her hands and slips backwards when her feet slide through a puddle forming on the cement. Her arms fly upward, launching the roast off the pan, on trajectory path headed straight for the bride and groom . . .

Pan to the bride and groom who have just reached the shelter of the canopy. A swift undercut of wind lifts up the bride's train and it billows like a sail behind her. With her back is to the barbecues, Margo lifted the roast from only moments ago. The burner is still on. And, no longer buoyed up by wind, the bride's train gracefully deflates—and a corner of it catches the grill on the way down while she is fussing about her hair and her make-up.

Then the corner of the train lights on fire.

Unaware of this, the groom steers his bride toward the buffet, trying his best to keep her calm. And as they edge away from the barbecue, the bridesmaids, who are admiring how glamorous the bride is, suddenly see the end of train on fire—and scream.

The groom turns. Just as Margo's errant roast beef missile projects towards him. When he sees the projectile coming, the groom's reflexes kick in. The star high-school quarter back of Crystal Lake High, braces his arms in a cradle posture, catches the projectile and hugs it to his body, as he would a football. Then he tucks and rolls—not because this is his next football play, but because what he has caught is not a football. It's a blazing hot roast, and he is feeling the burn through his suit jacket and shirt.

The roast rolls out of the grooms arms and under the table. He lays curled up on the cement, a roast-size blood stain blotting out the pristine white of his shirt.

Pan to Margo who has caught herself just before she fell. She stands paralyzed with horror watching the scene play out in front of her, a silent scream ricocheting through her head, unable to move.

Pan to Michael at head of the buffet table, knife in hand, bent down over the roast as he is about to carve a slice from for the bridesmaid in front of him. He hears the trio of screams and shouts to the bride and groom. He steps out into the aisle to see what is happening and spots the flames licking the fringes of white fabric train behind the bride. A hair's breath later, he sees Margo turn, slip on a pool of water brought in by the rain, then sees the roast slide off the tray, and fly towards the groom.

Now, a little background on Michael (that has

bearing on his next move) is that Michael is a hockey player. He has trained his eye to move, not just to where the puck starts its trajectory but to anticipate the target before it gets there—so he can intercept it's path. And when he's playing hockey, his peripheral vision is his super-power. It takes nano-seconds for Michael to determine the course of action he must take to avert not one but two disasters. And as he lunges toward the bride and groom, he yells out,"Fire! Fire! Clear the tent!"

Pan to the scene in the parking lot where the lilac-clad chorus of screaming bridesmaids swoop to exit through the back of the canopied tent. The groomsmen, who are still in the parking lot, smoking and drinking beers by one of their trucks, clatter back to the scene in their cowboy boots, shouting for help, water, calling Blade's name, asking if anyone is hurt. Shouting orders to get the fire extinguisher from the hall.

Hearing the commotion, a crowd has gathered on the steps. The mother-of-the-bride pushes her way past them to get her first glimpse of smoke and fire and her daughter screaming as her groom is doubled over on the cement in a bloodied shirt, groaning.

Pan back to the bride who lets out a blood-curdling scream when she sees her beloved, curled up in a fetal position on the ground, groaning, his shirt soaked in blood.

"Blade! Baby? What the hell? It's blood! My baby is bleeding! Help!" she screams out, and struggles to yank her train free of the grill. When she looks back, her eyes widen and she screams! "Fire! I'm on fire!" In that instant, Michael grips his free hand around her left wrist. The bride sees a man with a knife grabbing her arm and shouts blue murder.

Michael swiftly cuts through the loop around the bride's wrist that binds the train to her. Then, with one deft slash, he cuts the burning fabric away from the bride's dress. Goal accomplished, Michael steps back, drops the knife and puts his hands in the air. He says to the fear-stricken bride, "You are alright. I was just trying to free the loop that held the train to your wrist and cut off the burning end of the train."

Rubbing her wrist, the bride nodded and turns around to see what the damage is. Behind her two of the groomsmen are bravely stomping on a grey suit-jacket that overlays the smouldering bride's train, imprinting the fabric with sooty cowboy boot prints. Moments before, the groom had recovered himself, stripped off his jacket and thrown it down on the burning fabric, suffocating the fire.

Pan to the bride who has been led back up the steps by her groom, jacket-less, his bloodied shirt exposed. She gingerly places one hand on his chest. "Are you hurt? Are you bleeding? I thought you were murdered!"

The groom catches her hand in his, kisses it and says gallantly. "I'd take a bullet for you, babe. But no, I'm just singed. I intercepted a pass. A flying roast."

The bride looked at the rain-soaked canopy and the mess beneath it. The jacket and the train-fabric lay in a smouldering heap. Rivulets running down the sides of the canopy and onto the cement creating a stream that meandered through the aisle between the barbecues and the buffet. She thanks her lucky stars that her train was as long as it was, or it could have been her gown that had gone up in smoke. As it was, her $5000 designer dress was drenched and probably smoke damaged, and all that was left of her magnificent train was in a heap of smouldering ashes.

Michael stood in the parking lot for a while after the bride and groom went back into the hall, staring up at the canopy, wondering what the probability would be that the canopy would hold through this storm. He didn't like the odds. Making his way to Margo who was trying to salvage salads, trays of crudites and side dishes, awash with rainwater from the slanting deluge, he said, "I think we had better move this buffet inside. I don't think this canopy will hold."

Margo looked sideways at him. "Seriously? Like we still have a buffet to serve? One roast down. One roast on the floor, and three more on the Barbecues—that blackened and dried out while they waited to be eaten because I didn't turn off the barbecues. And for sides, we have soggy potato salad and shreds of carrots and cabbage with swollen raisins swimming in a watery dressing. What buffet? I think we have to call this a disaster!" Margo pushed her damp curls back from her forehead with the back of her hand and stomped up the stairs, going inside to look for Ronnie. She found her in the women's washroom with her daughter. Brittany held her father's tux jacket around her shivering frame. Ronnie gently wipe the streaming make-up off her face with a tissue, while making suggestions about what to do next. Margo coughed to make her presence known.

"Excuse me, Ronnie. But I think the buffet is toast." Bad choice of words, she thought. "I mean probably the roasts can be saved—for stewing meat maybe or left overs—but with all the commotion going on, they were left on the barbecues and I think they're way over done. And the salads and sides probably can't be salvaged. They're drowning in rainwater."

Brittany started to cry. Ronnie stroked her hair, cooing her motherly comfort in her daughter's ear. "It's going to be alright, my darling. All is not lost. Only the food was damaged—and your lovely gown of course. But I am so happy that you weren't hurt, or Blade. And we still have the evening ahead of us."

To Margo she said, "Thanks Margo. For everything you and Michael tried to do. Especially to Michael for his quick thinking with the knife. No one could have predicted this. It was just . . . a perfect storm of catastrophes." Ronnie smiled and tenderly stroked her daughter's hair as she sobbed into her own designer mother-of-the-bride dress.

Margo nodded, affecting agreement, but she was thinking, "Michael could have predicted this."

"Do you think you and Michael could handle the clean-up of the kitchen and salvaging of any of the food that hasn't been completely ruined? We'll call some of the family tomorrow to clean up the canopy and the unfortunate mess."

"Of course. And again, I am so sorry. The rain, the fire, everything, just ruined your perfect day."

Ronnie put up her hand up to interrupt Margo's speech. "No need to feel sorry. We're used to surprises in Wannatoka Springs. And we learn to roll with them. The young people will too. In fact, in a year from now I guarantee they'll laugh about it—or at least have other things on their minds—like addition to their family?" She hugged her daughter. Brittany sniffed and dried her eyes.

Addressing Margo, Ronnie said, "Thank you Margo. You and Michael were so courageous and gracious to take on this role. We are so grateful as a family, and as neighbours, for your willingness to help."

Brittany lifted her head and sniffed, while brushing back tears that caught in her false eyelashes with her fingers. "Please tell Michael thank you from me. He wrecked my dress, but he might have saved my life." She mustered a small smile while she blinked back the tears. "It's all good. We'll take it from here."

Margo and Michael spent the next two hours cleaning up the area, wrapping up the food that was still good and throwing away that which was ruined, washing dishes and scrubbing charred meat off the barbecues.

As they worked together, they overheard a group of boisterous young men talking as they clattered down the stairs—about going to Crystal Lake for pizza to take back to the party. Tipping their cans of beer back, they drank the last dregs, crushed the cans, threw them into the bushes, then clamoured into their cars and squealed out of the parking lot.

Much later that night, a weary Margo and Michael sat together on their deck swinging on their bench swing. Michael was sipping on his favourite single malt whiskey that he only brought out for special occasions and Margo was having a glass of wine. They drank in companionable silence for a while.

Michael broke the silence. "That was the best adventure we've had yet, Margo! It's one for your book!"

Margo allowed herself a small laugh but thought she would probably reserve her judgement of the scale of adventure it was until she took some distance from it. "And to think Ronnie gave us an honorarium for catering the wedding."

"What?" Michael sat up, surprised. "I didn't know that. We got paid for that? Ha! I would have done it for free—minus the knifing fiasco of course. That, I would have wanted a stunt double for!"

Margo didn't go back to the book she was writing until the end of July when she had, had her fill of soaking in the sun on the deck and reading in the shade of the garden.

***

On a cloudy day in August, she opened her laptop and rewrote the first paragraph . . .

It was a dark and stormy night. Rain ran down the window. A branch was tapping at the window pain. The crack of lightening shot through the air. Startled, Jessica took her eyes away from the mirror where she was trying on her veil for the umpteenth time, to see what effect it made.

A shiver went through her as she crossed the floor her bedroom in her parent's house. It was to be the last time she slept in her childhood bed. Tomorrow she would marry the man she had loved since they were children, growing up in a tiny community nestled in the valley of the mountains. She peered through the curtains to see the storm that was coming across the lake. Having grown up in this tiny village, Jessica knew that the weather could play havoc with well-laid plans. But she prayed a silent prayer that tomorrow they would be blessed with the promise of sunshine forecasted. The last thing she needed was a rainstorm to ruin her special day and her plans for a beautiful outdoor wedding.

CHAPTER SEVEN

The Cinnamon Bun Wars

The sunlight beamed through the windshield of Margo's car magnifying the layer of dust on the dash. As she opened the door and slid onto the driver's seat, Margo felt the sun-warmed leather seat on her back. She hadn't felt that sensation for months. Winter had been long and spring was late, but it had finally pushed its warm currents through the cutting cold air and prompted the spring bulbs Margo had planted in the fall to poke up through the soil their winter dormancy. A vibrant pallet of purple, red and yellow blooms paraded down the flower bed Michael had dug out the year before, in front of their house.

Margo rolled down the driver's side window. She wanted to feel the air around her as she drove slowly through Wannatoka Springs and down to the ferry ramp. It was the May long weekend, the start of the tourist season. She hadn't seen that many cars lining up for the ferry since last October when the shoulder season died down.

The ferry was in the middle of the lake, steadily making its way towards the dock on the Wannatoka Springs side, where Margo was waiting to cross. It would be less than five minutes before they would board. Another car pulling a trailer came up behind her and slowed to a stop. When it did, a couple of young boys ejected themselves from the back seat and ran up to the bathroom outhouses at the top of the hill. Margo thought they would have to be quick; the ferry would sail without them if they weren't ready to move when it was ready to load. But that would probably be OK. The ferry travelled back and forth every half hour. The family looked like they were on vacation, so wouldn't be in a hurry. They might even stop for lunch at one of the picnic tables on the grassy knoll that over-looked the lake.

Margo heard the boys slam the wooden doors of the outhouses and watched them chase each other down the hill, laughing as they raced. One stumbled but caught himself before he fell. That gave the other one the advantage. The pair touched the car—one just before the other, calling 'dibs!' as they did so. The ferry's brake screeched, and then a rigid boom of the ferry's metal bumper banged against the rubber bumper of the dock. Margo smiled at the boys' antics as each jerked around the back of the car to settle into his.

Sometimes the sight of children playing together brought up memories of her classroom. She missed teaching and the children she taught, but she enjoyed her freedom from schedules, staff meetings, and parent calls she had to make. After almost a year of retirement, those memories were fading. Seeing the boys scrambling up the hill and down again, so carefree and able-bodied, brought other memories into focus. She thought of her childhood, when she was free to making up games with her siblings, and play outdoors until their mother called them in for supper. She was free to dream then, dream of what she wanted to be when she grew up.

When she graduated from high school and it was time to consider a career path, her choices narrowed to the one path, becoming a teacher. She loved reading and she loved writing in English classes when she was in high school. Because of her natural inclinations, her parents steered her in the direction of going to university and becoming an English teacher. She followed that path all the way to the end . . . to her retirement. Then, one day, she woke up and realized that the door to dreams about what you wanted to be had opened again. She hadn't thought about her childhood dreams in years. Thinking of them now was confusing. What if she hadn't chosen the career she did? What if she had chosen something else? Where would she be now?

Margo's reverie was interrupted by the brake lights ahead of her. The ferry was loading. Smoothly gliding forward and onto the ramp, Margo found herself snugged up against a truck in front of her. The family with the trailer was parked closely behind her. She waved to Kyle, one of the ferry workers, who was also the volunteer fire chief. He was wearing a high viz vest and directing cars to park in one lane or the other.

When they were aboard, Margo opened her window and greeted Kyle with a friendly wave. "Hey, Kyle! How're the new fire-fighting recruits doing?"

"Learning as they go. Bound to make some mistakes, but at least we're not fighting fires while they're training".

Kyle looked up and noted the signal from the other member of the crew with a hand-up signal. "Duty calls," he said and tapped the door-frame. "Have a nice day, ma'am." He said with a wry smile.

"That's Margo!" Margo called out her window.

"Right. Margo. Have a nice day Margo!" Kyle quickly tapped her car's hood twice with his knuckles and then walked through the gap between vehicles. Margo smiled to herself. Kyle was saying 'ma'am' on purpose just to get a rise out of her. Now, it was an inside joke between them.

Margo's destination was a grocery store nestled in another tiny community across the lake called Crestview. On the other side, the countryside opened up to a wide valley and flat, arable land. The micro-climate tempered by the lake made Crestview a jewel in the crown of BC's orchard and farmland country. The small, family-run general store had become Margo's convenience store only twenty minutes later. She especially liked going there because she had come to know the woman who ran it. Kate was a hard-core back-to-the-lander.

During the exodus of young people from urban centers, Kate came to the Kootenays as a young woman in the mid-sixties. They had all left the city in droves, and some even left their country for various reasons—draft avoiders, hippies looking for freedom from the establishment, drifters, and migrants. The communities they established became part of the back-to-the-land movement that prized homegrown everything from food to shelter to sustainable businesses. Kate was one of the Canadian women who married an American draft resister to legitimize his immigration into Canada.

Kate and her husband, Beau, were in their early seventies now. They established and ran their store for thirty-five years. They were fixtures in the community of Crestview. These days, they didn't do much more than take inventory, haul groceries in sometimes, and help out in the back. Their daughter and son-in-law had taken over the day-to-day running of the store. It was a small-time country store, so there wasn't much variety. Most of their stock was locally grown, home-cooked, or hand-made. They stocked some of the staples the locals could buy so they didn't have to travel into the city or take the ferry across to Crystal Lake to shop all the time. But they didn't carry many specialty items.

For Michael's birthday, Margo wanted to make an angel food cake with strawberries. She called ahead to ask if they had an angel food cake mix. They didn't. But they had frozen strawberries. Margo looked up a recipe for shortcake and followed that recipe instead. She did find it satisfying to bake her own cakes from scratch rather than opening a box.

When she returned to the store the next time,

Margo raved to Kate about how good her shortcake was. And after she perfected the shortcake, she had tried other baking recipes. Slowly, Margo developed confidence in her baking.

Margo found that she enjoyed baking, but there was always too much for her and Michael to eat. Michael was always watching his weight, bragging that he still fit into the first suit he bought when he started working at age twenty-three. He did, but the buttons were strained when he closed the jacket, and the shoulders and arms looked like they had shrunk.

Because Michael was tentative about eating 'extraneous' food, as he called anything eaten for the pleasure of eating it, and because Margo wanted to overdose on them, she made a point of freezing her cinnamon buns in pairs, pulling them out to thaw on the counter for serving with coffee in the afternoons.

Afternoon coffee time had become a ritual for Margo and Michael, a way to mark the time of day. As a teacher, Margo had thirty-some years of bells to mark the beginning and end of school and switching classes and lunch. That meant she was accustomed to a bell telling her it was time to change activities eight times a day.

Not having any signals to tell her what time of day it was or when it was time to change up activities, took some getting used to. So she set up her own schedule. Michael agreed to have some markers (like afternoon coffee with Margo at two and dinner at six) but he didn't want to tie himself down to a set schedule and ate during the day when he was hungry.

At first, Margo would offer Michael a cookie or a cinnamon bun at coffee time, but he would often decline, complimenting her on how delicious they looked but patting his stomach and making the excuse that he had to watch that his waistline didn't hide his shoes. After a while, Margo stopped offering him her baking and only pulled out a single bun for herself for a coffee break.

Unlike Michael, Margo didn't mind if her waistline thickened a little. She had a mature figure that she thought suited her. She was neither slim nor fat. A few pounds had crept up on her over the last year, reshaping her waist and hips, so she found that her fitted professional clothes were a struggle to put on. "What the heck!" she told herself, "I'll just give them away. I don't need to wear them anymore. Let someone else wear them to work." And she folded them and put them in a large bag that she took to the thrift store.

These days, Margo wore casual clothes that smoothed over her body comfortably, wide-legged, loose-fitting pants with elastic waists and long shirts that draped over them. She felt her clothes now defined her relaxed lifestyle and attitude. Retirement, as she imagined it, was a life of no stress and no one to impress. So far, apart from a few surprises and a couple of curve balls, she had been getting used to life in Wannatoka Springs.

To fill the gap and spread her baking around, Margo started inviting neighbours over for coffee. Usually, she invited women, but sometimes, she invited couples. Michael joined in if it was a couple. But, when Margo invited a woman by herself, he often stayed to say hello and then excused himself, taking his coffee downstairs to his man cave. In this way, Margo would, on those occasions, serve her cinnamon buns.

By now, Margo had won the hearts of many of her neighbours with her friendly, helpful personality and her cinnamon buns. She was even asked, a couple of times, to supply them for fundraisers. Happy to bake and donate them, Margo was pleased that she had found a new hobby that was a hit with the folks in the community where she and Michael had settled into their retirement.

Margo hoped Kate was in the store when she arrived there. She wanted advice from a long-time local and a merchant. Kate's daughter, Brook, was ringing up a purchase when Margo walked through the door, jingling the bells that announced her entrance. "Good afternoon! Beautiful day!" Margo said.

"Hi, Margo," Brook looked up briefly and smiled. Then she turned her attention back to the customer in front of her and recited the total of the purchase. When she had concluded the transaction and the customer left, wishing her a beautiful day, she asked Margo, "What can I do for you?" as she was wiping down the counter and straightening out her selection of used bags that people sometimes brought in for others who didn't have one.

"I'm looking for Kate," Margo announced. "I want to run an idea I have by her."

"In the back." Brook pointed to the curtained-off doorway that led to the back room. Margo walked to the back and pushed through a faded flower sheet now used as a curtain. She could hear music softly coming from one corner of the room. She walked toward the sound and found Kate sitting on a milk crate, cutting off the green ends of wilting carrots and throwing them into another crate.

Kate looked up from her work. "Oh, hi, Margo. How's retirement life treating you there in Wannatoka?"

"Hi, Kate. OK, but I'm still finding my way. I'm hoping to talk to you about an idea I have." Margo said. "Can I help you with your pruning while we talk?"

"You'll find a knife over there." Kate pointed to a worktable that was stacked with vegetables in about the same state as the carrots. "Just cutting off the ends of these carrots. The local farm sells 'em to me. They come in fresh, but the tops go limp if they sit too long. No one wants a limp carrot, let me tell you!" Kate held up a droopy carrot. Margo laughed.

"Don't laugh. Limp carrots still have value. You just have to know how to pivot with age. I shred them, mix them with those vegetables, and sell them as a pre-mixed salad. They go fast. It's all perception, I say. People these days want everything done for them—fast food, fast salad." Margo picked up the knife and followed what Kate was doing. "Are you going to tell me what this big idea is?"

"I want to sell my cinnamon buns. I think I've perfected them to the point that they would sell like crazy. People in Wannatoka are asking for them all the time now. I'm supplying fundraising events and coffee times at the community center. I want to expand—become a cinnamon bun peddler!" Margo grinned at the image she conjured up of a nineteenth-century peddler on a bicycle with a rack of cinnamon buns on the back, crying out, "Cinnamon buns for sale! Get your cinnamon buns while they're hot!"

"There might be an opportunity to sell them here," Kate shrugged, "but you'd have to compete with the local baker. I have a guy who has delivered here for years. Makes the sourdough bread and regular buns. He also makes cinnamon buns, but not regularly."

Margo shook her head. "Thanks. I really appreciate the offer, Kate, but I want to go out on my own, not on consignment or wholesale. I've always wanted to be an entrepreneur. But my father said teaching was the way to go for women, not business. A secure wage, time off in the summers, and maternity leave were good jobs for women who wanted to have families. That's what I did for the past thirty years, but I have always wanted to run my own small business.

Kate laughed and shook her head. "And you think you can do that selling cinnamon buns? Do you realize how many cinnamon buns you would have to bake to make it worthwhile? Besides, you're retired. Let me tell you, I am a small business owner. I'm still working—no pension to speak of. I don't think I'll be able to retire, to tell you the truth. And you have to be self-reliant in the face of all kinds of ups and downs. Take my advice and put that notion out of your head. You're one of the lucky ones. You have a retirement income that will carry you through. Tell you what. Bake a few dozen cinnamon buns if you want. Bring them over once a week. I'm sure they'll sell if they're as good as you say."

Margo didn't look up. She kept cutting the tops off the carrots. She knew what Kate was saying was good advice, but she felt like Kate had just popped her balloon. She waited for a minute to speak when her voice was steady.

"I know what you're saying, Kate. And I'm grateful I have a pension and am comfortable. But I really want to try something different. And now that I have the means, what's wrong with chasing a dream?"

"Sure, go ahead. I always have time to listen to someone's dreams."

"You know we don't have a store or a bakery in Wannatoka Springs. However, we have an empty building where a bakery used to be. It's on the access road beside the Motel. I figure, with our savings, Michael and I could buy the building and bring it back to life. We could make it into an eat-in bakery, serving fresh coffee, tea, and all kinds of baked goods. People travelling on the ferry might stop if they knew it was there."

Kate held up her hand to stop Margo. "Whoa. Let me stop you right there. It's a good idea. Margo. In fact, when the bakery was running, it did a pretty good business, just as you imagine it would, selling to travellers. But only in the summer months. They couldn't make it work year-round because of the expenses of running a place like that through the winter. The locals likely won't support it. They probably bake on their own and certainly can brew their own coffee. We're not in the city, you know, where there's a Starbucks on every street corner because people are in a hurry to work and can't be bothered to make their own. So—long and short—good idea but wrong time and wrong place. And probably the wrong end of your life.

The reality of what Kate said sunk in, but Margo wasn't ready to give up. "I get it. I really do. But this might be my opportunity to build something I can say I built from scratch and succeeded at doing."

"I hear what you said about teaching not giving you that sense of satisfaction you might have had running a business. Your success might not have been visible, but I'm sure you made a big investment in your students' achievements. Can't minimize that."

"True." Margo sighed. "And I don't want to take away from my teaching career, but honestly, I don't think I know what success feels like in the end. Is it just getting to the finish line and then walking away to spend your golden years reminiscing about what you did?"

"Not so bad. That's more than most people can say they have accomplished in their life. Sounds like a success story to me. Listen," Kate went on as she picked up her crate of cut-up carrots and deposited it on the work table, "Why don't you make a compromise? Instead of your 'go big or go home' idea, why not scale it down to size."

"Like what?" Margo asked, interested now.

"I don't know. Like what you are doing—baking for your community. Baking for fundraisers. Hell, baking for my store if you want. Just start small. That's all I'm saying. And be satisfied with the success you have." Margo felt disappointed with Kate's advice, but she understood the wisdom of it.

Kate patted Margo on the shoulder affectionately and then began sorting the carrots on the table. "Believe me, a small-business owner's life is never done. And it isn't all recognition and praise either." Margo stood up. Kate wiped her hands on her apron and said, "I hope you don't take this the wrong way, but I'd trade shoes with you any day. And you'd get mighty sore feet if you had to walk a mile in my shoes."

With that, Kate hefted the crate of the carrots that could still be sold and walked with them to the vegetable stand. Margo's ego smarted from Kate's last remark. She was thinking of a rebuttal but thought better of it. Instead, as she followed Kate out into the store, Margo said, "Thanks for your advice, Kate. I'll think smaller."

"I'm here as a listening ear anytime," Kate said as she stacked carrots in the vegetable rack between the beans and the squash.

Margo left the store with the locally sourced eggs and salad greens and drove back home a little deflated. The day didn't seem so full of promise and possibilities on the way back home. When she got to the ferry crossing, the clouds had gathered, obscuring the sun. The fresh breeze turned brisk and smelled like rain. Kyle seemed to be all business. He directed her car on board without a sign of recognition and then disappeared until the ferry bumped at the other side. He reappeared to direct the cars off—just another routine day.

When the ferry reached the other side of the lake and she drove off, Margo noticed a long line to get on the ferry. Passengers stood beside some cars with open doors looking wearily at the creeping advance of the ferry and the slow offload. Others were still at the picnic table, getting up now to walk back to their cars.

The ferry made the crossing, fifteen minutes there and fifteen minutes back, making the wait half an hour if you didn't catch it. But it did seem like an eternity to some passengers, especially since there was nothing to do but wait in cars on hot pavement. There was a shady spot with a picnic table high above the line-up but no place to walk—except to the outhouse washrooms— and nothing to stare at except the calm lake and the ferry making its way, painfully slow, towards the shore.

Margo had an idea. She felt the goose bumps on her arms rise in reaction to her excitement. She drove as fast as she dared to her home and parked. Grabbing the cloth bag with the groceries she bought at the store on the other side of the lake, she skipped up the three front steps and burst into the house.

"Michael! Michael!" Margo called as she swung her bags of groceries onto the counter.

"I'm right here! No need to shout." Michael was at the fridge just feet away from where Margo stood, looking for something to eat for lunch.

"I'm going to set up a cinnamon bun stand at the ferry. I'm calling it 'Cinnamon Bun on the Run'. All I need is a trailer set up with a booth. I can use the side-by-side to tow it down to the ferry dock and . . ."

"Wait, what?" Michael was staring at Margo, eyebrows raised in the middle. "Slow down. A cinnamon bun stand?"

Margo took a breath and slowed herself down, paying careful attention to unpacking the items she bought. She kept her eyes down as she talked. She had always been a confident woman, but she felt vulnerable just now for some reason.

"When I came back on the ferry from Crestview, I had to wait nearly half an hour in line because I missed the ferry by five minutes. I saw a line-up stretching past the golf course when we docked on our side. It must have been at least a one sailing wait. Looks like tourist season is hitting its stride."

"Mmmmm," Michael nodded in agreement as he spread mayonnaise on a slice of bread with which he intended to make a tomato sandwich. "The usual long weekend traffic. Lots of campers heading out."

"Right. All those campers, families, and delivery trucks in between have to wait for a ferry where there's nothing to eat or drink, maybe for an hour or more."

"So . . ."

"So, I set up a cinnamon bun and coffee stand where people line up for the ferry. I thought we could rig something up to fit in the back of the side-by-side and then we could motor down to the beach to catch the ferry traffic and sell my cinnamon buns to hungry holidaymakers."

"Wait just a minute," Michael waved the knife he used like a baton, "By the first 'we,' I assume you mean me. I can rig something up to fit in the back of the side-by-side. And by the second 'we,'" Michael leaned into the 'we' and pointed his knife at Margo. "I hope you mean you." Then, he turned back to making his sandwich. "I have no inclination to sit on a side-by-side on a hot pavement in the summer selling anything when I could be out walking the golf course for a round or two. I'm retired."

Michael wiped his knife with a forefinger, licked off the excess mayonnaise from his finger, and started cutting the tomato with the clean edge. Margo winced. Michael was fastidious and had nearly perfect manners, but he had this idiosyncrasy, which he said was left over from childhood. He deftly sliced through the tomato as he conversed.

"Of course, I wouldn't dream of interrupting your daily walk around the golf course with a putter to ask you to work the business," Margo said with exaggerated deference. "I'll take care of everything from baking to selling. But I do want some of your input in building or rigging up some kind of booth to fit on the side-by that would be portable and light enough for me to set up and manage."

Michael was silent while he carefully placed his tomato slices on his sandwich, precisely four slices, evenly cut and spaced, and pressed down the top bread he had readied with more mayonnaise and a sprinkle of salt. He cut it diagonally as he always did. He said that ensured that the tomatoes would be evenly distributed and less likely to squish out the sides. Having completed the operation successfully, he set the two wedges on a plate with a space in the middle for his other condiment, mustard—which he liked to dip the edge of his sandwich in as he ate. Turning the plate around, the mustard facing him, he sat at the counter to eat. He lifted one half of the sandwich, dipped the tip of it in the mustard and paused, sandwich in his hand, mid-journey to his mouth.

Margo fidgeted with the groceries, waiting for Michael's response. She knew him well enough to know that, while she often spontaneously leapt into a new project, he would need time to absorb an idea before he acted.

"And you are doing this because . . ." Michael's eyes bore into Margo's. "I mean, it's not like we are impoverished and need a side hustle to get through month to month. We came here to retire. At least I did. So why do you want to start working again?"

"Because . . ." Margo blinked back the tears that were welling up in her eyes. "Because my cinnamon buns are such a hit with the community, it would be like providing a service and fun for me. I don't do half the things you do to get out into the community. I don't volunteer for the fire department, I don't play golf, I don't . . . I don't do anything social. I don't even drink beer! So maybe I feel like my retirement is a bit lacklustre and less sociable than my work life."

Margo paused and pulled herself together. "Because maybe I'm bored!" she said emphatically, twirling on her heel and rushing to the bathroom to dab her eyes. She didn't know why she was on the verge of tears. Maybe the admission that she was bored made her feel like a failure at retirement. Or maybe moving to a place with so few outlets was a mistake. She hadn't considered what she would do to fill her days. If you didn't knit, hike, camp, drink beer, grow an organic garden, or homestead, there weren't many options in Wannatoka Springs.

After spending a cold winter indoors, she realized she needed something to occupy her time and creativity, something that would also create a positive interaction with her neighbours, or she would be going south, in her mind anyway.

"Margo," Michael called from his place at the counter. "I can't find the salt." That was the best he could think of to draw his wife out. He always felt a little inept at dealing with her emotional crises. Especially the existential ones. "Do you know where it is?"

Margo slid the bathroom door open, sniffed and then walked out. When she reached the kitchen island where Michael was sitting, she grabbed the salt shaker well within his reach, lifted it, and set it down directly in front of him again. "At your elbow," she said matter-of-factly. "You never can see what's at a ninety-degree angle to you." She smiled wanly.

"What would Major Tom say?" He asked, grinning.

It was an inside joke about the RCMP officer they dubbed Major Tom, who had stopped them in their first month while driving the ATV for the first time down Maple Street, informing them that they were driving down the municipal street illegally and would have to have to have a ninety-degree permit to cross the highway.

"I don't issue ninety-degree permits," Margo said in a gruff, official voice mimicking the officer's response.

"Exactly my point. So how would you get the ATV across the highway and down to the ferry dock?"

"He'd have to catch me crossing the highway first!" She said coyly. "After that, I would be just another ATVer driving down the beach-front, aiming for the ferry landing. And parking in the picnic area.

"Clever!" Michael licked his fingers and chewed on his sandwich. "Out maneuvering the law just like a true Wannatokan. 'Margo's outlaw cinnamon buns on the run!'"

Margo laughed, but she blushed at the thought. She had never once thought about breaking the law. In fact, she always checked her speedometer to make sure she was well within the speed limit, especially in school zones.

"But let's be serious for a minute. Do you know anything about making a vending business? Taxes, licenses, product mark-up?" Michael set his sandwich down and listed the items he mentioned on his fingers.

"I'm serious, Michael. I'm sure I can learn what I need to do from YouTube." Margo's hands settled on her hips, a tell of her defensiveness.

Michael held up his hands in a gesture of surrender and smiled, "I am sure you are most capable, Margo. And I wouldn't dream of pouring cold water on your ambition. It's a clever idea and would likely fill a niche. It's just the logistics I am concerned about."

"And you're the very person who can help me figure those things out." Margo grabbed his hands and put them around her waist. "I could use a partner like you. A sexy numbers guy, a probability risk assessment analyst."

"Are you trying to seduce me with your flattery?"

"Is it working?" Margo looked up at Michael with a mischievous smile.

"Keep talking. Flattery will get you everywhere." Michael bent forward and kissed Margo, then turned his attention back to his sandwich. "I'll help you with whatever I can from behind the scenes—but there is no 'we' in selling cinnamon buns at the ferry dock. That'll be your baby. I have a golf game to improve."

It took Michael a week to fashion a portable vending booth out of plywood. Margo took another week to paint it in lively colours of sky blue with red and yellow trim. The sign above the window read, "Cinnamon Buns On the Run."

The booth itself was simple enough. It was three-sided with a roof that folded up and latched like the top of a box. A large window, through which Margo could conduct her business, had a shelf on both sides that could be collapsed or set up with hinges and locks. It was open in the back so Margo could easily walk in and out. Margo had a bar stool she could sit on while waiting for customers. The cinnamon buns would be packed into trays and kept in a closed container in the back of the side-by-side. Paper plates and a napkin dispenser were stacked on the inside ledge so they weren't exposed to the elements. Everything could be folded up and put away when not in use. Margo was delighted with it.

While Michael was building the booth, Margo researched business plans, mark-ups, and costing out her materials. She didn't want to include too much for labour because it was a labour of love. She handed the itemized pricing to Michael, who created a spreadsheet that determined how much each cinnamon bun cost and what they would cost the customer using various mark-up formulas. Margo had the heady feeling of starting something new. She fantasized about being the CEO of a fledgling baking company. Who knew where it would go?

By the long weekend of July, the plan was in place, and the booth and side-by-side were ready to roll. All she needed to do was follow the rules of driving an off-road vehicle. Margo thought the location was the perfect spot to give people the idea that they could jump out of their cars when they were waiting, buy a bun 'on the run' and either jump back in their cars in time to load or if they had time because they were waiting, they could sit in the shade enjoying their cinnamon buns. Margo made one more trip by herself down to the beachfront in the side-by-side and set up the booth to ensure she could handle it herself. The launch of Margo's 'Cinnamon Buns on the Run' business was set for July first.

She posted her launch in the Wannatoka Times. It read, *The launch of 'Cinnamon Bun On the Run' at the ferry landing is July first, 8am to noon. Freshly baked cinnamon buns! Hope to see you there, neighbours!*

The night before the launch date, she baked two dozen cinnamon buns. Each was the size of a side plate and slathered with her specially formulated gooey brown sugar and butter coating.

Margo woke up early on July first. She was too excited to sleep, and the sun shone through her bedroom window. She wondered if she had enough or too many buns and if she had thought of everything she needed. Michael assured her he was just a cell phone away, and if she needed anything, he could deliver it by car or walk over.

Margo squeezed Michael's hand when he loaded the last of the cargo in the back of the side-by-side.

"I'll be fine!" Margo said cheerily. "I'll be more than fine! I'll be great!" She carefully drove the ATV down the uneven beach trail to the ferry landing, careful not to upset the load in the back. She hoped to make it there without too much manoeuvring. She didn't want her cinnamon buns to get bruised and battered on the drive.

As she rounded the bend and started climbing slowly up the incline to the spot near the landing she had picked out to set up the booth, she was confronted with an unexpected sight that made her stop.

Right where she wanted to set up her booth, a white panel van with a hinged serving window propped up on the side, was parked.

A man was inside the van, scrunched down to fit his head and arms through the window and passed a plate with something on it to a woman and child standing before him. On the side of the van, a sign read, Crazy Dave's Travellin' Bakery'. The words traced in the script around the sidewall read, "Cinnamon Buns, Donuts, Hot Dogs, Coffee, Soft Drinks."

Margo shaded her eyes and squinted to ensure she read the sign correctly. *Who was Crazy Dave,*She wondered. She had never seen him or his van. In all the times she had taken the ferry, she hadn't seen any vendor parked at this spot or any spot along the route.

The ferry was a few minutes away when Margo drove up close to the van and parked. She could see it making its way slowly to the shore. Most of the people waiting in line to board were making their way back to their cars, so there weren't any customers at the truck.

Margo walked up to the truck with a smile plastered on her face. She didn't feel like smiling. Someone had taken her spot, a place she had carefully chosen. It was true that she didn't own it and wasn't entitled to it, but it did seem odd, not to mention aggravating, that someone just appeared out of the blue as if they knew exactly what she was about to do and got there before her.

"Hi!" Margo called out when she got close, "Crazy Dave, I assume."

The man nodded, and his face broke into a smile. "Yup. That's what they call me! Can I get you something?"

"This is your truck?"

"This is my baby, Jeannette." He stuck one hand out and patted the side of the truck, addressing it as if it were his girlfriend. "We've been travellin' together for about five years now."

"And you have a bakery in there?" Margo looked skeptical that a whole bakery could fit inside a van.

Crazy Dave let out a loud guffaw. "Hell no! My bakery is in the basement of my house. I usually sell wholesale to restaurants and stores in Crystal Lake and around the area and deliver them. But this summer, I thought I'd try something different. It's a nice spot, don't you think? Last summer, the fires were burning in the valley. It is a bummer trying to sell cinnamon buns to evacuees. Better if you were selling smoked sausage to the firefighters!" He laughed.

"Do you set up here every summer?"

"No. Not really. Last year I travelled down to the coast. I had to get out of the smoke. I mostly sold coffee and ice cream. I hit the farmer's markets on the island, met some nice folks, and stayed clear of the fires. I made some money but would rather sit here and let the traffic come to me. My cinnamon buns are the best. Would you like one?"

"Um, sure. How much for one?" Margo hadn't thought about competition. However, since there would be competition, she thought she should at least do the research.

"Five bucks."

"Oh!" Margo reached into her pouch. She had stocked it with small bills to make change for customers. She produced a five-dollar bill and handed it over to Dave.

"Bag or plate, ma'am."

Margo grimaced at the word 'ma'am' but held her tongue.

"Plate, please. And a fork and napkin."

"Comin' right up, ma'am".

That was twice. Margo couldn't contain herself. "Do you always address your female customers of a certain age as 'ma'am'? You know it's ageist and sexist. And so not politically correct," she lectured.

Dave scratched the stubble on his chin. "Thank you for informing me. I'll try to catch up on the correct appellation of my older female, non-binary, SIS and transgender women." He winked at Margo. "Will there anything else ma'am?" With that, Crazy Dave handed her a cinnamon bun on a paper plate and produced a fork and a napkin to go with it.

"Thank-you." She said, tight-lipped. Margo was fuming but didn't want to start a war of words with her competitor. A cinnamon bun war, maybe, but not a war of words.

She walked back to the picnic table to test her competition's bun. Crazy Dave's product wasn't as large as hers. It was also iced, not a sticky bun like hers. But people liked that, didn't they? Margo took a bite. She chewed it thoughtfully. It was delicious, she thought despondently. And the icing was maple syrup flavoured. When finished, she balled up the napkin and took it with the plastic fork and paper plate to the garbage. What a waste, she thought. There ought to be a recycling bin here or a more environmentally conscious way to serve a cinnamon bun to go. She thought that maybe that could be her edge. She pulled out her phone to text Michael to give him the news and to make a note that she needed to source a recycling bin.

Margo: Houston, we have a problem.

She heard the message swoop and saw 'delivered'

on her phone. She waited for Michael to get back to her.

Meanwhile, she watched the ferry unload its cargo from the other side of the lake. The off-loading cars clunked over the metal plate then picked up speed as they drove onto the open highway. Only one car pulled over and stopped at Crazy Dave's van. A couple headed over to see what he had for sale.

Ding. Michael's message lit up her screen.

Michael: What's up?

Margo: Did you ever hear of Crazy Dave's Bakery?

Michael: No.

Margo: He is here in the truck selling cinnamon buns!

Margo aimed her phone at Dave's van, snapped a photo, and sent it to Michael.

Michael: Oh?!

Margo: Exactly in the spot I was going to set up.

Michael: Did you set up somewhere else?

Margo: No. I couldn't bring myself to do it. I think this is his only source of income.

Michael: Did you ask him?

Margo: No.

Michael: I think you should.

Margo: OK, I'll talk to him. Wish me luck!

Michael: Luck! Let me know how it goes.

Margo: Thumbs up emoji, heart emoji

Michael: Thumbs up emoji, kiss emoji

Margo tucked her cell phone into her pouch and retraced her steps to Dave's truck. He was sitting in a lawn chair in the shade. "Oh, hi again, he said. "How was your first Crazy Dave Cinnamon Bun?"

"Delicious," she said with a forced smile. Again, she didn't feel like smiling but didn't want to start with negative energy. "I didn't introduce myself. My name's Margo."

"Glad you liked it, Margo. So where are you going? I see you got your side-by out. Exploring the trails?"

"Actually," Margo hesitated momentarily and then launched into her explanation. She told Dave how she had just thought of starting a cinnamon bun business because everyone told her that her cinnamon buns were unparalleled. She and her husband had built a portable stand so she could sell to folks travelling on the ferry. She ended her speech with, "Honestly, I had no idea you frequented this location. Or you had invested in the cinnamon bun business, or I would have talked to you first."

As Margo told her story, Dave sat back and folded his arms. With raised eyebrows and an amused smile around his mouth, he silently took in what she was saying.

When she finished and drew in a breath, Dave, still leaning back on his chair, said, "Well, I'm sorry to disappoint Margo, but I believe I have first dibs on this spot. First, come around here. 'Sides, I get a lot of repeat customers who stop just to get one of Crazy Dave's buns."

He looked at her with a kind of pity and added, "Sorry you went to all that trouble, Margo. You could try setting up on the other side of the lake. People are waiting to catch the ferry there, too. I bet you would find a nice little niche there."

"No, that wouldn't work for me," Margo said. "I'm driving an ATV and don't have a license to drive on the highway. The ferry is part of the highway, so I wouldn't be allowed to cross. But you could!"

Dave shook his head slowly. "Sorry, no can do. I'd lose my customer base." He shook his head.

"I see," said Margo. "Well, I suppose there's no compromise we can work out then."

Dave shrugged his shoulders. "Can't see one if you're talkin' about usurping my spot. But don't worry; I'll go back to my wholesale business in the winter months. This is just a sideline. Gets me out of the kitchen, so to speak. All yours after August."

Margo turned and walked away. She knew August would be nothing compared to the summer for tourists. She started to trek back to her vehicle. But ten steps in, she had a thought. She turned around.

"Hey, Crazy Dave!" she called out, hands on hips, 'Here's a crazy idea. How about I challenge you to a cinnamon bun contest? You think yours are the best, and I think mine are. Why don't we let the customers decide who has the best cinnamon buns?"

Dave laughed and waved her off like he was swatting a pesky fly. "Now, that IS a crazy idea!"

"You don't have to have a permit or lease to park here, right?"

"Haven't you heard? Wannatoka Springs, and virtually this whole Kootenay valley, is a 'less-law.' Anything's up for grabs until it ain't."

"OK. How about this? I propose that I set up across from you on THIS side of the ferry landing. You sell yours on your side, and I sell mine on the other. That way, you get the customers who are going across, and I get the customers coming back. We set this up for July. The contest will see who sells the most cinnamon buns between eight and twelve. I don't want to spend afternoons here. If you sell more cinnamon buns than I do, I will fold. That will be it for my business. I'll leave the beach to Crazy Dave's Travellin' Bakery."

Dave leaned forward in his chair. He was amused at the offer of a competition. "And what if you sell more than me?"

"If I sell more than you, I get to park my stand where you are now, and you have to move to the other side of the ferry."

Dave thought about it briefly while he scratched his stubbly chin and said, "You got a deal. But our product has to be the same price—five bucks a piece for cinnamon buns."

"You're on!" Margo replied.

Margo turned her side-by-side slowly around and crossed the highway to the other side of the on-ramp. The grassy area there was a little uneven, and she had a more challenging time finding a level area to park her stand, but she did manage to find a space close to the trees where there was some shade. She set up quickly and had everything ready and waiting for the next ferry to off-load. Of course, she was on the side of the oncoming traffic now, so they might be more focused on travelling to wherever they were going, but some might be tempted to stop if the attraction caught their eye.

She placed the brightly coloured sandwich board she hand-painted as close as she could to the ferry off-ramp, hoping the name "Cinnamon Bun on the Run" would convince travellers that they only had to stop momentarily and be on their way with a fresh cinnamon bun. Conveniently, there was a wide shoulder just before her booth so cars could pull over to the side safely. She gave her booth the once-over to ensure she hadn't forgotten anything and then watched from her stool as the ferry slowly but steadily docked.

While she waited, Margo texted Michael.

Margo: We've reached a deal—swoop delivered

Michael: Compromise?

Margo: Challenge!

Michael: Challenge????

Margo: The Cinnamon Bun Wars are on!

Michael: Wow emoji, wow, emoji,—That's my Margo!

Margo looked up from her phone when she heard the familiar metal bump of the ferry docking.

Margo: Show-time!

Michael: Go get 'em! Thumbs up emoji, heart emoji

Margo stuffed her phone back into her pouch. She stood up and walked towards the slow, steady line of cars that moved off the ferry and hit the pavement. As she walked towards the cars exiting the ferry, she waved cheerily at the drivers and passengers, pointing towards her booth. Crazy Dave, on the other hand, sat in his lawn chair, waiting for customers to come to him. *Who's crazy now*? Thought Margo.

The third car stopped, and the passenger, a young woman, leaned out and asked, "Selling cinnamon buns?

Are they fresh?"

"Fresh and warm!" Margo said, leaning forward, hands on knees to engage the woman eye-to-eye.

"Can I get a cup of coffee too?"

"I'll tell you what. I don't have my coffee urn set up yet, but if you buy one of my cinnamon buns, I'll buy you a cup." She pointed at Dave's van and said, "You see that van over there? Just tell Crazy Dave to put it on Margo's tab."

"Good deal!" the woman exclaimed and turned to the driver. "Pull over Winnie! We're going for a cinnamon bun on the run." Turning to Margo, she said, "Make that two —with two comp coffees."

Margo fairly flew up to her booth to get the order ready. She watched eagerly as each woman peeled off the first layer of their bun and popped it in their mouths. The expression on their faces told them what she wanted to know. They gave her two thumbs up! Margo thanked them for pulling over and asked them to please give her a 'like' or a comment on her Facebook page when they could. She gave them a card with 'Cinnamon Bun on the Run" with her site address and a QR code.

The two women then crossed the highway on foot between the cars lining up to board the ferry in the other direction. Crazy Dave saw them stop at Margo's first and could make out cinnamon buns in their hands. All they wanted was coffee, they said. He poured them each one and asked them for the amount.

"Margo says to put it on her tab," One of the women said, pointing back at Margo's booth. When Dave looked over her way, Margo waved and gave the 'OK' sign, followed by a thumbs-up! Dave shook his head. He had no idea what she meant, but he figured he would catch up with her later. The two women walked away with their coffees, back to their car and drove off.

When the traffic dissipated, Margo walked across the road and took Dave over one of her buns.

"What do you mean by telling those girls to put it on your tab? What tab?"

"Just an idea I had. I don't serve coffee, but you do. If a customer who comes to me wants a coffee with their cinnamon bun, I'll buy them one at your place of business. You make money on coffee. I get customers to try my buns!"

"I did not agree to that. I said the cost should be equal. Five bucks each."

"Of course!" Margo nodded seriously. "They pay me for the bun, and I send them to you for coffee and tell them to put it on my tab. At the end of the morning, I settle up with you. Win. Win. And here is your first payment—one of my cinnamon buns for two coffees." She handed the bun over to Dave, who frowned at her but accepted the offer.

"Guess it couldn't hurt to taste the competition," he said begrudgingly. He bit into it and chewed it contemplatively. "Pretty good!" he pronounced, and he licked his fingers. "But mine are better."

At noon, Margo walked over to Dave's to pay for the coffees on her tab and to compare notes. "Well, how was biz, Margo?, he asked. "I sold eight buns this morning! All with coffee or another drink." Dave crowed. "And you owe me ten bucks." He said smugly, holding out his hand. "I assume that means you sold four buns with coffee?"

"No, seven," Margo replied, digging into her pouch for the money. "But only four wanted coffees. Here!" She said lightly and handed Dave a ten-dollar bill.

Dave snatched it out of her hand and made a turn with his hand, "Nice doing business with you, ma'am—and thanks for the extra coffees! That's quite a technique. Take a loss on your cinnamon buns. Hope you made a profit."

"Not, but I will. After I get my own coffee urn." Margo said with a sly smile.

Margo found her coffee urn. She had not

unpacked it since they had moved in a year ago. She added coffee to her signboard: FREE COFFEE WITH A CINNAMON BUN. Not surprisingly, the sign offering free coffee with a cinnamon bun drew customers in. Crazy Dave also upped his game. Instead of sitting beside his van waiting for customers, he walked up and down the row of cars that had stopped to invite them to come and get a fresh cinnamon bun while they waited. He couldn't quite see the logic of free coffee. That would make his profit margin too small. But he did offer a small bun for kids and seniors, at a lower price. It wasn't against the rules, he figured, if the bun wasn't his signature 'Crazy Dave's Cinnamon Bun,' which he still sold for five dollars.

At first, a lot of customers went Dave's way, but then a few of them started walking across to Margo's and found that they could get bigger cinnamon buns that had the sticky, gooey topping they liked AND a free coffee.

Word spread on Margo's page as customers left rave reviews: You gotta stop at the ferry for a Cinnamon Bun on the Run and Free Coffee! She was quickly developing a reputation with the regular ferry commuters. And, when travellers waiting for the ferry saw the line-up at Margo's, they joined it—because that's what people do. They go to the vendor with the longest line because they figure they must have the better product or the best deal.

By the third week of July, Margo's energy was flagging. It was a lot of work getting up early to bake and then pack the buns so they would be warm and fresh, set up the booth and sell all morning. And then she had to go home and prep the next batch to rise in the fridge overnight. After she came home, she tallied her books, entering costs and sales to see if she made a profit. She began to doubt herself, especially regarding the stamina it took to be an entrepreneur. Maybe Kate was right. She was beginning to think she was too soft and maybe too old for this type of life.

One day before July 31, when the weather forecast predicted soaring heat, she decided it didn't matter anymore. She had given entrepreneurship a shot. Although it was a short one, it was a fair one. And she had proven to herself that she could do it—if she were a younger woman with more stamina. But now, she had everything she needed and didn't need to prove anything to herself or to Crazy Dave. Cinnamon Bun on the Run was going out of business.

With that resolve, she revved up the ATV and meandered down the beach route she had established, taking time to enjoy her surroundings. The breeze from the lake was refreshingly cool at that time of morning. The sky was clear, and the sun sparkled across the water. When the ferry advanced toward the shore, Margo felt a twinge of regret about her decision. Maybe she was giving up too soon, she thought. No, she affirmed herself, it was the right thing to do. Retirement was a privilege and a reward for the hard work she had already put into her career.

Margo rounded the corner and stopped at Crazy Dave's van. She noticed an RCMP vehicle parked beside it. Probably a customer, she thought. Cops were known to love their coffee and baking.

"Hey, Crazy Dave!" She called out as she hopped off her ATV.

Dave didn't acknowledge her. His arms were flailing and his voice was raised. He sounded like he was arguing with the officer. She walked closer and recognized the officer. The one who almost fined them for cruising down the street in Wannatoka Springs. The one she and Michael jokingly called Major Tom.

When she was within hearing, she heard Dave shouting, "I always come down to this spot in the summer! And no one has ever questioned me. I've never had to get a permit. Now, you tell me you will have this van towed to Crystal Lake and impound it? And how am I going to pay for that if I can't sell my baking? It's my livelihood, man. Tow away my van, and you take away my livelihood! Are you kidding?"

Major Tom didn't look like he was kidding.

"Excuse me, officer," Margo piped up. "Hi. It's Corporal Tom Majors, isn't it?"

The officer looked taken aback that she knew his name. "Have we met?"

"Yes. Last year. My husband and I were coming around the corner of Maple Street in Wannatoka Springs. You were talking to our neighbour in his driveway. We were new to the neighbourhood so we stopped to say hello because we thought you were there for a friendly chat. You took the time to set us straight on the rules and regulations for driving an ATV on a municipal road."

"Oh. . . I remember you now." He eyed her side-by-side, parked on the grass. "Did you ever get your ninety-degree variance?" He cracked a small smile.

Margo shook her head seriously. "No. Like you said, we'd have to apply through you, and you don't give them out." She smiled innocently. "We learned our rules of the road, Officer Majors. We come this way along the beach from our cottage—around the corner." As she pointed in the direction of her fictitious cottage, Margo felt like a kid telling a lie to a teacher, which was ironic since she was a teacher telling a lie to an officer of the law. She crossed her fingers behind her back.

Crazy Dave looked over at Margo with raised eyebrows. She continued. "I couldn't help but overhear that you are asking Dave to get a permit and I wondered if I could help explain the circumstances. I was the one who wanted to start a cinnamon business on the beach. I got my friend Dave here, involved in a friendly competition— just for the month of July. I called it the 'Cinnamon Bun Wars'. I had no idea that we needed a permit. He usually sells at markets, and I'm sure he always gets a permit for that. Anyway, lesson learned. Dave and I won't be setting up here anymore."

Margo put on her most winning smile and hoped it still worked the way it used to. "I came to tell my friend, who agreed to this friendly competition, that it's over. I'm done. Going back to retirement. You have a scheduled stop at the farmer's market on Saturday at Crestview, right?" Margo spoke those words directly to Crazy Dave.

Dave looked quizzical at Margo but went along with what she was saying. "Uh, yes, I do, Margo. And this misunderstanding would seriously impact my business, Corporal Majors. If I could humbly request a warning at this time, I would be most appreciative and will vacate the premises immediately—especially since my colleague will be vacating it as well." Dave eyed Margo sternly.

Corporal Majors rolled his eyes. He knew he was probably being strung along, but this was the Kootenays and these folks were more like pests than criminals. Plus, there would be the paperwork if he did go through with his threat of a fine and impounding the vehicle. He let Dave go with a warning and told him that if he saw the van parked there again, the vehicle would be towed and impounded, and he would receive a $625 fine unless he got a permit to vend there.

"But," he said as he opened the door of his vehicle, "You have to go through me to apply for permits to vend at the ferry dock. And I don't issue them."

Dave nodded and held his hands up in surrender. "Yes, sir!"

"Is that the going rate?" Margo asked innocently.

"Going rate?" the officer raised his eyebrows.

"I mean, that's what you said we would have to pay—$625—if you saw us driving our ATV on the road next time."

"Yeah—and it's two for one Friday." Corporal Majors said dryly, writing out the warning tickets and giving one to both, "And that goes for you too, ma'am. So don't let me find you out here either!"

Margo swallowed her retort. Another rule of the road: don't get into a war of words with the RCMP. Then she insisted Officer Majors accept a cinnamon bun. Margo assured him this was not a bribe as he had already issued her the warning.

"Thanks. I'll save it for my coffee break." Corporal Majors said with a half-smile, the first Margo had seen.

"If you love it, could you give it a 'like' on my Facebook page?"

"I don't give those out either."

As they watched the officer take a u-turn and glide back down the highway in the direction he came from, Dave said, "Thanks, Margo. I owe you one."

Margo shrugged. "Major Tom and I go back. Long story. But what I said to him is true. I'm folding. I didn't realize how much work it was, making a business from my baking. Long days on my feet. It's been exhausting! I admire your stamina!"

"That's why they call me Crazy Dave. The name comes from people saying, 'You're crazy, Dave! Who would want to do what you do when you have an accounting degree and could make a lot more money sitting at a desk counting other people's beans?"

"Really? You were an accountant?"

"Once upon a time, yeah. But I was dying stuck behind a computer all day, punching numbers. Now, I followed my heart. Talk to people. Make something with my own hands. Working my own hours. It's everything I want to do. I do get tired. But when I do, I can always curl up in the van or sit on the beach. It's my time, and I get to do what I want with it. Call me crazy, but it takes crazy to fit in here in the Kootenays. And you, Margo, have proven to me this month that you have that kind of crazy! Welcome to the neighbourhood!" Dave stuck out his hand.

Margo shook it and laughed. "I never thought I had to be crazy to be recognized as belonging here."

Dave grinned. "Now that the contest is closed and you have conceded, you can tell me how many cinnamon buns you sold."

"I'm not conceding, Crazy Dave. I'm just folding. And I don't want to embarrass you." Margo said with a smile that revealed nothing.

Dave shrugged. "Fine with me. I was gonna move on anyway at the end of the month. Like the sign says, it's Crazy Dave's Travellin' Bakery. I only set up here in the first place because I saw your launch ad in the Wannatoka Times. I thought I'd check out the competition and maybe run you off my territory."

Margo scowled. "Seriously?"

Dave held his hands up in surrender. "Hey . . . I didn't, did I? You held your own. You handled it like a born and bred Kootenayite. I tip my hat to you, ma'am." Dave tipped an imaginary hat and winked.

"A dubious honour, coming from a guy who goes by Crazy Dave. And don't call me ma'am!" Margo smiled and offered her hand to shake.

Dave reached his hand up to a high-five in response. Margo met his hand and slapped it.

"Got it!" he said "Enjoy your retirement!"

"And good luck to you—wherever your travelling entrepreneurial spirit takes you."

As she retraced her steps to her side-by-side, Margo tried to sort out her confused reactions. She was irritated that Crazy Dave had intended to drive her off. But she was proud of herself for not backing down and did what she set out to do. Did she actually get a Kootenayite endorsement? The thought made her mad all over again. She didn't have to prove herself to anyone! Especially not to someone who calls himself Crazy Dave!

Margo pulled out her phone to text Michael.

Margo: Ground control—Major Tom shut Crazy Dave's business down! No permit. Hands up surrender emoji, laugh emoji, Good thing I wasn't

driving the ATV on the highway!!! Anyway. I'm packing it in. So done with work! Garbage can emoji
Michael: What??? Why???
Margo: Crazy face emoji, sick emoji, steam coming out of ears emoji
Michael: Calm down.
Margo: I AM CALM!!! Laugh/cry emoji
Michael: Happy retirement!
Meet you in the backyard for a cold one. Cold drink with straw emoji, umbrella over chair in sunshine emoji

CHAPTER EIGHT

The Iconic Kootenay Village Contest

Margo stepped out the front door. She walked down Willow to Oak Street and, around the corner, past the motel to the only other business still thriving in Wannatoka Springs, Terry's General Store. She was meeting Tina there for a coffee.

The unincorporated community of Wannatoka Springs, population 207, was established in the 1960s when the British Columbia Kootenay Basin hydroelectric dam project was initiated. Wannatoka Springs (then simply called Site A) came into being as a purpose-built community for the workers and their families. At one time, in addition to the motel, there was a three-room elementary school, a restaurant, a bakery, and a convenience store and gas station that also served as a truck stop.

Truckers could pull off the highway, find room to park their rigs in a spacious parking lot, gas up, take a break, get a bite to eat and do their laundry before resuming their route by ferry across the lake where the highway joins a network of highways that run through the province.

The families who lived there were either displaced landowners who had been bought out when the government took over their land and flooded the valley to create the man-made lake, or the construction workers who relocated there with their families with the promise of years of work ahead of them.

A generation of children grew up in the tiny community, but most left when they graduated from high school, either to attend university or to establish themselves in larger centers where work was more readily available.

When the construction phase of the dam in this area was completed, the workers who were hired specifically for the project either retired or left. The jobs they held didn't exist for the next generation. The only viable work in the Kootenays, logging and mining, went through a downturn around that time, making it difficult for all but the most tenacious to find work in the area. With fewer resource hauling trucks frequenting the corridor, and fewer supply trucks servicing the area, the economy flattened.

The subsequent influx into the area came in the seventies when young people, including draft dodgers from the U.S., were disenfranchised by the government and the establishment, had a starry-eyed vision of living off the land in a remote, self-sufficient lifestyle, far away from the prying eyes of 'the man.' The land was cheap then, as it had little commercial value. And since neither the retirees nor the homesteaders tended to be vigorous consumers, the few businesses established in Wannatoka Springs either died or retired with their owners.

Terry was one of the second-generation Wannatokans. She left after high school to find work and established herself in Kamloops, where she met her husband. They raised two kids and bought a house. Her kids had flown the coop when her husband died suddenly, of a heart attack, at his job site while on his lunch hour. Finding herself alone at fifty, too young to retire but too old and wise to wish to remarry, she decided to sell the family home, cash in her husband's life insurance policy, and move back to the village she had fond memories of growing up.

She bought a house on Maple Street that she vaguely remembered as a double-wide trailer. The previous owners had put it on a foundation, gutted it, and renovated it in the eighties. They had built a shallow peaked metal roof over it so it would shed the snow and painted it white with blue trim. It looked like a rancher now, with a bed of flowers and shrubs on either side of the cement steps and metal railings leading to the front door in the center of it.

Scouting around for what she might do to support herself, Terry found the opportunity to take over the postal service contract from the retired couple who took it over for extra income. She also bought, for a song, the building beside the self-serve gas station, which had once been a convenience store, café, and laundromat. What was left was dilapidated, with no improvements made since the sixties when it was established.

The laundromat hadn't functioned in years, the couple who owned it found their business dwindling in the economic downturn. Finally, an injury and declining health made maintaining even minimal hours beyond sorting the mail difficult. In the past five years, when it was under their management, the stock and the upkeep of the store had been let go. When Terry took it over, it was a shell with empty shelves, broken appliances, and a counter behind which the incoming mail was collected, sorted, and stuck in the mailboxes outside and parcels held for pick up.

When Terry arrived, she held out hopes for restoring the village to its nostalgic past. With that in mind, she lobbied for a village name change, making the case that it was no longer a hydroelectric dam site. Single-handedly, she mustered a first-ever referendum—to change its name. She held a contest to name the village, and the prize for the name that the majority voted in was a lifetime coffee subscription at her newly established coffee bar.

People first joked that 'lifetime' was relative, depending on how long this proprietor would last. But soon, the spirit of Terry's enthusiasm caught on, and folks were dropping names into the box Terry set up at the counter where folks came to collect their parcels.

Terry posted the suggested names in her store window, attracting discussions and prompting more suggestions. When she thought she had enough and the suggestions were getting more outlandish, Terry posted the names on her storefront window and a metal box outside where people could vote for the name they thought best, and she set a date to announce the tally and the winning name. Whoever picked up their mail there was eligible to vote on the name.

Terry didn't hold out much hope for a turnout, but she advertised free donuts and coffee to the partici-pants who cast their votes. It might have been the offer of free coffee and donuts, or it might have been the fresh enthusiasm Terry brought with her when she came back to her childhood residence. Most of the folks who lived there and a number of folks occupying outlying homesteads who picked up their mail there cast their vote.

The names suggested varied. Some were tongue-in-cheek—like 'Last Resort' and 'End of the Road'; some were established family names—the name Vanhouten was posted as a town name option. And some were practical or landmark distinctive, like 'Ferry Landing', 'Damsite A' and 'Loggerville'. The name that garnered the most points (in a voting system that ranked first, second and third choices) was 'Wannatoka Springs'. The name came from the whispers of hot springs in the forested hills behind the village.

No one in the village admitted to knowing where it was, but a story circulated that it was once an Indigenous winter camping ground and was now a clothes-not-optional hippy hangout; the key to finding it or being let in on where it was to use the code words, "Wanna toke at the springs, man?" when addressing the right sort of person who thought you were the right sort of person to be initiated into the hippy hole.

When the springs were referenced in a conversation—wildly speculative talk about its possible location, it was shortened to 'Wannatoka Springs'. If the hot spring did exist, which no first-generation Site A resident could say for sure—regardless of how familiar they were with the terrain from crisscrossing it on their ATVs and hunting throughout the range—it didn't have a name other than that.

Terry and a few others in the town were surprised at the name that won the most points—a secret ballot vote. But they were not so surprised at the town's sense of humour considering the changing demographic in the last thirty years. And so Wannatoka Springs, est. 1998 became a dot on the map that Margo and Michael identified while searching for a retirement community.

Terry's trade was mainly in news. And she dispensed it for free. She would have been wealthy enough to retire long before if she could have made a buck for every tidbit of gossip she heard and passed on. As it was, words are cheap and plentiful if you run the post office, the only retail business in town.

Terry didn't mind. She liked talking to people. She didn't discriminate either—between visitors and locals. Anyone who inquired about the goings on in Wannatoka Springs out of curiosity, or stopped at the counter to politely ask "what's new" as they put their coffee and baked goods on the counter to pay for them got an earful of fresh gossip and updates on ferry schedules, wait times, and water meetings, as Terry rang them up. More often than not, customers left with more than they paid for.

Two booths in the back of the store were all that remained of the original café. Since she didn't want to wait on tables, Terry unbolted the other two and hauled them into the back room, where she could later decide whether to use them somewhere else or haul them to the dump. The only clue that there had been more booths there, was a yellow footprint on the linoleum tile around the whiter tile where the booths had been bolted for nearly 30 years.

Terry tried to salvage the two remaining booths so that customers could sit and drink their self-serve coffee. She scrubbed the yellowing Formica tabletops with a cleansing powder. That treatment removed the pen marks and shallow stains, but nothing could remove the deep brown burns from smouldering cigarettes in ash-trays, burning down too close to the surface. Nor could she cover initials and rude words carved into the table-tops over the decades. *Scarface was here* and *For a GUD TINE call. . .* (with subsequent penned spelling corrections erased) ending in a phone number worn away and probably not in service anymore. The tabletops were sanitized—the rest was character.

The brown Naugahyde bench seats were worn and cracked. Unable to afford new upholstery, Terry cleverly patched the cracks with vinyl stickers and decals meant to adhere to car bumpers and weather outdoor surfaces. Bumper stickers, outdoor stickers meant to cover signs, and car decals almost obliterated the brown vinyl on the backs and seats of the booths. They peeled eventually, but Terry had a supply of funny stickers and odd signs that travellers and truckers familiar with her practice gave her when they passed by. If you stopped to read the one in the first booth before you slid into your seat, you would read the bumper sticker that was covering a long horizontal crack: *Farts are from Uranus.*

That particularly amused the kids who scraped by on the seat with shorts and bare legs, purposely trying to make the seat squeak as they slid across it. On the back was a *Wide Load* sticker. Another bumper sticker said, *If you can read this, you're crawling up my ass. Back up!*

Margo's favourite sticker had a yellow background with a yield sign: *Slow Cat   Xing*. Someone had drawn in with a permanent marker between the words 'Cat' and "Xing' the silhouette of a cat, back arched and head turned sideways to look straight at you with a disdainful look on its face—daring you to drive over it as it crossed the road. Margo wondered where that sign was intended to be displayed. She couldn't recall ever seeing one like it on the highway. She surmised it was probably from a construction site with heavy machinery. Sitting on the opposite side of the booth, and staring at it one day, she solved the puzzle. She could see letters missing after 'Cat'—where the space was filled with the cat drawing. It used to read, *Slow. Cattle Xing*. Some clever customer had scraped off the missing letters and drew the cat on the sign between the letters.

The signs kept changing or overlapping as some peeled and Terry replaced them with new ones. Thus, some layered over each other, and the messages underneath were cut off, often in strange ways. For example, *S . . . ucks Coffee* (the overlapping sign cut off the t-a-r-b). Others were just messages where letters were worn out or scraped off and the words gaped like a smile with missing teeth: *FISH and . . . HIPS* and *. . . . do Drugs* (London Drugs).

The stickers, an expression of Terry's sense of humour, reinforced the store's novelty. Travellers crossing the ferry would stop in and buy a cold drink or a coffee, see the booths and want to sit in them, often reading the funny stickers or reminiscing about the nostalgia of café booths. Terry's store was the hub of local news and Wannatoka Springs's only tourist attraction.

When she entered Terry's store, Tina was already sitting at one of the booths, a cup of coffee in front of her, scrolling through her phone. Margo took a paper cup and poured herself a cup of coffee, doctoring it the way she liked it with sugar and cream. Terry came out from the back, carrying a tray of individually wrapped cinnamon buns she had baked.

"Hey, Margo!" Terry called out, "Help yourself. Fresh cinnamon buns if your sweet tooth is gnawing at you."

"Thanks!" Margo said, "But I'm trying not to pay attention to my sweet tooth." She opened the creamer and poured it into her coffee.

"Okay, then," Terry chirped, "but they're here to tempt you. Just help yourself."

Margo trashed the sugar packets and empty creamers and returned to sit with Tina.

The back of her legs rubbed against the Naugahyde, emitting a squeak. Recalling the bumper sticker behind her back that read, *Farts are from Uranus*, Margo lifted one leg and then the other away from the vinyl so she could move freely down the bench. "These booths, this place, is so ironic!" Tina's mouth twitched a smile. She looked up from her phone and cut her eyes towards Terry, who placed the cinnamon buns under the plexiglass display on the counter.

"Careful. Pitchers have ears." Tina said under her breath. Then, in full voice, she said, "You look nice, Margo. Very summery!"

Margo took the hint. Terry listened to every conversation she could, but neither wanted to say anything that might insult her host and neighbour. She might not think her booths were ironic and could take offence. Margo sucked in her lips and held her coffee up to take a sip.

Terry stood back to assess the impact of her display. Cinnamon buns, individually wrapped in plastic, were stacked in a pyramid. Judging it good enough, she turned and made her way to the booth at the back with a half-full coffee carafe in one hand. "Hey, girls," Terry said as she approached them. "Need a top-up?"

Margo shook her head. Tina laughed and said, "Terry! That's not like you! I thought you didn't serve! But since you're asking . . ." Tina offered her cup to be topped.

"I'm making an exception," Terry said and looked around surreptitiously to ensure no one else was in the store, although the jangling bell would announce anyone who came through the door. "Don't tell anyone. I have something I'd like to run by you two."

"Of course!" Tina smiled and slid over to give Terry room on her bench. Terry set the coffee carafe on the table and dug into her apron pocket, pulling out a folded square of newspaper. She looked serious. "Now I know you are both new to our little community. And I seen how both of you are taking care of your places. Your lawns and flowers—especially yours, Margo—are beautiful. It's not just me. There's been talk about it in the neighbourhood."

Margo raised her eyebrows. "My flowers? I hope I haven't offended anyone. I didn't mean to show anyone up. I just love flowers . . ."

"No, no, it's nothing like that. In fact, it's the opposite. Folks are admiring how you brought the old Wilson property back to life. God knows it sure needed it! So do a lot of our old houses. Nothing like they were when I was a girl growing up here. But that don't matter. What matters is that new folks like yourselves have moved here, spruced up your places, and have brought back some life to them.

"Thank you!" Margo beamed and glanced at Tina, giving her the nod that said, 'I told you so . . .' to Tina's poo-pooing of Margo's obsession with flowers. Tina liked a tidy outdoor space, but couldn't care less about ornamentation.

Terry went on, "So I was thinking. Maybe we could build on that. Wannatoka Springs could be the next place where retirees like you want to live or even get younger folks interested in moving here. Lots of them want to work remotely, and now that we have high-speed internet, that would be an option. A couple of young families have already moved into acreages down the road. Wouldn't it be something to build up some infrastructure so folks here have some things to do and places to be? Right now, there's just my store. I am grateful for and proud of being at the center of the Wannatoka Springs community. But there could be more here if we attracted more people to come and live and invest here. That sorry old school house, for example. It could be utilized for a lot more social events if the damn roof didn't leak, and you didn't have to pay a fortune to heat it."

"Interesting idea, but don't most folks like things the way they are?" Margo objected.

Yes and no." Terry shrugged. "Some like not to be bothered. But even some of the old ones complain that there aren't no connections or services like there used to be. And you can't have services and businesses in a place that has no population to speak of. Then there are folks like you who just might enjoy living in a community that takes pride in itself and has things to do and places to gather. But, that all takes money."

Margo and Tina nodded their agreement. Seeing that she had their interest, Terry leaned forward conspiratorially and tapped the newspaper clipping. "So, I got a project in mind that I think would put Wannatoka Springs on the map and get us some money for improvements."

"Ohhh . . . a project! I'm all ears," Tina said enthusiastically. Margo held back her opinion. She wanted to see where this was going before she offered one.

Terry unfolded the newspaper cutting, pulled her

reading glasses down from her forehead, and settled them on her nose. Taking a moment to focus, she read the headline aloud.

Cash prizes and a community development grant offered by the Kootenay Tourism Foundation, including a feature spread in our online site and in a national magazine for three villages to show off their iconic Kootenay character.

Terry paused, then leaned in to emphasize the following words: *The Iconic Kootenay Village Contest.* Terry looked up meaningfully. "I think, given the history of this village, and with what we could manage to spiff the place up, we could have a chance! So that's my plan. What do you think?"

Margo and Tina exchanged glances. Margo winced, remembering the word she had just used to describe Terry's store.

"I think it's a great idea," Tina enthused. Margo rolled her eyes. Tina was undoubtedly humouring Terry. She would find a way of squirming out of it after she puffed her up a bit with flattery, and here it came . . . "But I don't see how we would ever be able to raise funds to beautify this village, much as I would love to, or how we would even incentivize others in the community to go along with this project!"

"I've thought of that," Terry said, pushing the newspaper clipping to the center of the table, "First off— don't underestimate this community. There's already a community effort to restore the old school and playground for use as a community center–aimed at both community members having a place to gather, maybe play cards, knit, do yoga, take painting classes—whatever. They want to reno the playground, maybe even add a skate park for the kids they see riding their bikes and skateboards up and down the street. Somewhere to go for them so they don't end up vandalizing properties for entertainment. We got the land and the building—although it leaks and needs a new roof. But we don't got the money. So, there's the incentive. Cash prize, it says. And a community development grant." Terry's forefinger tapped the newspaper clipping as confirmation.

The tinkle of the bell at the front of the store severed the conversation. Terry slid out of her seat and grabbed the coffee carafe. Walking back towards the counter, she hailed the woman who came in. "Hello, Elmira! How are you today?"

"I'm very well, thank you, Terry. I came in to pick up a parcel."

"Be with you in a second, Elmira," Terry shouted. Turning to Tina and Margo, Terry said in a low voice, "Elmira's a little deaf. Anyway, girls. I'll leave you with that with that tip. Let it swill around . . . up here," she tapped the side of her head. "See what you come up with!" Terry turned to walk back toward the front of the store.

Margo lifted her eyebrows and mouthed, "Swill?" When they heard Terry start up a conversation with Elmira in a loud voice, Tina leaned in and whispered, "I think she meant 'swirl'." Tina made a twirling motion around her head. "Not swill—like a beer." Both women sipped their coffee to stifle the giggles that threatened to erupt. And they couldn't help but listen to the conversation between Terry and Elmira.

They heard Elmira report all about her neighbour Stella's cat's health. According to Elmira, Stella's cat was suffering from some severe form of arthritis that Stella was treating with steroids prescribed by the vet as well as various home remedies she had read about, including apple cider vinegar, turmeric, and glucosamine syrup. Apparently, the cat didn't appreciate the cherry-flavoured syrup and kept throwing it up, which only made Stella more worried about his dire state.

"Munchkins by proxy." Terry declared solemnly.

"It's poor Stella who's suffering. I've seen it before. She makes up fake symptoms for the cat. Always taking it to the vet. Must cost her a fortune! And her cat, well . . ." Terry handed Elmira her package shaking her head, "Poor thing looks worse every time I see it sitting on her porch. Its hair is even falling out in patchwork!" Terrible mental illness, Munchkins by Proxy. Poor Stella. Good that she doesn't have any children. That's all I can say."

Tina could hardly contain herself, "I think she means Munchhausen by Proxy. It's a mental illness where the caretaker makes a child ill by diagnosing fake symptoms or creating real ones to make them sick. I've seen a few cases of it in my time as a nurse. It is a terrible illness. But transferring hypochondria onto a cat? That's novel." Tina glanced sideways in Terry's direction and grinned.

"Oh! Thanks for the clarification. I thought Terry said 'Munchkins'—like the little people that populated Oz in the Wizard of Oz."

Tina sucked in her breath to stifle another giggle. "She did. Terry confuses words sometimes." The bells on the door tinkled again, signalling another customer entering the store.

"Let's scoot while we can," Tina said, glancing at Terry who was engaged with a conversation that involved the newcomer." She scooted out from the vinyl bench seat with a squeak when her bare thighs stuck to it. It sounded like a fart. Both Tina and Margo stifled a laugh and, picking up their garbage, walked back to the front of the store to deposit it.

When they passed by the counter, and threw their empty paper cups in the garbage, they waved good-bye to Terry. Without missing a beat, Terry called out in a cheery voice, " Don't forget your server, ladies. One tip deserves another." She winked and then fell right back into the conversation she was having.

Margo looked surprised. After having spent a

year in this tiny community, she was still learning the unspoken etiquette. And there were no shortages of teachers who unabashedly prompted her to do the right thing. Terry, apparently, thought the tip about the Iconic Kootenay Village Contest was a generous tip. They each fished out some change and deposited it in the glass jar labelled 'Tips for Tips!"

***

Margo walked down the street and turned the corner to pick up Tina who was standing in front of her house on Maple, shading her eyes against the bright summer sun. Tina waved and bounded off the porch and down the sidewalk. Five years younger than Margo, Tina was lithe and athletic. She had been her whole life. Being a nurse had kept her on her feet almost all day and when she wasn't working, she enjoyed outdoor sports and activities like kayaking and camping. She was the yin to Margo's yang. Opposite but complimentary.

Tina wore a light-coloured pair of Lulu Lemon yoga pants and a baby blue tank top that outlined her taut upper body and skimmed her waist. Blue complemented her blue eyes and blond-streaked hair. She bounced as she walked down the street in her ubiquitous athletic shoes. It didn't matter if it was hot as blazes or nearly cold enough to freeze your hands off; Tina wore her athletic shoes inside and out. She said she loved their support and feel and didn't feel that there was any occasion where they couldn't be dressed up or down.

"Hi!" Tina waved as she came towards Margo. "Ready for your induction into the Ladies' Garden Club? Like your dress. Very bright and sunny. Sunflowers! Good choice!"

***

"Too much?" Her sleeveless dress draped from her bust down to her ankles, the fabric widening generously so that it swirled around her when she walked. She found that since she had retired, she was enjoying more loose-fitting clothing that grazed her ankles. They made her feel free from encumbrances, unlike the clothes she wore to work as a teacher where every layer, from her tights, to her fitted skirts and pants with zip-up flies to the synthetic blouses and jackets that bound at shoulders. Margo was slowly letting go of her identity as a professional and refashioning herself as a free-er spirit. The freedom she allowed herself was not only freedom from constricting clothing but also a constricted diet. Her waist and hips appreciated her lax attention. She had just bought the dress online from one of those sites that targeted figure-flattering dresses for 'women of a certain age.' And though Margo doubted the sincerity of Tina's back-handed compliment, an open face and smile disarmed her. "It's the Community Service Club, Tina. Looks like you thought you were going to a yoga class."

Tina locked her arm into Margo's elbow and walked down the street with her friend. "Never mind how we look. As long as we're both comfortable in our own skin. Now, let's get this village beautified!"

When they walked into the old school house used for community events, village meetings, yoga classes and games nights, Margo noted the foldaway tables were formed into a horseshoe with chairs lining the outsides. At each place was a package of paper, no doubt meant to raise discussions and to be perused by everyone. At the side was a table with coffee and tea in urns, a delicious assortment of pastries, and a fruit bowl. Margo already knew what she would go for.

There were fifteen members already present—all women. No men, Margo noted. Margo was pleased that   Terry's word-of-mouth and her own Facebook posts on the Wannatoka Times community page advertising the *Iconic Kootenay Village* contest with cash prizes and a grant for community upgrades, had garnered support from community members but they needed a central committee to get behind the plan to organize the beautification of the village and get the village on board. Margo called Ronnie Vanhouten, the president of the Community Service Club, to ask if they could make their proposal to enter the contest at their next service club meeting. Ronnie had agreed to put it on the agenda. And now here they were, at the one pm Thursday Wannatoka Springs Community Service Club meeting.

Margo looked around at the women seated, cookies and coffee or tea in front of them, talking to their neighbours. She recognized most of them in passing when she and Chance walked by the houses on their route. At the refreshments table, Ronnie Vanhouten was talking with Terry. Ronnie's family played a prominent role in the community. Dating back to the original settlement of this area, when the government appropriated their land and moved it to higher ground so the valley could be flooded, the Vanhouten had owned and worked the land for two—going on three—generations. They still kept horses on their family ranch but had let go of their cattle and sheep a generation ago. Ronnie's husband owned a construction business. His company won most of the bids on local and government construction work, so her influence would go a long way to garnering support for this project.

Margo had engaged in polite conversations with Ronnie around the post boxes when they met. Still, she always felt intimidated by her, somehow.

"Hi," Tina said, holding one hand and addressing the room. "We're here for the Community Service Club meeting. Right place, I hope?" She looked around the room and smiled. Margo smiled, too, although she felt a little self-conscious in her boldly patterned dress. Most women looked to be in their seventies or eighties, with white or grey, short, curled or carefully styled straight hair fitting around their heads like helmets. The fashion statement for women of this age could be summed up in a description of short-sleeved cotton blouses with tiny floral prints over stretchy synthetic pants or capris in beige or white.

Ronnie stood out among them as much younger in her wheat-coloured linen tunic and loose-fitting ankle-length linen pants of a slightly darker shade. She wore her dark brown hair with threads of silver running through it in a shoulder-length bob that gleamed with polished perfection. Her hands ended in professionally manicured nude-polished nails, which drew attention to the sparkling solitaire ring and accompanying wide gold band on her left hand.

Margo wished she were a shrinking violet, not a blaze of sunflowers. Tina ignored everyone. She was comfortable in her own skin and her own style.

Ronnie waved back at Tina and smiled. "You are definitely in the right place! Welcome!" She walked toward Tina and Margo and offered her hand in a greeting. Tina clasped it briefly.

"Yes. Delighted to see you again, Ronnie."

Ronnie turned her warm smile and offered her hand to Margo. When Margo took it, she exclaimed with genuine enthusiasm, "Margo! What a boon you are to our community already. Terry tells me you have supported this contest idea and are here to contribute some valuable ideas."

"Thank you for inviting us, Ronnie. I'm pleased to be here!" Margo said. "Michael and I love it here." And she genuinely meant that.

"Come and sit down, ladies. You might want to pick up a coffee or tea and a snack if you like. And then join us."

"That's okay," Tina said. "I've eaten. And I don't

drink coffee after noon.

As she walked towards the table. Margo debated whether to go to the sweet-laden table to pick up one of those scrumptious-looking pastries but decided to follow her friend's lead. "I'm fine, too," she said, smiling back at Ronnie. Ronnie led them to the table.

"Why don't you sit here? She gestured to two empty seats nearest her and beside Terry.

Ronnie called the meeting to order. "I am so happy to see this enthusiastic turnout! We have a supportive community here, and I'm proud to be part of it. Before we start, I know all of us old-timers know each other very well, but we have two newcomers to our community who may not, so let's start introducing ourselves." Ronnie gave time for each of the women to introduce themselves, say where they lived, and provide any other information about themselves they thought was relevant.

Margo and Tina had their turn introducing them-selves. When each made their introductory remarks, everyone present was invited to turn to page one of the packages in front of them and thus started the proposal summary. Then Ronnie gave Margo the floor to introduce the project.

"We want to propose a project to enhance the beauty and value of Wannatoka Springs. Our project has the potential to raise funds to repair and refurbish this old school house, which I know has a lot of uses but is in dire need of repair—especially the roof, which I hear we have to use more than one bucket to catch the drips when it rains." A few listeners nodded soberly. "We've only been part of this community for a little over a year, but I already understand how the folks in Wannatoka Springs love their community. And I know, too, that some folks are wistful about how it was when there was a lively, family-oriented community. We all accept that it's a natural thing for communities to evolve. Children grow up and leave the nest. Families move away to find work and schools. Some people stay, and new people move in. Michael, I, my neighbours Tina and her husband Joel are examples. We discovered Wannatoka Springs and think it's a perfect place to make this our retirement home.

While we appreciate the welcome we have received here and wouldn't want to change a thing for ourselves, we do want to contribute—especially while we have the energy and enthusiasm as newly retired folks –to making Wannatoka Springs a livable place for all.

We all know that it takes money. We don't have money individually, but we may be able to raise it if we work together. That's why entering our beautiful little Kootenay village in a contest will not only put us on the map for future families and retirees to discover and want to live but also give us money and grants to improve our community assets. Besides that, I think working together as a community is a beautiful way to engage with our neighbours. I am, and I know my husband Michael is, and Tina and Joel are very much looking forward to investing in our neighbourhood and working with our neighbours.

The women applauded politely when she finished her presentation, but no one immediately spoke up. None wanted to be the first to support or denounce the idea. Ronnie stood up and stepped in to break the silence. "Thank you, Margo. I think the idea has real potential. I'd like to open it up for discussion. I am opening the floor to discussion and questions."

One or two at the table didn't relish change and felt it would be too much work upfront with no guarantees, and they had enough on their plate as it was. One said they didn't think entering a contest would fly with their neighbours. Some positive comments and questions demonstrated at least restrained interest in the idea.

After an hour's discussion, Ronnie called the meeting
to order and suggested the club take it to a vote on whether
they would support entering the contest and participating in Margo's beautification plan for Wannatoka Springs.
Since Margo and Tina were not officially part of the club,
although they were welcome guests, Ronnie stipulated
that they must leave the room while the club discussed
this further and took a vote.

As president, Ronnie reserved her vote unless
she had to break a tie. She invited Margo and Tina to
help themselves with the refreshments and perhaps take
them outside to the picnic table in the playground. This
time, Margo permitted herself to be herself. She told Tina
to go ahead if she didn't want anything. Before following
her outside, she would take a couple of samples of the
homemade goodies on display and fill a cup of coffee
with cream and sugar.

The ballots were collected and counted; Ronnie
counted them and then recounted them. She looked up.
"There seems to be a tie," she said when she looked up
from counting the ballots. "The club protocol is that the
president casts the final votes if there is a tie."

Tina paced while Margo sat at the picnic table,
biting into a creamy Nanaimo square and sipping coffee
between bites. Both were working out their nerves as
they waited. Presently, one of the club members has
called them back. Tina clapped her hands enthusiastically.
Margo tried to be indifferent to the outcome but was
nervous about how she would be perceived in her new
community. As she took her place at the table inside,
she realized that community support and inclusion were
important to her.

Ronnie looked at Margo when she spoke. "This is
an ambitious project, to be sure. But, as we have already
expressed, we welcome new ideas, and you, Tina and
Margo came to us with one heck of an idea for moving

forward with our agenda to beautify Wannatoka Springs and raise funds to support the work that we need to do, especially on this old school house. The vote is mixed, and I expect you will still have to do some convincing to get the community at large on board with your idea, but the majority has voted 'yes' to supporting your proposal. The Wannatoka Springs Service Club is at your service." Ronnie beamed her smile around the room.

Margo breathed a sigh of relief. Tina beamed and clapped. Half the board smiled and clapped, prompting the others to join in reluctantly.

Tina and Margo couldn't get over their coup. Had the newbies managed to win the confidence of the Community Service Club to beautify the neighbourhoods of Wannatoka Springs? And all in one meeting! Margo figured they must hold the record for initiatives approved and acted upon, not just for this board but any board she had ever been associated with. Margo and Tina joined the club that day as participating members. The next step was selling the community on their plan to beautify the community.

"What about this," Margo was trying out her ideas for beautifying Wannatoka Springs on Tina over coffee. One of the things on her radar was to get rid of the old junk cars and appliances and other machinery that was left where it stopped running. "Why don't we have a community-wide yard sale? We could call it the 'Got Junk? Sell it or Scrap it'—It's a community yard sale," Margo smirked.

"Love it!" Tina exclaimed, punctuating her enthusiasm by slamming her coffee cup on the counter and sloshing coffee on the surface. "Oops! I kinda get carried away." She went to the sink to get a dishcloth to wipe up the spill.

Margo and Tina clinked coffee mugs in high spirits, thinking they would rid Wannatoka Springs of the eye-sores in yards and then move on to phase two: beautifying those yards with flowers, plants and bushes, they could sell as another fundraiser. First, though, they had to convince their neighbours of the value of beautifying their yards by selling or hauling away their junk. Not surprisingly, when Margo and Tina presented their contest and the merits of winning a grant to improve their community to the neighbours at a village meeting, they were met with some resistance.

"What if we don't want to get rid of our so-called junk?" One man shouted from the back. "I, for one, intend to fix up some of those vehicles in my yard and cannibalize the others. Just haven't had time yet."

"Yeah—in which decade Harold!?" a woman snorted.

"One person's junk is another one's treasure," muttered a disgruntled woman in the front row."

"What if we like it just the way it is?"

"Yeah! I like looking at your old junk in the front yard, Shirley, just the way it is." A heckler from the back called out. Shirley turned around and balled up her fist but smiled, "I'll get you for that, John. Next week, install twice as many lawn ornaments in my yard!"

That drew a titter in the crowd.

"Now, folks, let's not let this get personal," Ronnie interrupted. "And we certainly don't want to encourage a junk collection competition!"

The woman, Shirley, laughed. "No contest. I'd win hands down every time!"

For the most part, the folks who came out were supportive of Margo's community yard sale plan. Getting rid of stuff, they no longer wanted would relieve the pressure of trying to do it on their own, and it would be nice to spruce up the neighbourhood. Also, the idea of supporting the community by contributing to a fifty/fifty profit for junk sold to the cause of restoring their old schoolhouse made sense. It allowed the residents to come together for a common cause. And enthusiasm builds enthusiasm.

So, the plan was agreed upon, and resistors were assured that they didn't have to participate or could reserve their participation until they saw how it was going for others. Margo was counting on group pressure to break down their resistance—at least partially. But it was Terry, the shopkeeper, who became the most vigorous proponent and the real mover and shaker of the community yard sale.

Not only did Terry spread the news she gathered, but she also invented the news and spread that, too. Some said she could start a rumour that would catch like a wildfire on a wet field. If she spread the rumour that Turner, up on the back of Willow Road, had contacted a collector to come and look at his old tractor, that rumour bolstered others to consider putting their collectibles up for sale.

Margo didn't know for sure but suspected that Terry had started a rumour pieced together with snip-its and conjecture that collectibles might visit the village show, like the Antiques Road Show. The buzz set the village on fire. Residents were coming to the store— the hub of Wannatoka Springs.

Terry sold a lot of coffee and cinnamon buns to folks who were discussing what they might want to put out for sale if that happened. Thanks to Terry, Margo's 'Got Junk? Sell it or Scrap It' community yard sale expanded into a yard sale and silent auction for collectible vehicles. Terry had all the connections. She worked with visitors to the store, put posters up in Crystal Lake, contacted independent car dealers, and posted ads on special interest groups touting the sale as a unique sale and auction of vintage automobiles and collectibles.

***

Margo had been scanning the weather reports for a

week, hoping the long-range forecast, which predicted a high-pressure system for July, would hold for the weekend of the community yard sale and silent auction.

Margo's stomach had been in a knot for weeks, worrying about the details of the beautification project. She and Tina had written the proposal for why their village should be considered for the contest and sent it off before the deadline. They heard back two weeks later that the village's application for entry into the contest was accepted and that they would be contacted about a time when the judges would pass through their village.

The community yard sale was the first step to beautifying Wannatoka Springs. With a little less junk and a little more enterprise and vigour, Margo believed the Wannatoka Springs might just win the title of Iconic Kootenay Village. The morning of the yard sale, Margo texted Tina to confirm their status.

Margo: How's it going on Maple?

Tina: Junk out on front lawns. Thumbs up emoji

Tina: On Spruce?

Margo: Good from what I can see. Most are just setting up, however. I'll do a drive around Willow.

Tina was stationed at a table at the entrance to Wannatoka Springs, just in front of the post boxes. Cars would be registered and parked up the business street and in the parking lot that surrounded Terry's general store and gas station. Chelsea, a woman in the community who worked on the ferry, volunteered to direct vehicles to their spots. Tina registered their names, phone numbers, and vehicle license plates on a clipboard and gave each one who asked for as many as ten square stickers—the kind that conventioneers wore on their lapels that read 'Hello. My name is . . .' Buyers were instructed to write their license plate number, where the name should go, and the time they made the bid. The potential buyers were instructed to stick the stickers on the auction sign

next to the item. At the end of the day, the highest bidder
would be informed by phone, given the owner's contact
details, and from there, they would make arrangements with
the owner to haul it away by the end of the week.

Anonymity was crucial for keeping the auction
civil. In a small community like Wannatoka Springs,
someone always didn't like someone else and didn't
want to sell to them or they would jack up the price
if they knew who it was that was bidding. People who
would fight over the top bid with their competition would go
to the lengths of tracking them down and bullying them into
letting them have the last bid.

By mid-morning, the parking lot was almost full.
People came from neighbouring villages, Crystal Lake and
beyond, thanks to Margo casting a wide net of promotion
on social media. Already, some cars were drifting away, and
the owners had walked the two blocks and found treasures
among the things that were for sale.

Someone asked Tina when she would announce
the winner of the silent auction for a rusted-out 1961
Chevy truck; he put in a bid for. He couldn't stay, he said,
but he wanted to come back and cruise through the
auction just before it closed to see if anyone had offered
more, so he could counter it if he wanted to. Tina told
him the cut-off time was four pm. That seemed to satisfy
the man, and he drove off in a dirty, old Ford pick-up that
looked like it could also be classed as a vintage truck if it
wasn't held together with solder and body putty.

Tina: Smooth operation here.

Margo: Busy but upbeat here.

Tina: Thumbs up emoji

Margo: Keep me posted!

Tina: A line of thumbs-up emoji and a smiley face emoji

The inventory of 'lawn ornaments' as Michael called
the junk cars and rust-eaten machines and appliances hauled
onto the neighbours' yards with 'for sale or bid' signs on

them, included vintage cars and trucks, one tractor dating back to the thirties, as well as smaller motorized items like rototillers, lawnmowers and washing machines. In all likelihood, they, like the old cars and trucks, did not run; the owners were hoping to take advantage of the hype to sell them cheap so they didn't have to pay the dumping fees.

Before the sale, Tina had visited the owners and listed the items and working order, printed stickers on them with brief information—mileage or hours and 'runs' or 'not running' along with a reserve price if there was one. On the day of the sale, Tina was in the parking lot, registering names and giving out numbers, which the bidders could use in place of their names beside their bids.

Margo assigned herself the duty of overseeing the collection from the sale of items the neighbours designated as donations to go toward the project. She and Tina had knocked on doors, inspected garages for likely sale-able items, and drank gallons of coffee with neighbours for two weeks prior to the yard sale in their campaign to support the cause of beautifying Wannatoka Springs.

The village had taken on a carnival air. Terry was in front of her store across from the community parking lot, roasting hot dogs and brats on a barbecue. The smell of roasting sausage wafted towards the parking lot and hit the nostrils of the visitors as they stepped out of their vehicles, luring them to make their first stop at the BBQ in front of the store.

Strains of pop music wove through the streets, coming from various neighbours' garages or portable sound systems, sitting next to the owners of the yard sale items, who were stretched out on lawn chairs, chatting amiably with passersby.

Whole families of bargain hunters made their way slowly and deliberately down the two parallel streets sipping on coffee or lemonade, their pacified children slurping on ice cream cones trailing behind. Clumps of people stood around tables sorting through buckets of treasures: china, crockery, tools, kitchenware, stuffies, children's clothes, platters decorated with hula girls and palm trees, memorabilia from holidays, and t-shirts of every description.

Couples stood in front of items parked on the lawn, examining them for quality and life left in them, discussing whether or not they would use this exercise bike or that outdoor table with an umbrella and four chairs. Wives pulled husbands away from the groups of men standing around a 1952 Chevy truck and a hollowed-out carcass of a 1972 yellow Corvette—fibreglass body still intact, talking about rebuilding engines and reminiscing about trucks they once owned, which were probably worth a fortune now that they were considered classics.

Margo was pleased to see purchasers hanging onto lamps and cloth shopping bags strung over shoulders, stuffed with bargains. They wheeled wagons full of purchased goods, their children walking beside their mama, holding her hand instead of riding in them— the way they came in. She was especially gratified to see the bare patches emerge on lawns where furniture, fixtures and tables of goods had been displayed.

Starting at four o'clock, Tina made the rounds of more oversized items entered into the silent auction. She was excited by the number of bids, some from repeat stickers, on some of the big-ticket items. The old tractor went for $300. The 1952 Chevy truck was bid up to $500. Even the 1972 yellow Corvette carcass was bid up with fourteen bids–the top bid, a whopping $1,100—placed at 3:59 pm—beating out the bid before it by $100.

Tina figured there must've been a car collector or two among the crowd, vying for the same prize. Most of the items were reserved at a base price, which the owner collected, and anything else that was donated to the Beautification and Recreation Society. The profits from the items that didn't have a reserve price were split fifty/fifty.

When Margo tallied up profits the society made from the yard sale and the silent auction, she was amazed that what she considered junk turned into a treasure trove of over $5,000. Equally crucial to Margo was the prospect that by the end of the weekend, all of the junk displayed in the yards and driveways would either be picked up by the purchasers or hauled away by the junk dealer they had hired from the proceeds of the sale that the participants all agreed could haul away to be dumped, recycled or sold for scrap, clearing the way for entering and hopefully winning the contest for the most desirable village in the Kootenays.

Watching the sun sink lower in the sky from Tina's deck, Margo and Tina clinked wine glasses and sipped. They were exhausted from talking all day to visitors and neighbours, so they lounged in Tina's plastic adirondack chairs, silently staring down at Maple St, now empty except for a few neighbours packing up their wares and taking down their tables.

After a while, Tina said, "I believe that was a success."

"Yes. Definitely a success." Margo agreed.

"The neighbourhood looks a lot better already."

"Not too shabby."

"So, are you up for phase two—Operation Lawn Ornament?" Tina queried and took a sip of wine.

Margo looked at Tina. She couldn't believe that Tina had the energy to even think about the next step. She was exhausted beyond the point of thinking about anything except finishing her wine and going back to crawl into bed—maybe for the whole week. But she realized that was a distant fantasy. If they wanted to beautify Wannatoka Springs, they had yards to go before she slept.

Tina's inspiration, 'Operation Lawn Ornament' would be the final phase of the campaign to beautify the village. Tina had secured coupons from the garden nursery and the hardware store in Crystal Lake that could be applied as discounts on plants, shrubs, and ornamental trees—anything to do with garden decoration that could be purchased from the garden center and hardware store in town.

Tina talked this idea up with the neighbours and went door to door to visit them. Her contagious enthusiasm and generous handout of green-bucks seemed to be catching on. Avid gardeners enthusiastically embraced the idea and went to the garden center to pick out plants that would brighten up corners or add to displays of colour along the front of their houses and along the walkways.

Not everyone was a garden enthusiast, however. So others in the community dragged their heels, reluctantly setting pots of bushes and plants on their steps and asking to be signed up for the garden squad to help plant them and spruce up their yards. Some refused to get on board at all.

While Tina created the buzz, Margo mustered the help of the ladies of the club, along with an army of volunteers, to help clean up yards and plant shrubs and flowers for neighbours who were reluctant to do the work or needed assistance. Tina and Margo and their small army of volunteers made headway, going from home to home, volunteering to weed, prune, rake and mow the lawns and gardens that were straggly and overgrown. By the end of the month, the two women had done as much as they possibly could. Both were played out.

Gazing out at the setting sun from her perch on their deck, Tina lifted her glass to Margo, "To you, my dear friend! I believe you have succeeded in making Wannatoka Springs an Iconic Kootenay Village!"

Margo clinked her glass but said, "It takes a

village. Here's to Wannatoka Springs!" Margo swallowed the last of her wine, set the wine glass on the table, then scraped her chair back and pushed herself up and out. "I'm done. I think I'll turn it in. See you tomorrow for coffee."

Still seated, Tina raised her glass. "Tomorrow is THE DAY! Get your beauty rest!"

Margo drifted off into a much sought-after sleep, reviewing everything in her mind's eye. She had found that it just didn't look like it on the outside, Wannatoka Springs was becoming the village she imagined herself moving to—a bucolic little village with quiet, tree-lined streets and tidy houses framed by neatly cut lawns and sweet little gardens and hedgerows. It was almost a replica of a perfect suburb she had imagined moving to but set against the backdrop of the natural world of forests and lakes in the interior of British Columbia.

That Saturday morning, the day of the judges' arrival, sunshine already streamed through her living room windows. Her backyard trees and shrubs and bee and bird-attracting flower gardens were alive with competing sounds of birdsong. She could hear the boisterous shrieking of children scraping wagons and rid-ing bikes down her street from her bed. But Margo could not rouse herself—not even to answer Tina's texts ping-ing on her phone, one after the other in swift succession.

Her energy was drained. She could hear Michael in the kitchen, unloading the dishwasher and putting coffee on. The smell of coffee filled Margo's senses and persuaded her to open her eyes and pull one arm out from under the sheet to reach for her phone. She picked it up and held it close to her face, focusing her eyes on the screen before her. Four notifications from Tina.

She pressed her finger on the home button. The screen opened. She reread the number four on the texting app. After a moment of hesitation, unsure of what to expect or if she wanted to find out, Margo tapped the app. The message simply shouted in all caps. "WAKE UP!" Margo scrolled up to the four messages Tina had sent in a row.

Tina: OMG! I can't believe this! Hands covering mouth emoji

Tina: Walk over here now. You have to see this! Wow' emoji. Wow emoji

Tina: Margo???

Tina: WAKE UP!!! Loudspeaker emoji

Margo sat up straight and blinked herself awake. Tina could be an alarmist sometimes, but these messages seemed to have reached a crescendo of panic. After struggling into her stretchy yoga pants and an oversized, long-sleeved t-shirt, Margo grabbed her phone and carried it into the kitchen.

"I smell coffee. Thanks." Margo pecked Michael on the cheek and reached into the cupboard for a coffee cup.

Michael turned around and looked up. "Good morning to you, Sunshine! It's your big day, so I thought I'd start you on the right foot. Coffee is on. Breakfast is being prepared . . . whenever you are ready."

Margo rubbed the bridge of her nose. "That's sweet, Michael. Maybe later. I'll take a cup of coffee in a to-go mug. Tina has summoned me." She showed Michael the texts.

Michael frowned as he read the texts. "Looks serious!"

Margo yawned. "Probably not. It's probably just a disgruntled neighbour making a stink about the neighbour's dog peeing on their newly planted bush or something. But Tina summoned, so I must go."

"OK. Your day. Your way. I'll do as directed and otherwise stay out of your way, ma'am." Michael held up his hands and returned to the dishwasher he was unloading.

Margo retraced her steps, stopping to use the washroom and then into the bedroom to get ready. "Thanks. And don't call me ma'am!" she said and swiped at Michael's rear end. It was their running joke. She hated being called ma'am and had upbraided every man who addressed her that way. Michael only used it when he thought she needed some lightening up. He had already read that in her attitude this morning.

"I'll take my phone. If it's a real emergency, I'll text you."

"Or call me. I'm a simple guy. Phone calls still work for me." Michael reminded her.

Engrossed in her thoughts, Margo passed the little white church with blue trim around the windows. It has been emptying of parishioners for three years now. An influx of new people might mean reopening the quaint little church. Margo, herself, was not a churchgoer. But she could envision families entering and leaving the church on a Sunday morning in this pastoral setting.

She was almost at the end of the connecting street, where it turned the corner onto Maple Street when something caught her eye. She was sure it hadn't been there yesterday. She quickened her step to get a closer look at the front of a house. An ancient, rusty garden tools and machinery procession stood on the yellow-spotted lawn. They were lined up neatly as if on display. She wasn't an expert on garden tools, but the first one looked like it might be a fencepost digger, the next a rototiller, and next to it, a tool used for poking holes in the lawn to aerate it. Margo couldn't tell what the next machine was. It was completely covered in rust from its handles to its engine box. It looked like it had been exposed to the weather for some years. One of the four wheels was off, so the box tilted to one side.

Pete and Birdie lived there and Pete stepped out of the open garage, wiping his hands on his shirt. "Quite a collection, eh?" He puffed up with pride as he gazed down the row of ancient tools. "Been collectin' them for years—using 'em till they died and then leavin' them to rust in the back yard." He laughed. "I couldn't bear to part with 'em, so didn't put them up for sale. Birdie thought I should put them out on display, seeing's how this town's bein' judged today for its unique lawn ornaments."

"What?" Margo scrutinized Pete's face. "How did you get the idea that we were being judged on 'unique' lawn ornaments?"

Pete frowned and rubbed the stubble on his chin. "Well, if this ain't makin' our village stand out, I don't know what will. Terry said you told her the contest was for the most iconic village in the Kootenays. Now, every village is likely to have nice flowers, and we have plenty of maple trees, so as neighbours on this street, we decided to go with something we thought would make our village unique. You're the one who inspired it with our 'lawn ornaments' yard sale. And then, Terry says she heard you say that her booths in the back of her store were 'iconic.' So, we thought, what better way to stand out than with our iconic lawn ornaments? Take a look!" Pete shuffled to the corner and invited Margo to come with him to look down the street. His gap-tooth smile widened with pride.

Margo lifted her eyes and choked back a gasp. "Oh, my goodness!"

Just yesterday, she had walked down Maple Street, pleased about how much work her neighbours had put into tidying up their yards and driveways. The village seemed to have rekindled its sense of civic pride. Wannatoka Springs' two parallel streets almost looked like they could be suburban streets somewhere with the gracious Maple trees lining each side, lawns mowed, new plantings in front of houses and vehicles neatly parked in driveways that were now clear of eyesores and junk.

This morning, as far as she could see down the street lawns were littered with all manner of old junk. "You all planned to put these . . . uh . . . lawn ornaments out—just for today?"

"Yup!" Pete looked like he would burst with pride.

"Thought we'd surprise you. It was all Terry's idea. Terry spread the word that we should all make a personal display with something iconic. She didn't want to say anything to you 'cause she knew how hard you were workin' to beautify the lawns and didn't want to add to your burden. So whadaya think? Maple Street will most certainly grab the judges' attention, don't ya think?" He spread his hands as if writing a sign in the sky, "Wannatoka Springs. Your destination for iconic lawn ornaments!"

"Terry was right! This certainly caught me by surprise! Wannatoka Springs will certainly be a memorable stop for the judges today. Iconic lawn ornaments."

Strolling down Maple St, Margo's eyes took in every cliché of organized gizmos and whirly-gigs she could imagine and some she could not. One lawn had a collection of bird feeders hanging off the branches of an apple tree. Another had a line of solar lights of every shape—flowers, wands, butterflies, crosses, and flames— marching up the sidewalk and outlining the front of the house. Garden gnomes with yellow and black striped hats and red noses peeked out from around the bushes, eying her with mischievous looks on their faces. Here, a bare-breasted mermaid spewed water into a stone fountain. There, a little boy with his pants down to his ankles peed into a flowerbed. Pale-coloured paper lan- terns in the shape of wasps' nests were strung under an eve, and un-naturally bright plastic flowers decorated the bare spaces of gardens between bushes.

Although it fought for first place in her assessment, Margo thought the prize for the unique display of lawn ornaments was a collection of moving lawn sprinklers. There was a nest of connected hoses running to a plastic candle tube with a sparkler at the top that created a prism when it spun with the water pressure, a miniature windmill that ran a miniature water wheel, a twirling copper gyroscope atop a copper stand, and a toy-sized red fire truck racing a yellow tractor up and down the hose tracks they ran on with the water pressure, spraying the lawn with water in both directions. Margo was mesmerized. Who thought that up? And who would buy it? Obviously, one of Margo's neighbours did.

Tina stepped out of her house to meet Margo and stopped to look at the front yard across the street. The lawn across the street from Tina had bloomed overnight into a field of plastic and wire flowers, larger-than-life bees and brightly coloured birds on metal stands poked into the ground, their wings and petals whirling lazily around and a round in the light breeze.

"Can you believe it? This morning, when I took a peek out my window to see how light it was, I couldn't believe what I saw! All this . . ." She swivelled around to take in all angles of her street, "was done last night!"

"How? . . ." Margo gestured up and down the street, her question unformed. "And you didn't hear anything?" Margo asked.

"Nothing unusual. I sleep with earplugs, and Joel is a sound sleeper. He wouldn't wake up even if the sirens went off and the house was burning down! I faintly heard some noise outside. I thought it was just kids fooling around."

"I just can't believe our neighbours came up with this! What were they thinking?"

Tina gave Margo a side hug. "Look on the bright side!"

Margo stared at her darkly, "What bright side?"

"Uh . . ." Tina looked around. Even sparkling Tina was struggling to find the bright side. "The lawn ornaments on some of the lawns are very creatively arranged! Look at that one on Mrs. Halverson's yard." Tina pointed to a row of twirling windmill ornaments in the shapes of flowers, birds, planes, and traffic cops directing traffic—sorted from smallest to largest, arms slowly winding around in the light breeze that ruffled the maple tree leaves.

Margo recognized some of them. "I saw those in some of the boxes on tables. She must have rooted through every box and bought every windmill lawn ornament she could find!"

"And did you see Fred's front yard? His wife, Evelyn, bought the plaster fountain with the mermaid with naked breasts, spitting out water from her mouth, and a unicorn that lights up with fairy lights."

"How is this the bright side, exactly?"

Tina smiled. "Because it shows the unique spirit of Wanatoka Springs. Wannatoka Springs—an iconic Kootenay village!"

"Beautiful morning, isn't it!" Tina waved at her neighbour, Evelyn, across the street. Evelyn was setting up the lawn chairs she and Fred planned to occupy while the judges came through. She told Margo they wanted to have a watch party when the judges passed by, so they were setting up half a dozen chairs on their lawn behind and around the bare-breasted mermaid fountain, with a couple of over-turned five-gallon pails between them for stands to put a beverage on an ashtray so visitors and themselves could toke and smoke and drink a cold one— like they liked to do on a summer afternoon. They said they might offer a cold one to the judges as they passed by. Nothin' more Kootenay iconic than that, Evelyn said with a broad smile and invited Margo to bring Michael around later for a beer.

Margo could envision the judges walking by Fred and Evelyn's place on Maple Street, pot wafting through the air, waved over to share a beer or a toke.

As for the judges. They came. They saw. They left. When Margo watched the rear view of the last car of the three judges leave the village and head down the highway toward Crystal Lake, she knew what their impressions must have been. And they would be unlikely to score the outcome she had such high hopes of achieving.

In the month following the competition, Margo's disappointment slid into resignation and indifference. She and Tina attended one last meeting of the Community Service Club. Margo put on a brave face, thanked everyone for their enthusiastic participation in her Yard and Junk Sale, and reported that $6000.00 was raised to support the schoolhouse roof fund. Then she announced that they had not won the Most Iconic Kootenay Village contest, but she was so proud of her neighbour's efforts and so happy to get to know the positive people of this town better.

Margo and Tina were commended for their efforts and consoled by Ronnie about the contest's outcome, "But Wannatoka Springs got a boost. And it brought out so much community interaction. It was wonderful to see our village get behind a common cause and move a lot of collectibles!" Ronnie shot a conspiratorial look at Margo when she said this. And Margo realized she had a lot to learn from Ronnie about acceptance of where she was and who her neighbours were.

***

"It's MY retirement! My time to do whatever I want to do. And it should be FUN! When it turns into work, I'm D-O-N-E!" Margo announced with emphasis.

Tina and Margo sat in one of the booths at the back of Terry's store, sipping coffee out of paper cups and unwrapping the plastic from a cinnamon bun they intended to share. They brought the coffee and bun with them, two paper plates, napkins, and two sets of plastic forks and knives, which they had helped themselves to from Terry's coffee bar at the front of the store. Under her arm, Margo carried a copy of this month's Kootenay

Voice, a paper published and distributed for free in the area.

Tina turned the pages. She read the headlines aloud: *Houseboat washed up on shore. Stuck in mud flats. Will be burned if not claimed, Local man wanted for stealing an ATV. Was last seen driving down Main Street in Crystal Lake around eight-thirty am.* "I guess he decided to stop for coffee before he hid the ATV," Tina snorted. Margo rolled her eyes—old news. "Oh. . . now this one's scary . . . A cougar was seen walking down Spruce St. in Wannatoka Springs late at night." Margo sat forward, alarmed. Tina looked up slyly and back down at the paper. "A witness said she was about sixty-five, wearing pink tights and hot pants and had curly red hair. Last seen walking . . ." Margo nearly spat out her coffee. She kicked Tina under the table. Tina burst out laughing.

"Stop! You had me scared for a minute."

"Oh! Margo! Look!" Tina's eyes widened. She laid the paper down and turned the page around so Margo could see the picture. Featured in full colour were the two booths, one of which they were sitting in, the cracked, torn vinyl seats patched together with bumper stickers and decals. A formica tabletop with etchings and cigarette burns stood between each bench on rust-spotted chrome columns.

The article's caption read, *Iconic restaurant booths makes a statement during the Iconic Kootenay Village Contest.* The article went on to describe Terry's General Store in Wannatoka Springs. *A must-stop on the way to the ferry. Buy a coffee and sit in the back, imagining you are back in the seventies sitting in a booth at your local truck stop.* Beside the picture of the booths was a picture of Terry with a coffee pot in hand, standing behind the counter of her store. A quote below the photo reads, *"'These booths are iconic!' So said my neighbour Margo Gator. That comment inspired me to tell her we ought to run for the most iconic village in the Kootenays! Too bad we didn't win. But it was worth the effort!"*

Margo looked up from reading the article and pointed at her name. "They spelled my name wrong! It's g-a-e-t-e-r. They spelled it like the abbreviation for the reptile!"

"They did," Tina said, squinting at the small print. "Oh well, Look on the bright side! At least you got your name in print! And it's attached to the story of our iconic village, Wannatoka Springs." Tina beamed.

Coffee carafe in hand, Terry swished importantly to the back of the store where they were sitting, "Yup! We're on the map!" Terry filled their cups without asking. "Don't expect this service every time, now. Even if Terry's General Store and Cafe *is* iconic." She extracted two packets of sugar and two creamers from her apron and set them on the table, "Well, maybe for my two favourite gals in Wannatoka Springs, but don't get used to it." She winked and then wheeled around when she heard the bells on the door clang announcing the entrance of a customer. "What can I do for you, dear?" Terry called out as she walked back to the counter at the front of the store, "Did you hear my store got written up in the paper? 'Iconic', they said."

"I said 'ironic,'" Margo said in a hoarse whisper. "I said her booths were ironic."

Tina propped her head to one side and said brightly. "One person's ironic is another's iconic,"

Margo snorted a laugh.

When they had drained their coffee and licked the last of the cinnamon bun syrup from their fingers, Tina and Margo claimed their paper cups, plastic wrap, and utensils and gave the counter a cursory wipe with a paper napkin. Terry's only rule: leave it like you found it.

Margo scooted out of the booth bench. Her summer dress had ridden up in the back, leaving her bare thighs to sweat against the non-porous vinyl. A farting sound ripped from the vinyl seat as she slid across it.

"Now that's iconic!" Tina said with a girlish giggle.

Margo glared. "I said—IRONIC!"

CHAPTER NINE

Father Bart Blesses the Animals on St. Francis Day

"What? *You?* Going to church?" Michael looked up from his phone. He was studying the stats of the rookie players in the preseason NHL hockey games. He wasn't much for watching a full game of hockey anymore—took up too much time and space, he said. But he still like to follow the stats and keep an informal ledger of who the best players on each team were, and, in preseason, evaluate the rookies and make calculated predictions about which ones would be contenders for rookie of the year.

Margo answered Michael's question with her question. "Why *not* me?"

"Just surprised, that's all. Never heard you mention any desire to go to church before. In fact, you have always tried to avoid 'churchy' people."

"This is different. This is a service for pets." Margo balanced her reading glasses on her nose and read from her phone, the announcement she had been reading in *The Wannatoka Times.*

St. Francis Feast and Blessings of the animals at our very own St. Mary's Catholic Church is sponsoring a special mass on Sunday, October

Margo swivelled in her recliner to face Michael and pushed her reading glasses up onto her forehead, pushing back stray curls that had fallen forward into her face.

"A pet blessing church service? That's new." Michael said indifferently and went back to scrolling through his hockey app.

"Not really," Margo said. "I looked up St. Francis of Assisi." Margo propped up her phone and extended it to Michael. "Patron saint of animals and the environment. See?" Margo held out her phone to Michael. Michael looked up from his phone and squinted at the sketch of a bearded man in a long robe with a circle of light around his head. His arms were outstretched heavenward and on one hand a bird perched. Other birds circled around him and, at his feet were woodland animals, a deer, a wolf, a raccoon and a rabbit—predator and prey encircling their patron saint in rapt attention.

"That's a fairy tale if I ever heard one. Just proves my suspicion that church is for children. And now we can add pets apparently." Michael looked down at his screen again.

"I think it will be nice. Another opportunity to meet the neighbours and socialize. And why not. What better things do we have to do in our retirement. It'll be fun!"

Michael grunted. The clincher of Margo's argument was always 'It'll be fun'. That's what they had committed to do their retirement: having fun. Making up for all the times they prioritized work over fun.

"OK. I'll come along. If only to humour you my dear." A half smile played on his lips. He was imagining the cacophony of neighbours and their pets filling the pews of the tiny white church on the corner of their street. "You're right. It might be fun."

"Good." It's settled. I'll talk to Eunice. She's the one who posted this. I'll ask her what I can bring and if I can help set up."

Eunice lived in upper Wannatoka Springs on Willow Street. Unlike the two parallel streets of Spruce and Maple with sectioned lots for single houses, upper Wannatoka was comprised of acreages ranging from half an acre to five acre properties. The partially forested area with cleared fields would have been where the original fruit orchards and mixed farms that sustained the families who were first moved here from the valley below. Most were just managed as acreages now.

Margo drove to Eunice's home. She could have walked but it was October and she was wary of encounters with bears. She had read in The Wannatoka Times that there was one large male black bear hanging around the old orchard up there and stuffing himself with plums from trees that had grown like weeds in the wildness of the neglected acreage.

Eunice was a widow. At eighty years old, she was slim, cheerful and always on the go. Whether it was attending a social event, driving or shopping for her elderly neighbours who were more housebound than she was, or working on her own acreage, she always kept herself busy. She still lived in the farm house she had her husband moved into when they were first married. When there was a school at Wannatoka Springs, she had been the school secretary and her husband drove the dairy truck, delivering dairy products from the farms on the other side of the lake to all the stores in the valley. When he passed away, he left Eunice to continue to care for their only son, a man who was now in his late fifties, but whose mental age was that of a ten-year-old.

Terrance had grown up in the relative safety and shelter of this tiny community. He knew everyone and their dog. And everyone and their dog knew Terrance. Going to school was a trial for him, as he only learned to read at the grade two level and his innocence and gullibility made him an easy target for bullies and pranksters. Eunice pulled him from school after he repeated grade three and grade six twice. She was a practical mother and didn't see the point in her thirteen-year-old boy repeating the same times tables, trying to read the same books he failed to grasp the first time around and repeating the same science and social studies curriculum.

An early adopter of homeschooling, Eunice determined that her son would learn more practical things by working around the farm. Terrance's mind was made for practical and literal learning. He learned how life began and ended and the value of produce by raising pigs and chickens and selling eggs; he won prizes at the local fair for his livestock entries. His father taught him to whittle and carve to enhance his fine muscle movement.

Terrance took an interest in nature, particularly birds. He identified birds that came to nest in the trees on their acreage and their migration patterns by what times of year they would appear and disappear. Carving real life likenesses of the birds he watched was a natural extension of his interest. He then taught himself to painted them in the colours he observed, with meticulous care.

In the summer, he would sit down by the ferry landing and sell his carved birds, telling anyone who stopped by his table waiting for the next ferry, about the birds in the area, their habitat, what kind of food they liked to eat, who their enemies were, and their nesting habits. Travellers often bought a bird from Terrance just to remember the occasion of meeting the young naturalist.

Not surprisingly, Terrance's observations of birds as he wandered the property, led to finding injured and abandoned birds. Babies who had fallen out of their nest too early, birds who had a broken wing or beak, or even puncture wounds from a fight with another bird or an injury sustained when a bird of prey attacked but failed to capture them.

Eunice coached her son gently to release the young ones when he had raised them to maturity, and the injured when they could become self-sufficient again. The lame or the blind, she allowed Terrance to keep in the old barn on their property as long as he cared for them humanely and kept the place tidy. Over the years, Terrance kept a menagerie of birds, both those he found, and brought there to heal from wounds or grow to maturity before they could be released and those that would not be able to cope in the wild, who would live with dignity, without fear of predators despite their disabilities.

It was Terrance idea to organize a St. Francis Feast day. Eunice, a practicing Catholic, had read stories to Terrance about the saints and martyrs, which she considered to be part of his religious education. She often paraphrased the stories, highlighting the charities and goodness of the saints, since Terrance wouldn't have understood the hard words, but always read them out of a book so Terrance wouldn't feel like he was less than anyone else because he couldn't read himself.

When he was a boy, he was enthralled with the gory stories about saints who had been beheaded or boiled to death for their non-repentance to the tyrants, although he hated hearing that their punishment was to be drawn and quartered because that meant that horses were made to inflict the suffering. He had a strong sense that animals would never hurt anything or anyone unless they did it to survive or to eat. He knew that only humans would hurt others for no good reason.

Of all the saints and heroes of the church, Terrance was particularly transfixed by St. Francis, a monk who talked to and prayed for the animals. Ever since the first time his mother read him the story of how he blessed the animals had wished he could be just like St. Francis when he grew up. He had cut out a drawing he found of St. Francis, a halo around his bearded face looking skyward with arms held up to heaven. Birds perched on his shoulders and woodland creatures gathered around him. He glued it onto a piece of wood he carefully sanded, and hung it in his room. Even after almost four decades, as mother and son observed saint's days, when it came to October's saint—St. Francis—Terrance made that declaration that when he grew up, he wanted to be just like his hero.

Eunice would hug her son and affirm his dream, but a pang of sadness because she knew her boy, unlike other boys, would never grow up to live out the fantasy of what he would be when he grew up. The thought was sweetened by the thought that Terrance would always be a boy living with the innocent hope for his future. In Eunice's mind, Terrance was been guided by his patron saint, St. Francis, to welcome wildlife around him and accept that their lives were valuable.

Terrance's father died when Terrance was ten-years-old. When he knew he was dying, Terrance's father said to his wife and son, "I hate the thought of leaving you, but it looks like I gotta go. But I take comfort in knowing you will take care of each other like always."

Terrance had seen death in animals so he knew his father was moving out of his home, his body, and he would not be able to talk with him or see him again. He felt sad and thought of the little birds he had buried behind the barn. He assured his father that he would take care of his mom. Eunice had shed her tears in private. She didn't want Terrance to be distraught over her own grief of losing her life partner and her uncertainty for the future being left the sole carer of their son.

Many years had passed since then and Eunice and Terrance fell into a happy rhythm that both supported and maintained their independence while caring for each other and, together, caring for the land they had always lived on together.

Margo stood at the white front door with an outer screen door framed in a light blue scalloped edge. When she opened the screen door, it squeaked on its hinges just as Margo imagined a farm house screen doors should. She rapped softly on the wooden door. Hearing no response, she knocked a little harder and called out, "Hello? Eunice?" Eunice's neat little grey Toyota was parked in the carport beside the house. When she stopped to listen, Margo could only hear the sounds of birds chirping and the distant sound of a chainsaw coming from up the road. Someone was bucking up wood for the winter.

She was about to go back to her car to see if she could find a piece of paper and a pen to write a note— something she rarely did anymore she realized—since the invention of the messages app on her phone. But Eunice was an old-fashioned woman. She had a land- line. No cell. And an answering machine that reported it was full when Margo had tried to call earlier. When she turned to go down the steps, a man she didn't recognize stepped out from around the carport.

"Hi!" he said with an open grin, one palm waving in an arc. "May I help you?"

Margo had never met Terrance, Eunice's son. But she had heard she had an adult son who was mentally delayed, who knew everyone by their dog's name. The man's boyish mannerism and openness in his face put her at ease immediately.

"I'm here to talk to Eunice. Would that be your mother?"

The man grinned wider and nodded. "Yes, Eunice is my mom." He stood there nodding but offered nothing further.

"Oh! Good! I have the right house then! I am a new neighbour. My name is Margo. My husband and I moved into the house on Spruce street."

Terrance nodded. "I seen you around. You have a yellow dog. I seen you walkin' him."

Margo smiled. "That's right. His name is Chance."

"Chance." He repeated and snorted. "That's a funny name for a dog. Did he take a chance on you when you adopted him?" He smiled into his hand, self-consciously concealing his delight at his joke. His pale blue eyes danced.

Margo returned his smile. "Something like that. Actually, we thought we took a chance adopting him. But, now that you mention it, he was probably thinking he was taking a chance on us!" Her smile broadened. The humour bridged the gap between them and they both relaxed.

"And what's your name?" Margo asked.

"Terrance."

"Pleased to meet you, Terrance. Is your mom home?"

"Yup. She lives here."

"Do you think I could talk to her? I read her post about the St. Francis Day Feast and blessing of the animals and I was wondering what I could do to help."

At the mention of St. Francis Day, Terrance's eyes widened and he lost every trace of shyness. "Oh! St. Francis Day. St. Francis my patron saint. He blessed the animals and prayed for them and the earth and every-thing. I want to be just like him when I grow up. And on St. Francis Sunday, we are allowed to bring our pets to church. Father Bart is going to bless our pets and the earth and everything." Terrance stretched out his hands to indicate the land and wildlife that surrounded him.

Margo could see that this day meant more to this

simple man than she could have imagined. Before her stood a true disciple of St. Francis. The thought moved her more than she expected.

Just at that moment, Eunice opened the front door. Blinking, she stared at Margo and then at her son. "Heard some voices out front. I was just lying' down for a nap. Who's here Terrance?" She rubbed the glasses she held in her hand on her shirt and fitted them onto her face while studying Margo's.

"This is our new neighbour. She has a dog named Chance." Terrance said.

"Oh?" Eunice looked from her son to Margo and then back at her son, "And does she have a name?"

"I'm Margo," Margo stepped forward. Unsure if she should extend her hand or not, she flexed her right arm but then clasped her left hand with her right.

"And she wants to help out with St. Francis Day at the church!" Terrance beamed at Margo and then at his mother.

Eunice stepped down the three stairs, and stretched out her right hand. "Welcome, Margo. Good to meet you." Margo extended her own hand and felt the older woman's cool dry papery skin for a moment, then released it. Eunice's smile crinkled her parchment face, all the way up to her eyes.

"So! You want to be a volunteer for St. Francis Day."

"I want to inquire if I could help in some way. I'm not a Catholic. I've never attended a St. Francis Day pet service before. Or, any Catholic service —or even a Christian one in a long time. Hope that' isn't an issue. The post did say anyone was welcome to attend. And I thought it would be a nice way to get to know more of our neighbours. My husband and I just bought the house two properties down from the church and well, it looks so inviting, but so empty. I just thought that was sad. And we would love to get to know more of our neighbours here, so . . . ." Margo knew her explanation was becoming too long but Eunice listened intently without interrupting. "So . . . " she stopped leaving the sentence hanging.

Eunice nodded and smiled. "Anyone in the community is welcome to get involved. It's not an exclusive club. Not enough Catholics left to make it that, even if we wanted to, which we don't. Well, you'd better come in for a cup of tea, then. I'll tell you all about it," Eunice said. And with a curt nod, mother and son turned abruptly and walked back up the stairs, expecting Margo to follow.

Margo looked at Terrance who was still standing in the same spot, smiling and bobbing his head in agreement. "Mom made blueberry pie today. I'll bet that's what she'll serve with tea. She makes the best pie in the whole of Wannatoka Springs."

"Sounds lovely! Will you be joining us for tea?"

Terrance let out a flighty giggle. "No. Tea is for mom's friends. But I might come in to get a piece of pie." And then, remembering his manners his posture and tone became more formal. "After you ma'am," he said, gesturing with an open palm towards the partly open front door.

"Thank you, Terrance." Margo said and then added, "you can call me Margo or Ms. Margo. But please don't call me ma'am." She patted his arm for emphasis.

Terrance nodded soberly and repeated. "After you . . . Ms. Margo," He enunciated her name clearly and held the door open for her like the perfect gentleman his mother had taught him to be.

Terrance led Margo into the small living room and asked her to please be seated; his mother would join her soon. Margo sat down on the worn grey-blue sofa that was flanked by a smaller sized rocker-recliner upholstered in a rose print with a knitting bag beside it filled with pastel coloured wool. Opposite the sofa sat a dark brown leather recliner, creased and cracked with age. A a magazine holder beside it held a picture book with birds on the cover. That must have been where Eunice's husband when he was alive, Margo imagined. And now, perhaps, judging from the subject of the book in the magazine stand, the chair Terrance sat in when he kept his mother company.

A wooden upright piano at one end of the room took up most of one wall. Three framed photos sat on it, one was an old-fashioned black and white wedding photo of a young couple that Margo assumed that was of Eunice and her husband. One was of a young mother sitting with baby in her arms—Eunice with her son Terrance. The third the third was a coloured photo of a boy in a maroon sweater, white shirt and tie, hair parted neatly on one side, staring seriously at the camera. Margo recognized the school photo format.

The rest of the piano shelf was crowded with woodcarvings of birds. Birds of all species, sizes and colours, carefully painted to capture their natural colouring and features. Margo stood and walked over to the piano to have a closer look. She was admiring the skill and detail put into each one when Eunice came in with a silver tray bearing the tea things and pie.

"Those are Terrance's. Aren't they just beautiful? Such a talent that boy has for carving. Self taught you know. When he was nine his father gave him a pocket knife for his birthday and taught him to whittle. When Terrance was about twelve, he started carving birds—the birds he observed. I wish his father had lived to see his accomplishments." Eunice shook her head sadly and set the tray down on the coffee table then walked up behind Margo to explain her son's hobby. "When he really got into it, I found a book for him that had detailed pictures on carving. After that it was 'I need this tool to carve the eyes and make the feathers,' or 'I want to paint my birds but I need this paint'. I always said he had to work for whatever he wanted, so he would do chores around the house at the beginning to earn the money for tools and paint, but soon he began to sell them. He's sold enough over the years to not only pay for his hobby but to put a little away so he always has an independent income. He uses some of his money to equip the bird sanctuary he has fashioned out of that old barn out back. Have you seen it? It's been the temporary home of all sorts of hurt, fledgling, or lost birds he somehow comes across in his wanderings. He rehabilitates them if he can, and then sets them free to live in the wild again. Or if the disability cannot be rehabbed, he manages to find space in sanctuary for them."

"That's remarkable!" Margo said, still looking over the bird collection.

"Come and sit down dear. I've made a pot of tea and happened to have a couple of slices of blueberry pie left. Good thing, too! Terrance doesn't leave fresh pie sitting on the counter very long." On the coffee table, Eunice arranged a fine china tea set with a pansy floral pattern, and two matching plates each with a slice of blueberry pie and a silver fork—on the coffee table in front of the sofa.

"Blueberry pie from fresh picked blueberries this summer—and frozen," Eunice said proudly. Margo took a bite. The pastry was exquisitely light and flakey; the blueberries plump and juicy in a light syrup

"Delicious." Margo complimented Eunice.

"I bake a pie every week. Terrance likes pie. He can put a whole pie away in one sitting if he were left to it. But I've told h he's not a growing boy anymore. It's got to be a balance or he won't fit into his clothes! And if that happens, I won't be baking any more pie. He's learned to restrain himself, but its not been easy."

Margo's fork paused half way to her mouth as Eunice explain that, silently wondering if she should imposed the pie restraint order on herself. "Mmmm . . . " she said in acknowledgement, and resumed eating her pie.

As Margo drank her tea and listened to Eunice explain their history, her eyes drank in the setting. Here was a woman who had been content to be what she was her whole life, and took pride in her home, her possessions and her family. And who effortlessly shared her gift of hospitality. Her housekeeping was immaculate, as if it was ready anytime to entertain visitors. Even the most humble, impromptu visit was an invitation to bring out the best china and silverware.

When the wall clock chimed four, Margo signalled her leave taking by setting her empty cup and saucer and well-scraped pie plate on the tray. "This has been a wonderfully visit, Eunice, but I really hadn't intended to take up so much of your time. I do apologize for interrupting your afternoon nap."

"Not at all, my dear!" Eunice retorted. "The Lord gives us the day to work and the night to rest. I just like to cheat a little in the afternoon these days. But I'm sure it will catch up with me when I finally rest in peace!" Eunice chortled, then crossed herself and winked, as if to sign that God was complicit in her joke."

***

The fall in Wannatoka Springs is a cornucopia of splendid colours. The maple trees lining Maple Street turn a burnished shade of red, complemented by the yellow and orange leaves of the hazelnut, oak and birch trees. The sky-scraping dark green sentries, sixty-year-old coniferous trees that grew up with the community form a somber backdrop. Eunice had been praying earnestly for a splendid sunny, fall day for the St. Francis Day blessing of the animals, one that would invite admiration for the glory of the earth. Despite her earnest petitions, what started out as a promising dawn with clear skies and a glorious sunrise, disintegrated by mid morning into a murky, glowering cloudscape that threatened rain.

Margo, Eunice and three other volunteers including Terrance had worked hard all morning to set up for the pot-luck feast on the church lawn. The night before, Michael and Joel used Joel's truck to pick up and deliver chairs and nine collapsible tables from the community hall. They had set the tables up in a square formation. The chairs lined each side of the long tables. Another table off to one side, would be used as the buffet table for folks to drop off their goodies to share for the pot luck. The volunteers had rolled out and taped down sheets of white plastic around each table. Now wind gusts ruffled the edges and ballooned the spaces between the tape threatening to tear the table covers off. Terrance patiently reinforced the tape, and smoothed the plastic out again. Despite the increasing threat of foul weather, Eunice marshalled the small crew with her optimism and enthusiasm. "It can't rain on the Lord's day! Especially not on St. Augustine's Blessing! He wouldn't be pleased.

Margo wasn't so optimistic. But she kept reminding herself that she didn't have any sway with the powers that be, so she may as well go along with those who thought they did and be there to volunteer to help if things didn't quite work out as anticipated. After two years year of retirement and living in her newly adopted community, Margo had learned that outcomes were not always predictable. More than once, she had to adapt her plans and make the most of the ride! This was a big step for Margo, the teacher who had lived by setting outcomes and planning lessons to meet them.

As the crew was setting up, a sleek grey early

2000s Crown Victoria pulled up and parked beside the church lawn. Eunice glanced up from her work. Recognizing the occupant, she waved as enthusiastically as a child.

"Father Bart!" She called and scuttled toward the car, holding down the hem of her knee length dress with one hand, as a gust of wind threatened to lift the hem. "Praise the Lord! You are safe and sound!"

First to emerge was the crown of a man's head, a cap of short brown hair, neatly parted on the side. Next, his upturned face, round and cherubic, gave him a boyish appearance, although clearly he was a man in his late fifties or early sixties.

"Safe, to be sure! But sound? I'll not be taking bets on that!" The priest slid with some effort out from behind the steering wheel of his car which scraped his belly, and heaved himself out of the car holding onto the door with one hand, the other gripping the frame. The suspension sprang back up with the relief upon his exit.

Dressed in a black suit jacket and black pants which did very little to disguise his rotund figure, with the traditional black clerical shirt and the white band at the neck indicating his vocation, the priest mopped his sweating forehead with a white kerchief he produced from his pocket and then touched his cap of brown hair, seeming to adjust it, ensuring his hair was in its place. He wore a smile that reached around his face and raised his cheeks into two bright red balls. His dancing blue eyes found Margo's inquisitive ones, immediately endearing him to Margo.

Lifting his arms, embracing the air he called out. "I'm here by the grace of God to celebrate with you God's presence!"

Eunice clasped both of her hands in front of her and beamed. "So good to see you made it here." Eunice said. "I hope your journey went well."

"As well as it could be," Father Bart replied, "But

I can't say the same for this weather! Looks like a storm is brewing!" He glanced up at the darkening sky. "And we all know the Almighty doesn't adjust nature to suit our plans! But we'll make do. We'll make do." He affirmed himself. Then he noticed Margo.

"And who might this be?" He asked, extending a hand. "A new member of the flock?" Margo automatically stuck out her hand in exchange and he grasped it with both, pudgy hands now clammy from the brief exertion. "Father Bartholomew," he introduced himself warmly, "But please call me Father Bart. Everyone does. Although I'm not as popular as the famous Bart Simpson, but I'm blessed with that name and I claimed it first!" He chuckled and held her hand while he talked.

"Pleased to me you Father Bart." She said and smiled. "Margo Gaetor. We are practically neighbours—I mean your church is. My husband, Michael, and I live two houses down from the church, not that we attend church. Well, I suppose no one does now. I mean, Eunice and Terrance would of course, and I'm sure there are other faithful members of the church who would if there were services. But my husband and I aren't Catholic. Or anything really, so . . ." She didn't know quite how to go on from there. She thought she had already spoken too much, as was her habit when she was nervous. Meeting a priest made her nervous. She had never met one before. Did he have some kind of spiritual x-ray vision? Could he see directly into her soul?

Father Bart came to her rescue. "It is lovely to have you in attendance today, neighbour Margo. We are all part of the family of God in some way or another. We don't have to practice to be part of that family. Just welcome God's love." He released his hands and turned to Eunice, both arms outstretched. She almost stumbled in her eagerness to connect with Father Bart. "Eunice, my daughter. How are you?" Father Bart held both of

Eunice's hands and leaned towards to kiss her lightly on both cheeks while he said softly and kindly, "I greet you in the name of Christ."

Eunice blushed a little. "And you also, Father," she responded. Pulling herself straight, she gestured toward Terrance whose long shadow was cast over both of them as if in a group embrace. "You remember my son, Terrance?"

"Indeed I do!" Father Bart squinted up at Terrance and stuck out his hand in a formal greeting. Terrance shook the Father's hand once and let it go. "How are you my son? Still whittling those most exquisite bird carvings?"

Terrance grinned at the acknowledgement. Although he wasn't sure what 'most exquisite' meant, he took it as a compliment. "Yes Father." he nodded.

"And still caring for God's sparrows?"

Terrance frowned. "More than just sparrows. There's wrens and jays, and winter robins, and, oh—I got a pet crow."

"Of course my son. I only referenced sparrows because "God keeps his eye on the sparrow . . . so much more will he care for you."

"Oh, I keep my eye on them sparrows, too, Father. You should see my barn." Terrance puffed up with pride.

"He has more injured and disabled birds than ever! Don't you dear." Eunice filled in, looking at Terrance and nodding approvingly.

Terrance grinned and looked down shyly, stubbing the toe of his boot in the grass as a distraction.

Father Bart put a hand up and, reaching Terrance's shoulder, he offered an impromptu blessing. Bowing his head he recited, "For caring for all of God's creatures, we are grateful and bless this, your humble servant, Amen." With that he squeezed Terrance's shoulder firmly and lowered his hand. A smile flickered across Terrance's lips. He looked down at Father Bart's benevolent smile as he pronounced "Amen" and then, embarrassed, he stared at the ground again and mumbled, "Amen".

"Now then," Father Bart said as he clapped his hands together and rubbed them in anticipation, "Where are we with the blessing of the animals? Can you show me around, Terrance? I trust that you will be my assistant as you have the gift of caring for animals. Will the service take place outdoors?" He looked around at the tables set for the luncheon to follow.

Terrance snapped out of his bashful self. His eyes lit up with excitement. This was to be his moment. Assisting the Father with the blessing was akin to enacting the role of St. Francis when he prayed and blessed the animals outdoors in the picture his room that Terrance had studied so many times it was etched in his memory. He imagined himself calling a group of birds and woodland animals around himself, with his pet crow, JJ, sitting on his shoulder.

"This way Father." Terrance led the priest toward the entrance of the little white church. He had planned it all out weeks in advance. The animals would be grouped around the steps of the church, arranged by species and size. Terrance didn't want to mix dogs and cats together or cats and rodents so he had used a chalk line marker used for marking out strips of sod, to create a half pie sectioned off into places for where people with the various categories of pets could stand in the grass. Little plastic signs used for identifying vegetables in a garden were stuck into the ground at the apex of the triangle, identifying the group of animals that could stand with their human in that area.

"You see, Father," Terrance explained as he took the two steps up to door in one giant step up, "You will be standing on the steps, here." Terrance turned on his heel to face the priest and his invisible audience. "So, you can look down on the animals as you bless them." To demonstrate his point, Terrance outstretched his right arm and, palm down, rotated it around slowly as if performing a blessing over the heads of his parishioners.

"That's just the thing, my boy! Ingenious! Delightful!" He clapped his hands and punctuated his commendation with hearty laugh.

Terrance looked down, embarrassed at the priest's enthusiasm. He held his hands behind his back, a half-smile played on his lips. Eunice made a triangle with her hands, held them over her nose and pinched the corners of her eyes to stop the tears that had formed unexpectedly. She was so proud. Her boy had won the Father's praise.

Standing a little farther away, Margo looked on, and then up at the troubled sky and frowned. She wondered how long it would be before the thunderstorm she heard rumbling in the distance would be upon them.

Father Bart, who had positioned himself on the steps where Terrance had shown him to stand, solemnly bowed his head and murmured a prayer, then lifted his head, made the sign of the cross and clapped his hands together and he merrily threw out the words. "Now let's get this party started!" as he opened the door and launched his unwieldy body into the sanctuary. Eunice and Terrance followed not far behind him.

Just as the door closed, Margo heard a rumble of thunder. Closer than the last, but still far away. An ominous sign, she thought. Perhaps the god of thunder was just getting the party started. She walked into the church herself and shut the door behind her, just ahead of the storm.

An hour later after the storm abated, as storms in the Kootenays will, leaving the church lawn soggy and the neatly chalked lines Terrance marked, smudged and all-but erased in places. A small, nervous crowd of neighbours accompanied by their beloved pets were assembled in front of the church. So, today, the normally quiet, sedate church grounds were inundated with the chaos and language of dogs straining on leashes: yipping Shiatsus and Chihuahuas, barking Terriers, growling cats, rodents scrabbling in their carriers, and one parrot squawking out obscenities— whose owner kept telling her to mind her manners.

With his pet crow sitting on his shoulder, complaining loudly Terrance tried to organize the chaos into tidy quadrants. Like a ferry guide loading cars onto the ferry, he pointed with one arm straight out at one pair at a time, calling out the name of the dog he recognized, and signalling the dog with their owner to come forward.

With hand gestures signalling them to move to the left or right of the pair already in place and holding his hand up for them to stop when he thought they had parked close enough, Terrance directed the participants into the categories he had planned out. After the dogs were in place, he called out to the cat owners to take up their space, pointing to the far end. In between he sandwiched the various other pets in their cages along with their owners. Margo was impressed at how calm Terrance was, and how he took charge and how the gathering formed into an orderly audience around the steps, without question or argument.

Margo stood at the back of the small crowd, collaring her dog Chance who was restlessly surveying the other dogs. She took her place at the back since her dog was a larger breed than most—and Terrance had indicated that the little ones should come to the front.

Michael was directed to take his place with his cat in the carrier on the opposite side to the dogs. His weight shifted from one foot to the other as their large cat, Roscoe clawed at his carrier and threw himself from one side to the other, uttering imprecations and threats, indignant that he should suffer this incarceration.

As he approached the cat area, Michael slipped on the wet grass. Roscoe's carrier swung forward, as he slipped backward. It upended to the front when Roscoe slid forward and landed on the barred and latched entrance barrier. Michael looked down at the upended carrier and imagined for a split second Roscoe face-planted into the grass, forepaws struggling to hold his obese body up far enough so his nose didn't press against the bars.

"Oh, poor baby!" The exclamation came from above Michael who had fallen backward onto the ground. He shook his head and made a mental check of his body. Everything was intact. "Oh dear! My goodness! Here! Let me help you!" He heard Birdie sing out.

"I'm alright," Michael muttered and rolled over to kneel and then stand up. When he did, he saw that Birdie was not addressing him. She was talking to Roscoe whose cage she had set upright. Rosco had caught one paw outside the metal gate and was shaking it, in an effort to retract it.

Birdie had just squeezed the two spring latches that held the metal gate closed in order to open the gate so she could get Roscoe's paw out, when the thunder boomed and a sheet of lightning lit up the sky and rain started to pour out of it as if some capricious god had turned the cold water on the gathering.

The orderly formation Terrance had created broke into chaos. Owners shouted to take cover. A few owners, holding tightly to their pets' leashes and cages, stormed the front door of the church. Pets barked and screamed and yowled according to their vocal affinities. Dogs pranced and squirmed on their leashes and pets in carriers scrabbled to escape or tried to dig themselves in deeper in their instinctive fear.

On her shoulder, Birdie's parrot, Precious, let out a screech that sounded like a woman's scream, likely imitating her owner. Birdie's hand jerked away from the gate, flinging it wide open. Roscoe's paw was pulled forward. He pulled himself back, throwing his weight into it and extracting his paw from the grate. He cursed. Then, shrewdly assessing his chance of escape as he leapt out of the carrier and jumped into the low growing juniper hedge that skirted one side of the church steps.

When Michael recovered himself, he glanced at the carrier. The door was wide open and Roscoe was not inside. His eyes darted through the crowd and then searched the perimeter of the church. Just before he disappeared around the side, Michael spotted Roscoe wrestling his way through the juniper. He made his way as fast as he could through the maze and confusion, stepping over carriers, and playing hop scotch around leashes attached to small dogs frantically trying to escape to somewhere they would feel more safe. On the way, he bumped into Margo who was trying to quiet Chance. Not at all a calm dog, upon hearing the thunderclap, Chance went into paroxysms of fright. Margo was doing her best to calm him, one hand hanging onto his leash close to his collar and giving him soothing strokes on the head and behind his ears with the other, while muttering soothing words into his ear.

Roscoe's escaped!" Michael said, panting, as he approached the pair. "But don't worry, I got this."

Margo glanced up at Michael, then she quickly turned her attention back to the shaking and struggling dog in her grip. She didn't have time to worry about the cat.

A moment before the thunder struck, Terrance glanced nervously at the sky. He sensed that the heavy clouds were about to break and dump their amassed water. But before he could act, the thunder boomed at close range and a downpour followed with such force, it drowned out his command to take shelter.

Father Bart rocked to one side as the first of the dogs with owners in tow pushed past him, jockeying for position inside the sanctuary. He stumbled backward, grasping at the doorpost to keep himself upright.

Terrance's pet crow, JJ, who was perched on Terrance's shoulder, stopped screeching abruptly when the thunder roared and the lightening shuddered across the sky, wildly flapping his wings and winding himself up for flight.

As the priest leaned back, holding the doorpost, the crow lifted off Terrance's shoulder, flew through the open door, and landed on Father Bart's head. Disoriented and panicked, Father Bart, wobbled and clutched his hair. Then, showing surprising agility for a man of his girth, he pivoted and lurched up the aisle, holding both sides of his hair in his fists. The crow's claws locked into the priest's hair with a death grip as he rode atop the priest's head, flapping his wings as if to take off and propel both of them airborne. But the cargo was too much for him.

Terrance followed the priest and his crow with his eyes. Thoughts of putting the animals in order evaporated and were replaced with hurriedly assembled thoughts about how to extract his crow from the Father Bart's hair without injuring either of them. In hot pursuit, Terrance ran unceremoniously into the sanctuary, stopping himself just before he ran into trembling priest leaning against the baptismal font, hanging onto the sides of his hair, shaking his head and crying for help to get this damn bird off him.

Suddenly aware of where he was, Terrance stood back, crossed himself and then stepped forward. He held out an outstretched arm, standing still in the pose he had memorized; St. Francis blessing the animals and murmuring a blessing to his friend. The crow wasn't having any of it. He squawked back in return. Alarmed at the outburst, Father Bart's fists uncurled from his hair and began swatting the bird on his head. Wings still beating wildly, JJ was unexpectedly airborne. The beating wings launched the crow, a cap of brown hair clutched firmly in his curled his claws.

"Help! Oh my goodness! My hair! Stop that bird!" Father Bart cried as he clapped both hands on his bald crown.

Terrance froze, mouth agape, taking in the reality of the scene. His pet crow had taken off with Father Bart's hair! The priest rocked to one side and then gripped the font to steady himself, splashing holy water on himself.

JJ the crow, squawked loudly and dart back and forth through the sanctuary, looking for an escape, grazing Terrance's head with Father Bart's hair still clutched in his claws, as he flew over him.

Although he was brought up to be well mannered and respectful especially in church, Terrance still possessed the humour and amusement of a twelve-year-old boy.

When he grasped the scene before him, Terrance's face first broke into a grin. Then he slapped his knee and let out a peal of laughter. His body doubled over, then he took a deep breath in and continued to laugh as he held his stomach with both hands. He laughed so hard his eyes watered.

Shocked at first by Terrance's reaction and affronted by his apparent rudeness, Father Bart caught himself and remembered that inside, this polite, gentle man was a harmless boy with a boy's sense of humour. He started to see the humour himself, and a tentative laugh escaped and built itself in into open-mouthed, head-back, double chin waggling, belly slapping spasms of laughter.

This was the scene the pet owners and their pets witnessed when, without direction from either priest or his assistant, pushed through the doors in no particular order to escape the sudden downpour that followed the rumbling thunder and the sky-illuminating lightening show.

Peels of laughter coming from the short, rotund priest, his a bald head fringed with sparse strands of greying brown hair—while clutching the font to steady himself. And a lean-framed, middle-aged man with closely cropped greying hair, dressed in clean jeans and a newly ironed plaid shirt, standing beside him, a wide open smile displaying gapped upper teeth, wiping the tears streaming down the creases of his lined face with the back of his calloused hand.

Margo looked around her in the sanctuary for Michael. She and Chance were squeezed into the last pew. She stood on the bench to see what the commotion coming from the head of the church was, Chance's lead twisted tightly in her grip. Like everyone else, she gawked at the site before her. Then she scanned the audience for Michael. Michael was not among the congregation. Possible worst-case scenarios popped into her head. As quickly as they came, she dismissed them, telling herself that Michael could handle Roscoe, and in any event, Roscoe could handle himself.

When he became aware of the gathering in front of him, Father Bart pulled himself together, gasping for breath. He pulled out a large white handkerchief, mopped the sweat that had beaded his bald dome and then honked into it, clearing his nose and wiping his tears.

Terrance, too, steadied himself and looked around. When he saw that he had an audience, he immediately felt embarrassed. His mother would surely be ashamed of his behaviour. That sobered him up quickly. His eyes darted around the church, looking for JJ, but could not spot him. Thinking he must have escaped through the open doors, Terrance felt relieved that the show might be over. He backed away from the font, genuflecting and whispering a penitential prayer in case God was also cross with him.

Then he turned around, his eyes following the pattern in the carpet as he made his way to the first pew and sat down. There was no one in the first pew—there never was—so Terrance felt strange sitting there, imagining all eyes staring at the back of his head. But he was too ashamed and embarrassed to walk any further. If it wouldn't have attracted further attention to himself, he would have crawled right under the pew, like some of the animals had done to feel safe. Instead, he slumped forward and laid his hands on his lap and stared at them.

Father Bart straightened out and stood tall—as tall and straight as a pudgy man of his diminished stature can stand. He, too crossed himself and genuflected, facing the font and then took his place on the stage behind the podium. He touched his collar to make sure it was straight and surreptitiously patted the sides of his head where his hairpiece should have been. He smiled sheepishly, looking down at the podium and then up at the expectant congregation who had quieted to a whisper, save the disturbed animals.

Clearing his throat, he began. "Now that you know my vanity, I hope you regard me as a simple man who still holds the vain hope that his whole body will be resurrected on that day—including his hair." A titter waved through the congregation and the tension eased. Father Bart raised hands toward the ceiling and bade the congregation who were still standing to take a seat. There was a shuffle in the church as people and pets settled.

Outside, the gusting winds had died down. The thunder was a distant rolling drum. The storm had passed. And calm also washed over the audience when Father Bart uttered his first priestly invocation to worship. Even the little dogs were quiet. Only one yipped, but was quickly hushed with her owner's hand clamping over her muzzle.

Raising his hands, Father Brown uttered the first prayer that marked the beginning of the service. Upon his uttering, "Amen" an echo of amens followed. The few Catholics in the sanctuary crossed themselves.

"In keeping with the day of St. Francis Feast," said Father Bart, "and because we are joined here today with not only our friends who are not yet part of this family of parishioners, but also our four-legged—and two legged friends (here he smiled at Birdie's parrot, Precious who cocked a suspicious eye at him) we will dispense with the conventions of the liturgical order and get straight to the blessing of the animals in the name of St. Francis who was the first to bless the animals and the earth and whose example and tradition we follow on St. Francis Feast Day." Here he paused, as if in thought.

Then looked up and queried. "I don't suppose the bounty of pot luck lunch items were saved from the rain?" He looked for Eunice. She found her seat beside her son. Eunice shook her head sadly.

"Ah, sister Eunice has indicated that, sadly, no, the bounty did not survive the flood. Oh well, the best intentions of mice and men, so to speak . . ." Father Bart grinned. "But we will get on without it. God knows I can survive without another church luncheon! Though I was fully looking forward to it, and will still bless the hands that prepared it." He patted his belly and chortled.

His down-to-earth manner and easy humour at his own expense, went a long way to putting his audience at ease in most situations. On this occasion, however, his audience was not only made up of humans who understood his language, but also restless creatures that were unaccustomed to their surroundings. A cat yowled from his cramped quarters. A dog barked at the cat. The priest grinned and looked around at the sanctuary, pet cages on benches beside their owners, dogs on leashes. Some sitting in anticipation on the floor or at the feet of their masters, some sitting nervously on laps, and one or two squirming and sniffing at the cage beside them, their owners trying to pull them back and settle them down. Precious, sitting on Birdie's shoulder scowling, let out a warning screech in response to the dog bark. And, from somewhere in the rafters, a crow cawed.

"Thank you for the reminder, dear creatures. You must be getting cagey—and no doubt hungry. Without further adieu, my friends, let's get on with the blessing of your precious gifts from God, and all of us who are creatures of the natural world."

Margo looked around furtively for Michael. Chance sat beside her feet, fully alert, waiting to see what would come next in this unfamiliar place. Michael and Roscoe were still missing.

Father Bart commenced his blessing. "Today, on this, St. Francis of Assisi Feast Day, we celebrate God's creatures and the bounty our natural world provides for them and for us, and we bless those who nourish and care for these innocent creatures and our earthly home. I invite you to sit, stand or kneel and while laying a hand on your dearly beloved pet or pet's carrier, I will offer this blessing of the animals in the tradition of St. Francis."

At the prompt, there was a shuffle as prayer kneeling benches were pulled out, as devotees assumed their practiced posture of prayer. As she sat, Margo felt the prayer bench being slid out from the pew in front of her. She took that as the cue to kneel on it. Chance took that as his cue to move out of the space he occupied. He backed out of the row and sat quietly at the end of the pew still attached loosely to the leash Margo held in her hand. Margo rested one hand on Chance's head and gripped the back of the bench in front of her with the other. She hadn't been on her knees since they had pulled up and tided the garden a month ago. Her aging knees strained to hold her weight. She hoped the priest wouldn't take too long with this prayer.

Sensing the settling of the congregation, Father Bart raised his hands and his eyes to the heavens—or in this case, the rafters—and began his blessing.

"We invoke your blessing St. Francis and pray for your intercession for our furry friends. May you watch over them and keep them safe from harm. Guide their footsteps and protect them from danger. We ask that you bless them with good health and vitality, and that you ease any pain or discomfort they may be experiencing."

Then he lowered his hands and crossed himself solemnly as he uttered the invocation, "In the name of God the Father, the Son and the Holy Spirit, amen."

Margo closed her eyes when she listened to the prayer. She opened them now and breathed out a sigh. It seemed to her that a hallowed hush had come over the furry and feathered friends and their caretakers. For a single moment there was not a peep, squeak, squawk, meow, or bark. A sacred moment, Margo thought.

Then—just as the hush had settled over them—the bubble of tranquility popped. Father Bart stretched out his hands to the side to invite his audience, pets and owners to line up in the aisle so that, one by one, they could join him for a personal blessing if they wished. In response, feet shuffled, prayer benches squeaked across the floor, pets, now alert, began a cacophony of motions and sounds signalling their restlessness.

And, above them, the distinct caw of a crow trumpeted from the rafters. Terrance, who'd been standing in front of his pew for the prayer, turned and began to search with his eyes for his pet crow. Thinking he spotted his companion perched upon one of the rafters, beady eyes looking down at the audience, he lifted his finger and silently pleaded with him to land on it. But JJ had another idea. JJ saw his moment. With his claws he Picked up the hair-piece resting beside him on the beam and dove from the rafter in a smooth glide down towards the front of the sanctuary.

Margo ducked when she felt the swoosh of air rush over her head. Someone screamed. "It's that crow!" someone else shouted, and pointed at the black bird moving swiftly and purposefully across the sanctuary, a pelt grasped in his claws.

Terrance's eyes widened and he managed a throaty croak and a squawk, with which he meant to communicate in crow language to come to him. But if he understood what Terrance was saying to him, JJ took no notice, intent as he was on a target. With a caw that sounded like a laugh, he released the hair piece his from his claws. It landed unceremoniously on Father Bart's head, partly covering his eyes. Then JJ swooped back up again toward the rafters. A safe distance away, he cackled and croaked in laughter as he watched the mayhem below that his practical joke had created.

In reaction to the piece landing askew on his pate, Father Bart clapped his hands to his head and ducked below the podium for cover.

In response to the crow's jeering caws, the cats screeched in their crates and the dogs barked. Some of the dogs, including Chance, who were loosely held by their leashes, broke free during the commotion and started to run around the sanctuary, barking with the pure joy of children being let out of their classroom for recess.

While the pets chased each other up and down the aisles and under the benches, their owners desperately grabbed at whatever leash was closest to try to catch the dogs, tripping and tangling their legs in one or another's leash in the process. The sanctuary air was fouled with imprecation and curses from the owners at their dis-obedient dogs.

Unsettled, Birdie's parrot dove at any beast or person who came anywhere near Birdie, giving them a sharp pinch with her beak—which added howling to the barking, yowling, squeaking and screeching as people and animals scrambled to find each other and, if that couldn't be accomplished, find safety from the enraged parrot.

After much squawking from Birdie, the parrot cam back to rest on her shoulder, parroting some of the language she heard in the sanctuary.

JJ dove down from the rafters, to claim his spot on Terrance's shoulder, smugly chortling to himself.

Terrance glared at JJ, thinking of how to rebuke him later. But he knew that 'later', with animals, means nothing. They have no memory of misbehavior, and so have no recognition of what they are being punished for. Or so they lead humans to believe.

Mutely Terrance worked his way through the chaos of people and pets moving out of their pews and making their way to the back of the room. He felt responsible to try to re-establish peace and order in honour of his patron saint, St. Francis. When he got to the church door he opened it wide. A watery sun gleamed through thinning clouds. A few owners and their pets were regrouping outside in the fresh air. Soon the sanctuary emptied and people stood around in small groups, releasing their tension by laughing and quipping back and forth about the antics of their pets—and especially recounting the JJ incident with stealing and then resetting Father Bart's hairpiece.

"Did you see that? Swooped right down. Fitted it to his head like he knew exactly where it went!" Said one man, gesturing clownishly with his hands grasping both sides of his head and waggling it back and forth.

"My Precious wasn't impressed," Birdie piped up. "She thought that crow was being impertinent. And she knows how crows can be!"

Father Bart stepped out of the church last, blinking as his blue eyes adjusted to the light. He strutted like a bandy rooster back and forth on the stoop, an amused twinkle in his eyes and smile playing on his lips. Not one to lose the moment, he clapped his hands together and continued to clap in appreciation of his feathered friend's trick.

When he caught Terrance's eye, he bowed toward JJ who still sat on Terrance's shoulder, and tipped his toupee to him, as if it were a hat and then rocked back on his heels and laughed heartily. A smattering of claps and laughter lifted lightly from the displaced congregation when they saw the priest laughing the hardest.

Having regained the attention of the crowd, Father Bart took a deep breath in and resettled his face, "Well that was quite the benediction! I must apologize, however, that the feast Eunice and the ladies worked so hard on to lay out for us that has been sadly drowned in the rain. Be that as it may, "Bless the hands that prepared it. And the peace of God be with you and your furry and fine feathered friends." He meant that to be his benediction.

While he was pronouncing his benediction, an obnoxious odour wafted across the front of the church, past the priest, and into the loosely gathered crowd of humans and animals.

"Skunk!" Someone shouted pointed at a hole in the side of the church's foundation. Out of it squirmed a fat skunk, and after her came three kittens. They waddled around the perimeter of the church as if they were out for a Sunday stroll. A beat or two after the skunk family emerged from under the church, a very large black cat with white paws and a white tuxedo ruff on his chest walked out too. He solemnly followed the skunk family— keeping a safe distance.

"Roscoe!" Margo called out.

Terrance saw the potential chaos that could erupt. He stood between the skunks and the people and their pets and pleaded with his hands, "Stay calm. Let the skunk family pass by. Please. Keep your dogs close. Don't let any of them chase the skunks. It will be bad if they do. A big bad stink."

His words held the crowd back for a split second and then they dispersed—as quickly as they could, some leaping into waiting cars, others running and dragging their dogs, or carrying their carriers along as they ran in the opposite direction.

Still entranced by seeing her cat parading calmly in the line with the skunks, Margo didn't see Michael approach her from behind. "Michael?" She said when she turned to see him standing there a distance away from her. Then she turned up her nose. "You missed the whole service! Where were you? And what's Roscoe doing following the skunks?" She sniffed the air and smelled the acrid smell coming from her husband. "Eww! You got skunked!"

"Stay there," Michael said holding up his hands. Margo had no intention of getting closer, but appreciated her husband's warning just the same. "Yeah, the good news is—I found Roscoe. Apparently, he has found new friends—a family of skunks who have made their den under the church. When I followed him in to see where he had gotten to, I got skunked."

The skunk family crossed the road and disappeared into a ditch opposite the church. Roscoe, a huge black shape mounding over the tall grass, followed. Father Bart rocked back on his heels, an amused expression on his face. The only ones left of his morning congregation were Margo, her dog Chance, Terrance with JJ on his shoulder, and his mother Eunice at his side. Standing a respectable distance away, Margo's skunked husband Michael looking dishevelled and disheartened.

"I see we are down to the usual number of parishioners for a Sunday morning," the priest said lightly. "Would anyone be so kind as to offer me tea before I leave to depart to offer mass to the next church in my parish circuit?"

Eunice stepped up, cooing and coddling like a mother hen. "Where are my manners. Father Bart, would you please come and enjoy a light repast with us on this Sunday morning?" She turned to Margo and said, "I'm so sorry, Margo. I'd invite the two of you back to the house but in light of the situation . . . why don't I drop some sandwiches and canned tomatoes off at yours. I have a dozen quarts left over or so from last year's harvest. I'm up to my elbows in canning now so I'll be happy to donate them to a good cause. He must strip first outside and then, if there is some privacy, douse him well outside with strong detergent. Gardener's soap if you have it. Then, run a hot bath about half way, and pour in the canned tomatoes. He should sit in that for at least a half hour." Eunice was talking to Margo as if she were giving her instructions on how to take care of her dog, not her husband. As she was speaking she cast a sympathetic glance toward Michael who stood apart from them, undecided about which was more humiliating, being ostracized because he was smelling of skunk or the anticipation of the bath Margo would give him in a tub of canned tomatoes and their juice.

Margo waved good-bye as Eunice and Terrance loaded themselves into their car, telling Father Bart to follow them in his.

JJ flapped off Terrance's shoulder and ducked into the passenger seat of the car, presumably to make his own way back to his roost in the barn.

Margo walked down the street ahead of Michael, calling for Roscoe who poked his head out of the grasses he was exploring.

A rainbow appeared between clouds and a shaft of light framed the straggling family who were walking with as much dignity as they could muster, to their home two doors down. If anyone was on the street to witness the scene, they would have seen a woman in her sixties, a mass of curly reddish hair tentatively held in place with two combs. She was wearing a loose dress with orange and brown and turquoise colours in abstract patterns swirling around her generous figure. A curious golden retriever sniffed the path along the ditch that the skunks had taken. Behind the dog, a slightly built man with thin grey hair, balding at the crown, looked uncomfortably dishevelled in a soiled sport jacket and khaki pants muddied at the knees. He reeked of skunk when he walked, and looked just as one imagined the Charlie Brown character, Pig Pen smelled—with a whirling cloud of filth around him wherever he went. Bringing up the rear—a cool two car lengths behind—a large, some would say, obese, black cat with white paws and a tuxedo ruff of white on his chest, nonchalantly walked down the middle of the road pretending that he didn't even know that family walking ahead of him.

CHAPTER TEN

Santa Gets Caught with His Pants Down

"Ho! Ho! Ho!" The voice boomed out from behind her. Margo was bent over the stove, opening the oven door with one mitted hand and pulling out the pan of just-baked Christmas cookies with the other.

Without turning around, she recognized the voice as her husband, Michael's. Cookie pan with fresh baked cookies in hand, Margo straightened up and pivoted to the counter where she slid the cookie pan onto the cooling rack. "And Merry Christmas to you Santa!"

When he left for the Wannatoka Springs Fire Brigade training, Michael told her that they were getting the trucks ready for the Christmas parade. He was excited that he had been asked to play the Santa role this year.

Michael clumped into the kitchen in his heavy firefighter boots and wrapped white work-gloved hands around Margo's waist from behind. He leaned into her ear and said, "Have you been naughty or nice?"

Margo squirmed away when she felt the fake beard tickle her ear. "Santa! Watch yourself!" She wiggled around to face Michael and tugged on his furry white beard. The elastic around his ears stretched out so Margo let go and the beard snapped back. "Oh, sorry, Santa. I thought it was real!" She giggled.

Michael straightened out his elastic-bound white whiskers so he could talk through the gap. "So? Whaddya think?" He took a step back and rested his fists on his hips, striking a pose.

Margo laughed. "I never would have thought you would fill Santa's boots, but I believe, with a little more padding in the right places . . ." she pulled out the baggy jacket at the belly, "you just might pass!"

Margo took in the special fire brigade Santa costume Michael was wearing. The red fire chief bucket helmet sloped in the back with a crossed-axe insignia on the crown, topped a wig of curly white hair that massed around his shoulders. Twinkling blue eyes peering over oval gold wire-rimmed glasses perched on a reddened nose and cheeks. The rest of the face was covered with a curly white mustache and beard set, that ruffled around the neck and covered the open yellow-lined collar of the fire-retardant red suit. The jacket, closed with brass buckle fasteners, was trimmed with two bands of reflective yellow stripes—one wrapping around the chest and one just above the flared hem. A thick black leather belt buckled with an oversized, square silver buckle cinched the folds of extra fabric together. The effect was like a firecracker cinched in the middle on Michael's slim frame. Below the jacket, he wore a pair of suspendered overalls of the same red fire-retardant fabric, three sizes too big for him. The hems of the baggy pant legs were rolled up to form a wide cuff of yellow lining, atop a pair of large black rubber boots with yellow soles and toe topper trim. White work gloves completed the Santa costume.

"Turn around," Margo said, pulling out the extra fabric, and appraising the costume. Michael turned slowly.

"Eek! There's a split in the pants along the back seam!" Margo declared.

"Oh, yeah. Joe got too big for his britches. He said he split the seam last year, bending down to give a kid a handshake."

Margo laughed. "I can fix that."

"Santa would appreciate that. I can feel a draft. Can't imagine how cold it would be standing on a fire truck in the middle of winter." Michael smiled. "Do you think you could take it in a bit too? Joe was a big guy! He filled out this costume with no padding. Unlike myself." Michael smoothed out the front of his suit, proudly profiling his nearly flat stomach.

"No, no, no! That would not do!" Margo waggled her finger, "Santa stands for Ho! Ho! Ho! And, eat, drink and be merry! Wait here!" Margo commanded and dashed off. Michael sat down on the bend and took off his hat, wig and beard. Sweat was streaming down his cheeks. He wiped around his face with one gloved hand. "Can you get back here a little faster? It's hot under here Margo!"

"Coming!" Margo called out. "Just a sec." Margo's return seemed like an eternity, even to a patient man like Michael. When Margo emerged from the basement, her arms were full of an assortment of decorative pillows and a ball of string. She liked to change the decorative cushions in the living room and the pillows on her bed every year or so, but didn't have the heart to give up the old ones to the thrift store so she had accumulated quite a collection.

"Now stand up and take off that jacket!" She ordered, dropping the pillows on the floor.

"Gladly. Do you have any idea how hot and unbreathable fire-retardant gear is?" Margo helped him unbuckle the brass buckles. "Pretty sexy . . . undressing Santa." She said as she unclasped each buckle.

"Yeah, and hot! Real hot!" Michael smiled and

winked. "I need a shower."

Margo loosened the last buckle and opened the jacket wide to reveal the top of the overalls and the black body suit Michael was wearing underneath.

"Ohhh . . ." she said as she ran her hands across his shoulders and under the jacket, removing it. "And sexy underwear, too!" A playful smile tracked across Margo's face.

Michael felt himself blush but Margo didn't notice. His face was already beet red from wearing the wig and false beard. For all the years they had been married, Michael had always been the conservative one. He still felt awkward reacting to Margo's playfulness. But he wouldn't have it any other way.

Margo worked around Michael, tying cushions around his arms, then pushing his padded arms through the sleeves, and making adjustments as she went. Then she tied cushions on to the front of his stomach. Next, she worked cushions down his pant legs and around his backside, to fill out his seat and around his thighs. Michael squirmed a bit when she was reaching her hands down his pants.

"Hold still, Michael!" Margo yanked the legs of his pants over the cushions. By now, Michael was sweating profusely. He just wanted the ordeal to be over.

"Enough already!" he broke away from Margo's grip just as she finished tucking in the pillow in front of his stomach into his pants. "This Santa costume is deadly hot!" He couldn't see over his belly. And Margo pushed his fumbling hands away, laughing as she released buckles, stripped off the jacket, pulled the pillows out of their binding and tossed them aside. Next, she deftly released the clips on overall straps. Michael pushed the pillows in his pants down with the overalls and hopped one leg and then the other until both legs were free. "This is the worst, Margo. I don't know why I let you dress me! What if there was a real fire! I couldn't go anywhere!"

Finally, when the pillows had been untied and extracted, and his overalls pulled off, Michael stood in his black, sweat-soaked wicking underwear. With hands on hips, Margo commanded: "Now my darling man—strip and hit the shower!"

***

The winter scenes of this tiny village with its two parallel streets on which most of the residents lived, reminded Margo of the old-fashioned Christmas cards with twinkling glitter on the snowy landscape and the cheerful houses all in a row, aglow with Christmas lights. As Margo walked down the street, the hard-packed snow crunching under her boots, she admired the lit-up houses, some with smoke trailing upward from the chimneys, and thought smugly about last year's Christmas light competition between Michael and Joel.

This year, it seemed as if more of their neighbours were lighting up their houses and decorating their yards. It could have been their influence. She smiled at the pulsing light displays and lawn ornaments—a blow up Santa on his sleigh with presents in his hand was in Mabel's snow-filled yard. Barney with a present in his mouth and three blowup snowmen in Ivan's yard. A plastic nativity scene lit from the inside, and a unicorn figure outlined in white lights in was front of Birdie's house. And on Buck's porch a giant set of antlers with coloured lights twisted through the branches, rippling through their sequence.

In the past year, Margo had come to embrace her neighbours' styles. She was proud to say that she had met and knew the names of the individuals who occupied each unique home—something she had never accomplished in all the years they lived in their house in the suburbs. They, like most suburbanites lived in satellite communities; work and home life circled two different orbits. Friendships were made in cohorts; Margo's teacher friends and Michael's hockey buddies and golfing partners from work. Neighborhoods in the suburbs had become more transient over the years. Established owners sold after they had raised their kids, taking their equity out and moving farther away. The buyers were often people who were taking advantage of the slightly less expensive housing in the suburbs, building up equity to invest in their next in their home in a preferred neighbourhood closer to the city.

The difference here, in Wannatoka Springs was that people stayed in the homes they raised their children in, and in some cases the second generation came back or remained in the area, finding or making work for themselves. There had been a recent influx of new buyers. Five homes, including theirs, changed owners two summers before. Not surprisingly, they were retirees who were looking for a place to live out their retirement dream of living in a peaceful community that was less transient and more stable.

Wannatoka Springs, an unincorporated cluster of eighty-two properties on the water line, had no mayor or town council, but it did have a community service club that made connections, wrote grants for support, and otherwise supported their community with projects and goals for the betterment of the community.

Margo was beginning to feel that she and Michael were becoming part of the fabric of this patchwork neighbourhood. If they were first seen to be outsiders, now they were affectionately referred to as 'those city folks from the coast'. Their neighbours had endeared themselves to Margo and Michael with offers of support like bringing them a load of firewood, taking garbage to the dump if they were going, sharing the over-abundance of fruit that grew on nearly everyone's property. Not to mention, all manner of practical advice about how to get along in the hinterland—including back-road ATV driving lessons.

Michael had joined the volunteer fire brigade the summer before last. He, along with several other new transplants—including his new friend Joel—took a more active interest in the fire brigade when they resettled after the evacuation order due to an impending wildfire striking their community was rescinded. The department had swollen that year to seventeen members—then, as the urgency diminished, and with attrition settled into a steady twelve-member crew of both women and men, ranging in age from nineteen to seventy-three, each committed to defending their community's properties should the need arise.

Margo was walking towards the fire hall to join the team and their significant others for the potluck tonight. The Fire-hall was a squat, rectangular brick building with an oversized garage door and a regular sized door used to enter the building. A sign above the doors read "Wannatoka Springs Fire Hall" painted in red letters on a white background. The humble building was erected in the mid-seventies. It housed the two fire trucks which served the community. The yellow one, considered the 'new one' was a 2014 model. The red one, Michael's favourite, was thirty-five-years-old. They both fit snuggly into the garage side by side if backed in carefully. The scrapes and dents on each side of the truck cab doors told a story of attempts by trainees that weren't so accurate.

Michael was the one of the eldest members of the crew—besides Joe who was retiring this year at age seventy-three. But he felt confident that he could take on any of challenges they practiced when they took out the trucks for drills. His friend, Joel, was the next oldest in the team at age fifty-six. Freedom fifty-five looked good on him. He had worked for a power company in Los

Angeles, installing and repairing transformers on power lines. His high-power job had kept his mind and body responsive. The rest of the crew was composed of men and women of different ages, backgrounds, and abilities who wanted to offer their service to protect their tiny community. Among them was a local man who lived with his mother on an acreage on Willow. Terrance, was in his fifties's with a delayed mental age of twelve. He was a shy man but he enjoyed being part of the team and willingly did whatever job he was assigned.

Kyle, the volunteer fire chief, age twenty-nine, was probably one of the youngest fire chiefs in the Kootenays, but he had been the chief for the last three years and a volunteer for seven. He was experienced and cautious, and had good rapport with the crew. He was thoughtful when assigned jobs to each member of the crew according to the abilities they demonstrated. But he insisted that everyone rotate through all the roles on the truck, including driving and operating the trucks. After all the volunteers tried their hand at driving, and Kyle had observed how they handled the pressure of driving, he assigned four drivers to be the primary drivers.

Terrance was one of those who didn't qualify in Kyle's mind to be one of the four drivers—although he had learned to drive on the acreage he lived on, and was fairly competent. He was disappointed, but Kyle told him he needed Terrance to do a very important job. He made him operations engineer, which meant Terrance was responsible for starting the truck and monitoring the dash instruments, particularly the fuel gauge. If it was low or out of fuel, he reported it to Kyle, who would assign someone to drive it with Terrance who would pump the gas. Terrance was also responsible for turning on the siren and lights and turning one or both off at appropriate times. The siren assignment thrilled his boyish heart, but he took all of his responsibilities seriously and was eager to perform his duties.

Kyle took care to assign tasks and responsibilities to each of the crew members, drilling into them the essential importance each person's contribution to the team effort and effectively handle a fire, should it come to that, which he dearly hoped it would not. With the emphasis of the importance of every role, and interaction and cooperation of the team, a bond created by a common mission was formed among disparate crew members.

Michael and Joel qualified as drivers. Michael was ecstatic the evening he came home and shared the news with Margo—that he was the designated driver of the red truck. It was the older of the two and the most temperamental, but it tickled his childhood nostalgia of becoming a fireman one day and driving a red fire truck.

On the night of the light-up parade, however, Michael would defer his role to Joe, the oldest serving member of the crew, who, said this year he thought he should hang up his overalls. Joe was a corpulent and jolly man. His drinking habit dovetailed with his eating habits, which ran to red meat, eggs, bacon, and pan-fried potatoes. He proudly claimed the title of iron skillet chef. Although he suffered from gout and arthritis, he never let the pain dampen his spirit. He was always cracking jokes; everybody's day was made when Joe was in the house.

For ten years in a row, Joe had played Santa Claus for the Christmas parade. Given his size and his demeanor he was a town favourite. This year, he admitted his gout and arthritis were making it hard for him to move around. He showed off the split in the seat of his pants as proof, having a laugh at his expense, as usual. When he announced his retirement he made a case for Michael, was the second oldest member of the crew, to play the role of Santa and carry on the tradition. Michael reluctantly agreed to the unanimous vote by the other members of the crew.

It was established that Michael, playing Santa,

would stand behind the cab, waving at the onlookers and dipping into his bag whenever he saw children lining up along the street as the fire truck passed, to throw out candy and party horns, and Joe would drive the truck, one final time, just for the parade.

It wasn't until he came in to dress for the parade that Joe realized the only overalls that would over his oversized body, were the ones he had worn for the last three years. That last-minute change meant that Michael had to scrounge for another set of overalls to wear as Santa. He didn't have the heart to communicate this with Margo. She had stitched up the seam where it was split in the back and resewn a rip in one of the pockets. She had taken such care of them, even washing them and hanging them up in front of the fire to dry. Michael found a XX size pair of overalls that were hanging in the back of the equipment room. They weren't claimed, so Michael assumed they had been worn by a someone who had already given up their duties—or perhaps had outgrown them. He was in the annex, climbing into the overalls he found and stuffing them with pillows when Margo came through the open garage door, and into the hall, carrying her contribution to the potluck.

"Hi Margo!" the high, thin voice of the youngest member of the crew, Sanji called out. Sanji was twenty-one and came to the Kootenays with her partner, Kayla to escape from urban life. They had bought an uncleared forested property on a back road and were committed to living 'off the grid' which meant, for now, living in a fifth-wheel they hauled up there. Sanji worked as an Emergency Medical Technician. She was on call with rescue crews and at the Crystal Lake hospital. Committed to service, especially emergency medical service in the hinterland where ambulances and doctors were a long way away, she served as a volunteer on the fire brigade.

"Where should I set this down?" Margo lifted the pan covered in tinfoil she held firmly between her two gloved hands.

"Oh . . ." Sanji, smiling widely, came towards Margo arms extended and hands open. "I'll take that from you."

"Careful! It's hot!" Margo cautioned.

"No problem," Sanji said as she stuffed her hands into the pockets of the open firefighter's jacket she was wearing. She lifted her pocketed hands and took the casserole dish off Margo's hands. Deftly maneuvering around the volunteers standing around the table, she set the dish down on a long table that was already crowded with a cornucopia of delectable dishes. The yellow truck had been moved out of the garage in order to make room for the table and the team and their guests to congregate. Still, it was standing room only. But that didn't seem to deter the festive atmosphere, as folks stood chatting and forking in mouthfuls of stew, crunching cookies, and sipping non-alcoholic beer. There was a strict no-alcohol rule while in the fire hall—for obvious reasons. Michael was the hero when he introduced a brand of non-alcoholic beer, he found at the supermarket that he thought tasted pretty good. He kept the fridge stocked with near-beer, his contribution. And like the near-beer it went down well with the crew.

Margo looked around for Michael. She had come, not only to bring her dish to the potluck, but also to help Michael suit up in his Santa costume. Everyone seemed engaged in their conversations so she thought she would just look around. The red fire truck, the one he would ride at the back of as Santa was still in the garage—off to one side. *Michael may already be on the truck*, she thought. Margo greeted familiar faces as she made her way through the gathering towards the truck. The truck's hood was wide open. As she approached it, her eyes focused on the very large backside covered in pair of extra-large red fire fighter coverall pants straining at the center seam. The yellow cuffs were rolled up above thick black fireproof boots. The rest of the body was covered by the hood but Margo recognized the over-stitching of black thread she had reinforce the seam with when she sewed up the split.

'Michael?' Margo queried when she recognized the Santa costume. A muffled response came from underneath the hood. She thought she heard "don't peek." A mischievous grin playing on her face. Margo stepped forward, reached out and goosed him. She giggled and ducked behind a tall volunteer and then turned and skipped through the door to the annex, to hide.

Letting out a sharp yelp, the man bent over the engine shot up and bumped his head on the rim of the hood. He then slumped forward—his body bent over the frame. Several volunteers who noticed the reaction, rushed to the slumped body and called an alert.

Hearing a commotion out in the garage, Margo opened the door a sliver to see what was going on. "Margo?" She heard Michael's voice behind her. "What's going on?"

Margo froze, then slowly turned around, eyes wide, mouth shaped in an O and covered with one hand. "Michael? What are you doing here?" She saw Michael half-dressed in red overalls clutching the pillow in front of his belly with struggling to grasp the strap to his overalls with the other.

"Getting suited up. What do you think? Glad you're here. I'm having trouble getting the pillows to stay in place in these overalls. We had to switch out the overalls for the costume because Joe wanted to wear his fire uniform while he drove the truck in an honourary farewell so I found these in the equipment room." Michael strained to get the legs of his overalls over the pillows wrapped around his thighs. "I think these are a size too small for all the pillows you stuffed me with!" He groaned and gave the overalls one more tug.

Margo held her hand up over her mouth. "Oh, Michael! What have I done?"

"It's nothing you did, Margo. It's the overalls. You just need to help me adjust the pillows to fit. It was a last minute thing. Joe couldn't fit into any other overalls than the ones he usually wore. The jacket doesn't matter. He has a regular jacket to wear. Sorry, I didn't want to tell you about the switch before you came over, because I didn't want you to be disappointed with all the work you put in to mending those overalls and adjusting the stuffing. I thought I could manage this myself.

Margo sunk back against the door, "But you're in here."

"Yeah, so. Its more private. I get enough ribbing from the others. I don't need their jokes about how to stuff my costume. Are you going to help me?" Michael pleaded.

"If you are in here, who was that out in the garage with his head buried under the hood of the red fire truck? All I could see was red firefighter pants with the seam I patched, and the yellow cuffs. I thought it was you!"

"That was Joe. He was checking out the truck fluids. Why? Margo? What did you do?"

Her eyes widened and she shook her head. "Oh no. Oh no, no, no, no!"

Without answering Michael's question, Margo turned around and squinted through the crack in the door, to take in the scene in the hall. Someone shouted for Sanji. Someone else asked if they should call an ambulance. Joe was propped up against the fire truck, rubbing the back of his head. Kyle was standing beside him, supporting him with one arm. When Sanji arrived, her voice changed from the thin, high voice she used to greet Margo, to a firm, confident voice that commanded attention.

"Joe we are going to get you to sit down. Kyle and

Joel get a hold of Joe under his armpits. We'll walk him to the bench." Sanji instructed.

"Are you feeling, dizzy Joe? Can you walk?" She asked, tucking her thin arm under Joe's thick one.

"'T'ain't nothin'" Joe was saying, "Jist a goose egg."

"We don't know if you have a concussion." Sanji said gently but firmly, "So you had better sit down and let me examine you. Joe acquiesced and sat down with an "Umph". The group stopped talking and followed the action as Sanji followed the procedure she was taught, awaiting further instructions should Sanji require assistance.

Michael peered out the crack of the window above Margo. "What's going on?" he whispered. "Is that Joe? Looks like he hurt his head. Step out of the way, Margo. I need to go out there."

Margo slid out of the way and clenched her eyes shut. "Please, God. Let it be superficial." That was the second time since they moved to Wannatoka Springs she had prayed. Serious injuries were the community's nightmare. It would take an hour just to get an ambulance to Wannatoka Springs and then at least another forty minutes to an hour to get the injured person back to the hospital in Crystal Lake.

Joe was seated on the bench and holding a bag of frozen French fries to the back of his head—that Sanji had ordered one of the crew to fetch from the freezer. The fries were left over from their last BBQ fundraiser along with a box of frozen hamburgers. Joe was answering Sanji's questions. "Four" he said when she held her fingers in front of him. Then he tracked her finger left to right and back. "Told ya. I'm OK. Just a bump on the noggin. But that girl—an' it better have been a girl. . ." He scowled and looked around at the faces staring back at him, "who pinched my behind. She had better watch out!" Then he grinned and started to sing in a lusty voice, "She better not cry. I'm tellin' you why. Santa Joe is comin' to town!"

His grinned, displaying a nearly toothless smile as he pointed his finger at all the females in the room and said, "And he's going to find out who's been naughty tonight". A titter ran through the room. Some of the men feigned mock horror. The women shrunk away or put their hands up, shaking their heads vigorously. Michael just stood there with his arms crossed, expressionless.

Margo! He thought. Worried that Joe might eliminate all the women present, he thought the best way to shield his wife from the embarrassment of being found out as the one who goosed Joe, was a distraction, so he announced in a loud, jovial voice: "Ho! Ho! Ho! There's only one Santa here tonight. And if anyone's going to deliver anything to nice girls and boys, it will be THIS Santa!" He poked a finger into his pillow-stuffed breast for emphasis. "So, keep your britches on Joe!" He stood with his hands at his hips, puffing out his chest.

Seeing the Michael standing in front of him with pillows strapped to his arms, stomach and thighs, looking more like the Michelin Man that Santa Claus made Joe roar with laughter and slap his ample thigh. If Joe could laugh, he was alright. The mood broke and the group went back to their conversations about how they were going to get this show on the road. Sanji just shook her head, said something to Joe. And with a squeeze on his shoulder, walked away to put her first-aid kit back in the truck.

Michael joked about having to get stuffed and exited the hall, through the door to the annex. Margo was there, cringing with embarrassment. Michael looked at Margo and let out a real, hearty laugh. He leaned against the wall and gasped for air, "You should see your face, Margo! If Joe spotted you right now, he would know you were the naughty girl who goosed him."

"I'm so, so, sorry!" At first, she felt chagrinned,

and then she couldn't help herself when she conjured the scene in her mind, and she joined her husband laughing at the mistake she'd made.

"I honestly thought it was you under the hood, Michael. I recognized the pants and the seam I stitched up. And when I heard, 'Don't peek' when I called out your name, I thought you were playing a game so I goosed you—or rather I goosed Joe. I'm so embarrassed!"

Michael straightened his face. "That's so weird, Margo. You know I never play those games. You thought you heard 'Don't peek'?" Michael queried. Then, Michael slapped his forehead, "Oh! Joe was testing the lines in the truck. He must've said something like 'It don't leak'!"

Margo sucked in her breath. "Oh!" She covered her mouth and stifled a laugh.

Michael reached out and pulled his wife towards him and embraced her with his overstuffed arms. "You're naughty girl! And Santa knows it!" He whispered in her ear and tapped Margo's bottom. "Now come on. We'd better get this Santa stuffed!"

Michael bent down and struggled out of his overalls once again so Margo could help him stuff them. Margo gasped when she saw her husband standing before her in only the boxers she had given him for Christmas the previous year—with Rudolf the red-nose reindeer face and the words "You light up my life" printed on them. Michael shrugged "Well you told me the long underwear would be too warm. I thought this would be more appropriate considering the occasion." Michael smiled.

While Santa was being suited up in the annex, the rest of the crew were going through the checklist Kyle instituted to be done every time they took the trucks out on practice runs. They would be riding along on the trucks during the parade waving at the crowd as the trucks drove slowly down both Maple and Spruce and up the Willow loop, circumnavigating the community they proudly served to protect against potential fire. Sanji gave Joe one more check-up and determined that he was too hard-headed to be damaged. She gave him the OK to step into the red fire truck and ease it out of the hall onto the paved driveway. When everything looked like it was in place, Kyle blew his whistle and called the crew to order.

"Listen up!" Kyle said, "You have all worked hard to do your part for this parade, now let's review one more time how it's gonna go down."

Michael kissed Margo on the forehead and let her slip out the back door before he stepped into the hall as Santa—so she wouldn't be noticed. The crew clapped and whistled their delight at Santa's appearance. Joe patted him on the back. "You'll do young fella! Your sleigh awaits!" He gestured towards the red fire-truck. "Better you than me climbing up that ladder. When he climbed into the driver's seat of the truck, Terrance tooted the horn and Joe waved and shouted, "All aboard? Let's light up this old town tonight."

***

It was a postcard perfect light-up parade. Kids in parkas, toques and winter boots stamped around in their snowy yards and threw snow at each other, impatiently waiting for the parade to come down their street. They stopped their games and ran to the edge of the street when they heard the siren and saw the blue and red lights of the RCMP vehicle roll slowly down the street, followed by the first responder truck, then the yellow fire truck, and finally the red fire truck with Santa standing behind the cab, throwing goodies from his bag.

In the Wannatoka Springs tradition, some of the locals decorated their vehicles with lights and ribbons and bows, and joined in as the parade, honking as they passed. Kids ran alongside of and behind the red fire truck with open arms waving to Santa to aim the treats their way.

Like the Pied Piper, Santa in the red truck led everyone down one street and up the other. At intervals, as the convoy made its procession, Terrance wound the siren up, the signal for the neighbours turn on their festive lights as the parade passed by. Coloured lights came on in house after house until the whole street was lit up with an array of festively outlined roofs and windows as well as lit up displays on the lawns out front.

No two houses were the same. Joel had erected the surfing Santa on his lawn again, and one wall flowed like a waterfall with blue and white lights. Next to him was Birdie's house with a unicorn outlined in white lights, a stone mermaid holding up a birdbath wearing a string of red and green lights like pearls around her bare breasts. The neighbour across from them had set up a life-size silhouette Nativity scene lit from behind with white floodlights. Some houses were decked to the halls. Others took a minimalist approach: a star or a wreath on the front door, a lit-up Christmas tree seen through an open window. Nearly every house had some arrangement of lights to turn on when the parade passed by.

Taking in the scene through Santa's eyes as he waved to the children and adults who waved back, a warmth came over Michael. It was different from the overheating he felt in the suit, it was the warmth of the heart. *How far he had come*, he thought, *in a year and a half, from being the out-of-place city yuppie who didn't have a clue how to drive an ATV or how to mingle with the guys who gathered on the neighbour's lawn—to taking center stage in the Christmas parade, riding on the Wannatoka Springs fire-truck.*

When the parade had made its second loop,

participation dwindled as folks dropped out. Some went home, others walked or drove to the old school house behind the fire hall where a bonfire was set up and with provisions made by the community service club for a wiener roast, hot chocolate and s'mores.

It was a given that there would also be tailgate gatherings, with adult beverages being consumed and truck stereos blaring sassy country music as the night wore on and the fire burned down. In the wee hours of the night, the sounds of gleeful children would be replaced with the sounds of engines revving up and tires swirling concentric rings in the field between the old school house and the fire hall. Some truck, without four wheel drive, would inevitably get stuck out there and be found in the morning, in the middle of the field with footprints leading out of the field and back to the road. But it wouldn't be long before a neighbour would volunteer to help the owner who overestimated their truck's track-ability on ice and snow, by hitching one end of a rope to the bumper and the other to their rig, and haul them out. Support was woven into the fabric of this community. Even for the dumb asses that got themselves stuck.

Michael remembered well, that he and Margo were in that category the last Christmas when they tried to cut down their first Christmas tree in the bush.

The red fire truck was the last member of the parade to trundle down the hill back to the fire hall. Kyle's instructions to the team were to drive the yellow truck directly to the pavilion and the red truck to the fire hall. Except for Michael, the team would attend the function in their gear to reinforce their commitment and receive the appreciative comments and the slaps on the back they deserved from grateful community members. Kyle and a couple of the others would stay until the wiener roast and bonfire wound down, and make sure the fire was properly extinguished. Michael was to be dropped off at the hall so he could change out of his Santa costume before joining the group at the old school house—to preserve the mystery of who played Santa Claus.

Still in his Santa suit, Michael climbed down from the red fire truck carefully. The stuffing around his thighs and belly had sloughed down the suit and made it awkward to find purchase. He was hot and uncomfortable and could hardly wait to take this get-up off his body. He wasn't at all convinced now that the light shorts he wore under his suit, and nothing else, was such a good idea. All the sweat that might have been wicked away with his moisture-wicking body suit was now coursing down his back and soaking into his cotton boxers or was sucked into the pillows that drooped around his middle and his thighs, making them even heavier. When he reached the ground, one rubber boot slipped on a patch of ice and he felt his ungainly body gyrating. Moments later, he fell backwards on to his roundly padded rump.

"You OK Santa?" Terrance called from the cab, genuinely concerned. Michael struggled to right himself, which wasn't easy given the unwieldy girth Margo had added to his waistline. He had to crawl to the hand rail and pull himself up. Once he did, he raised himself up to the cab and grinned, "You bet! Can't keep this Santa down!"

Joe tooted his horn and started down the road to meet up with the rest of the crew and the neighbours at the old school house. "All in a night's work Santa, my boy! We'll see ya down at the weenie roast—that is if yer not too roasted yourself!"

Terrance waved through the window as the truck pulled back out onto the road. Michael, Santa, was left standing under the single streetlight, waving goodbye to his ride. From the field, he could hear children squealing as party goers chased each other and pushed each other around in the snow.

When the tail lights grew smaller, Michael doubled over his fat belly for a minute, leaning his hands on knees to catch his breath. Breathing out a cold cloud of air he stood up straight and waddled toward the fire hall entrance door. It was locked. He had a key. But it was deep in the pocket of his overalls, beneath the fabric of the oversized jacket and a layer of stuffing. He tore off his right glove with his teeth and fiddled with the freezing cold brass buckles on the jacket. Then he rummage around in his overall pocket until he felt the key and then extracted it. His hand felt slippery with sweat. Every step, every task, every move he made was so much more work with all the extra padding.

By the dull yellow glow of the yard light, he groped around the lock until he managed to feel the key-hole. He inserted the key. With a satisfying click, the door unlocked. He cranked the latch and pushed the door inward. He was in.

There were no lights left on in the hall. Michael wondered whose responsibility it was to leave one bank on when they were out on manoeuvres. He fumbled along the wall until he came to the place where he knew the bank of switches was and turned the nearest set of lights on. The oppression of the internal heat beneath his gear was compounded now that he was inside a building, not outside in the cold. He had to get this sweat suit off! Scooping the fire chief helmet with the wig off his head, and pulling the beard down around his neck so he could breathe, he hobbling over to the familiar bench against the wall where he suited up before fire practice. There, he kicked one and then the other of his boots off as he sat down. He sluggishly peeled off the jacket and slung it on the bench. Then he wrestled the pillows, still tied to his arms and belly, off his body, shedding and pounds as he stripped down. He was loosening his pants off, while pushing the pillows down his legs when the alarm sounded. Michael froze when he heard it. *Dammit!* In his rush to get the suit off, he had forgotten to disarm the alarm.

From the time the alarm was tripped by the movement of the person entering the building, the intruder had three minutes to enter the correct code and disarm the alarm before the alarm was set off. After the alarm was triggered, there was a thirty second interval during which it could be disarmed in case it was missed when it was silent. After that a signal would be sent to the alarm company and an operator would call in for a verification code. The operator would ask the person who answered the phone to give a verbal code, which was not the same code as the code to disarm the alarm—as proof that they had authorization to be there. Failure to answer, or to quote the correct code triggered the next step—a call to the police, to inform them of a breech in the security of the fire-hall.

The alarm panel was on the wall beside the door. Each member of the team had been trained to be the first to exit and enter the hall and each one was given the code to arm and disarm the alarm with instructions to memorize it. Wanting to ensure all possible gaps in security were closed, Kyle changed the code on a regular basis. Some of the team complained that he changed it more often than they changed their underwear. And if they couldn't remember the last time they changed their underwear, how were they supposed to keep up with the codes? Michael was a numbers guy and memorized each new code using a mnemonic trick he learned many years ago.

Gathering up his extra-large overalls which he had rolled down to his waist with his fist, and draping the bib over his arm, Michael stumbled back towards the entrance. The keypad panel light pulsed red to the beat of the piercing electronic alarm that assaulting Michael's ears.

Michael put his hand up to the pad. His fingers stopped in mid air. He drew a blank. No code came to his mind. *Think!* Michael prodded his brain. Numbers tumbled through his head like a slot machine, but whenever a series settled, Michael dismissed it. *No. That was last month's numbers. No. That was the number to his house keypad. No. That was the series Margo used for her ATM card.*

What's happening to me? Michael's mind raced. *Has the heat gone to my brain and melted my memory? Think!* He tried one sequence. The button continued to blink red and the alarm continued it's incessant shriek. It seemed to him that he was standing there for an hour sweating, but it was no more and no less than thirty seconds later when the phone in the fire-hall meeting room rang.

Michael spat out all the words he could think of to curse the shrieking alarm and ringing phone in the empty hall while he hopped and ran in fits and starts towards the room where the phone was ringing. In a panic to answer the phone, he nearly tripping over the legs of his baggy pants. The phone was still ringing when he opened the door to annex.

The landline was plugged into the wall behind a steel shelf where boxes and bins holding, fire extinguishers, electronics, radios and other fire accessories were stored. Michael could hear the phone, but couldn't see it. He had to use both hands to pull out a box, then remove a fire extinguisher and follow the cord he discovered dangling down the back of the shelf, to the phone. His overalls slipped down to his ankles as he reached for a grey hand set, camouflaged on the steel shelf.

"Could've been red!" he spat out in an angry voice when he finally traced it and lifted up the receiver. The voice he heard coming from the hand set in his hand said, "This is AMC security. We are calling because the alarm in the Wannatoka Springs fire-hall has been set off. Do you have the code to disarm the alarm?" The voice paused. Along with the code, Michael couldn't find his voice. When he didn't answer, the voice on the other end continued. "Hello? Is anyone there? This is AMC security. Do you have the code to disarm the alarm?"

Michael was sweating profusely now.

A picture of how he must look suddenly flashed before Michael's eyes: a disheveled, slimmed down, shirtless Santa, red pants down around his ankles, standing in his Rudolf-the-red-nosed reindeer boxers, and a white fake beard and mustache ringed around his neck. He started to laugh.

The voice at the other end of the phone repeated her message impassively. "Please recite the telephone authorization code for this building. If you do not recite the code, I must alert the police of a breech. If you know the code, please recite it now"

Michael sucked in a breath to calm himself. "You won't believe this," he started, "I'm standing here in the fire-hall—a half-naked Santa Claus in my boxer shorts." His face turned red.

While he was talking the female voice on the other end of the phone-line repeated her message. "Sir, if you know the code, please recite it now. Failure to do so will result in an immediate alert to the RCMP that this building's security has been breached."

Michael gurgled and choked as he tried to talk and laugh at the same time, "You should be here, see who you're talking to. Half-naked Santa, stripped down to his shorts. This is the funniest thing you've ever seen. I can't believe it myself . . ."

"Sir, if you know the code, please recite it now."

Michael caught himself and inhaled, trying to wrestle his brain back to his senses. "Uh. . . the code." His mind was blank. He could not think of one number. Not his shoe size. Not his postal code. Not his phone number. Nothing.

"I give up. Call the police." He said and hung up. *This has got to be the most irresponsible thing I've ever done,* Michael thought. And the worst senior's moment of my life! He shook his head and, grabbing his pants, he pulled them up to his waist again and awkwardly walked back to the bench to wait to face the consequences.

When Corporal Tom Majors pulled up outside, he radioed in to report that he was on the scene of the Wannatoka Fire Hall. An active alarm was signalling from within the building and a light was on. There were no cars or trucks parked out front. When he tried the door, it was open so he stepped in.

Michael was sitting on the bench, resting his head on the wall behind him. The fake white beard and mustache ringed around his bare chest like a white wreath. When he saw the familiar officer, he stood up and held up both of his hands in surrender. When he did that, the over-sized red overalls slumped down to his ankles. "Evening Tom!" he said, "You got me. Santa has broken into the building." Michael smirked. He shifted his weight from one foot to the other in his discomfort as the officer's eyes slid down Michael's body, taking in the bare chest and the Rudolf-the-red-nosed reindeer boxer shorts with the message 'you light up my life'. When he got that far, he quickly refocused his eyes back on Michael's.

"Evening Michael. It's Corporal Majors when I'm on duty." He said in a deadpan voice. "What's going on? Forgot the code?"

"Guilty." Michael replied sheepishly. "I was so hot when I came back to get out of this Santa suit after the parade. I forgot to disarm the alarm. Then I forgot the code! Codes! I can't believe it. Never in my life have I forgotten numbers. My mind just went blank. Call it a senior's moment, I guess."

"Can't say I can relate. Not being a senior. But it happens." Corporal Majors replied. "I'll call it in. You can—uh—finished getting undressed or—dressed—or whatever you were doing."

"Right," Michael grabbed his overalls to pull them up again and then, thinking better of it, kicked them off. Corporal Majors talked into his radio. The alarm went silent.

He turned his radio off and said, "See you at hockey on Wednesday,Michael?"

"Yes! I'll be there with bells on—so to speak." Michael smiled ruefully.

"OK then. See you Wednesday."

"Good night, Tom—uh, Corporal Majors! Thanks for the break!"

Tom turned and smiled. Pointing his radio towards Michael he said, "You're never going to live this one down in the hockey dressing room, buddy! Cops don't have client confidentiality rules about Santa getting caught with his pants down."

Michael heard a snicker as door clicked shut. Standing there in his boxer shorts and socks, Michael felt the woosh of cold air rush in when the door opened and shut. That triggered something in his brain. He remembered the code: 092921—the date of the fire evacuation for Wannatoka Springs.

Margo's New Retirement Dream

"Michael! Wake up!" Margo nudged her husband who had nodded off in his reclining lounge chair. Michael groaned and smacked his lips. His eyelids fluttered, but didn't open. Margo figured he was faking sleep so she went on.

Standing at the window, with her back to Michael, and staring into their backyard Margo announced her new plan. "Tina and I are going to buy a property with cabins on it. It's been abandoned for years, and the cabins are in really bad shape. But the infrastructure is still intact. An you won't believe this . . . it's near the elusive Wannatoka hot spring! We found it! Well, Old Man Keppler told us where the hot spring is and drew us a map. It was originally some sort of settlement. Maybe an old settlement from the 1800s or maybe a hippie colony—can't be sure until we see it, but it's listed for sale . . . as a property with five log cabins, zoned commercial/residential. A potential income property. And it's near the hot spring! This like finding a goldmine! The fountain of youth! The holy grail! We're going to buy the property, fix up the cabins and dam the spring or whatever we have to do to make a hot spring pool. This is it, Michael. This my new retirement dream. We're going to call it Wannatoka Springs Resort.

Michael pulled the lever on his recliner and sat upright. He wiped his face and blinked his eyes into focus. Seeing Margo in front of him, he said "Oh! Margo. When did you come in? I didn't hear you. Must've dozed off." He shook his head as if to shake off drowsiness. "I just had the weirdest dream. I dreamt that you and Tina are going to build a resort at Wannatoka hot spring." He grinned. "Now that would be something! A couple of old gals who've never used a power tool in their lives, building a resort."

Margo stood with her hands on her hips. She was livid. "You didn't dream that, Michael. I've been standing right here talking to you about my dream. I thought you were awake.

And us old gals are not too old to learn new tricks. Tina and I are going to build a resort. Without you old guys!" Margo pumped her fist in the air. "With our two hands, power tools and girl power!"

Look for the next series of stories of
The Margo Chronicles– Girl Power
coming out next year
(hopefully)

Author's Note

If you haven't read my first book, *The Margo Chronicles*, don't worry, you can always catch up on Margo and Michael's adventures in the first year of their retirement after you read this one. Or read it first and come back to this one! If you have read The Margo Chronicles, I hope you'll enjoy reconnecting with your new friends as they continue on their quirky retirement journey.

The village of Wannatoka Springs, its history, the situations and the characters come directly from my fertile imagination, but of course, I don't live in a vacuum so there will be similarities to things I am familiar with.

Sometimes, I feel like Margo and Michael live 'in the walls' of my house. Their house is a lot like the one we live in. And the layout of Wannatoka Springs is remarkably similar to the tiny village in the Kootenays where my partner and I moved four years ago, to live out our retirement.

But that is where the similarities end and the adventures begin. I've had a lot of fun, sitting in my twin lounge chair recliner, looking out my oversized living room windows imagining what Margo would see when she looked out of them, and what their neighbours might be up to or, more importantly, how she would involve herself in her neighbourhood.

Nothing she gets into is ever straightforward, though. Where would be the fun in that?! But it turns out that Margo has had a pretty good reception in Wannatoka Springs, and has started to feel comfortable in her neighbourhood and in her own skin. And I'd to think that I have too.

New for Margo fans!

I invite you to like and follow: _The Margo Chronicles_ Author Page on Facebook.

On it, Margo and I (CJ) will post more information about life in the Kootenay village of Wannatoka Springs.

So, check in for recipes, gardening tips, fashion advice for retirees, gossip about the adventures and misadventures of Margo and her friends—**and an event schedule in case you should want to attend a reading sometime.**

See you there!